tryst

Also By S.L. Jennings

Sexual Education Novels

Taint

Fear of Falling

Afraid to Fly

Dark Light

The Dark Prince

Light Shadows

tryst

A Sexual Education Novel

S.L. JENNINGS

wm
WILLIAM MORROW
An Imprint of HarperCollins*Publishers*

HarperCollins books may be purchased for educational, business, or sales promotional use. For information please e-mail the Special Markets Department at SPsales@harpercollins.com.

FIRST EDITION

Library of Congress Cataloging-in-Publication Data has been applied for.

ISBN 978-0-06-238973-2

15 16 17 18 19 DIX/RRD 10 9 8 7 6 5 4 3 2 1

To Tim.

Thank you for loving me so beautifully.

tryst

Prologue

I could have easily told him what I wanted. I should have. I see that now.

I could have reached across the white-linen-covered table, grasped his large hands, and leveled my stare with his, before spilling my guts all over my half-eaten, olive oil–poached branzino.

I could have said, "Tucker, I love you. You're a wonderful husband, partner, friend, and lover. And my life would be empty without you. But honey . . .

"I need to be fucked.

"Not your version of fucking—which is great, and all—but fucked like you hate me. Not like you love me, because I already know that. I've always known that. And as much as I wish that love was enough . . . it's not. So please give me what I need. Please do to me what you deem dirty and disrespectful. I need you to understand that. *I need you.* But I need this too."

It would have hurt him, but he would have understood. He always did.

Then we wouldn't be where we are now.

Scared. Excited. Naked.

My loving husband and me.

And him.

Maybe I should have told him what I wanted from the start.

But then again, maybe not.

Chapter One

He was doing it again.

Analyzing every word, every inflection of my voice. Trying to read my body language for any sign of discontent. His lips are smiling. But his maddeningly perceptive gaze is burning right through my impassive expression, boring straight into the root of my unease like a drill.

I huff out an aggravated breath and take a sip of my martini. If I couldn't keep him out of my head, I'd just drink until I didn't care anymore. Until my thoughts slurred together and edges didn't exist to contain logic.

"Stop it," I finally say, looking down at my menu to hide my aggravation.

"Stop what?" I can practically visualize him narrowing

those cunning eyes, causing the space between his brows to wrinkle with age and misplaced concern.

"Shrinking me. I'm not your patient, Tuck. Stop it. I said I was fine and I meant it."

I look up just as he places his elbows on the table and leans forward. Sincerity rests on those lusciously full, bowed lips, fashioned into a comforting smile. "You're right; you're not my patient, Heidi. You're my wife. And I'm worried about you."

That's right. He said wife.

I am somebody's wife. And the somebody sitting across from me—a tall, tan Adonis with cornflower blue eyes, bourbon brown hair sprinkled with the first signs of maturity just at the temples, and a pronounced, chiseled jaw—is my husband, Tucker DuCane. The best man I know. The man I've loved and devoted my life to for the past ten years.

"Ever since all that shit blew up with Justice, you've been busier than ever," he continues, peering at me over the dark rims of his glasses. "The long hours, the trips every other week . . . you need to slow down. You're a publicist, babe. Not a superhero."

I set down my menu and look away, unable to face his condescending stare. He doesn't mean to be a patronizing ass, but he can't help it. He's a psychiatrist, and a damn good one at that. He gets paid hundreds upon hundreds an hour to listen to New York's famously fucked up bitch and whine about their trivial, self-important lives. And he actually cares enough to help them. The man is practically a shoe-in for sainthood.

Then there's his most demanding case of all—me.

I've been known as a lot of things—the Ice Queen of the North, a shark in stilettos, the Big Apple ball-buster, and my personal favorite, the blonde Olivia Pope. But I'm rarely known as a happy, doting wife. And that's not a matter of negligence. Simply circumstance.

Being married to the top publicist in New York is no picnic, especially one as notorious for her razor-sharp tongue as her colorful clientele. So it's no surprise that most of this city wouldn't make the connection between us. Tucker DuCane, serenity-inducing shrink to the upper crust married to Heidi DuCane, PR pit bull in a skirt? Doesn't make sense.

Except it does.

Well, it did.

A tall, tuxedo-clad young man with angular features and the smoothest, darkest skin I have ever seen approaches our table with a blinding white smile. "Dr. DuCane, Mrs. DuCane. Lovely to see you again. Another date night?" he asks in his intriguing accent that boasts of his Nigerian heritage combined with years of schooling in England.

"Bilal, great to see you, young man. Sick of us already?" Tucker jibes, successfully smothering all signs of seriousness and using that blithe tone reserved for patients and the press.

"Absolutely not, sir. I could never tire of my favorite guests, especially with Mrs. DuCane helping me nab the biggest campaign of my career." He beams, casting brilliant light into the dimly lit dining room.

"Don't tell me you landed the Versace campaign. That's amazing, Bilal!" I smile, stowing my Bitchy Resting Face and grasping his hand. I'm genuinely happy for him and I'm human enough to let it show.

"I did! And I owe it all to you, Mrs. D," he says, completely covering my much smaller hand with his long fingers.

"Nonsense. You're the one with the gorgeous face. I just simply made a call. It was nothing."

And I mean it. Bilal has been serving at our favorite steakhouse in the city for the past two years, and I've always felt he was way too pretty to be pushing pretentious plates of porterhouse for stuffy, old businessmen and groups of gal pals à la *Sex and the City*. But the fashion industry here is fiercely competitive, and even an extraordinary beauty like him was struggling to get seen by the right people. So I made a quick call, no biggie. Donatella owed me a favor anyway.

Bilal makes quick work of taking our order, not even bothering to ask the desired doneness of our prime steaks—he already knows—before thanking me again. After checking on his other tables, he returns with a stellar bottle of Cab.

"On the house," he says with a wink as he fills our glasses. He doesn't pause to give us the standard taste, either. He already knows that we'll love it.

Goes to show just how steeped in routine we are. Same restaurant, same food, same wine every third Friday night.

Sometimes we mix it up and try the specials rather than our usual filet, but that's as risky as we get. Which is good considering that I'm throttled into constant chaos Monday through Friday for twelve hours a day, as well as weekend galas, press junkets, and premiers.

Routine is good. Constant is good.

And Tucker . . . Tucker is the king of constant. And he has been for the last ten years.

"Any exciting plans tonight after dinner?" Bilal asks, making small talk.

"Exciting? No," I answer. "But I do need to have a late meeting with a band that's in town tonight for a concert. Business as usual, of course."

"A band?" he inquires with a raised brow as he uncorks the wine bottle. "Anyone I know?"

I glance over at Tucker with a tinge of nervousness. He hates when I talk business at dinner. It was the one concession I allowed him considering the other twenty-three hours of the day I eat, drink, and sleep all things work related. "Ransom. Heard of them?"

His face is saying, *Are you shitting me?* but he's much too polite to ever utter those words. "Yes, definitely. I was hoping to get tickets to tonight's concert, but, of course, duty calls."

"I'll let them know you're a fan," I offer before Bilal tips his head graciously and returns to the kitchen.

"Awfully kind of you," Tucker muses as he brings the rim of his wineglass to his lips. "And blasé, considering how much of a Ransom fan you are. Admit it, you're dying to meet them. Or should I say, *him*?"

And there he goes again. Shrinking me.

See, Tucker is good at that. Better than good. He's a goddamn walking mind fuck draped in a charcoal Brooks Brothers suit and Tom Ford readers. He looks like he's itching to pick you apart just for the fuck of it. Only you're too enthralled with the pretty packaging to realize it, let alone attempt to stop him from rummaging around in your head like a back-alley scavenger.

To the untrained eye, he appears as the regally handsome man that he is. But to me—the woman he's loved since I was just a jaded undergrad and he a young, ambitious psychiatric resident—he's a high-paid emotional coddler.

Of course, I'd never say that. To his face, at least.

I roll my eyes before downing what's left of my martini, the sear of the liquid stifling the anxiety rising in my gut.

"I don't know what you're talking about." Lies.

"Oh, come on, Heidi. Isn't he on your list?"

"It's business, Tuck. I'm not going there tonight to live out some crazy fantasy that was merely meant to be a joke. Come on, you don't actually think I take that stuff seriously?"

He shrugs, giving me a knowing smile. "Your list, love. This was your idea, not mine."

I look down at my empty glass, already missing the burn of vodka on my tongue.

He's right. It was my idea.

Some time ago, I asked Tucker who was on his Fuck-It

List—women he could have a free pass with without repercussion from me. There were rules, of course. It's not like he could include his hot, busty secretary or the young, perky shop girl at our favorite gourmet cupcakery. They had to be unattainable women that would be virtually impossible to meet, let alone sleep with. And the same would go for me.

It started off as just pillow talk—playful banter as we kissed and flirted between the sheets of our bed, tucked away in our tiny shoebox of an apartment on the west side. This was when our marriage was still fresh and new. Before reserved date nights, scheduled sex, and secret eye rolls behind menus.

"No one," he'd said. "I could never imagine being with anyone but you."

I'd known he would say that. Tucker had always been furiously devoted to our marriage and me. "But come on," I'd urged anyway. "There's got to be some sexy model or actress that you wouldn't mind spending a wild night with, no strings attached."

"Nope." He'd smiled, causing the little crinkles at his eyes to only make him seem even more charming. "You're all I want, Bunny."

I always softened when he used my childhood nickname, which I inherited from my family, along with two front buckteeth that stood so far out of my mouth they practically had their own zip code. Dr. Sawyer and two years of braces were able to fix the chompers, but the nickname stuck.

"Ok, fine. You don't have a list. Then what's your fantasy? And don't say me."

"I can't say that I have any besides you. You have and always will be the keeper of my deepest desires. There is no one else." He gave a passive half shrug before turning my words right back on me. He was good for that. "But since you brought it up, how about you? That list of yours must be pretty notable."

I gave a wave of nonchalance. "Not at all. Hardly worth mentioning."

"Oh, I seriously doubt that." Tucker eased up on one elbow so his face hovered over mine. He looked genuinely interested. Maybe even a little fascinated.

"I don't know about this, Tuck."

A slow, lazy smile spread across those too-full lips as mirth danced behind his heavy-lidded eyes. "Come on, Bunny. Tell me. I promise I won't judge."

I took a deep breath in an attempt to muster up some courage. He didn't realize what he was asking for. But if honesty was what he needed, I'd give him just that.

"All right, fine. Mark Wahlberg."

Deep, baritone laughter filled our modest bedroom, loud enough that I was sure Mrs. Epstein from downstairs could hear. Any minute now and she would be jabbing the ceiling with the blunt end of her broom and yelling Yiddish obscenities.

"Marky Mark? You want a hall pass for Marky Mark?"

I scoffed with feigned outrage and smacked his bare shoulder. "Hey, this is my list. And you promised you wouldn't judge!"

"Awwww, baby." He pulled me into his arms and made quick work of dotting soft kisses along my neck and shoulder. "I'd never judge you, I promise. Go on, tell me the next one. I won't even laugh."

"Ok, ok. Fine." I'd surrendered with a heavy sigh, peering at him with one eye closed, bracing myself for his condemnation. "Gerard Butler."

Brows raised to the sky, Tuck peered down at me in surprise. "Wow. You really have a thing for older men." Which had been a valid observation, considering he had more than a few years on me.

But instead of agreeing or shrugging my shoulders, I gave him the third and final name on my list. The one that was sure to shock those tiny smile crinkles right from his handsome face.

"Ransom Reed."

And like I had imagined, Tucker didn't disappoint. *"Ransom Reed?"* he scoffed. "That little rocker punk? Sheesh, babe, what's he, like, nineteen?"

I waved off his disdain. "He's legal. And it's only a foolish fantasy. No way in hell I'd ever actually meet him."

That was before the PR agency I worked at put me on the fast track, letting me take the lead and prove myself with a couple of their elite clients. Before Tucker's hard work and diligence had truly paid off, and word of mouth had tripled his annual intake. Back then we were just two bright-eyed, viciously determined professionals, working our fingers to the bone to try to just . . . make it.

And we've made it.

I look across the table at my husband—the man who had literally force-fed me bites of grilled cheese at my desk when I'd get too focused on work to stop and eat. And when I'd fall asleep at my laptop, my face pressed against the keys, he would carry me to the bed and strip me out of my work clothes. I'd feel him gently kissing the little square indentions on my cheek, his lips coasting across the phantom letters as if they were the sweetest braille.

I never have to wonder if he loves me, if he cares for me. If he'll be waiting for me when I get home, lounging in his favorite chair, a book in those massive hands and his readers pushed down to the bridge of his nose. And even when the media paints me as ruthless and opportunistic, he still manages to see the woman within—the one he fell in love with despite all her reasons why he shouldn't.

He's the one thing I can always count on. The one person who's become as predictable as the sun's rising every morning, and its descent every evening.

That should be cherished. Celebrated even. And I do.

I did.

I look up at my husband, almost forgetting entirely what we were discussing over drinks and an artisan breadbasket. His probing stare tells me that he hasn't.

"You're right, Tuck. It was my idea . . . my list."

Just as the words leave my lips, Bilal returns to our table to present our appetizers. I place a hand on his forearm before he turns away.

"If you haven't fired that steak yet, I'd like to change my order," I say before sweeping my amused gaze to my husband's perplexed expression. "I've got a taste for something different tonight."

Chapter Two

Despite my offer to have our driver drop him off at our condo on Park before heading down to Madison Square Garden, Tuck insists on accompanying me to the Ransom concert. It's completely out of character for him for various reasons. For starters, Tucker despises the concept of digital music. "Music should be felt," he's always said. "You should be able to hold it, smell it, taste it. You can't do that with some goddamn download."

Considering himself a true purist, his record collection resembles that of a small vinyl shop, minus the choking dust and decaying scent of days gone by. He refuses to succumb to this generation's need for instant gratification and will very gladly settle for his Sunday morning trips to various vintage music retailers. So to say that Tucker is a little behind the times when it comes to what's new and notable is an understatement. Not that he minds in the least. He'd much rather trade Iggy Azalea and Hozier for B.B. King and The Beatles.

Also, NYC nightlife has never been his scene, even when we were younger. Back in undergrad, I'd try to drag him away from boring medical texts on the scarce nights he was off work on weekends and push him right into the heart of his unease—a nightclub. He'd be a good sport, but after watching him guard the wall for hours while I danced with my friends, I knew I had to accept that he would never be the partying type. Which was cool with me. I would much rather have the settling-down type. And eventually, the marrying type.

Even with all those reasons why Tucker probably would have preferred a prostate exam over attending the Ransom concert with me, there is one factor that should have surely sealed the fate of our evening.

Tucker hates my job.

Don't get me wrong—he loves me. But he hates what I do. He hates that I have to constantly jump through hoops for a colorful array of celebutantes and entertainers. I guess one would say he does the same, just in a more personal, intimate capacity. He keeps secrets, while I expose them. And Tucker's afraid that putting out so many social fires will one day leave me burnt and raw with bitterness. I can't really blame him. He hears my bitching about the ridiculous demands and expectations of my clients. He sees how it physically wears on me to keep everyone happily relevant and in the public eye. I live in the land of the self-important, and I am their wizard. I swear most of these people wouldn't wipe their own asses unless I advised them of its social benefits.

I suppose I should be happy that Tucker is taking one for the team, especially after he's worked his own grueling, sixty-hour week. Yet, I can't help but be suspicious of this sudden interest in my career. Or maybe it's interest in Ransom Reed.

I gaze out the window of our town car, watching as the city lights stretch thin like illuminated lines of neon cocaine. Even with us slithering at a snail's pace in bumper-to-bumper Friday night traffic, everything seems like a blur. The street vendors with their carts of peanuts and waterlogged hotdogs. Makeshift booths with peddlers selling everything from knockoff handbags to bootleg DVDs. Tourists of all walks of life capturing treasured moments through the lens of a Nikon. Annoyed locals brushing past stupid tourists as they fumble with their fucking cameras in the middle of the damn sidewalk.

This is my city. Always has been. And even though my Louisiana transplant husband would much rather rip me from Manhattan's clutches, carry me down south, and knock me up faster than you can say, *Gotcha, bitch,* this will always be home. And the baby thing? Don't even get me started on that.

We turn onto Fifth, giving us a view of Central Park. I smile at the memory of our first date at this very location.

I had lived in the city for months yet had never been on a horse and carriage ride. I don't even remember telling him that during one of our countless meetings. Talking to him had become so seamless; I could almost forget why I was there to see him in the first place. But he listened, he remembered. And that was the very second I knew I could let myself fall in love with him.

"Remember that time . . . ?" I whisper, my head still turned toward the window.

"I do," he replies. He doesn't even need to ask me to specify. He already knows what memory has stolen me away from reality. "I remember thinking you had the longest legs I had ever seen. And against the moonlight, your skin looked like porcelain and that white-blonde hair turned to spun silver. You were so beautiful. You wore black tights, a pleated skirt, and a sweater. I told you you'd get chilly and tried to give you my jacket but—"

"I said I knew I'd never be cold. You'd never allow it." I turn to him and smile, enraptured by the memory of his warm body folded around mine protectively.

His fingertips slide against the soft leather of the bench seat and find mine in the dark. He's still so warm, even after all these years. "Then afterward, you wanted to go to FAO Schwarz and play Chopsticks on the giant piano mat like Tom Hanks in *Big*."

"I loved that movie. Must've watched it at least a million times as a kid. I couldn't wait to grow up."

"I know. And you did. Maybe too fast."

I turn my gaze back to the cacophony of lights and sounds as we ride in strained silence with only our fingertips touching. Stardust touches my cheeks, turning my face from pale peach to iridescent periwinkle. I'm so lost in thought that I can barely hear the blare of horns and sirens on the other side of the tinted glass.

"That was a good day," I remark after a long beat. "The best day."

"It was," Tucker agrees, letting his fingers slide over mine with just the barest of touches.

"We were so young. So free and adventurous. So . . . happy." My voice breaks on the last word, knowing exactly what I'm implying. But he doesn't withdraw. He simply twines his fingers through mine. Holding me. Keeping me warm and safe like he always has.

"We can be like that again, Bunny. We can go back to that."

I turn my face to his to find that he's closer than he was just moments ago. It's dark but I can feel those knowing eyes on me, studying me. Stripping me naked and exposing all my scars.

"Can we?" It's barely a whisper. If I say it any louder, maybe he'll detect the uncertainty in my voice. Maybe he'll hear the yearning.

"We can. Starting tonight. Starting right now."

THE RIDE TO MSG is far too short, yet I find myself springing from the backseat as soon as the driver opens my door. I smooth down the bodice of my pearl white Gucci jumpsuit in an attempt to collect my bearings. That moment with Tucker—whatever that was—has left me open and raw, emotions brimming right at the surface of my stoic guise. I can't have that right now. I need my head in the game, not crammed with bittersweet memories of how we used to be. Broke, but in love. Struggling, but happy.

I feel him behind me, yet I walk ahead to the side entrance of the massive building. Throngs of screaming, adoring fans are held at bay by a partition, but I approach the wall of beefy security like they are nothing but ants under my strappy, metallic Jimmy Choos.

"Heidi DuCane," I say with all the arrogance of Donald Trump on a good hair day. "The band is expecting me."

The guy directly in front of the door—a bald, seven-foot beast of a man with a crooked nose—studies a clipboard using a penlight. He thinks I don't see the way his hand is trembling as he searches for my name. As usual, my reputation precedes me, as it should.

"Here you are, ma'am," he says, with an almost audible sigh of relief. He peers over my shoulder and looks back down at his clipboard. "And he is . . . ?"

"My guest," I reply tersely, without an ounce of hesitation or remorse.

"Guest?"

I roll my eyes at his questioning tone. "Yes. Guest. Is there a problem?"

"N-n-no, ma'am," he stutters like a cowering toddler. "I just need his name and you can—"

"Not important," I huff out, crossing my arms over my chest. "But since you want to keep us out in this stifling heat all evening, why don't I call Mr. Berke out here so he can join the party."

The giant visibly trembles before looking back down at his clipboard. "My apologies, Ms. DuCane. That won't be necessary. Please, proceed."

He steps aside, waving us toward the door and the solace of central air. Yet, even with unrelenting humidity sticking to my body like hot honey, a startling chill passes through me.

I don't turn around as we walk through the door that leads to the backstage common area and dressing rooms. As expected, it's swarming with roadies, sound techs, and stage grips, yet it is nothing like the usual preshow scenes I'm accustomed to. For starters, there are no skanks. Not one. The only women in sight are fully clothed professionals, and not of the slutty persuasion either. Not one colossal silicone titty or fake mink lash for miles.

There's also a lack of alcohol or any signs of drug use. I don't condone the behavior by any means, and have been known to rip a few new assholes because of it for some of my more reckless clients, but I kinda expected the whole Sex, Drugs, Rock 'n' Roll persona from Ransom.

"I don't see your boy anywhere," Tucker says, coming to stand beside me. It's the first time he's spoken since the car.

I'm just happy he's speaking to me at all, considering how I completely belittled him at security. But this is a business call. And in this industry, the only marriages that count are the ones that come with the right name and a black card.

"I don't either. But there's his agent."

Caleb Berke is the epitome of what you expect from a successful talent agent—fast-talking, manipulative, and about as honest as a three-dollar bill. He's made his millions from representing some of the hottest young talent, from pop princesses to hardcore rap artists. Imagine Ari Gold from *Entourage*, but taller, fitter, and gayer. Caleb is my most trusted frenemy. Friend, because I genuinely like him. Enemy, because he's a big, flaming pain in my ass on most days ending with Y. He's actually the person that tipped me off about Ransom Reed's desperate need for a new publicist, so on these rare occasions that he actually acts more like a friend, I make note and take it seriously.

"About time you got here," he gripes just as we approach. "I swear, bitches are always late. And the few extra minutes didn't do you any favors."

We fake air kiss before I fire back with, "You're one to talk, Queenie. Any more bronzer and someone may mistake you for the Tanning Mom. Or a piece of beef jerky."

Caleb snickers and greets Tucker with a handshake. "Tuck, good to see you, handsome. I'm surprised this old harpy let you out of your kennel." Tucker laughs off the comment, accustomed to the way Caleb and I tease each other.

"So where's your client?" I ask, jumping right into business. "You did say you were desperate, correct?"

"In his dressing room. You'll have to meet him after the show."

I prop my hand on a slender hip and narrow my wicked, silver gaze at him. "No," I retort with the frightening calmness of an assassin. "I'll meet him now."

Caleb isn't even phased. "No can do, Blondie. Ransom has a strict routine for performances. He demands that he and his bandmates be left alone to meditate and mentally prep before every show. No partying, no groupies, no business. So yes, you'll wait."

"Then why the hell did you insist I be here *before* the show?"

Caleb shrugs before inspecting his perfectly trimmed cuticles. "Thought you could use some fun, is all. Plus I want you to *get* him. To know him is to know his music. Without that, you're just scratching the surface." He buffs his nails against the lapel of his blue metallic suit jacket. "He's the real deal, Heidi. But the kid needs help."

With that, Caleb flicks his eyes up to Tucker, signaling that whatever he needs to say isn't for public knowledge. And although the good doctor is bound by his vow of confidentiality, Ransom Reed is not his patient.

"Excuse me. I'm going to grab us a few bottles of water before the show starts," my husband says, taking the hint. He kisses my cheek before giving Caleb and me our much-needed privacy. God, that man is a saint.

Caleb digs right into the dirt as soon as Tucker is out of earshot. "Girlfriend, what's with the ball and chain tonight?" he probes, his stare burning into Tuck's retreating back.

I shrug. "He wanted to come. I don't know, maybe he's warming up to all this," I suggest.

"Humph. Or he feels the need to mark his territory."

I roll my eyes. Leave it up to the drama queen to create some make-believe conflict. "Whatever. Can we get off my marriage and get back to business, please? Or would you like to crawl into our bed tonight too?"

"You wish, bitch," he fires back, although he quickly switches up his demeanor. "The kid is stupid talented, but he's a magnet for trouble. Paternity rumors, bar fights, rocky relationships—he's like candy for TMZ. And that's just the U.S. tour."

With a sobering air, Caleb steps forward and rests a hand on my bare shoulder. "Once it's over . . . I'm worried for the kid. His entire identity is wrapped up in his music. It's who he is to the core. And with such a long break between this final show and the world tour, I'm not confident that he'll be able to keep himself out of trouble."

"Wait," I say, taking a step closer. "What kind of trouble are we talking about? Is there something I need to know about him?"

Caleb gives me his usual cocky grin and waves me off. "Nothing to worry that pretty little head over. Anyway, I have a band to corral for a concert. Enjoy the show."

With that, he air kisses my cheeks once more and turns

toward the mass of frenzied activity. But before he can get more than a few feet away, he turns back to me, wearing a peculiar, almost jolted look. As if a very important notion has just struck him over the head.

"Heidi . . ." He calls me by my name. Not "Bitch" or "Blondie" or "Legs." Whatever's on his mind must be serious. "Just be . . . smart about him. Be careful." And without waiting for a response, he disappears into the crowd.

Huh.

Be smart. Be careful. What the hell does that mean?

Before I can pick his words apart and concoct all kinds of silly notions about the elusive Ransom Reed, my ears are suddenly bombarded with wild, hyena-like screeches and shrieks, along with the thunder of clapping hands. My eyes search for the source of the rapid change in atmosphere, but keep colliding with a quickly forming wall of bodies, humming with excitement. Instead of moving closer to the scene, I take a step back toward the entrance of the stage where I can blend into the shadow of heavy curtains and dim lighting. But that doesn't obstruct my view. Not in the least. If anything, it gives me the privacy I need to mentally process what I'm seeing.

Emerging from the crowd first is a tall, shirtless man, twirling a pair of drumsticks between long, thin fingers. Striker Voss, Ransom's drummer. He's lean, almost lanky, yet hard ripples of muscle lie just under his taut, tanned skin. His hair is cut short, leaving just dark peach fuzz over his scalp. But what he lacks in hair, he more than makes up for in tattoos and piercings. His eyebrow, nose, septum, lip, ears, and even nipples are all adorned with silver rings or barbells, and every inch of his chest and arms is covered in ink. And that's just the parts of him that I can see as he stalks past me to the stage.

Right behind him is Cash Colby, lead guitarist and bona fide manwhore. The only thing more infamous than Ransom Reed's bad boy persona is Cash's penchant for young, hot bimbos with low self-esteem and daddy issues. And looking at him, I can see why. Think a taller, edgier, hotfuck version of Justin Bieber, minus the douchiness. He's got the sandy blond hair that's long enough to fall in his eyes, just begging to be flipped back while he fingers the strings of his Fender with the sensuality of a skilled lover. Rumor has it, those fingers have expertly played with a few of America's sweethearts, soiling their (manufactured) good girl images.

Following Cash is Gunner Davies, rhythm guitarist and the more mysterious of the bunch. He isn't adorned with dozens of tattoos or piercings. His clothing is black and nondescript, as well as his hair. He's not in the press every week, if at all. Come to think of it, I can't think of a single woman he's dated or even a story that's remotely touched on his private life. However, the second he passes me, I feel the temperature drop in the atmosphere, and a sense of danger snakes through me, causing me to physically shrink back a foot and divert my eyes to the tips of my Jimmy Choos. That kid's got menace in his veins. I can smell it.

The very second I force myself to look up, badassery renewed, I know that he's emerged. Every cell in my body tingles with expectation and the very breath in my lungs catches on a gasp. No music video, no magazine spread—shit—not even the dozens of pics I've Googled could have done Ransom Reed justice. He's taller than I expected, and he has the lean body of a rock star who can command a stage. And he struts with all the confidence and swagger of a man who knows he's a big fucking deal—in and out of the bedroom. Dressed in ripped, worn jeans that look as if they were made for him, a V-neck white tee and black leather jacket adorned with silver zippers, he's the epitome of rock godliness. He runs a hand through his dark brown hair that he wears haphazardly slicked back. Still, a rogue lock of hair falls over his forehead, just short enough to stay out of his eyes, yet long enough to allure the fuck out of me. I swear, that move must've been rehearsed. Caleb is beside him, walking double time to keep up with Ransom's long, leisurely strides. The closer he gets, the less I breathe. And now that he's so close—close enough that I could reach out and touch this beautiful urban legend of a man—I don't think I'll ever take another breath.

I find the courage to look up into his face as he approaches, and I completely lose the ability to process intelligent thought. His features are severe and angular, from the intensity of his dark, slanted eyes to the gold hoop threaded through his slender nose. The only word to describe his lips is sensual. And his tanned, golden skin speaks of foreign roots—maybe South American.

He's exotic and enticing and terrifying as hell. And everything that my husband isn't.

Just as the thought seizes me with a jolt of guilt, Ransom Reed is right in front of me, making his way to the stage where nearly twenty thousand fans are screaming his name. He turns to look directly at me, a smirk on those lips that were designed for kissing a woman's most intimate parts, and he winks. Then all I can do is watch him disappear from sight as I try to remember how to inhale oxygen again.

"Taller than he looks on TV, huh?"

The sound of Tucker's voice nearly makes me choke on the electrified air. Seeing me flounder for words, he offers me an ice-cold bottle of water, which I gladly accept and drain in thirty seconds flat.

"Yeah, he is," I shout over the raucous screams and cheers of adoring fans. The band is hyping up the crowd, thanking them for coming to the last stop on the Hostage tour, which incidentally is being filmed for HBO.

"Your face is red. You all right, Bunny?" he shouts back.

I turn in the direction of the stage, my eyes trained on the lithe movements of Ransom Reed. The band goes into their opening number, a fast paced, sexy song about a man's yearning for a woman that he shouldn't have. Although Ransom sings to the crowd, I can hear him as if he were right beside me, whispering those lyrics in my ear. Singing in that raspy tone for an audience of one.

"Yeah, I'm fine. Just fine," I finally remember to answer.

I know that after tonight, I'll never be *just fine* again.

Chapter Three

Somewhere between me losing my composure and Caleb escorting us to Ransom Reed's dressing room, there was a concert. I know it was amazing—evidently Ransom brought the house down with their best show yet—but I couldn't tell you what songs they performed or how many bras were thrown at their feet. Honestly, I can't even remember my own name.

What happened out on that stage was no concert. It was no simple, rehearsed performance. Every note was a raspy moan on the back of his throat. Every lyric was a threat of pain, violence, and pleasure so deep and fulfilling, it should be illegal. And every movement of his hips was a jolt of adrenaline straight into my core.

Yet, even with concentrated sex racing through his veins,

his songs were about so much more than the physical. I felt pain in his words. Loneliness, heartbreak, joy, fear. I listened to his life story and lived within the sultry timbre of his voice.

Ransom Reed is no singer. He's a magician. And his greatest trick of all is hypnotizing the masses with the tip of his golden tongue.

I anxiously pace the floor, awaiting his arrival. I can feel Tucker's eyes on me—he's never seen me this nervous to meet a potential client before. Even Caleb couldn't stop giving me the side eye at my jittery behavior.

"Just relax, babe. He'd be a fool not to hire you," Tuck assures me, using that soothing shrink voice reserved for his patients.

"That's not what I'm worried about," I confess. He raises an inquisitive brow but doesn't press for more. He doesn't want to hear that I'm worried that Ransom *will* hire me.

"You know you don't need to do this," he says, leaving his spot on the leather couch and coming to stand before me. He gently grasps my shoulders to halt my incessant pacing and levels his eyes with mine. "You don't need him. Hell, with the client list you already have, you're already too busy. Taking on another client, especially a musician, will only ensure that we never see each other."

I know he's right, but I don't have the nerve to tell him so. Tucker is always right—he's always the voice of reason. And being married to someone who is always right makes you realize just how wrong you always are.

The dressing room door opens, unleashing a barrage of voices battling to be heard. Although Tucker's body is blocking my view, I can clearly hear what sounds to be an entertainment reporter, asking for Ransom's thoughts on the end of the Hostage tour.

"The whole experience has been absolutely incredible," he answers, the smoothness of his speech completely contrasting the almost rugged rawness of his singing voice. "And to end it here in New York City is the icing on the cake."

"What about the rumors of you leaving the band? Any truth to that?"

I clearly hear Ransom huff out a half chuckle. "None at all. They're just that—rumors. My bandmates are my family. We are absolutely devoted to each other and our music."

Good answer. Maybe Ransom isn't a lost cause after all.

"So the story about you and Cash Colby getting into a physical fight are untrue? And that you have supposedly slept with Striker's wife? Rumor has it, you're the biological father of her unborn child. How do you feel about becoming a daddy?"

An audible gasp escapes the lips of half a dozen groupies that have been hanging on to their rock god's every word. I peer around Tucker just in time to see Ransom visibly freeze mid-step. He slowly turns back to the reporter behind him—the guy who's itching for an ass kicking. And the way Ransom's fists close at his sides and his angled jaw tightens, he's just the one to scratch that itch.

"That's enough questions for now. Please direct any further

questions to my assistant sometime next week," I find myself saying without fully thinking it through. I can't fully justify my outburst, but I know the look on Ransom's face was just a prelude for trouble. And the publicist in me couldn't sit idly by and witness the press-provoked shit-storm.

Of course, every eye draws to me, wondering where the hell I came from and who the hell I am. Back straight, I step around Tucker and approach the group at the door. Yet, for all my confidence, I can't find the nerve to look up at Ransom as I come to stand between him and the reporter.

"And you are?" the reporter asks. I recognize him—someone from VH1. He's short, plain, and about as nondescript as you can get. But one tweet about how Ransom Reed violently accosted the press after the biggest show of his life, and he could successfully destroy the rocker's already questionable image.

"Heidi DuCane." I extend my hand and he takes it, just as recognition sets in.

"Ah, Ms. DuCane. I wasn't aware that you repped the band. While I have you here, do you mind if I ask you about one of your other clients?"

I roll my eyes. These press assholes are fucking, life-sucking vampires. As soon as they smell blood, their fangs come out. And I don't have to guess which *client* he's talking about. Ever since the news broke about Justice and his relationship with Park princess, Ally—formerly Allison Elliot-Carr—my phone has been ringing nonstop, every vulture in town just dying to know the scoop on the two of them, and

Oasis. My answer is always the same: "We refuse comment at this time" aka *"Fuck off!"*

And that's exactly what I'd like to say to this little weasel of a reporter right now.

"I do mind actually. This is Ransom's night. Let's keep it about them and their music. The operative word being *music.* That is what the VH1 brand is based on, correct?" I reply, not even bothering to mask the annoyance in my voice. I don't know why, but I feel the need to protect Ransom. And considering that I've never even met him, let alone don't represent him, I have no right to feel that way about him.

Caleb and his shiny suit step up and, with a little more diplomacy, ushers the reporter out of the room, along with the crowd of awaiting groupies. A simultaneous, disappointed *Awwww* resounds from the other side of the door.

Without the distraction of the reporter, I'm forced to look up at Ransom, realizing that we are much closer than I'm comfortable with. Still, I stay planted where I stand, refusing to be intimidated. He must've gotten the same memo because he stares back at me, intensity simmering behind those dangerously dark eyes that seem to study me with rapt attention.

"Publicist, huh?" he says, his lips moving into a sly smile. "I wasn't aware I had hired one."

"Ransom, we talked about this," Caleb speaks up, moving to inspect the spread of gourmet cheese, fruit, and premium alcohol. He picks up a bottle of champagne and proceeds to pop it open. "After Ingrid quit with your last social media snafu, I told you that you'd need to hire a replacement ASAP."

That social media snafu being a very detailed, up-close-and-personal dick pic taken by some random hookup while Ransom was asleep. Ingrid Carlsbad, a pretty solid publicist and rival, was able to get it removed just hours after it made its big debut (pun intended), but the damage was already done. So she took the coward's way out and quit, rather than appear incompetent by her peers.

"I know that, Caleb," Ransom retorts. "I just don't recall hiring *this* one."

With that, he tears his eyes away from mine and walks to the back of the dressing room. Not in an act of retreat. It's as if he's dismissed me, yet I'm too goddamn dumb to realize it.

"Heidi DuCane is the best in the business. You need someone who is willing to protect your image, and at the same time, make sure Ransom stays trending. If you couldn't tell from how she just handled that reporter, Heidi is who you want."

Ransom pulls a beer from the fridge and pops it open, taking a long gulp. When he pulls the bottle from his lips, he spies Tucker quietly standing just feet away. Ransom frowns slightly, blinking his heavily lashed eyes rapidly before bending down to retrieve another beer. Then without a word, he offers it to Tucker, who accepts with a thankful nod. After that . . . nothing. Ransom doesn't even glance in my direction.

Head high and shoulders pressed back, I go to stand beside

my husband, the only person in this room who doesn't have an interested stake in Ransom's career. Yet, he's the only one that seems to be gaining his attention. If I didn't have built-in gaydar, I would totally be giving Ransom the side eye.

"Mr. Reed, you need a publicist—yes—but you also need someone who knows her shit and is willing to go to bat for you." I take a step toward him and meet his gaze, which seems more . . . bored . . . than anything right now. Still, I soldier on. "I am that someone. I know this business like the back of my hand. I've made some incredible connections within the music industry and the press. And I protect my clients like my life depends on it. You won't find a better publicist than me, I can guarantee you that. But I'm not here to beg for your partnership. I don't need to. You know as well as I do that you need me."

Ransom studies me for a long beat while he takes another sip of his beer. Even when he tips the bottle up, displaying his smooth, tanned throat, he keeps his eyes on me. When he's swallowed his fill, he turns to Caleb, who is frantically texting while helping himself to Ransom's rather expensive champagne.

"Where'd you find this one, Caleb?" he says, completely ignoring my whole spiel.

"I told you I'd bring you the best and I delivered," Caleb answers without looking up from his phone. "Heidi is who you want. Trust me. Have I ever steered you wrong?"

"Today?" Ransom laughs, the sound husky and deep. It causes the tight knot of irritation to unfurl in my gut.

He looks back at me, regarding me with a look that I can only describe as contemplative, as if he's analyzing everything about me. Self-consciousness snakes up my spine but I deny the urge to look down at the ground. His gaze quickly sweeps to Tucker for just a second, and then back to me. "Bring her to the suite," he says to Caleb, his eyes still studying me intensely.

"You got it," Caleb replies, stowing his phone in his suit jacket. "Ok, you've got the fan meet-and-greet and a briefing with the guys. We need to get moving."

Without another word, Ransom strides to the door. Before his hand touches the knob, he looks back at me and smirks. "Nice to meet you . . . Heidi." Then he launches himself into the fandemonium.

"Hang out here for a bit, if you can," Caleb says, quickly following his client. "Drink the champagne—Ransom demands it, but doesn't like the stuff. I think he only requests it for me. And help yourself to anything here. I'll be back as soon as I can to escort you to the after party."

I screw my face in annoyance. I'm not used to taking orders from anyone, especially Caleb. He notices my scowl and shoots me a knowing smile, his dick growing an inch, no doubt. "You're in, Heidi. He likes you. He just likes fucking with people." And he heads into the hallway, ducking and dodging worshipping band sluts in ripped Ransom tees and short skirts.

"That was . . . interesting," Tucker says, as we both stare after the closed dressing room door. We can clearly hear the sheer fuckery on the other side, but we stand completely frozen in shock, as if we're in the wake of a tornado. That tornado being Ransom Reed.

"Interesting? That guy's a dick! He should be lucky I'm even entertaining the idea of representing him." I go straight to the champagne with every intention of draining the entire bottle. This whole situation has got me wound so tight, I don't even bother with a glass. I just take it straight to the head.

"Relax, babe. You heard Caleb—he likes you. You know these entertainer types are all about dramatic effect," Tucker reasons. "Besides, he'd have to be a fool not to hire you."

Tucker finishes off his beer in a few hearty swigs and chucks the bottle in the nearby trashcan. Then he comes up behind me, sliding his hands up my bare arms before resting them on my shoulders. When he begins to knead, I feel the tension slowly ease out of me.

"Just listen to what he has to say," he coos, bringing his lips to graze the shell of my ear. I lean back into his touch, until my backside hits his groin. "And if you don't like what you hear, we will at least get a nice night out together."

"And free booze," I add, taking another drink from the champagne bottle.

As always, Tucker is right. After several more swigs of bubbly, I'm feeling relaxed and optimistic about my next interaction with Ransom Reed. I mean, so what, he's ridiculously sexy and so drop-dead gorgeous that it makes my eyes hurt. Even if he's been cursed with the dreaded asshole gene, he'll be pretty to look at. And let's face it—I'm used to dealing with assholes. *Hello,* Justice Drake, anyone? And I'm two parts asshole myself.

When Caleb reenters a good while later, both Tucker and I are pleasantly tipsy, having raided the dressing room's mini fridge. We're noshing on a cheese and fruit platter when he tells us it's time to head to the after party.

"Where's it at?" I ask him as he leads us outside where his ride awaits.

"The Royal. Penthouse."

The Royal? That's a modest choice, considering that most entertainers would surely choose the swankier offerings, like The Plaza or Ritz-Carlton. But, then again, the papzz would expect that.

"Which penthouse?" The Royal has three of them, all boasting a nightclub sorta vibe.

"All of them," Caleb answers, pulling out his phone to reply to a text.

We ride the short distance in companionable silence until we reach our desired location, which, honestly, isn't much to look at from the outside. Caleb leads us to the elevators, stopping briefly to greet a few industry folks. We take the ride to the top where the party is already in full swing.

What the preshow festivities lacked in booze and boobs, the after party more than makes up for it. We step into the largest suite, which is crammed with wall-to-wall partygoers who look as if they've been at it for at least an hour. Everyone is beyond toasty, the music is loud and the lights are dim. I can barely make out anyone familiar, although I suspect the largest packs of girls have band members smuggled between them.

"Where's Ransom?" I shout at Caleb over the music.

"He's here somewhere. Grab a drink, have some fun. He'll turn up somewhere."

I turn to my husband, who looks just as out of his comfort zone as I am. Don't get me wrong—I haven't always been this square. But penthouse parties haven't been my thing since my twenties.

"Come on," he says, grasping my hand and leading me through the crowded room. We stop at what appears to be a bar. It's littered with various bottles of alcohol, champagne, wine, and beer. He finds a clean flute and pours me a glass of bubbly before snagging himself a beer.

"When in Rome," he says, smiling in a toast. That smile is a picture of beauty. And unfortunately, I don't see it half as much as I used to. I take a sip of my drink and grin right back at him.

Ok, maybe one night of fun won't hurt. What's the worst that could happen?

Chapter Four

It's close to midnight, and Tucker and I are three sheets to the wind, and one sip away from being pissy drunk. Surprisingly, we're having fun. The music and jovial atmosphere are infectious, and by the second drink, we find ourselves moving together to the rhythm, our bodies pressed close together. I can feel Tucker growing against my backside as he sways to the beat, and I encourage it by rubbing my ass against the threat of his erection. We shouldn't be doing this—someone could see us. But with the lights this dim and the room this crowded, we can't find a good reason to stop. Especially when Ransom Reed, the whole reason we're here, is nowhere in sight.

As if he's heard his name in my thoughts, the crowd parts, and I glance up to find him across the room, sitting on the back corner of a couch. He's ditched his stage clothes and is dressed casually in worn jeans and a white V-neck that's just tight enough to display cuts of impressive, lean muscle. A slouchy beanie sits on his head that reveals longer front layers of dark brown hair. He's leaning forward, elbows on his knees and a beer in his hand. And he's staring right at me. Even with scantily clad women hanging all over him, vying for his attention, his intense, dark gaze is pressed solely onto me. I'm not sure what I should do, so I keep moving side to side with Tucker right behind me, flexing his hips into the curve of my ass seductively.

I feel soft lips moving along the side of my neck and I melt into the enticing touch, yet keep my stare trained on the exotically alluring man across the room. There's a woman sitting between his legs, her body angled so her face is in his crotch. I can see her hand moving against something, but I don't *see* anything nor does he react to what she's doing. Another woman leans over to whisper in his ear before letting her tongue trace the line of his jaw. Yet another desperate groupie is behind him, rubbing his shoulders. He doesn't move. Hell, it's hard to tell if he's even blinked since we locked eyes.

I know whatever is transpiring between us right now is inappropriate, both professionally and personally. Tucker could look up at any moment and easily see Ransom eye-fucking his wife. And if that weren't enough, he would see his wife . . . taking it. Eye-fucking him right back while her loving husband sweeps tender kisses up and down her neck.

This isn't me. I'm not irresponsible or reckless. I never put my own personal feelings before business. And sure, I've had plenty of opportunities to explore the prospect of sleeping with other men. I just never truly craved the feel of a stranger's body pressed against mine, touching me, kissing me, filling me. Until now.

A look of resignation flashes in Ransom's eyes and he suddenly climbs to his feet, leaving his harem lonely and dejected. My heart pounds faster, harder, as he stalks toward me, and everything around me ceases to exist. The music, the people, even my husband. I shouldn't let him have this power over me and my body, but he already does. And he's never even touched me.

I hold my breath, holding back frustrated tears as fear and guilt spike in my veins. I don't understand what's happening. Is it the champagne? Quite possibly. But I've never behaved like this before, and I've always been able to hold my own. No, alcohol is no excuse for what I'm feeling.

When he's standing directly in front of me, his towering frame eclipsing the party before us, I hesitate to look up into those dark, hypnotic eyes. But I can't help myself. He completely disarms me of all good, God-given sense.

"Come with me," he demands, before turning toward the exit of the suite.

"But . . ." That single words stops him in his tracks but he doesn't face me. "But what about my husband?"

I'm cringing before the sentence has even fully escaped my lips. *What about my husband?* What the fuck am I saying?

If Tucker wasn't standing here, would I have posed that same question?

Ransom looks over his shoulder and shrugs. "Bring him too."

Of course. Of course, I would bring him. Why wouldn't I? And why would I ever put myself in a position where I'd even have to question that?

When it seems like I'm still debating the decision in my mind, Tucker takes my hand and gently pulls me toward the direction of Ransom's retreating back. He doesn't wear the same awkward look of confusion as I do. Maybe he's much more sober than I, able to sift through whatever illusion I've created in my head.

I allow Tucker to pull me out of the suite as Ransom leads us to another room, away from the drunken fray of sweat-slickened bodies and vibrating bass lines. We're far enough that the crowd has thinned and we're able to slip in the unoccupied suite undetected. It's one of the smaller penthouses, and while it is just as luxurious, it's much more understated in its décor.

"Have a seat," Ransom mutters, his voice low and serious. He makes a beeline for the wet bar and grabs two beers, handing one to Tucker. Then he turns his attention to an ice bucket cradling a chilled bottle of champagne. Odd, considering that he doesn't like the stuff, according to Caleb. He pops the cork and pours a single glass, and brings it over to the couch where I sit, my legs and arms crossed over my body in nervous defense. I take the glass thankfully, although

I don't need it, and soothe my suddenly parched throat with a large gulp.

"So . . ." Ransom begins, settling into an armchair across from the couch Tucker and I occupy. The way his body slides into the seat so gracefully, as if he's so sure of every bit of his body, evokes thoughts in my head that I have no right to think. He positions his left ankle over his right knee. "Why do you want me, Heidi?"

I choke on my champagne.

Full on coughing, sputtering, retching choke. Tucker pats my back, which is completely unnecessary, and I wave him off. When I lift my reddened face from my hands, tears smudging my mascara, Ransom is standing in front of me, offering a bottle of water. I accept it with a nod and down half the bottle.

"Thank you," I croak, my voice hoarse. Oh my God, this is a disaster already, and I still haven't figured out what the hell I'm doing here. I clear my throat a few times and look up at Ransom, head high despite my watery eyes. "What do you mean?"

Ransom raises his brows and looks at Tucker and then back to me. "Um, why do you want me . . . as a client? Why do you want to work with me?"

I let out a relieved sigh. Business. We're here to talk business. Of course. Why the hell else would we be here?

Feeling foolish, I muster up a confident smile. "Suffice to say, you've been in the press quite a bit, and not all of it positive. Not a big deal, because we all know that any kind of publicity is good publicity. But there's a fine balance between the effects of good press versus bad press. And I want to make sure that even your bad press is shown in a positive light."

"Such as?" He sits back in his chair and takes a swig of his beer.

"Your feud with Cash Colby." I hold up a hand before he can even attempt to explain. "It's not my job to prove if it's true or not. It's my job to ensure that whatever it is generates record sales. That's it."

"But that's not even the issue. Cash and I are fine. He's an attention whore and I'm a cocky asshole. That's our dynamic and it always has been. It works for us."

"But does it?" I inquire, raising a brow. "That may be how you see things, but is that what everyone else sees? Because to your fans—the ones that purchase concert tickets and buy albums—there seems to be discord, which results in breakup rumors. And breakup rumors gets people imagining that they can actually hear the disconnect in your music. Which, inevitably, makes them not want to support you. Following my drift, here?"

Ransom touches his index finger to his lips, contemplating my words. Then he sets down his beer bottle and begins to fish for something in his back pocket. He pulls out a small cigarette case and opens it up on the coffee table between us, revealing a neatly wrapped joint.

"You mind?"

"Not at all," I answer. Tucker shakes his head beside me.

Ransom sparks it up and takes a long, deep pull. The potent smell of marijuana hits me hard, heightening my champagne buzz. Still, I grab my glass and take a nervous sip. After another drag, Ransom leans over and offers the joint to Tucker, who looks at it as if it's a crack pipe. His gaze wanders to me and I shrug. I can see it in his eyes—he wants to be young and reckless again. He's tired of playing it safe. So with the very tips of his fingers, my husband accepts the joint.

At first, he takes a tentative pull, just enough to fill his lungs with the aromatic smoke. After exhaling, he brings it to his lips again. Ransom and I are both watching him, waiting for him to freak out, but that moment never comes. Instead, he releases a chest full of smoke and passes the J to me.

Let's get one thing straight. I'm never the type to engage in irresponsible behaviors with my clients, let alone illegal ones. But as it stands, Ransom Reed is not my client. Not yet, at least.

I take the small, thin joint between my manicured fingers and bring it to my MAC Russian Red painted lips. Inhaling deeply, I let the sensation sweep through me, disarming all the anxiety rattling my senses. I take another puff and pass it back to Ransom before relaxing back into the couch cushion.

"You know that shit's not true," he says, his voice strained from just taking a hit. Smoke billows out from between his lips. "That rumor about me being the biological father of Striker's unborn child? It's not true. I've never touched Trudy."

"I believe you," I say, going for the last of my champagne, my mouth growing unbelievably dry. I drain it in one gulp. Tucker, being the caregiver that he is, gives me a quick peck on the side of my face and jumps up to retrieve the bottle. He refills my glass just as Ransom passes him the joint.

"And that bullshit with Cash . . . that's just us. Ever since we were kids. So whatever bitch is claiming that we brawled over her, she's a fraud."

"Could it be possible that you both slept with her?"

Ransom frowns, but now that we're all feeling pretty nice, it just makes him look adorable. His already slanted eyes are just mere slits but I can still feel the intensity of his gaze on me. What is it with this guy? Why does it always seem like he's studying my every move, as if he's trying to figure me out. Tucker studies my words, my expression, trying to get into my head. Ransom . . . it seems like he's trying to get into something else.

"What do you mean?"

"Did you both fuck her?" I ask flatly. No need to beat around the bush.

Ransom makes an amused face. "Like a threesome?"

I shake my head, feeling hot blood rush to my cheeks. "No, no. Not like that." A lazy smile slides onto my face. "Or maybe . . . yeah. Exactly like that. Like a threesome."

Both Tucker and Ransom break into chuckles, and for

some reason I can't comprehend, I join them. It's ridiculous—I'm smoking weed with a potential client, asking him if he had a threesome with a bandmate? This is so not me. But fuck it, why can't it be?

Tucker passes me the joint and I take a long hit. It's almost dead and Ransom gestures for me to go ahead and finish it.

"Have I had threesomes? Yes," Ransom muses, hands folded behind his head as he reclines in his seat. "Have I had threesomes with Cash? Yes. Was that girl involved? No."

My steel-gray eyes grow in size. "So you had a threesome? With Cash?" God, that sounds . . . hot. Cash is commercially beautiful with his longish, sandy blond hair and perfectly proportioned features. But Ransom . . . he's dangerously good-looking. The type of beauty that you know means trouble. The two of them together? Holy Hot Rock Gods, Batman.

My face flames and I look down at my champagne flute, suddenly bashful at my own thoughts. I feel warm fingers slide down my cheek and I look up to find Tucker wearing a sluggish smile.

"That excites you, doesn't it?" he asks quietly, his speech falling into that Louisiana accent that I love so much. It comes out whenever he's tired or drunk, and in this case, high. I've always told him he was my very own Harry Connick Jr. The wavy, russet hair and blue topaz eyes, the full lips and sexy, southern drawl—everything about him screams ruggedly refined sensuality. And the way he's looking at me right now—like he wants to take me right here on this couch, no matter who's watching—I can't really say that I would hinder him from doing whatever the hell he wanted.

Eyes low and hooded, Tuck leans over to gently kiss my bare shoulder. The soft brush of his lips feels like silk on my already tingling skin, and I suck in a breath. Face red with both embarrassment and desire, I glance up to find Ransom staring at us intently. Not disgusted or even amused. He's . . . enthralled.

"Threesomes," he replies, accentuating the *s*. "Don't tell me you're a prude, Heidi. Because whoever I work with needs to be able to keep up with *any* and *all* aspects of my life."

I answer with a shake of my head. How the hell did we get on this subject? Weren't we just talking about . . . oh, shit. What were we talking about?

"I'm not a prude. But . . . how would something like that work?" I ask, too intrigued to stop now. "With you and Cash? Do you two . . . ?"

"Do we fuck?" Ransom tacks on when I'm too ashamed to finish my thought. "No. The girl gets fucked, but we don't touch each other. It's not like that. Sometimes we take turns while the other watches. Sometimes we're both inside her . . . at the same time."

Mouth beyond dry, I reach for my champagne, which thankfully, Tucker has refilled. It's gone in less than three gulps.

Ransom's gaze sweeps to Tucker, then back to me. "Does

this subject make you . . . uncomfortable?" He grins crookedly like he already knows the answer.

I glance up at my husband, whom I half expect to be wearing an expression of shock and repulsion. But he seems . . . fine. More than fine. If I didn't know any better, he looks flushed with craving. And what he's craving can't be found in the wet bar.

"No," I answer, turning my attention back to Ransom. "I'm not uncomfortable. Not at all."

Over a few more beers, champagne, and another joint, we talk about the most random shit ever. I laugh when Ransom reveals some pretty bizarre stalker occurrences, involving his missing, worn underwear and shaved pubic hair. Tucker chuckles through a story about his days playing college football before he blew out his knee and I have to admit, the groupies were almost just as bold. I like this side of Tucker. Being open and honest and carefree, without worrying about what's appropriate or professional. And he and Ransom seem to really get along, despite being totally different in every way, shape, and form. Sitting next to them is like being caught in freeze-frame between night and day. But oddly, I don't prefer one over the other. It just seems natural to want them both.

"Wait. Does that even count?" I ask, after Ransom shares the story of how he lost his virginity.

"If it gets hard and can slide into pussy, it counts," he replies smugly.

"But you were twelve! You were a baby! How is that even possible?"

He shrugs before taking a swig of his beer. "It happens. A lot more than you think, actually."

"But she was sixteen! She knew better," I scoff.

Ransom shrugs. "What can I say? I've always been drawn to older ladies."

His statement sets my skin aflame and I look away, trying to hide my ridiculous grin. When I feel more in control of my erratic hormones, I look back only to find that he's still staring at me. His intensity makes me feel . . . uneasy. Like he knows exactly what I'm feeling. Like he can tell that every word he speaks sends shockwaves between my thighs.

"How about you, Tuck?" Ransom says, releasing me from his hold. "Spill it."

Tucker leans back into the couch, gathering me into his arms and taking me with him. I kick off my heels and curl up at his side, tucking my bare feet under me. Feeling the full effects of alcohol mixed with pot, I let my eyes close and just enjoy the high.

"Can't say I've ever done the older woman thing," he replies before kissing the top of my head. "But blondes . . . I've always had a thing for blondes."

"Yeah . . . me too."

My eyes pop open and dart over to Ransom, who is wearing that same cocky grin. Did he just say . . . ?

"They've always been my weakness," he continues.

I self-consciously touch my own white-blonde hair and

smile. He's gotta be fucking with me. Maybe he gets a rise out of knowing he's completely unattainable to very married women like me. But then again, those groupies in the other suite—the ones that were damn near giving him a hand job and licking the sweat from his brow in public—were all various shades of bottled sunlight.

"What? No young girls with big boobs and perky, little asses?" I jibe. "Old blonde chicks do it for you?"

But even with me chuckling at my own lame, self-deprecating joke, Ransom looks at me with genuine seriousness, as if he's completely sober.

"No. Girls don't do it for me. But real women do. Women like *you*."

The emphasis on the last word has me nearly shaking like a leaf. Not because I'm nervous that he's admitted to being attracted to me, but because I feel Tucker stiffen beside me. I risk a peek at him and find him looking down at me, an unnamed expression on his face. It's not anger or agitation. It's . . . No. It couldn't be.

"Funny you should say that," my husband says, his eyes on me, but his words for Ransom. "Apparently, you do it for her too."

Face on fire, I turn to interject, only to be stunned by Ransom's brilliant smile. "Oh, is that right?"

"No . . . no, it's not like that. I, um, I," I stammer. Dammit. For someone who's been known to castrate people with just her words, I find myself completely incoherent, which only makes Ransom smile wider.

"So you're not attracted to me?"

"I didn't say that," I manage to spit out.

"Then you are? Which one is it?"

Tucker chuckles softly beside me, just as amused by my fumbling. "You're on her list," he reveals slyly. I sit up straight, eyes wide, and smack him playfully across the chest. He feigns injury, but I know he hardly felt it. His college football career and highly paid trainer have kept Tuck's body impressively hard and toned. If it weren't for the tiny bit of gray around his temples, he could easily pass for twenty-nine.

I can't even look at Ransom now, let alone explain. However, I can damn near feel his stare burning straight through me.

"List?" he drawls. "What kinda list is this?"

"Her Fuck-It List," my (soon to be deceased) husband explains. "Men she's allowed to sleep with if the chance presents itself."

"Huh," Ransom snorts. "Interesting. And I'm on this list?"

Gathering what little bit of liquid courage I have left in my system, I look up at him and nod once. "Yes."

"And you have a free pass with me, without any repercussion from your husband, if we agree to sleep together?"

I swallow, my tongue suddenly feeling too thick in my mouth. "Yes."

Ransom sits forward, resting his elbows on his knees. Getting as close to me as he can without leaving his seat. All traces of humor are wiped clean from his gorgeous face, and I'm left only to take in that dangerously intense stare.

"So, Heidi . . . if you had the chance, would you sleep with me?"

Even with Tucker's arm around me, his fingers lightly stroking the skin of my shoulder, I am lost to the stranger in front of me. And like the golden-tongued sorcerer that he is, he conjures a single word from my body and casts it from my lips.

"Yes."

Chapter Five

"Let's play a little game."

Ransom Reed, sex-on-fire rock star, leans back in his seat once again, regarding me with an almost cocky air. I should be pissed off at both him and my husband, but I'm not. And judging by the wicked gleam in his eyes and his recent suggestion, he's not bothered in the least.

Fuck. What have I gotten myself into?

I don't even have a right to be angry. This was *my* fantasy. This is what *I* wanted.

And I do. I think that's what messes with me the most.

Heidi DuCane, PR powerhouse and devoted wife, wants another man.

"And what game is that?" Tucker asks, a hint of excitement in his voice. A jolt of fear and exhalation fills my belly, making me feel a bit queasy. Shit, I wish I'd finished my dinner.

"Think of it like Truth or Dare, but with an edge. You don't get to choose whether you do a dare or tell a truth, but you can always opt out. Anyone who works with me needs to be able to keep up. And if you can't roll with this"—he waves a hand along his taut torso, a gesture that makes it seem like he's offering himself to me . . . to us—"then I can't trust you to represent me in a way that's honest to who I am and what my music is about. So you're either in, or you're out. And if you're out, there's the door."

Tucker nods before looking down to meet my timid gaze. "Yeah. I think I can deal with that. How about you, Bunny? Sound good to you?"

I look back at the gorgeous, smiling man beside me, and wonder where the fuck my husband went. This isn't Tucker. He isn't spontaneous or risky. He doesn't play juvenile games or drink in excess or smoke pot. He's safe and responsible. The peanut butter to my jelly. The yin to my yang. He's my constant. And this . . . this is about as erratic as one can get.

For a second I wonder what his motivations could be. Do I really know Tuck? Sure, we've been together since I was in undergrad, nearly ten years ago. But do I *know* him? Does the sudden change in his once mild demeanor stem from a fantasy of his own? A fantasy with another man?

Seeing the confusion in my eyes, he leans down and whispers in my ear, "This is all for you, babe."

I'm still staring at him, mouth agape, when Tucker turns to Ransom and nods. "Yeah. We're game."

It starts off innocently enough, and soon I feel my nerves unwind and actually start to enjoy all the silly little questions. That is, until things take a turn down a slippery slope. One that I knew was coming, yet was too caught up to hit the brakes.

"What's your favorite position?"

"Me on top."

"Why?"

"I'm a dominant bitch. In every way. Plus the friction it creates . . . down there . . . Oh God."

"I dare you to kiss your husband."

I lean in to press my lips against Tucker, who eagerly accepts.

"No," Ransom says, shaking his head. "Really kiss him. Fuck his mouth with your tongue."

His brash words rattle me, and I pause to blink a few times before I turn back to Tucker, who is looking at me expectantly. Shit, why am I even nervous? This is my husband. My *husband.* The man I've loved for as long as I can remember. The man who knows me inside and out, and adores me anyway. He's seen me at my worst, at my best, and everything in between. Kissing him is easy.

Seeing the resolve in my eyes, Tucker moves in closer, yet doesn't bring his lips to mine. Instead, his hands slide from the top of my shoulders down to my waist. With a swift movement, he pulls my body to him, until we're chest to chest. Seeing the awkwardness of this position, I rise up on my knees and steady myself by placing my hands on his shoulders. Warm, strong hands slide up my back, urging me closer, closer . . .

Our lips collide, moving slowly at first, just tasting. I open my mouth just a fraction to welcome him inside, and he accepts the invitation, parting me wider to stroke his tongue against mine. What begins as soft and sensual quickly erupts into something wild and hungry. Tucker devours my mouth, drinking in my desire as he eases me back onto the couch. Our lips still moving together, our tongues still exploring, I feel his fingers roam my chest and ribs before sliding up to my breasts. He palms them gently, applying pressure at my nipples through the thin fabric. I moan into his mouth, which only spurs him on. I feel the silken straps of my jumpsuit slip down over the tops of my shoulders and cool air hits the top of my chest.

I should stop this right now. It's indecent and inappropriate and everything that *we're* not. But I can't stop now. I can't even attempt to push him off me when his lips move down my jaw to my neck. He sucks my throat gently, raking his teeth over the sensitive, thin skin. I shiver under his body and pull him down closer. There's something about being loved by Tucker that softens me. His touch makes me feel so tender, so absolutely feminine. I want to be soft and pliant for him. Hell, if I'm really being honest, I want to be weak for him. Almost submissive. I want him to dominate me until I can only mewl and moan at his feet.

When I feel Tucker's mouth meet the swell of my breasts, I gasp for breath. The sound is so raw and erotic against the quiet of the room, and it startles me, bringing me back to my senses.

We're not alone.

Feeling me stiffen, Tucker lifts his head and looks down at me, still panting with need. I gently push him back and shift into a sitting position, fixing my disheveled clothing.

"That was . . . hot. As. Fuck," Ransom declares, his own voice husky and thick. Forcing myself to look up at him, I can see why. He looks so . . . aroused. His face is flush, his chest moves up and down with his labored breathing, and a thin sheen of sweat covers his forehead. Which is just a fraction of what Tucker is dealing with. His arousal is a little more . . . obvious.

"Thanks," is all I can manage to say. Why am I thanking him? I don't know. With my head still spinning from the kiss and my skin still burning with Tucker's touch, I don't know much of anything right now. But as I look over at my husband, I know that something has changed between us, sparking this undeniable need that we both thought had been lost years ago. It's been so long since he's kissed me with that level of fervor. I felt wanted by him—desired. And while I knew I was safe in his arms, everything about his touch was verging on madness.

It's my turn to ask a question, and I turn to Ransom, who gazes at me expectantly. "How many women have you slept with?"

He smiles like the cat that ate the canary, as if he knows the answer will shock me. "I don't know."

"You don't know?"

He shakes his head. "I don't. It's not something I keep up with."

"I guess when you go around sticking your dick in anything that moves, keeping tally could be troublesome."

I chuckle sardonically at my tasteless jibe, but stop short when I see a quick wince of pain on Ransom's face. It only lasts a second before he schools his features back into the cool, impassive guise that I've grown used to seeing. I cock my head to one side. Could I have . . . hurt his feelings?

"I didn't mean it like that," I try to explain, but he quickly waves it off.

"No. You're right. I'll fuck anything that walks and is halfway decent-looking. I am a musician, after all. I usually have to wear a baseball glove on stage to catch all the pussy that's thrown at me."

He seems satisfied with himself—proud even—so I let the subject drop. Tucker goes next, asking me to name my naughtiest fantasy. I shrug my shoulders, not willing to divulge my secret. He kisses my shoulder as he begs for the truth, but there's no way I could tell him what I really want. That'd make me seem dirty and immoral. Not to mention make him feel inadequate.

When Ransom takes control of the game next, I know for sure that whatever he has up his sleeve will leave me humiliated and exposed. I hold my breath and await his retaliation, yet he looks at Tucker instead. Still, he doesn't hold back on shock factor.

"I dare you . . . to let me touch your wife."

An audible gasp escapes my kiss-swollen lips and I turn to Tucker, awaiting his wrath. He returns Ransom's intent stare, his expression unreadable. Yet, the younger man doesn't back down, cocking a challenging brow at Tuck's silence. He remains unmovable, a master at the art of restraint from his years as a shrink. No doubt he's had to answer some odd questions, but never any involving his wife.

"I don't *let* Heidi do anything. She has her own mind . . . her own body."

"So maybe I should be asking her." A sinister smile on his lips, Ransom angles his focus on me. "Heidi, would you let me touch you?"

My first reaction is to say no—*hell no.* But Tucker quickly grasps my knee, capturing my attention.

"This is what you want," he whispers. "He . . . is what you want. And I can accept that. This is your fantasy, baby. Let me help you make it come true."

I search his face, waiting for him to break into laughter, but he's completely serious. My husband is telling me to let another man put his hands on me—his wife. This isn't right. This isn't what married people are supposed to do. But even as that rational part of my brain lists all the reasons why I shouldn't allow this to go any further, my body is already tingling with anticipation. My face and chest are flush. My nipples harden in exhilaration. And my mouth waters with the prospect of tasting Ransom's skin.

Oh, God. I *do* want this. And now the decision is mine and mine alone.

"So?" Ransom asks, awaiting our fate.

Say no.

Say no.

Grab Tucker's hand and get the fuck out of here. Go home and make love to him. Let that kind, good, gentle man be enough.

Once again, Ransom Reed steals the truth from my lips, forcing me to abandon all decency and sanity. Making me take the sanctity of my marriage and soil it with my own slick arousal.

In one single breath, I shatter ten years of devotion, trust, and love. And although I know what I'm destroying by lighting this fire, I can't do much more than stand back and watch it all go up in flames.

"Yes."

He's on his feet, stalking toward me before I even get the word out.

Chapter Six

I'm not supposed to like this.

I'm not supposed to feel like I'm dying every second that passes without this stranger's hands on me. I shouldn't shiver as he towers over me, dissecting me with the darkest, sultriest eyes I've ever seen. And my breath shouldn't be coming out in short, eager pants.

I'm not supposed to be here. But I am.

I'm not supposed to want this. But I do.

And even knowing my husband is merely a foot away, glaring at us so intensely that I can feel the burn of those bright blue eyes, I can't force myself to be ashamed enough to stop. If anything, it just makes me want this more.

I gaze up at Ransom and wait, unable to do much else.

The first stroke of his hand against my cheek is gentle, tender. His fingers lightly graze a path from the bottom of my jaw up to the shell of my ear. I exhale and let my eyes close, wrapped up in the feel of his skin. His hand is warm, his fingers strong and slightly callused, probably from years and years of playing guitar. They glide down to the nape of my neck before tangling in my hair. I open my eyes and gasp when he gently pulls at the strands at my scalp and I raise my chin in defiance. Or to give him better access.

My nipples strain against silk with every erratic breath. He seems bigger this close to me—taller. His tanned arms are roped with muscle and I can clearly see defined abs through the white cotton of his tee. Oh, how I want to reach out and rake my fingertips over that stomach. Desperate to be closer, I turn my head toward the bare skin of his forearm and inhale his intoxicating scent of spiced smoke and clean sweat with a heady, masculine undertone that makes my mouth water.

I'm inhaling once more when Ransom quickly pulls away, taking the haze of passion with him. His demeanor is cool and collected yet the fire in his dark eyes rages with uncontained chaos. I swallow down the disappointment at the loss of contact and try to steady my breathing. Now that I'm not completely wrapped up in his touch, my head swims with a tidal wave of emotions—guilt, excitement, shame, fear. But mostly need. The need to feel those hands on me again. The need to abandon all my inhibitions and be totally unchained in my desires. But I need my husband too. As much as I want to explore this . . . this thing . . . with Ransom, I need Tucker just as badly.

As rejection and confusion set in, I gaze over at Tucker, who continues to watch us with rapt attention. I expect him to be angry at my reaction to Ransom's touch, but he isn't. He looks just as aroused as I, and again, I question his motives. But his eyes aren't on Ransom at all. He's staring at me, studying the pink flush that contrasts with my pale skin. Watching the way my chest rises and falls rapidly. Yearning to touch my slightly parted lips with his own. Aching to run his tongue over my pebbled nipples that are clearly on display through my flimsy jumpsuit.

Tucker hasn't looked at me this way since . . . since before I can remember. And it took another man touching me to bring him back to me. It took another man touching me to bring me back to *him*.

"Tucker," Ransom rasps, cutting into the tense moment. "Your wife is exquisite."

"She is, isn't she," my husband agrees.

"The things I would do to her . . . the pleasure I could bring her. Oh, how she'd sing." He turns to me, a dark hunger in his eyes. "Do you sing, Heidi?"

Sing?

I'm not even sure what that means, or if I should want it. Who am I kidding? Of course, I want it. I want whatever he's willing to give me.

"What?" I breathe, unable to ask him more than that. A sinister smile appears on his lips.

"When you come . . . do you sing? I want to know if you sing when you come."

"I don't know. I don't think so."

"Well, I'd like to find out."

I don't even know what to say to that. *He wants to know if I sing when I come?* For *him*?

I'm hot all over, my core burning up with need. Between the kiss with Tucker and Ransom's touch, I know I am living dangerously close to the edge. It's been so long since Tucker and I *really* made love, and my Battery Operated Boyfriend, aka BOB, has been no real replacement for the real thing. I need a man between my thighs, on top of me. Behind me. Under me. And at this point, with more champagne in my belly than food, I can't decide which man I want more.

The room is silent aside from the pounding of three hearts, racing with anticipation. Maybe this was all I needed? To be desired by another man. Maybe this will be enough to get Tucker and me out of the rut of our marriage.

I tell myself it's all in fun. That Ransom is just fucking with me and Tucker is somehow in on the big joke, when suddenly the young, hot rocker extends his hand to me. I look at his long fingers, the memory of them ghosting across my cheek still replaying in my mind, and try to determine what this means. I look to Tucker, who gives me just a simple, encouraging nod, and back to Ransom. He still wears that smug smile that he always plasters on, but there's something else lurking in his impassive guise.

"Shall we?"

This is it. This is what I've been waiting for. And I can't think of one good reason why I should deny it anymore.

I place my hand in Ransom's, giving over to the current of lust. He wraps his long, agile fingers around my hand and pulls me to my feet. My legs should be shaking, yet oddly, I feel completely calm. I'm filled with nervous energy, but it's out of elation, not terror. There is no more doubt in my mind.

I look back at Tucker, who still sits on the couch, watching, waiting. With my other hand, I reach out for him, urging him with steel-colored eyes to take it.

"I need you with me. I can't do this without you."

Varied shades of shock, surprise, and admiration play on his features as he pauses to digest what I've said. He looks . . . touched. But that expression quickly morphs into hunger as he laces his fingers with mine and climbs to his feet.

I'm not sure what we're doing, and how this will work, but I'm intrigued enough to find out.

The three of us make our way to the bedroom just a few yards away, yet every step feels like I'm walking the green mile to a beautiful death. Tonight will be my sexual suicide.

Ransom leads the way, ushering us into a room that is decked out like much of the hotel—chic, modern, and dark, with just a touch of rich color from jewel-toned tapestries. When we cross the threshold, Ransom goes to a little side table and picks up a tiny remote. With a push of a button, soft, sensual music flows throughout the room. He's setting the mood. The mood for what? I'm not exactly sure.

He comes to stand before us, his gaze trained on me then Tucker. Something passes between them, and before I know what's happening, we're in motion. Tucker goes to sit in an armchair a few feet away against the wall. Ransom takes both my hands and leads me to the bed. The back of his legs hit the foot of the bed, and he pauses, looking down at me to await my reaction. When I don't protest, he slowly sits down, aligning his face with my belly. I feel his hands burning through the thin fabric on the backs of my thighs, gently coasting up and then down to my calves. He keeps his eyes on me, his stare so intense that I can barely breathe, let alone blink. I force myself to look away, and seek Tucker's comforting smile. His hands clutch the arms of the chair, yet he's not angry. It almost seems like it's an act of restraint.

"I want to see you," Ransom murmurs, bringing my attention back to him. When I frown in confusion, he answers the unspoken question on my lips by letting his hands slide up my back to the clasped zipper. He waits for me to tell him to stop, but I don't. I don't even know if it's possible at this point.

The soft rustle of fabric, a gentle pull and my jumpsuit is undone. Oh, the irony. To begin the night in pristine white, only for it to end up pooled at my feet at the hands of another man. My morals aren't the only thing being tarnished.

With the straps loosened, the bodice barely contains my

breasts. Just a small shrug and I'll be fully on display. Using the lightest of touches, Ransom grazes the silken skin right above my nipples. Then he's easing it down, over the swells, down my ribs, my belly, my thighs. When my clothing hits my feet, he takes a moment from undressing me and takes me in, standing only in a nude, lace thong. His intake of breath and smoldering stare give me a little jolt of satisfaction.

I've always been slender and long, which left me a bit deprived in the curves area. My breasts are small handfuls, granting me the ability to go braless when necessary, and my hips are delicately subtle. I'd consider my ass to be the most substantial part of my body. Plus I have legs for days.

Truth be told, I've always been insecure about my slight frame. I never felt womanly enough. The word voluptuous has never been used to describe me. But the way Ransom is looking at me—like I am the juiciest piece of filet he has ever seen, and he is dying to sink his teeth into me—makes me feel utterly sensuous.

His hands—those magnificently large callused hands—slide from my ankles to my calves to the backs of my knees. His eyes are still trained on me, looking like midnight against the dim lighting. It's unsettling, almost scary, but I don't look away. I just keep watching him watch me as his scorching touch languidly dances over my thighs to my hips. When I feel his fingers dig into the softness of my ass, he leans in and presses his lips to my navel. I begin to pant, dizzy with the need for more.

He sits upright and continues to explore my body with his

hands, giving me so little yet successfully driving me wild with craving. A tiny smirk appears on his lips as if he knows just how much he affects me. As if he can literally smell the arousal pooling between my thighs, staining my lacey strip of underwear. Maybe he can. Considering how turned on I am right now, maybe my husband can too.

When his fingers meet my breasts, I can't hold back the moan that rumbles from my chest. He touches me like I'm delicate. Like I'm merely made of silken butterfly wings. And while I love it—while his control is maddening and alluring—I want him to break me. I need him to tear me in two, rip me apart until I'm raw and ruined. I don't want delicate and sweet. I've had enough of that. It's all I've had for years, leaving that shameful, carnal part of me neglected.

Without warning, Ransom turns our bodies and flips me over so I am on my back on the bed and he is looming over me. The look on his face is a mix of desire and corruption, his smile just as vicious. He grasps my hips with rough hands and pulls me to the edge of the bed until my aching, lace-covered flesh hits the coarseness of his denim-clad legs.

"Tell me, Heidi," he rasps, standing between my open legs. I struggle with the need to squirm against him in a quest to create friction. "Do you want me?"

"Yes."

"And if I want to fuck you right now, would you let me?"

"Yes."

"And would you let me do it right here in front of your husband? Do you want him to watch me fuck you?"

"Yes." I can't even tell if the word is audible through the moan in my throat.

He looks over at Tucker and raises a brow. "What do you say, Tuck? Do you want to watch me fuck your wife?"

I swallow, letting the guilt and shame slide down my throat like warm butter, and look to my husband with timid eyes. His gaze is already fixed on me, his jaw clenched with tension. Every second that he stares at me, I feel dirtier and dirtier. I want to run and hide from him, but not as much as I want to stay.

Finally, he releases a hissed answer between his teeth. "Yes."

Yes.

He said *yes*.

He wants this. Maybe just as much as I do.

Ransom nods once before turning his attention back to the heated space between my thighs. "What do you want me to do to her first?" he asks my husband, hiking up my arousal by ten more notches.

Tucker clears his throat, yet his voice still comes out husky. "Kiss the inside of her thighs. She's ticklish there but she loves it."

Without further preamble, Ransom sinks to his knees. It starts as a soft brush up my left thigh. Then my right. Sweet, sucking kisses run along the sensitive skin until I'm squirming at the sensation. Tucker was right—I am ticklish. But knowing that Ransom's head is between my legs—just centimeters from my swollen clit—creates a different type of tingle.

Just as I am adjusting to the foreign feeling of a stranger's lips on me, he bites me. Hard enough to make me yelp, yet gentle enough not to break the skin. I jerk reflexively but Ransom roughly holds my legs open. He bites me again, this time on the opposite thigh, then again, and again. I'm reeling, completely befuddled in my haze of violent passion, when he begins to kiss me again. His soft lips and tongue are such a vast contrast from the sting of his teeth that the change makes me cry out.

He's tonguing the edge of my thong when he asks, "What's next?" I'm not even sure what he means until I hear Tucker answer, "Her breasts. She loves to have her nipples sucked and played with."

Slowly, like a vicious jungle cat crawling over its scared prey, Ransom climbs onto the bed to hover over me. He's still fully dressed, but with him at this angle, I can see hard planes of ripped muscle down his shirt. He dips his head to take a pink-tipped nipple into his mouth and I moan loudly, arching my back to offer him more. He answers my proposition by sucking harder, so hard that it nearly hurts. His fingers find my other nipple and he pinches it with the same ferocity, eliciting downright disgraceful sounds from my mouth. Then he switches, laving its twin with teeth and tongue.

"Next," he groans, my nipple still in his mouth. He then pushes the two petite mounds together to suckle them simultaneously. He's so hungry; I can feel his growls rumbling from his chest.

"Taste her," Tucker pants. I can't even look at him. I'm too lost to Ransom. Too lost to the pleasure he's giving me. "Taste how fucking good her pussy is."

Without wasting a second, Ransom drops to his knees and rips my thong from my body. Then he's slipping his tongue between my folds with a frenzied hunger, claiming my orgasm within the first few minutes. I'm clawing at the comforter, calling for God, Jesus, and all the disciples, yet he doesn't relent. He doesn't give me a second to breathe before he sinks a long finger inside me.

Ransom's teeth pinch my clit ever so gently as he slowly fingers me. He pauses to insert another finger and the soft nibbling turns into a hard suck. When he adds a third, speeding up the tempo, he licks me to the rhythm of each thrust.

I reach between my legs, searching for my captor, the man who binds me with such pleasure. My fingers run over the rugged knit of his slouchy beanie just as he thrusts his tongue inside me to join his fingers, causing me to crush the hat in my tight grip. Silken, dark brown hair tickles the inside of my thighs, only heightening the intense sensation.

Just as I am on the cusp of another orgasm, he asks Tucker what he should do next.

"Fuck her. Fuck her now."

We're in motion again, as Ransom rises and flips me over onto my stomach in one swift movement. My head is spinning, and I'm dizzy with the remnants of my first orgasm. I hear the clink of a belt buckle, the rustle of clothing and then the undeniable crinkling of a small, foil wrapper. Oh my

God. Am I really doing this? Can I truly live with knowing that another man other than my husband has been inside me? And Tucker . . . will he be able to accept this—accept me? How will he ever look at me the same? I mean . . . why wouldn't he? *He* told Ransom to touch me. *He* told Ransom to taste me. And, *shit,* he told Ransom to fuck me. He damn near demanded it.

I don't get a second more to ruminate the dozen what-ifs and regrets jumbling my head before I feel his hands on my hips, pulling me up to rest on my knees so that my ass is fully on display for him. He pivots my body and places a hand on the back of my neck to position me just how he wants me. And how he wants me is cheek pressed into the mattress, my head turned to the side so I have a full view of Tucker. So I can watch my husband watch me being fucked by another man.

I whimper, feeling completely helpless and weak. The look on his face tells me that he feels the same. He's helpless to stop this—we both are. Because as uncomfortable as this should make us, as downright disgraceful as this is, we're both too invested to turn back now.

I feel Ransom's hands palming my ass as he spreads me wider, revealing my wet, swollen sex. He runs his fingers down the seam, stopping at my entrance to dip into my slickness. My eyes widen with horror as I realize what he's doing. He's prepping me. He's feeling how ready I am for him . . . how badly I want him. How desperately I need him to fill me and make me whole. I don't want to moan, but

I can't help it. I don't want my body to ache for him, but it does.

I find that I'm not the only one who is aching for relief. To my surprise, Tucker is fully erect inside his slacks as his palm runs along the strain, seeking release from its wool captivity. His blue eyes sparkle like angry fireworks, and his mouth is fixed in a hard line. But the way he's touching himself—grasping the thick base and sliding his fingers along the swollen tip, growing more and more frantic with every stroke—is 100 percent, unadulterated desire.

Sin-slickened hardness presses at my entrance, opening me, stretching me like a rubber band that clasps around him greedily. We both groan as he pushes inside, and I let my eyes close in ecstasy, just relishing the feel of complete fullness. When he's completely submerged within my walls, Ransom grasps my chin roughly, leaning over to press his chest to my back.

"Open your eyes, love. Look at him. Let him see what I can do to you."

And then he really performs for me—for us. Long fingers dig into my hips, holding me to meet every single hard thrust. He isn't gentle or tender. He's not loving or romantic. Ransom is proving to be exactly what I've learned of him thus far—severe, harsh, and undeniably sexual. And I am loving every second of it.

My hazy eyes find Tucker and I see that he has unsheathed his rock-hard erection from his slacks and fists it in time to the rhythm of Ransom's strokes. It's as if the three of us are one—one panting, moaning, fucking entity.

With one hand on my hip and the other gripping the back of my neck, Ransom plows into me, grunting with every forceful surge of lust. The room is filled with the sounds of skin slapping against skin and our indecent groans of pleasure, creating a personalized soundtrack of sex that completely drowns out Jay-Z's "American Gangster." Even the noises hissing between Tucker's lips are explicitly erotic, as he coaches Ransom in the art of claiming me.

That's right. Fuck her hard. Harder.

Pull her hair. He does, causing my scalp to prickle with the pain of a thousand tiny daggers.

Slap her ass. He does that too, stealing my breath. *Again . . . slap it again. This time make it hurt.*

It's all so much. All so overwhelming. And all so different from what I'm used to feeling. Tucker has never expressed himself this way during sex with me. No, everything is so sweet and romantic, as he murmurs words of endearment, telling me he loves me, adores me. Telling me I'm the most beautiful thing he's ever seen. And I love that too. But this . . . this is taking me higher than I've ever been, awakening a beast inside me that I never even knew existed.

I've never been this wet before. Never been this vocal.

I've never felt anything this . . . *good.* Because Ransom is so fucking good.

The little monster in me thrashes, coaxing me to buck against him and meet him punishing thrust for punishing thrust. I feel an intrusion in my belly, sparking a sharp stab of pain, but I keep going, needing more. The ache just spurns me on and I spread my thighs wider, welcoming him to crawl in deeper and never leave.

My knees begin to quiver under me with the first signs of climax. Ransom places a hand on my bare belly, and—surprisingly gentle—eases me down flat onto the mattress. He keeps moving inside me, but he slows his pace, focusing on the depth this angle allows. In this position, where his body is wholly pressed against mine, I can feel every solid, sweat-slickened inch of him. The hard planes of muscle straining with every languid stroke. His soft hair tickling my cheek and shoulder. His warm, ragged breath fanning over my face. It's so much more intimate than I expected from him, and although I can do intimate, I just don't know if I *should* do intimate with him.

I think I hear him whisper something in my ear, yet I don't hear him. Before I have a chance to ponder it further, he does it again, and I realize . . . he's not whispering.

He's singing.

His voice is breathy and light, yet I'd know that sultry rasp anywhere. And I've heard those lyrics before. Hell, I heard them just hours ago.

Shatter me with lies
You beautiful monster
Feel like I could die
Let you pull me under

Holy shit.

Ransom Reed, founder and lead singer of the Grammy-nominated band Ransom, is *singing* to me while *fucking* me.

Even with him nine inches deep inside me, I feel like a line has been crossed with those hypnotic words of surrender. He said he wanted to make me sing when I came for him. Maybe I misunderstood the meaning behind those words. Maybe it was *he* who wanted to sing for *me*.

I look to Tucker, wondering if he feels it too, yet his eyes are half closed as he strokes himself eagerly. With a pained groan, milky white droplets spurt from the head of his cock. Yet, he doesn't stop, rubbing his hot release into his still hardened, jerking flesh.

God, that's fucking hot. Hotter than anything I've ever seen. The sight brings me back into the moment, and I give in to the pressure between my thighs that now pulses out of control as those lyrics replay in my head on repeat.

Shatter me with lies
You beautiful monster
Feel like I could die
Let you pull me under

I'm breathing erratically, feeling like I may pass out from the Category 5 orgasm that's creeping up my thighs. I begin to shiver despite Ransom's hot body pressed into mine, and he somehow wraps me in his arms even tighter. His hand snakes under me and cradles my face, tilting my head up toward him, gazing at me lovingly through hooded eyes, caressing the edge of my mouth with the pad of his thumb . . .

He kisses me.

It's soft, almost timid at first, but even more intimate than his whispered song in my ear. At first I don't know what to do, but then hunger and craving set in, and I realize I am kissing him back just as eagerly, savoring his taste of sin and salvation. I reach back to thread my fingers through his sweat-dampened locks and open my mouth wider to give him full access to my tongue.

I'm drowning in him, eyes closed, breath stolen, utterly dying as this man fills me up and drains my very soul. I tremble around him, growing wetter, hotter. He feels it too, and responds with swift, jerky thrusts that nearly break me in half. Ransom releases my lips and sinks his teeth into my shoulder as his orgasm pours out of him. Hearing that erotic grunt of surrender and feeling him pulse wildly inside me as his seed spills into the thin barrier of latex is my undoing, and I cry out with my own climax, sobbing as my body quakes in beautiful agony.

We lay there together, utterly spent and broken. We breathe the same breath, our chests moving in tandem. He releases my shoulder from his teeth and tenderly kisses the stinging skin with swollen lips. I turn my face as far as it will go in hopes of basking in one of those kisses. That's when I see him.

My husband. Staring at us.

His lips are merely a thin, white slash across his hard face, and his shrewd eyes are made of sapphire. Although his erection is long gone, he still hasn't bothered to redress. I open my mouth to explain, but quickly snap it shut when I realize I have nothing *to* explain. He wanted this. He asked for this, just as much as I did. And now he's looking at me like he just caught me cheating on him.

Ransom eases off and out of me, causing me to wince. My whole body hurts—the back of my neck where he held me down, my hips where his fingers dug into the soft flesh, my ass that he slapped without remorse, my shoulder where he bit down as he rode out his orgasm. My joints are pure mush, and I struggle to roll over, taking the comforter with me to cover myself. Suddenly, I feel too exposed, too vulnerable. Even the room seems too quiet.

Without a word, Ransom dresses hastily. He doesn't even look at me or Tucker. His expression is blank, and it drives me positively mad not to know what he's thinking.

After he's secured his gray beanie over messy locks, he finally looks down at me and says, "Caleb knows how to find me." Then he walks out of the room and out of the suite. I wouldn't be surprised if he left the hotel altogether.

Reluctantly, I look over at my husband. He stares at me with such unrelenting coldness that I physically shiver, even though my skin is burning up.

I swallow.

Shit.

What have we done?

Chapter Seven

Ten years ago . . .

It's Thursday.

I always look forward to Thursdays.

Not because I love spilling my guts about shit that I really don't want to talk about—I hate that part. But because I get to see him.

Dr. DuCane. He told me I could call him Tucker.

Tucker is way too young to be a shrink. And way too handsome. I know he's got a few years on me, but he honestly doesn't look it. Who am I kidding? The man is fucking hotter than sin. Although he doesn't act like it. If anything, he acts like he doesn't realize he's the walking epitome of sexy. And if he does, the news doesn't seem important to him.

No. What are important to Tucker is his work and his patients. And I happen to be one of his patients. Of course, none of that was truly my decision.

I was only three weeks into my second year at Indiana State, and I was already failing Econ. I didn't get it—I loved money. Making it, spending it, stashing some away for a rainy day. So I should've been totally acing the hell out of this class, right? Well, not according to Professor Geldman.

So in a quest to save my stellar GPA, I sought out help—something that was just as difficult for me to do as admitting I was failing. There was this guy in class . . . Patrick Keller. He had taken an interest in me since the first day I strolled into the lecture hall, and while he was nice and not bad to look at, I really wasn't interested. I busted my ass to score a scholarship there, and I wasn't about to get blindsided by a pretty face in khakis. However, Patrick was killing it in that class, and lucky for me, agreed to tutor me. So twice a week, we'd meet up for a study session at the library or Starbucks or anywhere else we could find a vacant table. But never in our dorms. I made it clear that our relationship was strictly platonic.

I thought Patrick was a pretty cool guy. I could always count on him to have candy, especially Starburst. Once he realized that I would steal every piece he had on him, he started bringing more so we could share. Super considerate. So I didn't begrudge him the pining glances he shot me whenever he thought I wasn't looking.

After weeks of working side by side over cups of cold

coffee and Patrick's candy stash, I was finally making strides in Econ. Midterms were approaching, which meant longer hours hitting the books in preparation for the killer exam that Professor Geldman was sure to throw at us. The woman was a sadist.

We stayed later than usual at the library that evening, and when we finally looked up, the place was empty. I gathered my things as quickly as I could in hopes of making it across campus to my dorm before it got too late. However, Patrick said that he would drive me to ensure I got in safely.

"You don't have to do that," I assured him, shrugging on my jacket.

"Nonsense. I'm taking you, Heidi. You don't know what kinda crazies are out there at this time of night."

As we were making our way to the car, I began to wonder what motivation Patrick had for going out of his way to take me home. I mean, yeah, he was a nice guy and I considered him a friend. But it wasn't that long of a walk, and he never offered before. I let him help me into his Honda, which was small, yet new and clean, considering he was a college student, and I pondered whether he felt this little act of chivalry would score him brownie points with me. Oh hell. What if he thought this meant something more than it did?

Patrick said he didn't need directions to my dorm, which didn't arouse any cause for concern. But when he started taking a detour, I knew something was up.

"Where are we going?" I asked when he missed the turn that led us straight to the other side of campus.

"Shortcut," he said. But it was all wrong. His voice was all wrong. His face was all wrong. And he wouldn't look at me.

Looking back, I knew I should have never gotten in that car. And when he turned onto a tiny dirt road, miles away from campus, I should have taken the opportunity to jump out of the car, moving or not.

You hear about rape. You read about it. You see it in movies and on TV. But you never truly know the brutality of it until it happens to you. You may tell yourself that you would never be stupid enough to be put in that situation. You may vow to kick and scream and fight within an inch of your life. But even if you take kickboxing three times a week and drink nasty ass wheatgrass shots, nothing will make you strong enough to fight off an attacker who's sick enough to violate you.

I bled from almost every orifice for nearly a week. I had hypothermia from being dumped outside in the cold afterward, my nearly lifeless body too weak to even move for several hours. Some hikers found me trying to crawl to the priority road the next morning. I was told they saved my life, immediately wrapping me in their own coats and calling for help. According to the doctors, I probably would have only survived another couple hours in my condition.

The rape kit showed that I suffered severe vaginal and anal tearing, as well as three broken ribs, a fractured femur, a shattered cheekbone, broken nose, broken wrist, and wounds that required more stitches than I could count. Patrick had hoped he killed me or beat me badly enough that I wouldn't survive long enough to tell. Wrong, motherfucker. I told the police everything, from the make and model of his car, to his class schedule. The cocky bastard didn't even bother threatening me. He knew for sure he'd shut me up for good.

Patrick Keller was found guilty of first-degree sexual assault and received the maximum sentence in prison. I didn't expect him to make it that long, and vehemently prayed for some gang member to make him his bitch.

Regardless of the scars I bore from the attack, I busted my ass to finish out my sophomore year through online correspondence. My instructors gave me extra time to finish assignments and some even visited me at my parents' home while I healed. I had a long road ahead of me, but luckily, the reconstructive surgeries to fix my mess of a face and body were all sponsored by a foundation for rape victims. I was grateful; my parents could hardly afford my medical bills, even with insurance. I couldn't even leave the house, let alone get a job to help out.

By the fall, I had earned a scholarship at a school in New York and was looking forward to a fresh start. People thought I was crazy; no one bounced back from such a violent attack like that. No. They were left riddled with fear and hatred. They dropped out of school and shut out the world. They cried for hours, wondering what they had done to deserve such brutality.

I did none of those things. I had accepted what happened to me, and I chose to be better for it. Patrick may have broken my body, but he couldn't break my spirit. He couldn't. It didn't belong to him. And to prove that, I was more determined than ever to grow stronger—mentally and physically. After moving to New York—something I was deemed certifiable for—I buried myself in schoolwork. I didn't make friends. I didn't need them. However, my roommate, Keyanna, had worn me down, and I had to admit—I kinda liked having a girlfriend.

Keyanna, or Key, was completely different from me in every way. Where I was tall, thin, pale, and blonde, she was short, curvy, mocha-skinned, and wore her dark, curly mane au natural. But that's where the differences stopped. Key became my best friend. My *sista from anotha mista*, as she would say. And I grew to love her.

One night, after one too many shots of Fireball while watching old reruns of *Fresh Prince*, she asked me about my life back in Indiana. I frowned, not knowing what she meant by that. She had met my parents and siblings during a rare visit. I told her about my pathetic love life. Hell, she'd even seen baby pictures when I was once a cute, chubby kid. I couldn't say I understood where she was coming from.

"What did you leave behind?" she asked me. "Or better yet, what were you running away from?"

And right there, in her twin-size bed, I sobbed as I regurgitated memories of the most horrific night of my life. She held me and smoothed my thin blonde hair over my head. She didn't ask questions or interrupt me. If it weren't for the trickles of moisture that had wet my scalp, I would have thought that awful story hadn't affected her at all.

When I was all cried out and exhausted, she looked at me and smiled, but not out of happiness. It was the kind of smile someone gives you when they try to break some really bad news to you.

"You need to talk to someone," she said.

"I just talked to you."

"No," she replied, shaking her head. Pretty ringlets whipped at her damp cheeks. "You need to talk to someone that can help you through this. To help you make peace with what's been done to you."

I frowned. "I have made peace with it."

She shook her head again. "No. You haven't, Heidi. You keep people at arm's length. You never go out. All you do is study. Outside of me, you have no connection to the outside world." She grasped my shoulders, aligning her teary gaze with mine. "That fucker took something from you. I get that. But he didn't take everything. Not the very best parts. Don't let him have anything else."

Those words did something to me. They woke me up. They made me see that I *had* let Patrick win. I thought picking up where I left off proved that he hadn't completely ripped me to shreds, but in fact, I was letting this bastard dictate every freakin' day of my life. I didn't date; hell, I didn't even look at guys. I stayed away from parties and social events. And I rarely went out after dark. He was winning. And I had let him.

That week, Key talked me into seeing someone at our campus crisis center. They had shrinks come in on three month rotations—part of a local hospital's program for unlicensed doctors to gain more field experience. I figured, what the hell . . . what could it hurt? I wasn't tied to the program. There wouldn't be any note of this in my school records. And after three months, that doctor would be gone and someone new would come in. And honestly, I wanted to do this for Key. I couldn't stand her worrying about me. She was my only friend, and I didn't need her looking at me like I would wither away and die at any minute.

That's how I met Dr. Tucker DuCane. Young, ambitious, smart. He really is a good doctor. But more than that, I can tell he's a good man.

The first thing I noticed about him was his lips. They were the fullest lips I had ever seen on a Caucasian man. He later told me that he's from Louisiana and his great grandmother was Creole. Explains that sexy, southern twang. Every word he spoke sounded like jazz.

After I got over the shock of those enviable lips, not to mention those gorgeous, blue eyes that shone with wisdom and sincerity, I realized something. I was attracted to him. Huh. Go figure.

But attraction didn't mean anything, considering I was there for him to assess what a train wreck I was. Who in their right mind would choose to take on that type of obligation? And once he heard my story, he was sure to look at me the way everyone else did: with pity. And I honestly couldn't stand that shit.

However, Tucker never did. He never made me feel like

an escaped mental patient. And when I told him about what had been done to me, and how I chose to overcome it, he didn't try to tell me how I should feel. My healing was mine alone. And he respected that.

Even if Patrick hadn't made me a victim and I wasn't his patient—let's face it—the chances of Tucker and me hooking up were pretty slim. I've read enough romance books during my seclusion to know that I don't fit the profile. Guys like Tucker—gorgeous, smart, kind, warm—were the heroes. And I am anything but a heroine. I'm not quirky, or awkward. I'm not beautiful without knowing it. I don't listen to classical music or have some tragic backstory. I don't need to be saved. I don't need a hero. I can fare just fine on my own, fuck you very much. And Tucker is most definitely the kind of guy—*man*—that needs to save someone. No thanks, I'll pass.

And aside from being too cynical to be considered pleasant and as stubborn as an ox, I'm just not interested in dating. I think.

Yet, here I am, putting on my favorite jeans that make my ass look fabulous and spending more time with the flat iron than I usually do. For Tucker. The man that I absolutely don't want to date.

I think.

Chapter Eight

Now . . .

We sit across from each other at the breakfast bistro made for two, like we do every morning. Tucker has his usual: steel cut oats, a drizzle of honey, and freshly squeezed orange juice that our housekeeper, Lucia, prepares for him daily. I'm having my breakfast of choice: coffee and half of a grapefruit. We are creatures of habit. And while we may smile at each other from over the rims of beverages and newspapers, what's really on our minds is completely a break from the norm.

Friday night. The night I slept with another man, while my husband watched as he pleasured himself.

It was . . . intense. Exhilarating. Wrong.

And while we can both agree that it was totally not something that should ever happen again, we can't deny the impact it's had on our sex life.

When we left the Royal hotel in the wee hours of the morning, we didn't speak. I don't even remember us looking at each other. I was ashamed, I was scared. I didn't know if Tucker would hate me forever for what I had done. And more than ever, I knew that I loved him. That I needed him. And there was no way I could survive losing him.

The cab ride was silent. When the morning doorman smiled and lifted a brow at our disheveled appearance, I was too embarrassed to even cast him a greeting. Every step toward our home felt like a death sentence. Every breath felt like I was already dying.

Silently, Tucker let us into our condo, stepping back so I could enter. I walked in tentatively, awaiting the shouts, screams, tears. But they never came. Instead, I heard the front door slam shut behind me, causing me to flinch. And in the next second, I was pressed against the wall and my clothes were being ripped from my body. My already soiled panties were next to go.

I groaned with shock and relief as I realized what was happening. And when I felt the hard tip of my husband pushing at my still sore sex, the groan became one of desire.

He didn't kiss me. He didn't tell me he loved me or that I was beautiful. I don't even think he looked at me.

Tucker took me. He took back what belonged to him.

And with my cheek pressed against the wall, my knees trembling with exhaustion and ecstasy, I let him have me.

I look across the table as I take a small teaspoonful of grapefruit to find that he's staring at me. His gaze is hot, molten lava sliding down my lips and neck before slipping between the crevice of my breasts. His tongue snakes out to lick his bottom lip and I imagine that tongue laving my already hardening nipples. I want them between his teeth, as he applies the perfect pressure to make me squirm. It would sting so good. Good enough to cause wetness to dampen my French lace panties. And when I'm hot and ready for him, he'd slip a hand between my thighs and paint music notes with those long, callused fingers. Then I'd sing for him, just like he wanted me to . . .

I blink rapidly, tearing myself from the trance of my fantasies. I shouldn't be thinking like that. I shouldn't be looking at my husband while imagining Ransom's hand between my legs, his skilled fingers caressing my silken folds while I hit every note in every octave. I shouldn't still be able to feel the tug of his teeth on my nipples. I shouldn't still be craving the taste of his kiss—so sweet and tender, yet viciously hungry—or the scent of sex and sweat on his skin.

Jesus, what has gotten into me? Wasn't that why we did what we did? For me to get this ridiculous fantasy out of my system? It was supposed to be a good time. Something we'd look back at and laugh about when we're old and gray, reminiscing about the days when we were young and beautiful.

But my body just won't let it die. It's not ready for Ransom to become merely a memory.

Relieving me from my reverie, Lucia comes to refill my cup of coffee before I even have to ask. She's been with us for a little more than a year now, and I honestly don't know how we ever made it without her.

"So how was your weekend? Do anything fun and exciting?" she asks like she does every Monday morning when she comes back to work. She expects us to answer politely as we always do, reciting the recent events of our mundane life as we always do.

Tucker and I share a glance and a secret smile. And we say nothing at all.

MONDAYS ARE LIKE a weekly reoccurring nightmare for publicists. All of our clients have behaved like fucking snot-nosed children over the weekend and left a burning, brown paper bag of shit on our doorsteps to deal with. I've got Betty Ford on speed dial and most of the staff at the *Post* knows my home number by heart. So, I'm at my desk, starving because I've had to skip lunch, trying to put out some media firestorm revolving around my attention whore of a client and her arrogant prick of a musician husband. Oh, and her bubbalicious ass, which coincidently, is my *biggest* client of all.

"The photos were doctored. How can you prove that some horny little shit in his parents' basement in Connecticut didn't just Photoshop their heads onto some random porn stars? You can't, can you? Therefore, you're just spitting vitriol into the ether, in hopes that some sex-starved moron will actually be dumb and desperate enough to believe you," I say into the receiver of my office phone, while simultaneously tapping on the keys of my cell. Get rid of the original photos!!!! Wipe every fucking phone & computer NOW!

The journalist—which I say with sarcasm because no one at TMZ gives a fuck about journalism—snickers and pulls a trusted source out of his ass. I call his bluff, challenging him to reveal this *close family friend* that supposedly has proof. At that, he stammers an empty threat and I hang up on him.

I rub the bridge of my nose, feeling the first pricks of a migraine creep into my temples. I really should've grabbed something to eat. God only knows how long I'll be here at the office, which usually isn't a problem, considering it's my home away from home.

My office is fashioned much like my luxury high-rise condo. The walls are coated in a clean dove white, as is the upholstery, with just a touch of metallic color lent by stainless-steel accents. It's modern, chic, and painfully orderly, yet somehow it exudes warmth. That could be attributed to the massive windows that make way for brilliant bursts of sunlight to peek through, and for me to indulge in a killer view of the city.

I love my life. However, on days like this, I have to constantly remind myself of that fact.

There's a soft rap at my door and it opens before I can muster up an answer. I look up to see my assistant, Tamara (formerly Thomas, but that's neither here nor there), sashay in with a small stack of papers. She juts out a narrow hip and rests it on the edge of my desk, before gazing down at me with pursed lips.

"Mmmm hmmm. Honey, I told you about working these long hours without taking a break. What happened to that yogurt and granola parfait I brought you?"

I arch a slender brow and flick my gaze to a side table a few feet away where my now warm yogurt and soggy granola begins to decompose. Tamara rolls her mink-lashed eyes.

"It is three in the afternoon. No wonder you ain't but a tiny, little twig. *Girl*, that fine husband of yours wants to knock boots. Not knock bones. If he wanted little chicken wings, he would go to KFC, *ok*?"

She goes full on *sista girl*, complete with a neck roll and Z-formation snaps, leaving me in a fit of weak giggles. "Ok, ok. Have one of the interns run down to the deli on the corner and grab me a half turkey sandwich on rye and a banana. And someone needs to make a Starbucks run too."

"Done. Now, *after* you get some food between them ribs of yours, *People* needs a comment on the Allison Elliot pregnancy rumors, Page Six wants you to verify some info that surfaced about a potential Destiny's Child reunion album, *Bravo* needs an answer about you joining the cast of Real Housewives of NYC next season by the end of the week, and Caleb Berke had some documents delivered by messenger."

She sets the hand written messages on my glass-topped desk, along with a standard-size manila envelope. I go for that one first. The first thing I notice is my company's header. Then I realize what I'm looking at.

A contract.

Signed by Ransom Reed.

My trembling fingertips let the contract tumble from my grip and then float to the ground like paper parachutes. Tamara gives me a narrowed look before scurrying to pick them up as I sit wide-eyed and speechless.

He signed them. Ransom wants me to represent him. Even after what went down between us. I can't deny that it is a complicated conflict of interest, but it's not like I can explain the whys of that decision. And even if I did take him on as a client, how could we ever work together without it getting awkward?

Tamara finishes gathering the documents and leaves them in a neat stack on my desk. "Mmmm hmmm. Look at you. Too weak to hold a piece of damn paper. Let me go send someone before you pass out on me. I love you, girl, but I ain't mouth-to-mouth resuscitating a goddamn thing."

I shoot her a nervous smile as she walks away, fat-injected hips swaying. Then I look back down at that chicken scratched signature, running my fingers over the scrawled letters. Only two Rs are legible, but I can clearly make out his name. Why did he sign it? Because I slept with him? Suddenly, I'm pissed, and I pick up the phone to let someone know it.

"Caleb, what the fuck is this?" I spit out as soon as he answers.

"I'm fine, thank you for asking, Heidi. Now if you're quite done being a rude bitch, might you elaborate on your dilemma?"

I huff out my frustration. What exactly had I meant to say when I called? "The contracts, Caleb. They're signed."

"Isn't that what you wanted?"

"Yes, but, why did he sign them?" Shit. What if Caleb knows exactly what persuaded Ransom? My reputation would be as laughable as Shaquille O'Neal's music career.

"Well, you went to the party. He got a chance to hang out with you, and he likes you. End of. Geez, Heidi, if this is your version of gratitude, you are in serious need of an attitude adjustment. Maybe that sex doctor of yours can teach you some manners."

"Well, did he say anything?" I ask, ignoring his comments. He always manages to bring up Justice whenever we talk. Mostly because he's hoping I'll reveal that JD's secretly gay and wants to bang him. I guess being delusional doesn't interfere with Caleb's work as a top entertainment agent.

"Nothing." I can hear the shrug in his voice. "He said you were cool, and told me he'd sign. Fuck, Heidi don't tell me you have a pitiful little crush on the kid, because that would be—"

I hang up on him. I'm actually surprised I didn't do it sooner.

Fifteen minutes later, I'm still looking at the contracts in disbelief, but I have nourishment to counteract the swarm of butterflies in my belly. I take a bite of banana and contemplate my next move.

I can do this. I'm a professional, goddammit. So what—tons of industry pros have slept with their clients. I'm not the first and I won't be the last. And since he technically wasn't my client then, I should feel zero guilt about this.

I hurriedly wrap up my meal, take a swig of caffeinated crack, and get down to what I'm good at—launching careers to the next level. The plan of action is simple. Ransom needs to be on every talk television show, promoting the album and the upcoming tour. We need to show that the guys are united and there are no signs of discord within the ranks. And while I don't represent the rest of the band, I'm sure I can get them on board with this plan.

I shoot Caleb a text and tell him to send over Ransom's schedule for the week so I can get a few appearances lined up. He replies with a smart-ass comment and a set of numbers that tilts my world off its axis.

Tell him yourself, bitch.
555-844-6730

I don't call. But I save it under my contacts and assign it to *RR*. That's all I need to see—those two little letters, and I know it will all come rushing back to me.

Chapter Nine

It's Wednesday. And I've decided to put my big girl panties on and meet my newest client for lunch.

As unprofessional—and quite frankly punkish—of me as it is, I reach out to him by text, extending my invitation and relaying my intent. The text takes me nearly half an hour to generate, and another ten minutes to gain the nerve to just press fucking *Send.* He responds with two letters, five minutes later.

Ok.

I look good today. Chic, fashionable, yet smart, in a white, fitted wrap skirt, black silk blouse, and white, lightweight blazer. I've left my hair down so it falls in long, voluminous waves, something I rarely do during the week. And while my metaphorical big girl panties are on, my ass is delicately wrapped in La Perla.

I suggest Sage, a modern American restaurant in Midtown that I frequent often. It's my go-to spot for client lunches, and since Ransom is a client, and nothing more, it makes sense to meet him here. Plus, the owner is privy to my high-profile clientele and the staff always knows to seat me in a private area. However, Ransom texts me twenty minutes before our meeting to tell me to meet him in Tribeca at a modern French bistro called La Charcuterie. I huff out my frustration at the plan's deviation, although I'm inwardly grinning. I had heard great things about that place, yet my schedule permits little time for social lunching. And Tucker usually likes to frequent the same five restaurants on date nights.

By the time the driver pulls up to the curb in front of the bistro, my cool, confident demeanor is simply an afterthought, and I'm left standing on the sidewalk, trying to remember how to put one stiletto in front of the other.

The place is crowded, seeing as it is a popular hotspot, but the host leads me to a semi-private area that's occupied by mostly high-powered business types, trust fund babies, and homebred celebs. From what I can see, there are no windows in this section, blocking out the intrusive flash of paparazzi photogs, and I'm certain there's a separate entrance. No wonder Ransom chose this place.

The moment I spot him, sitting at a table dressed for two,

my heart hiccups into my throat. His roguish beauty is still alarming to me, those dark eyes and sharp features making him appear cunning and slightly villainous. He wears a pair of faded black jeans, a heather gray V-neck tee, and his hair is in a messy coif that leaves a few locks to fall over his forehead. It seems pedestrian, however, I can bet that every stitch of clothing that falls on that luscious body was created especially for him. I wouldn't even be surprised if the antique wash of his jeans was deliberate.

He doesn't see me right away, since his head is down, and I can't tell if he's on his phone or counting the threads in the white linen tablecloth. But he must sense my approach, because without cause, he lifts his head and his eyes immediately find me.

My step falters for just a half second and I pray he doesn't notice. His gaze sweeps over me like a gust of Santa Ana wind—hot, dry, and remarkably strong, so much so that I heat from the inside out. The back of my neck feels clammy and I can feel sweat beading on the bridge of my nose. A smile as slow and lazy as a house cat creeps onto his face as if he can smell my perspiration from feet away.

"Mr. Reed," I say in greeting, standing opposite from where he sits. He doesn't stand. He's no gentleman. Tucker would have been on his feet the moment he set eyes on me.

"Mr. Reed?" He raises a brow, yet his grin is still fixed on his face. He's baiting me; he knows I'm thinking about all the reasons why we should be on a first name basis.

"Yes, thank you for meeting me." I should reach over and

shake his hand, but I can only manage one movement at a time. So I sit down, entering his space. Sharing his air. And Ransom seems positively delighted at that prospect.

"So you received the contracts. I'm glad." His tone is polite, although I get the feeling he's hinting at something devious. I go for the untouched glass of ice water that sits on my side of the table and wet my suddenly parched mouth. Ransom follows my every move with a gaze so smoldering, you would think I was skating an ice cube along the column of my throat instead. It's unnerving.

"I did. Just one question though: Why?"

He narrows his eyes as though he doesn't follow so I continue. "Why do you want me as your publicist?"

The thought that Ransom could have agreed to work with me as a thank you for our night together, or in hopes that there'd be an encore performance, definitely crossed my mind. I had assumed he was done with me, seeing as he barely said a thing after we were done and couldn't get me—*us*—out of his sight fast enough. Yet, here he is, signing up to be in my presence on a much more frequent basis.

Ransom takes a moment to contemplate my question as he reaches over to retrieve his own water, yet he doesn't bring it to his lips. "Isn't that what you wanted?"

"Yes, of course, but . . ."

"That is why you came to meet me Friday night, correct?"

I nod vehemently. "Of course."

"You wanted me, so here I am," he replies matter-of-factly with a blasé wave of his hand.

I'm stunned speechless as the waiter takes that exact moment to ask us if we'd like to order drinks. Ransom orders a beer for himself. When I don't answer right away, he tells him to bring a bottle of champagne.

"I'm working," I manage to stammer. "I can't drink in the middle of the day."

"You'll have one glass," he retorts. He's not asking me. He's not even telling me. He's stating a fact. This smug bastard actually thinks he knows me.

I cross my arms in front of my chest, preparing to tell him just how misguided he is, when he gives me a shrug and a smile meant to completely disarm me. To my chagrin, it's working. "I've seen you drink much more and still have total control of your body . . . your mind. One glass won't leave you defenseless and at my mercy. Unless you want to be, Heidi."

I flinch at the sound of my name sliding over his skilled tongue, embedding itself into the warm womb of his mouth. When the waiter returns moments later with our drinks, I'm more than thankful for the sparkling liquid courage, downing my first glassful within seconds.

Ransom refills, watching me watching him. When he nestles the bottle back into the ice bucket, I finally allow myself to breathe again. Maybe speaking won't be so bad either.

"I have some ideas on what we can do to launch your career and really promote the tour and the new album."

"New album?" he asks, a jolt of surprise in his voice. "Who said anything about a new album?"

I furrow my brows in confusion. "Caleb. He said you wanted to record again. Said that you were excited about a song that you needed to get out. I just assumed . . ."

Ransom nods, but doesn't confirm or deny the rumor, and I don't push him to. With these creative types, you have to let them do things in their own time, in their own way. They don't respond to pressure unless it's self-inflicted.

With the break in conversation, the waiter comes to take our order. Even though the aromas wafting from the kitchen are downright heavenly, I hadn't even thought about food, let alone picked up my menu. I quickly flip it open and request a spinach salad, settling on practicality over desire. Ransom asks for some type of gourmet burger with a side of truffle French fries that'll probably cost more than what most people in this city pay for groceries for a week.

We discuss the Euro tour that's coming up in the fall. He tells me his plans for the summer and asks if I'll be like the rest of the urban zombies and escape to the Hamptons. I blush with embarrassment; that was exactly what we had planned to do, at least for Memorial Day weekend and the Fourth. I'm not sure why it embarrasses me or why I feel the need to seem much more cool and blasé than I really am.

We sip. We talk. We laugh when necessary. Ransom is . . . not what I expected. He's young—nearly eight years my junior—but he's lived more than most. He released his first album while still in high school. He's traveled the world. And I'm not naïve enough to ignore the fact that only a man with a lot of experience fucks the way he does.

By the time the waiter arrives with our meals, I'm on my third glass of champagne and probably having the best conversation I've had in months. But the moment I get a mouthwatering whiff of sizzling Kobe beef, melted cheese, and crispy potatoes, I realize just how hungry I really am.

Not wasting any time, Ransom takes a bite and an erotic sound slips between his lips, causing the heat between my thighs to fluctuate into my stomach. He chews, slowly, deliberately then looks at me expectantly.

"How's your salad?"

I look down at the plate of greens topped with bleu cheese, candied walnuts, and house-smoked bacon. Any other day, I would have found it fulfilling. Today, it seems as empty as my stomach. Still, I nod and reply, "Good."

Ransom smiles as if he's on to me and holds out his burger. "Do you want a bite?"

"No."

"No? Are you sure? Because you're staring at it with lust in your eyes."

"No," I repeat. Frustrated heat floods my cheeks, giving them an angry pink tinge.

"Why not?" He has the nerve to look sincerely confused, which only makes this situation even more awkward.

"Why not?" I mimic incredulously. "Because not only is it extremely inappropriate, it's grossly unsanitary."

Ransom laughs heartily, loud enough to draw a few eyes. He continues to hold that damn burger, bite side up, making me appear as some type of anorexic model he has to force-feed before she withers away. Meaning, no one in the restaurant deems this whole scenario as out of the ordinary and they go back to their meals. Still, I tuck my chin and avert my eyes, praying that no one will notice.

"I do not want to eat that," I rage whisper between a clenched jaw.

"Why not?" He stuffs a few fries into his mouth to prove his point and continues his campaign with a mouthful of food. Nope. Definitely not a gentleman. "It's probably the best thing you'll ever put in your mouth . . . to date."

I don't miss the teasing wink of his eye, which only flares my temper. "I'm not eating after you, Ransom."

A wolfish grin spreads his lips and he leans forward on one elbow, closing the space between us by inches that feel like miles. "Heidi, we've kissed. We've touched. We've fucked. I've sucked those pink-tipped nipples like twin cherry-flavored lollipops. I've had my tongue so deep inside your cu—"

"Ok!" I nearly shout, rocking my chair. "You want me to eat the damn burger? I will eat the goddamn burger!"

I lean over and take a small bite, which he happily offers. Once the juicy, premium beef, creamy Gruyère, black truffle aioli, and—oh my God, is that foie gras?—hit my tongue, I nearly have a mini orgasm right there at the table. I swear, my eyes even roll to the back of my head. Oh, sweet Jesus and all his disciples, it *is* the best thing I've ever put into my mouth. Like so fucking good, I'm pissed, because now I'll never be able to eat another burger again.

"You have got to be shitting me," I say flatly after chewing.

"Right?" He smiles broadly before taking his own bite. Right in the place I took mine. "I told you it was insane. Here, try these."

He finger-feeds me French fries topped with fresh shaved parmesan, roasted garlic, and white truffle oil, and I'm all too happy to oblige. Of course, they are just as amazing, and I fight the urge to suck the salt from his fingertips.

"Oh, God. Those should be illegal," I moan.

"Agreed. You should have ordered the same thing. The place is famous for it."

"I know."

Ransom brings a few fries to his lips, but stops before letting them tantalize his tongue. "Then why did you order a boring ass salad?"

I shrug. "It's similar to what I usually order for lunch."

"But it's not what you want."

I shrug again. "It's practical."

He looks affronted, and lets the fries fall from his fingers and back onto the plate. "Where the fuck is the fun in practical?"

Before I'm left with the awkward task of answering, the waiter comes to check on us, asking how we're enjoying our meals. I try my best to compose myself, while Ransom just seems . . . put off.

"You can take that salad. It's not what she wants," he says, his tone tinted with aggravation.

"Certainly, monsieur," the poor server replies, hurriedly

taking the offensive plate of greens from the table. "Would the lady care for something else?"

I open my mouth to tell him that's really not necessary, when Ransom speaks for me. "No thanks. She'll share with me."

I'm staring at him, quite gauchely with my eyes wide and mouth agape, when the waiter asks if he should bring another plate.

"No need. I'll feed her," Ransom answers, ignoring my glare. And with that, he scoots his plate closer toward the middle of the table.

I chuckle and shake my head, reaching for my glass of champagne. Ransom raises a curious brow. "Care to share with the class?"

"Nothing," I reply, still shaking my head in disbelief. "It's just . . . my friend—well client, really—has this theory about salad girls and burger girls."

"Salad girls and burger girls?" He leans forward, planting his elbows on the table.

"He said that salad girls are the ones that will never keep you satisfied. They're the ones more concerned with maintaining an image than being happy. It's all about appearances. But burger girls will always be real with you. They're comfortable in their skin. And because of that, they'll always be confident in you as their partner and friend. And you'll always be content—or satisfied, if you will—with them."

"Humph," Ransom muses, picking over the fries. "Sounds like a smart guy."

"He is," I smile. "Maybe you'll meet him one day."

"Maybe."

That's how we finish lunch—eating off the same plate and talking about everything from music to movies to books. To avoid further humiliation and hunger, I eat more than I probably should. Every bite seems to loosen the tension, and I find myself being more casual than I should with Ransom. He's easy to talk to. And considering he's an insanely gorgeous twenty-something-year-old man that has seen me naked, I know that can only be trouble. For me and for him.

By the time we finish it all off with dessert—a chocolate ganache confection that's good enough to make angels weep—I almost forget that Ransom and I have shared so much more than a burger and fries and cake.

Almost.

Chapter Ten

With a full belly and a midday buzz, I decide to call it a day. I have no more appointments, and all correspondence can be done through text or email. I call Tamara and let her know that she can leave just as soon as she emails Ransom with the Plan of Action and forwards all my messages so I can take care of them at home. She's delighted, of course, and prattles on about being able to make it to her favorite happy hour spot, which pretty much means she'll be on the prowl. I tell her to have fun, yet threaten bodily harm if she comes into work hungover and/or in the same clothes. She tells me to stop being a hater and to let my *"sexy ass husband"* uncork the stick out of my ass.

I'm laughing as we hang up. Normally, I wouldn't allow this type of familiarity with employees, but Tamara is different. She's incredibly efficient, professional, and knowledgeable. I've been grooming her to take on a junior position, although I'd hate to lose the best assistant I've ever had. And to be honest, she's my only friend in the city. Those are hard to come by, especially for me.

After tying up loose ends, including giving Lucia the rest of the day off, I decide to grab the book I've been dying to finish for the past month and take advantage of the quiet.

I only get three paragraphs in before I'm dead to the world, sprawled out in bed with the sheets tangled around me like ivy.

That's how Tucker finds me hours later when he gets home from work.

"Oh, my God, babe, what time is it?" I yawn after he gently wakes me. He looks handsome as always and genuinely happy to see me, but I can tell he's tired.

"Just a bit after six." He brushes his hand over my forehead and I instinctively lean in to his touch. "You ok, Bunny? Are you sick?"

"Yeah." I yawn again, before stretching my limbs as lithely as a sleepy feline. "Just thought I'd take a half day. Had a lunch meeting that lasted longer than I expected and I was beat afterward."

He loosens his navy blue silk tie—a gift from *moi*—while simultaneously kicking off his shoes. "Oh yeah? With who?"

My body begins to react reflexively, but before I can release the name from my tongue, I pause. Shit. How would he react if he knew I had met with Ransom? Would he question me about him? Would he suspect more than just a business lunch went down between us? I mean, if I'm truly being honest with myself, that meal had little to do with business. And if someone had seen us together, and it was splashed on the front of Page Six, do I really want my husband finding out this way? I hadn't even told him that I had taken Ransom on as a client. How would he feel about me withholding that information from him?

I know how he would feel. Pissed. Betrayed. Hurt. All the emotions I would be struggling to swallow if the shoe was on the other foot.

"Um," I stammer, as I climb out of bed. "Ransom Reed?"

"Ransom?" The name sounds more like a curse, more like an accusation.

"Yeah. He agreed to work with me. Crazy, right?" If I look as guilty as I sound, I'm screwed.

I force my eyes from the floor, where they have been fixed since I mentioned the illustrious rocker, and look to my husband. His expression isn't one of outrage or jealousy. More than anything, he seems shocked. So much so, that he's gripping his half-fastened shirt, hard enough to snap off the buttons.

"Yeah. Crazy." I can see he's trying to seem casual about it, but there are questions swimming in those deep blue eyes. Doubt. Perhaps even fear.

In an attempt to ease the discord that is undoubtedly tensing his broad shoulders, I plaster on a fake smile and traipse over to where he stands as still as stone. I place my lips to his cold, rigid mouth. At first, he doesn't reciprocate, but as my warmth thaws his chilly demeanor, I feel him melt into me, responding with a firm yet sweet kiss.

"Are you hungry?" I ask, in my most appeasing voice—the voice I only unleash whenever I feel guilty or remorseful. "I could make you some soup and a sandwich. I'm still pretty full so I may just have a salad."

"Soup and sandwich?" He frowns, and it's the first sign of discontent that he's shown me. For fucking food. "Where's Lucia? It's Wednesday."

Right. Wednesday.

Every Wednesday, like clockwork, Lucia makes Tucker's favorite, chicken enchiladas. She's Dominican, but she loves him, so she makes it a point to fix him his favorite feast weekly. She goes all out too—rice, beans, homemade guacamole. They're downright sinful, and Tuck hits the cardio extra hard on Thursday morning to afford them.

I hate enchiladas. Always have. So I usually end up eating salad, or settling for a liquid dinner consisting of fermented grapes.

It's been like that for as long as I can remember. And like a bad wifey, I just deviated from the routine.

"I sent her home early, Tuck. I told her not to worry about it this week."

He looks wounded, as if I purposely deprived him of his favorite source of sustenance. And maybe on some fucked up level, I did. Maybe I wanted to ruffle his damn rituals and push him just a bit to see how he'd react. To see if that same fire exists in those eyes that pierced right through me as I lay writhing on a borrowed bed last Friday night. The fury that forced him to roughly push me against the wall and fill the same space that Ransom had owned just hours before. I knew what he was doing—Tucker was marking me. Erasing the remnants of that stranger inside me with his dick. Cleansing my sullied shame with his hot seed.

I need to feel that again. I need to see that hunger and desire for *me.* Not some goddamn enchiladas.

"Yeah, sure," he grumbles, as he continues to undress. He won't look at me. I've offended him. Out of all the things I could have done and said today—out of all the reasons to hate me—it takes a lost pile of cheese, meat, and sour cream to insult him.

I throw together a sandwich for him with little finesse, not even bothering to dress it with his favorite condiments. There's some leftover tomato bisque in the fridge and I heat that up too. When Tucker emerges from the bedroom, I've got his food waiting for him at the bistro table, along with a cold beer. See, I can be domestic. I can pose as the perfect wife that's perfectly content with caring for her perfect husband.

"Looks great, babe," he smiles before kissing me tenderly. The taste of irritation no longer rests on those too-full lips. He sits down and digs into his pedestrian meal as zestfully as if it were Lucia's home cooking. Even when I give him a reason to be pissed at me, he doesn't take the bait.

"Where's your dinner?" he asks around a mouthful of pastrami.

"I ate too much at lunch. I actually want to get a little work done before it gets too late. Then maybe we can watch a movie?"

"Sure. Whatever you want, babe," he nods, digging back into his food.

I ruffle his soft, brown waves and kiss the crown of his head lovingly. Tucker's a good man, and I love him. And I'd be a fool to think that he doesn't love me, considering what he's supported me through . . . considering what he's given me. And what have I done? Lusted for another man. But maybe it's not the man that I want. Maybe it's that brash, careless attitude. Or the arrogant swagger. Or the feeling of being soiled by him with just a vulgar word.

That's just not Tucker. I knew that ten years ago, and I loved that about him. He never made me feel anything but safe and cherished. I didn't have to worry about whether or not he was being honest about his feelings. There were no complicated layers or minced words. He was always Tucker—kind, generous, and compassionate.

Just as I will always be Heidi. I'm just not sure who that is anymore.

TONIGHT ON E! News . . .

A drug-related arrest, leaked photos with a suspected prostitute and a possible stint in jail.

Good evening, everyone. We're talking about Evan Carr's sudden fall from Manhattan royalty, and what may have caused some of his recent erratic behavior.

After his very public divorce months ago, Evan's friends and family are truly worried for his life, saying that he's "out of control" and in a "dangerous, self-destructive state of grieving." Later on, we'll hear from the woman rumored to have been his mistress during the time he was married to America's sweetheart, Allison Elliot, who is now linked to intimacy coach and Evan's half-brother, Justice Drake.

But first, we'll get a behind-the-scenes sneak peek into the world of Ransom, the band that's known for their sizzling sound, as well as their ubersexy style. Find out how you can get their smoking hot look at home—

I click off the television and release a resigned sigh. That's enough Ransom Reed for one day. But just as I look over to my husband's sleeping form, my cell vibrates on the nightstand at my side. Who the hell could that be? It's not dreadfully late, but definitely past social hours.

Got your email. Food Network? Really?

It's Ransom. Holy shit.

My finger hovers over the message field on my iPhone, but I don't tap in a reply. Not yet, at least. I know I need to; this is strictly a business matter. But why does it feel like I'm doing something wrong?

Thought it'd be perfect for you, seeing as you love to eat good food. They're always looking for celebrity judges.

There. Short and sweet. That should answer his question. And if he fights me on it . . .

The phone vibrates again before I can consider his reaction any further.

Yeah. That's true. And if all else fails, at least I'll get a free meal out of it.

Like you hardly need to worry about that. I'm still pissed you didn't let me pay for lunch. It was a business expense, after all.

I'm smiling down at my phone, thinking about his earnest attempt to be a gentleman. Just as the waiter was approaching with the bill, Ransom quite literally shoved a wad of bills at him before I could object. He didn't even see what the damage was, but I'm guessing it was enough to cover our meal, and a hefty tip.

Don't worry about it. Next time.

Next time? Will there *be* a next time? Other than business-related meetings, can I allow myself to break bread with him again?

The answer is a resounding no, but I'm trying not to hear it. I don't respond.

You ever seen the movie Edward Scissorhands?

I nearly chuckle aloud.

Uh. Who hasn't? It's only one of the most iconic films of the 90s.

Johnny Depp fan, huh?

I wouldn't kick him out of bed.

I blush. Oh shit. Just the mention of a bed brings back memories of those dark satin sheets. I may not be able to listen to Jay-Z ever again.

I'll keep that in mind. It's on TBS right now. Watch it with me.

I know I really, really shouldn't, but—*Hello!*—Johnny Depp. So in essence, I'm not doing this for Ransom. I'm doing it for my own selfish reasons.

I turn on the TV, just in time to see Edward, in all his Goth glory, give some poor, sex-deprived lady a haircut so good that she moans in ecstasy. My cheeks flush in the dim lighting of my bedroom, and I glance over at Tucker to see if he's noticed. Of course, it's just paranoia; he's dead to the world, snoring softly on his side like he has since 10 P.M.—bedtime. I turn my eyes back to the movie and am quickly engrossed in the story and that strange, sad, beautiful man.

It's fucked up, you know.

I frown down at the cryptic message, wondering if Ransom accidently texted me something that was meant for someone else.

What is???

He answers immediately, as if he was already typing in an explanation.

To be wanted and celebrated by everyone, but be completely misunderstood. To be a novelty. Nothing more than a show dog.
Did you just compare yourself to Edward Scissorhands?
Idk. Guess I did.
Someone thinks an awful lot of himself.
LOL. But it's true. No one really knows you in this business. They know what they see on TV and in the tabloids. But you're a stranger, surrounded by people who think they love you.

His words bring me up short, and I take a few extra moments to formulate an appropriate response. I don't want him to think that his honesty has scared me away, so I hurriedly tap in some stupid emoji that I instantly regret.

:-/

Sorry. I can't imagine. But at least you have your band. And what about your family?

I don't know why I ask him. It's way too personal and something I shouldn't give a damn about. I'm his publicist. Not his shrink. If he wants to talk about his feelings, I happen to screw a pretty good shrink twice a week. Three times on holiday weekends.

Still, I stare down at my phone, waiting for a response.

They're not around anymore.

Shit. I didn't want to know that. I didn't want to feel . . . anything . . . about him. But now I know that he's alone in this world. And I can't *unfeel* the twinge of sympathy that seizes my chest.

I won't respond. I won't let him believe that I care, even if I do.

We continue to watch on, and young Winona's bitch of a boyfriend cons Edward into getting in trouble. I've always hated this part. It wasn't fair—he did nothing wrong. Yet, the townsfolk's perception of his crime has caused them to all turn against him in a vicious witch hunt. They loved him before when he seemed exotic and mysterious. They all couldn't wait to covet his talent. They all wanted a piece of that strange, sad, beautiful man, but not to love. To own. And the minute he fucks up, he's no more than a freak. An animal they just want to put down.

After the movie is over, I look to find that Ransom hasn't written more. I turn off the TV and the lamp on my nightstand then settle into bed. Just before I drift off to sleep, I reach over and power down my phone.

Chapter Eleven

I don't hear from Ransom all day Thursday, so I definitely don't expect to on Friday. However, I can't help but feel somewhat slighted that he hasn't texted, emailed, sent a carrier pigeon—something. Not that he should. Not that I should want him to. Which really is just poetic justice, considering that apparently I am on a roll when it comes to rejection.

I woke up oddly refreshed, ready to make Friday my bitch and start my weekend. Maybe I was still on a Ransom Reed high or just excited for some downtime. Either way, it was odd for me, seeing as I was not a morning person.

Tucker was already up, of course, and had just finished his 6 A.M. workout with his trainer. I could hear the shower beating down against sweat-stained skin and frosted glass, and a jolt of excitement ran through me like electricity, lighting up my nerve endings like a Christmas tree. I slunk to the bathroom and silently slipped out of my nightgown, and joined my husband under the steaming hot spray. He started at the first feel of my arms wrapping around his taut torso from behind, but it took him only a second to realize my intentions, and he turned to face me.

"Good morning," he murmured against my lips before capturing them between his. I opened for him—morning breath be damned—and let him drink in my desire. My nails ran a slick path up his back before raking down to the dimples above his ass. I felt him grow between us, nudging my belly, and I brought one hand to that rigid intruder. I began to stroke him—softly, at first—letting the water collect in my hand to heighten the feeling of warm slickness. He moaned and delved into my mouth deeper, his hands grasping my hips, my ass, my breasts.

I wanted him. Needed to feel him filling me in the worst way. I turned around and pressed my chest to the cool tile of the shower wall, my back arched to give him better access to the heat between my thighs, not that he's ever needed help finding it. His hands were on my shoulders, gently gliding down my spine to the arch of my ass, then . . .

Nothing.

I turned around to see what could be the hold up, to find Tucker studying the mosaic rocks of the shower floor. A frown dimpled his forehead and he panted, causing the water dripping down his face to shiver before dissolving into a thin spray. Then without looking up at me, he turned back to place his face under the hot spray.

"I have a client first thing, babe," I thought I heard him say. I can't be sure. It was hard to hear over the roar of blood rushing my face. Moments later, he stepped from the shower, abandoning me to the heavy veil of steam and water to hide my frustrated tears.

By the time I had collected enough dignity to step out of the humid safety of the shower, Tucker was gone. And I was left with the blaring reality that my life—my boring, mundane, beautiful, stable life—was trickling down around me, pooling at the soles of my bare feet.

I file the morning's incident under *Shit I need to deal with but am too chicken shit/busy/stubborn to do so*, and turn my attention back to my cell. It remains silent aside from Tamara's constant updates on the event my firm is hosting for a premium tequila launch tonight. I let her take the lead on this one, forcing myself to resist the need to micromanage and give her enough space and opportunity to flourish on her own. She has it in her—we both just need to trust it. However, I insisted on updates on everything from the catering to room layout to the swag bags for guests. My name was still stamped on this party, and I would demand no less than perfection.

I'm punching in a reply to Tamara's inquiry on the guest list when a deep, sinuous voice stops me dead in my tracks, leaving my finger hovering over the Send key.

"You know, you really should hire reliable help. Anyone could just walk in here."

I look up to find Ransom filling the space of my office entrance, leaning against the doorjamb with the grace and swagger of a man who knows and loves every inch of his body. I don't doubt that he does. I've only had the pleasure of seeing a glimpse of it, and I still can't erase that image from my mind. Who would want to?

"Anyone like you?" I quip, schooling my features into a cool expression. I don't smile. I won't let my happiness be manipulated by this man.

He's unruffled by my cold demeanor and enters the room without invitation or apology. The best way to describe it is saunter. Ransom saunters into the room, but there's nothing flamboyant about him. It's as if he's completely unbound by bones or skin, the way he moves as fluid as the silk of his voice. He stops in front of my desk and regards me with a devious smirk before folding himself into the chair across from me. He doesn't play by the rules. He just creates the game. At some point, I need to stop being such a willing participant. I need to quit playing myself.

Neither of us speaks for a hot minute. We just stare each other down as if we're seeing one another for the very first time. Or for the last time. Before I can find good sense enough to clear my throat and question him on his presence, he speaks up.

"Exactly like me."

I blink half a dozen times, causing the hardened ink on my lashes to gently bite my eyelids. "Excuse me?"

"Anyone like me could just walk in here. And you don't need that. You don't want that."

What the hell do you know about what I want? I silently ask him. He smiles as if he's stolen the question from my lips.

"You're right," I say, not meaning a word of it. It still doesn't dissuade his grin. "What can I do for you, Ransom?"

Relaxing, he folds a leg over the other so that his knee juts out to the side. His fingers rest atop his knee and begin to tap rhythmically. "Your POA proposal."

"What about it?" I set my phone down and give him my undivided attention. Business. This is about business. I can do that.

"We're doing *SNL* tomorrow night."

"I'm aware of that." Obviously, that had been in the works for weeks, at the hands of his agent.

"I want you there."

I pause, snapping my lips shut on my initial response. Why does he want me there? Why would he need me there? The band is performing—that's it. And from what I've seen, they make a cameo in a short skit alongside featured host, Rebel Wilson. Essentially, a publicist wouldn't be needed.

"I'd feel better if you were there," he shrugs, reading the questions escaping my expression.

"Why?" *Why me? Why now?*

I don't say it, but I know he can see it. I know he can see *me*.

"Why not?" *Because I want you.*

Suffocating silence lies between us when my cell rings,

and I scramble to answer, assuming it's Tamara. I don't even think I replied to her text earlier.

"Bunny, I've only got a quick minute." I can hear the urgency in Tucker's voice, and it instantly sobers me.

"What is it, Tuck?" Instinctively, my eyes drift over to Ransom and I cringe. I don't know why I do it; I don't know why there's the distinct knot of guilt caught in my throat, but there is.

"I've got to work late tonight. Something's come up." Translation: One of my patients is in the midst of a crisis, and they need me more than you do. "I know you have that thing tonight. Will it be all right if I pass?"

Without rhyme or reason, my gaze goes to Ransom, who lifts a curious brow in response. "Sure, honey. Not a problem."

"I'm sorry. I can try to make it later. It's just . . ."

"It's fine, Tuck. I'll be fine. I'll make an appearance and head home. No need to come, I promise. Go on . . . go be amazing." There's a smile in my voice, but it doesn't touch my face.

"Ok, babe." There's a rustle on the other end as if he's on the move. "You know I love you, Heidi."

I suck in a breath, drawing in those sweet, tender words and letting them fill the space he left empty early this morning. The space that's remained empty since he pressed me face-first into the wall almost a week ago.

"I know," I respond on an exhale. "I love you too."

When I look up, Ransom is regarding me with unmasked wonder.

"What?" I ask, almost annoyed with his candor.

"What can't he make?"

The papers on my desk serve as the perfect distraction, and I focus on shuffling them into neat piles. "My firm is handling the launch party for *Lujo* Tequila. I have to actually head over there soon to ensure everything is set for tonight before getting ready."

"Really?" I can't tell if his interest is feigned or genuine, but he suddenly sits up straighter. "What time does it start?"

"Eight P.M. Why?"

Ransom climbs to his feet just as lithely as he sat, and I am hurled back into the memory of his body sliding out and off of mine. I shiver, the need to feel that heat again fresh on my mind.

"Because I'll be in front of your place at seven thirty."

"What? Ransom, no. I don't need you to do that." I'm already moving around my desk to stop him from leaving with that crazy notion on his brain. He turns just as he hits the doorframe.

"I know. But I'm doing it anyway. So be ready."

He doesn't explain himself. He doesn't give me a chance to refute his offer—no—his demands. He just turns around and walks away, taking my good sense with him.

I finish the afternoon in a robotic, yet efficient, haze, which isn't far off from the norm for me. When I stop by the venue to ensure all is set for tonight, only Tamara notices that I'm less than present. But even she's too preoccupied to give a damn.

By the time I head across town to our condo, I'm seized with nerves. I don't know why. I could easily text Ransom right now and tell him to forget it, that his presence isn't welcome. That it is highly inappropriate for us to carry on so casually. But as I step through the threshold of the front door to see that Tucker isn't home, I release a sigh of shame-laden relief.

I dress in a simple black dress with a modest neckline and a back dip so low that my entire spine is on display. It's the mullet of dresses—business in the front, and all party in the back. I can get away with it at a function like this, but just barely. Still, I clip my ice blonde hair up to show off the dramatic plunge. If there's one advantage of having fun-size breasts, it's definitely being able to rock a daring outfit sans bra.

I'm anxious as I make my way downstairs. Part of me hopes he was just bluffing. A much larger, more physical part of me hopes that the black limo at the curb in front of my building contains one Ransom Reed.

It doesn't.

Instead, the driver opens the door to usher in Mrs. Worthington from downstairs, who is dressed to the nines in a cacophony of silk and sequins.

"Good evening, Mrs. Worthington," I manage to smile through my disappointment. The much older woman nods at me fondly, taking in my equally formal attire.

"Oh, good evening, dear. I see you have a steamy rendezvous tonight as well." She gives me a conspiratorial wink before dipping into the backseat of the dark car, leaving me surprised and a little envious. I snap my mouth closed and turn to the doorman of my building to ask for a cab when the seductive purr of a V8 engine captures my attention, just as a black metallic Maserati GranTurismo pulls up to the curb. Without even seeing his face through the dark tinted windows or smelling his scent of spiced smoke and earth, I know Ransom is behind the wheel. No one else could drive a car this sexy and pull it off so flawlessly.

With almost feline elegance, he unfolds himself from the car and comes around to where I stand on the sidewalk. He's dressed in all black—tailored black slacks, black dress shirt with the top few buttons undone, and clean, black boots. And although this is the most dressed up I've ever seen him, he wears the tighter clothing just like he does his worn jeans and tees—like they were made to grace his body.

"You're here." What was supposed to be skeptical is masked by the breathy sound of my voice. Dammit.

"I said I would be."

He doesn't greet me or tell me I look beautiful. He hardly even looks at me. He just opens the passenger side door and steps aside to let me in. Reluctantly, I slide onto the crimson leather seat, taking extra care with the hem of my dress. He doesn't want to look, so God forbid I give him something to look at.

"Nice car," I murmur as he filters into bumper-to-bumper traffic.

"Thanks. It was a birthday present to myself," he replies

stiffly, keeping his eyes on the road. Somehow, he seems to find every open spot and zips his way between lanes. I'm pretty sure the sweet ride has something to do with it too. Respect must be paid when a Maserati is on the road.

"Well, you sure know how to spoil yourself." It's a lame comment. Lame. One out of nervousness just to fill the empty space. Music plays quietly in the background, and I take it upon myself to turn it up, breaking cardinal rule number 1: Never touch a man's stereo. Nev-er.

"What are you listening to?" I ask, as the enchanting sounds of a male voice comes through the speakers. I feel like I've heard the singer before, but I can't pin down a name. The musical accompaniment is minimal, as it should be. The man has a beautiful voice, his upper register so impressive that it's almost feminine. However, there's a raspy attribute to it that gives it a certain edge.

"Matthew Koma."

I nod but silence the questions on my tongue to take in the music. His song is one of desperation, pain, and surrender. It's heaven to my ears, yet stirs something dark and hot within me. I know the name, I just didn't know he could sing like this.

"We've been working with him on our new material," he answers without me asking.

"New material?" That gets my attention and I turn in my seat to gaze at him through our capsule of darkness. Shadows play across his sharp features, brilliant, neon lights brushing kisses across the edge of his jaw. His hair is completely slicked back tonight, making him seem even more severe. Almost menacing.

"Yeah. We've been writing. Got to step into a booth earlier. Felt good."

"Wow."

He doesn't miss the hint of disbelief in my voice and turns momentarily to face me, his brow furrowed in offense. Artists are sensitive motherfuckers. "What?"

"Nothing, that's great," I quickly assure him. "It's just . . . his sound is so different from yours. The artists he works with are just . . . not like Ransom."

He shrugs with nonchalance, yet the tick in his jaw gives him away. "We sing—we play—what we feel. Change is good. Growth is good. Especially when it's felt. We're still Ransom. We're just evolving. Shouldn't that make you happy?"

Make me happy? Why would he even care about my happiness?

"Stay off of Page Six with drunken brawls and sorority girl hookups, and that would make me happy." I tack on a nervous laugh, which Ransom doesn't return. Damn. Something surely crawled up his ass.

Luckily, we pull up to the venue, which is a popular hotspot in the Meatpacking District. After his baby is secured with valet, Ransom comes to stand beside me, of course, drawing every flashing camera and catcall on us. I keep my head down and go to stand off to the side so Ransom can do his thing, but find that he keeps perfect pace with me, gently placing a hand on the bare skin of my lower back to guide me into the building. I'm flattered for a hot minute before full-on terror coils in my gut. Well, *that* surely will be front-page news. *Ransom Reed Steps Out with Older Woman.* The press will not be kind.

Once we cross the threshold, servers with shots of the featured tequila bombard us with offers. We each take one to be polite, especially since my clients are in attendance. Ransom looks at me expectantly, waiting for me to join him in a drink.

"What? You don't actually expect me to drink this, do you?" I say low enough that no one hears.

"Why not? It's free booze . . . that you happen to represent. Shouldn't you have faith in your client?"

I roll my eyes, all the while shooting fake smiles and waves to familiar faces around the room. I don't want anyone to think that Ransom is any more than a business associate. "Forget it, Ransom. Tequila and I don't mix."

"Just one drink, Heidi. Just have fun with me. Loosen up. Please?"

I finally allow myself to gaze up at him, and I plunge into the dark depths of his onyx eyes. Even with the nose ring and keen features, there's something soft and vulnerable about him. Something that I can only unravel when I get this close to him. I saw it that night we spent together, right after he sang to me while stroking me from behind. And when he kissed me, I felt it too. I felt it all over me, intoxicating me. Filling my lungs with his own brand of potent smoke. I inhaled deep and held it in, refusing to let it go. And when it hurt too much to hold on to, I exhaled, gasping his name in my desperate need for air.

"Yes."

It seems like I'm always saying yes to Ransom Reed. I can't fathom any woman ever telling him no.

He taps his shot glass against mine, and then raises his glass in salute. But instead of tipping it to his lips, he brings it to mine. Eyes locked, breaths ragged, I let him feed me a sip of the fiery elixir. It burns all the way down, but I lick my lips in craving, needing more. Just one taste is all it takes to hook me. All it takes to break me down.

"Heidi! Girl, where have you been? The caterer thinks we're going to run out of crab cakes within the hour. We got some stragglers outside trying to get in with fake invitations. And I swear, some of these old ass rich bitches are smuggling bottles in their bags." Tamara throws her hands up dramatically and wraps me in her thick arms. Luckily, I hand my shot glass to Ransom before she spills it.

"Ok. Calm down. I can handle this." I pull away from her and nod toward Ransom. "Tam, this is Ransom Reed. Ransom this is my assistant Tamara, the person who usually keeps *just anybody* from walking into my office."

Ransom nods and smiles to a starstruck Tamara, who gushes and squeals like a brace-faced Belieber. Ransom accepts graciously before excusing himself so we can get down to work. Which, coincidentally, is exactly what I need if I want to get through this night unscathed with my dignity in check. I have the caterer put out bacon-wrapped scallops to replace the loss of crab cakes to the menu. I double up on security at the entrance. And I make sure the staff keeps the alcohol behind the bar when they pour, replacing the ones on display for decoration with empty ones filled with colored water. Let those cheap old biddies steal that. Ha!

I don't even realize how much time has slipped by when I am done putting out all the PR fires until I look up to find that Ransom is nowhere in sight. I swallow down the knot of disappointment when I realize that he's left. I'm not sure why it bothers me—I've hardly paid him any attention. And it's not like I can't get a ride home.

I'm directing a few partygoers to the swag table to grab a few freebies when I hear the faint, melodic sounds of piano coaxing me from the pounding rhythm of Top 40s pop anthems blaring from speakers around the room. I follow the sound, sniffing it out like a hound in search of sustenance, and find that it's generating from a smaller space reserved for special events. Tentatively, I push open the door, and my gaze eagerly discovers Ransom sitting at a Steinway, his eyes closed as he regurgitates his soul through black and white keys. He doesn't look to me when I enter and shut the door behind me, but I know he feels my presence. A slight smile falls on his lips as he continues to play without falter. I know this tune—it's one of my favorites that Tucker plays at home on his record player. And even though Ransom isn't singing the words, I can feel the beauty of those lyrics as if they were etched on my heart.

Ransom finally opens his eyes when I sit down beside him on the bench, and his smile stretches wider. I can't help myself. I smile too.

"I didn't peg you for a Stevie Wonder fan," I say as he restarts "Ribbon in the Sky."

"My parents were . . . deeply religious when I was growing up. He was one of the few secular musicians they allowed in their home."

I nod, soaking it all in. Ransom Reed is telling me personal information about himself. He's opening a wound to let me in. Why?

"I learned every one of his songs. This one was one of my favorites."

He begins to hum, the sounds feral and intimate, like the way he sings seductively on stage in front of thousands of fans, grinding his hips to the beat of an equally suggestive Ransom tune. Or the way he moans when he thrusts deeper, until he's completely embedded in me, the tip of him stroking the sweet spot that causes me to clench around him.

Heat explodes in a swirl of red and pink and coral on my cheeks that I know he can see even under the dim lighting. Yet, he just continues to play, every skillful finger pressing the keys perfectly to produce magic. His fingers were one of the first things I noticed up close about him. They're long and slender—perfect pianist fingers. They were created to make love. To fuck. To create.

I don't realize I've closed my eyes until I hear him singing beside me, causing me to wake from my dream. It's just the first line of the first verse. But it's enough to have me panting with the need for him to trace those lyrics with his tongue all over my body. I have to get out of here. I have to get away from him. If I don't, I'm not sure what I will do. And I'm even more unsure whether he would stop me.

Ransom reads my frantic expression like sheet music and smiles. He slides those long, magical fingers from the keys and places his hands in his lap, turning to me with wonder resting on his brow. I stare back, my lips parted and my breath shallow. I stare and I wait and I beg.

"Heidi." My name is like an elixir on his tongue, potent and sweet. Too strong to swallow all at once, but intoxicating enough to crave it inside him. I move in a fraction closer, wanting to taste it. Wanting to smell my scent on his mouth.

A hiss filters between his teeth, and Ransom abruptly turns back to the black and ivory keys. A frown shadows his smile for just the barest of moments, but it's long enough to break the spell.

"Come on," he rasps in the voice reserved for the secrets he sings in the dark. "Time to go."

Chapter Twelve

We weave through streets as slick and black as oil, bypassing partygoers and club-hoppers and late-night diners. Ransom doesn't speak as he drives, but he leaves the music up. I close my eyes and lay my head back against the butter soft leather, and replay our last moments, our last words, our last touch.

What have I done?

What am I still doing?

We pull up to my building, and Ransom is already out of the driver's side door before I can collect myself enough to search for the handle. He opens it and steps aside, offering me a hand to aid my shaky efforts. Still, he says nothing. Even his fingers—those long, dazzling fingers—seem cold.

Maybe I was wrong about him. Maybe he is a gentleman, in his own unconventional way. But he isn't Tucker. And furthermore, Tucker isn't him.

"Thank you," I murmur, feeling self-conscious. I hug myself and shiver despite the warm, late spring temperatures.

He nods in response. That's it. That's all he has for me, reminding me that I am not entitled to more. I shouldn't crave more.

I turn to the door of my building, when he turns my limbs to stone with just a single whispered word.

"Heidi." His mouth cradles that word—cradles *me*—like a razorblade under his tongue. So careful, yet so dangerous.

I turn around despite the lead in my six-inch heels, but I don't respond.

"If you wanted me . . . If you were . . ."

That's all I need.

I nod, and bid him good night, and leave Ransom standing at the curb. It's not until I approach the elevator that I hear the roar of 8-cylinders drift away into the night.

My condo is dark and empty when I enter, but I'm not surprised. However, I am shocked by a beautiful spread situated on the kitchen table. I pick up the white notecard and recognize that messy doctor's scrawl that I've learned to decipher over the years. I smile as I read the haphazard lines and loops, and realize that, no, Tucker isn't Ransom, and he never will be. And I've never been more grateful for that.

Bunny,

It's going to be a long night, baby. But hopefully this makes up for it.

I love you.

Tuck

I set the note aside and see that he's arranged to have a bottle of my favorite Cab, truffles and chocolate chip cookies from Jacques Torres, Laura Mercier bath milk, and the softest, silkiest pajama set from La Perla.

He's thought of everything, and must've planned all this hours ago. He knew he wouldn't be able to make it tonight, and he still wanted me to feel special. He still wanted me to feel loved and cherished, despite what I've done. Despite what I wanted to do tonight.

Guilt seizes my chest, and I clutch my throat. Alone and in the dark, I choke on the shame and let it roll down my face, stealing my mascara with it. I suck in a few breaths to compose myself and quickly swipe away the tears, before grabbing the basket of goodies and taking them to our room. That's enough humanity for one night.

Gorging myself on wine and chocolate, I take the most luxurious bath known to man. Luckily, Tucker, being the kind, considerate man that he is, even thought to uncork the bottle for me and include a glass. I soak until the water runs cold and I'm all out of cookies. And after I get out and swath myself in ribbons of pale pink silk, I polish off another glass of red too.

Although I shoot Tucker a text to thank him and wish him

good night, I'm not tired enough to sleep. Wine and sugar spike my bloodstream like adrenaline, and I feel more wired than before my bath. I grab the remote and flip through the channels to find that one of my favorite movies has just come on, and I settle in with another glass of wine and what's left of the truffles. My ass may pay for this tomorrow, but I'm too distracted to care.

I'm sympathizing with Lester Burnham, understanding his desperation, his frustration, when my phone chimes beside me. I expect it to be Tucker—who else would be texting me at close to 1 A.M.?—but it's not. Of course not. That would be too much like right.

What are you doing?

My fingers hover over the keys, wondering if I should reply or just pretend to be asleep. But I can't find the strength to deny him. To deny myself.

Watching American Beauty. You seen it?

With Kevin Spacey? Yeah. What channel?

Showtime

There's a pause, and I imagine him flipping through the channels.

Got it. Great movie.

Weren't you like 5 when it came out?

8. And?

Seems a little cynical and morbid for an 8-year-old.

Not when you're a cynical and morbid 8-year-old kid.

I take a sip of wine. Another personal detail. One that would make me imagine a little, round-faced Ransom Reed, with shaggy dark hair and eyes too old for his young years. I could have done without it. Nothing good could ever come of it.

I used to have a crush on Ricky.

I don't know why I tell him that.

The weed smoking creeper kid with the camera?

Yeah.

Makes sense.

Why do you say that?

Because he's dark and dangerous. He doesn't fit in or conform. He's the complete opposite of you. He's the bad boy you want but will never let yourself have. Not completely.

I nearly drop my phone. Did he just . . . try to *shrink* me? Are we still talking about the movie?

So you think I liked him because he's the quintessential bad boy?

No, H. I think you want him bc you want to be bad too.

I reach for my wineglass and take a huge slug without even tasting it.

Then . . . I smile. He called me H. No one's ever called me H. Not to my face at least. And I think I like it. Not because it's simple or charming. But because he gave it to me.

What makes you think I want to be bad?

Bc you want me.

Seeing those words on the screen of my phone incites fear and excitement so deep that it literally shakes me to my core, and I drop the wineglass, ruining the beautiful bodice of my pajama top. I curse and toss my phone to the side to save it from sudden death and jump out of bed. Fortunately, there wasn't much vino left in my glass and my bedspread is unscathed. Unfortunately, my lovely new sleepwear is ruined. I strip and kick it into a pile, too lazy and, honestly, too tipsy to care enough to try to salvage it. Then I climb into bed completely naked, and pull the covers up to my breasts.

When I look back at my cell, I see there's a new message.

Did I scare you off?

No. I spilled my wine. Had to take off my clothes.

I could have left that part out, but fuck it. There's no such thing as a little wrong. Just like there's no such thing as a little pregnant. I was wrong the moment I replied to the first text message two nights ago. Just as wrong as I was to agree to one night of drunken debauchery. This is wrong. We're wrong. But I don't know how to be right. Not anymore.

You're naked?

I'm in bed.

I'm assuming your husband isn't home or asleep or you wouldn't be texting me right now.

He's working.

So you're all alone. And naked.

I snort out a laugh, knowing exactly what game he's playing. *Nice try, buddy.* He's trying to unnerve me. Get under my skin, in every way possible. Truth is, it's working.

Yes. How about you?

Naked? Yes.

Hmmm, interesting.

Alone? No.

I read his response again. And again.

He's naked, but he's not alone.

He's with someone. Right now. And he either just fucked her or is about to fuck her. Shit, he could be fucking her right now as he watches Kevin Spacey lift weights and smoke pot in his garage! All while texting me!

I don't know why this bothers me, not when I have zero right to feel a damn thing about him. When just this morning, I had my hand wrapped around my husband's dick, all but begging him to fuck me up against the shower wall. When I'm married to the man of my dreams and he is just some twenty-four-year-old horny kid who would probably fuck a tree hollow if he was drunk and desperate enough.

This should not affect me. This should not hurt me. But dammit, I can't help the heat that flames my face, leaking into my eyes until it gets too blurry to see the words on the touchscreen of my phone. I can't control my hands that shake so badly that my fingers go limp, dropping the device in the tangle of sheets swathing my naked body. And I can't tame the overwhelming nausea that roils my gut, creating a hot, soupy eddy of wine and chocolate.

Clutching my mouth, I run to the bathroom and make it to the toilet just in time. I empty myself of this illness, this frustration. I purge him from my body and my soul. And when I'm finished, I brush my teeth and spit the remnants of Ransom Reed into the sink. I'm done.

I climb back into bed and shut off the television just as Ricky's dad beats the shit out of him. Poor Ricky. He wasn't a bad boy or a creep. He was just bored. He was lonely. And loneliness and boredom combined will push you to the most extreme of extremes. All in a quest to find some semblance of normalcy. An inkling of freedom. A glimmer of life.

I think I hear my phone chime somewhere between reality and the fiction of my dreams, but I tune it out. It's much easier to deal with the truth on this side. I can make it up as I go along.

Chapter Thirteen

Then

"Are you sure?"

I look up at Tucker and smile before my fingers drift up to the collar of my white cotton shirt. My fingertips touch the smooth surface of a pearlescent button and free it from its noose. Then another one. And another.

"Wait, Heidi." Tucker swallows and I watch the way his Adam's apple bobs up and down, pushing through the tightness in his throat. He scrubs the back of his neck nervously and turns his head, yet his eyes are still on me. He can't *not* look.

"No," I say, going for the fourth button. The button that

will give him his first view of my bra. "We've waited long enough."

I keep going until my entire shirt is undone, keeping my eyes trained on the man in front me. Showing him that I want this, that I want him. I don't want there to be a single ounce of doubt in his mind. Because it just doesn't exist in mine.

I knew that Tucker would be the one I'd give my heart and body to freely. I wouldn't have to fight him. I wouldn't have to fear him. Because he knew me. He knew how to love me, how to hold me. He was good and kind and gentle. He was safe.

I let my shirt fall to the floor and stand before him, silently pleading for him to touch me. It only takes him a breath before his hands are on my skin, his fingertips sliding over my collarbones, down through the middle of my chest. I feel the soft bite of his nails rake over my ribs, like he wants to claw his way inside, yet he's holding back. He doesn't want to hurt me.

"I'm not going to break," I whisper, touching the backs of his hands. I press them hard into my skin, using every bit of my strength so he can't pull away. "You can touch me."

"I am touching you."

"No. Touch me, Tucker. Feel me."

I grasp the bottom hem of his shirt and wait for him to lift his arms. He closes his eyes and, with a huff, allows me to shed it from his body. His chest is magnificent. Hard and rippled and broad. A sprinkle of light brown hair trails his pecs and circles his nipples. I taste him and he flinches as my tongue flicks across the sensitive skin. But his hands grasp me harder, fingers digging into my skin, desperate to be inside me. I don't make him wait any longer. I reach back and unzip my skirt, and hooking my fingers underneath my underwear, I let them join our shirts on the floor.

"I want this," I reassure him. "I want this so bad."

Want and longing wage war against the uncertainty and fear on his face, so I take his hands in mine and lead him to my little twin-size bed. Keyanna won't be home until morning and the door is locked. I'm not letting this rare night alone go to waste.

Naked, I sit on the bed and pull Tucker to stand between my legs. He tries to sit beside me but I refute his efforts by grasping his hips. I take a deep breath. Then another. And I begin to unbuckle his pants.

He's ready for me, proud and hard and scorching in my palms. I slide my fingers over the satin skin and watch as the thin layer ripples over veins and ridges. I don't expect it to be darker than the rest of him—almost pink—but then again, I've never been this up close to a man before. Boys, yes. But never a man.

I slide my tongue over the tip of him and feel him tremble in my hand. The flavor of salty citrus tingles my lips and I suck more of him to taste more. He smells how he tastes, tangy and spicy, yet there's a musky undertone. I want more of him in my mouth. I want all of him in my mouth. And I take all that I can, all that he can give.

Tucker's trembles evolve into jerky movements of his hips, as he begins to thrust in and out of my mouth, keeping time with the suction of my lips. He groans with each stroke, growing longer and harder, and my mouth aches with every greedy suck. I pull back just to catch my breath, but before I can take a single gulp of air, he's pushing me back onto the bed and spreading my legs. He tastes himself on my lips before his mouth roams the slope of my neck to the small mounds of my breasts. He licks my nipples with rose petal strokes, and continues to paint my skin with his warm, wet venom. I arch into his touch, needing to feel more. He rewards me with a kiss at the top of my pubic bone and spreads me even wider, seeking the damp swell between my thighs.

His fingers follow the path of short blonde hair before whispering across my heated flesh. I moan at the almost-touch, the phantom penetration, hoping to inspire him to go farther. When his fingertip runs along my clit, a shiver runs through me so strong that I feel it at the very tips of my curled toes. He does it again, pressing harder, causing pressure to build inside my womb. I gasp his name and claw at the soft strands of hair that have fallen in his eyes as he studies my sex with wonder in his gaze. Wonder and hunger and an emotion so raw, there isn't a word for it. But when he presses his tongue against my slickness, I feel its meaning. I feel it become a part of me, digging into my soul like a branding iron. I ingest it, take it within me, and covet it like a sacred jewel. And when it is ready, ripened in madness and beauty, I release it and let it slide down his eager throat, so he can know and taste that feeling too.

I'm still panting when I hear the rustle of clothing hitting the floor and the crinkling of foil. I'm still shaking when he takes my thighs in his palms and pulls me to him so my legs cradle his hips. He brushes the hair from my face and kisses my tears with lips coated with my scent.

"Why are you crying, Bunny?"

"Because . . ."

"Did I hurt you? Did I do something wrong?" He's pulling away from me so I clutch his forearms and lock my ankles around his waist. He's mine now. He'll never get away.

"No. Never. You did everything right."

I kiss him deep enough to smother every doubt, every fear. And when he pushes inside me, stretching and breaking the tender flesh that was once surgically mended, I cry out. Not because of the pain, both physical and emotional. But because I knew that I would love this man until my dying day. This man who was making me bleed as he made love to me. This man whose agony was slow and sweet and sensual, and just what I had always imagined it would be. He was slicing me open and repairing all the damage, all the wrong. He was making me pretty and neat and shiny again.

I became the good doctor's greatest accomplishment. His little Frankenstein. What was once a monstrosity has been given new life.

"You're so beautiful," he whispers against my lips. "God, you feel so good. I love you, Heidi."

I kiss him so hard it bruises my lips and let the tears slide down the sides of my face. He wipes away every single one, his languid strokes not hindered in the least. If anything, he reaches deeper, pushing through the barriers of my heart and body until there's enough room for him to dwell forever. I thought it would hurt me, more than just the initial tearing. I was so convinced that I would never find joy in intimacy again, that I had just wanted to get it over with, so I could accept it and move on. But I was wrong. Tucker's body is therapy to mine. There's a stiff soreness at first, but even that feels good. And after those muscles have grown warm and loose, all that exists is pleasure. So much of it that my knees shake to the point that he has to grip my thighs as he delves farther and farther into never-ending wetness. It goes on forever, slicker with every thrust. It's just me.

He waits until I come before he allows himself to let go inside the warm safety of my body. Even with the latex separating us, he fills me up. But it's not enough. Not enough to make me complete. I need more of him.

"Next time," I pant, my breath ruffling his sweat slickened locks, "no condom. I hate that there's something between us."

He lifts his face from the soft pillows of my breasts and looks down at me. A single bead of sweat slides down his nose and lands on my chest. I even want that inside. I want his everything. Maybe that'll make me whole again.

"But what about . . . ?" He doesn't want to offend me, so I do it for him.

"I had a full, mandatory workup since the last time to ensure that bastard didn't give me anything. But what he did leave me with is scarring so bad that I will never conceive naturally. So you don't have to worry about me."

My tone is so cool and matter-of-fact that he flinches. I can see the concern etched in his face, but I can't return it. There's nothing to be upset over. This is my life, this is who I am. My rapist took away my ability to have children. I'll be damned if I let him take away anything else.

I pull Tucker's face to mine and kiss him, licking the seam of his tentative lips. He reluctantly opens for me, and within seconds, he's growing hard inside me again. With all my might, I push at his shoulders so he rolls to his back, taking me with him so my knees are on either side of him. I look down at the place where we are fused and back up to his worried expression.

"It's ok," I assure him. "I want this. I want all of you."

He closes his eyes when he nods, unable to look at me. I don't know if he's ashamed of me, or himself. But I still lift my body from his to scoot down his legs.

Tonight I saw a man up close for the first time. And now I'm seeing what a man can do to me . . . to my body. Tight latex hugs Tucker's semi-erect penis, glistening with pink blood and my slick, milky release. I'm all over him, from base to tip. But not really. Underneath that thin barrier, he's free of me. He's as clean and pristine as he always is. The urge to make him dirty with me is overwhelming, and I pull off the sullied condom and toss it to the floor, revealing his thick, long, swollen erection, painted only with his seed. I take him in my mouth, desperate to taste him. Desperate to take all I can from him. He twitches against the back of my throat, and I moan. The image of it choking me, of him choking me, disturbs and excites me all at the same time.

Wetness coats my thighs, and I reach back to feel it on my fingers, but it's not nearly enough to give me what I need. The friction, the fullness. The pain. I need it so badly. It's the only thing that can heal me.

I position myself over his saliva-slickened cock and slowly impale myself until I can't take anymore. Until his dark brown curls fuse with my short, blonde ones. Until I can't tell where my body ends and where his begins.

Tucker looks up at me like I am a goddess and my body is his only religion. For twenty minutes, I let him worship me with his hands and tongue and praise. And when pressure collects inside that little knot inside me that urges me to take him harder, faster, deeper, I bless him with an orgasm so intense that neither one of us can move, let alone talk. We can barely even breathe.

He kisses the top of my head, murmuring words of adoration and amazement. Telling me how happy I've made him, and how he only wants to do the same for me . . . forever. I turn into his chest and inhale the scent of his sweat, and I resist the urge to lap up every salty drop. I tamp down the desire to bite his humid flesh, to rake my fingernails over his skin until it blisters with tiny droplets of blood. And in turn, he would flip me over and fuck me like a wild dog, punish me for my transgression until I cry from the brutality. I'd trade all his sweet nothings and replace them with vile slurs said in a frenzy of violent passion. He'd spank my bare ass as he fucked me until my skin was bright pink and burning with his handprints. He would pull my hair until my scalp stung with red-hot needles. And just before I found sweet relief in all the pain, he'd grasp my throat until I came so hard that I'd lose consciousness.

That scares me. *I* scare me. Because if he knew what I really wanted, what would really make me lose myself in a haze of pleasure, he would realize just how sick and wrong I am. And he's worked so hard to make me right again.

I can be good for him. Whatever I'm feeling, whatever I am . . . it's just a phase or remnants of PTSD. It's not the real me. It's not what I really want. What I want is Tucker—sweet, safe, stable Tucker. And dammit, he wants me. And I'd be damned if I lose him over imagined affliction inside my twisted mind.

I prop my chin on my hands and look down into sky blue eyes, and smile. He smiles back, causing those too-full lips to fall into a smile too pretty for any man to possess. And I know right then and there, exactly what I want. And what I will always desire from this gorgeous man that has taken the scattered pieces of me and put me back together into something more beautiful than it was before.

Love me.

Hate me.

Chapter Fourteen

Now

It's the middle of the night when I realize I'm not alone. There's someone stalking in the shadows of my pitch-black bedroom. Someone watching me sleep, counting each inhale and exhale. Admiring the way the moonlight casts tattooed ghosts on my hauntingly pale skin. Breathing in the scent of my naked sex, still slick with a salacious dream.

He touches my shoulder, brushing the skin so softly that his fingernails feel like feather vanes. The whispered caress moves down my back, deliberately stroking every column of vertebrae until his hand stops at the top of my ass. He gently probes my seam and applies just a breath of delicate pressure at my puckered place before moving down to the wet, hot swell just below.

I wish I had the nerve to tell him not to stop. To go back to that little slice of exile and make it his. To rip me open and make me cry and scream with the pain of intense pleasure. But alas, I stay quiet. Because there is nothing decent or romantic about wanting a man to fuck your ass so good and deep that you can't sit the next day. And Tucker is a champion of decency and romance.

He slips a finger inside me and it goes in easily. He fills me with another and I take it with an encouraging moan.

"You're wet, baby," he whispers.

"I was dreaming of you."

"Yeah? Well, let me make your dream a reality."

Tucker removes his fingers and flips me over onto my back. I find that he's already naked too, as if he had been anticipating this moment since before he found me sleeping in the nude. His hot mouth finds my pebbled nipples, and he licks and sucks his way down to my navel, all the while positioning himself between my legs. When I feel the first stroke of his tongue against my clit, I reflexively grasp a handful of his hair and pull him in closer, grinding my sex into his mouth, seeking teeth, rigid tongue, and the roughness of stubble. Yet, before he bestows me with the insanity I crave, he crawls up my body and aligns himself with my entrance.

"You want this, don't you, baby?" he asks, looming over me.

"Yes."

"Already so wet and hot." He wraps a hand around his

hard cock and guides the head up and down my slick folds. "Tell me how bad you want me inside you."

"So bad, Tuck. It hurts. The emptiness aches so much," I cry.

He relieves just the surface of my suffering by pushing in an inch, just enough for my body to suck in his swollen head. I know he wants to go deeper but he is a master of restraint and order. He's never lost to passion or imprisoned by lust. He never wants me so badly that he can't control himself.

"Please," I beg. But I know it falls on deaf ears. He thinks this is what I seek—the chase. But what I'm begging for has nothing to do with his dick inside me. I want his madness. I want his rage and hysteria. I just don't think he's capable of giving it to me. Not when it doesn't exist.

He watches me as I pant and whine and paw at his chest before giving in to my plea, and filling me to the root. I cry with glee at the first initial jolt of pain. The first stretch of my flesh around his rock-solid cock and the invasion of it stabbing my womb. He pulls out to the tip and thrusts in again, this time even harder.

"Yes," I moan. "Yes, again. Harder."

And after a marriage—a life—of order, routine, and restraint, my husband fucks me.

Finally. He's finally heard me. Maybe last weekend didn't hurt us like I initially thought. Maybe he just needed to see what I needed. See what I want with *him*.

I moan louder than I ever have. I tell him how good he's fucking me, how big he feels inside me, how badly I want to taste his seed all over my tongue and tits. He's silent, for the most part, with the occasional grunt. He looks as if he's concentrating, like he's focused on not coming too soon and ending the moment. I don't question it. I just want him to keep pounding me into the headboard and keep squeezing my tits hard enough to bruise.

When the feeling goes beyond splendid to the place where ecstasy can't be defined, I take his hand and wrap his fingers around my throat.

"What are you doing?" He's still stroking but his rhythm has slowed.

"I want you to choke me when I come for you. I want you to squeeze my neck so hard I see stars. Then fuck me until I black out."

He stops.

He pulls out of me like my body is fueled by scorpion venom.

"What's wrong?" I ask, sitting up.

"You want me to . . . ?" He can't even say it. A grown fucking man pushing forty and he can't even speak candidly about sex with his wife.

"It's no big deal, Tuck. Lots of couples enjoy erotic asphyxiation. It heightens the orgasm." I reach out to pull him back to me, but he retreats even farther.

"Heidi . . . that's sick. That's wrong. How can someone like you . . . ?"

"Someone like me?" I scoff. "Someone who has been raped and beaten?"

"Don't say that."

"Why not? It's true! That's what you think of me, isn't it? That I'm sick and fucked in the head."

I climb out of bed, the delicious soreness between my legs forgotten and make my way to the bathroom. Tucker is right on my heels, his penis looking just as sad and pathetic as he does.

"Heidi, that's not what I'm saying. This . . . thing . . . it's not healthy. You're acting out sexually because you refuse to confront what's really troubling you. And knowing what I know . . . seeing what he had done to you . . . I can't perpetuate some violent fantasy that you need to reenact in a quest for control. I can't do that to you, baby. I love you, don't you see that? I love you so much, Bunny. I'd rather die than hurt you. Just the thought of inflicting pain on you makes me sick."

I cross my arms over my bare breasts. "That's all you think this is. Residual effects from my attack? Is it inflicting pain that makes you sick or the fact that I want it?"

Ignoring my questions, Tucker offers his hand, and musters up a reassuring smile. I ignore both. "Come on, let's go back to bed. It's been a long week for both of us. We're probably just both exhausted and on edge."

"You're right. I will. But first, I need you to leave."

He frowns, dropping his hand. "Leave?"

"Yes. You refuse to fuck me, so if you don't mind, I'd like to fuck myself. In private."

Shock slaps him in the face so hard that it turns bright red.

I step forward so that he has to step back and don't stop until his bare feet hit the carpet of the bedroom. Then I slam the door, locking it behind me, before sliding down against it.

I sit on the bathroom floor for forty-five minutes, the sounds of my sobs muffled by the running faucet. By the time I climb into bed, Tucker is already fast asleep, blissfully ignorant to my discontent. Some things never change.

Chapter Fifteen

It's late when I wake up, but I feel like I haven't slept in days. My head is weighted with lead, my mouth is lined with wool, and my eyelids have been fused together with Krazy Glue. Still, I know I'm alone without even having to reach out and touch Tucker's pillow, his body merely a faint, warm memory on the palm of my hand. However, there's a white notecard, ink-stained with his messy chicken scratch.

Heidi,

Got called in early and didn't want to wake you.

About last night . . .

I think we should talk.

Dinner tonight?

Just the words *last night* nearly cause me to break into hives. I can't forget the look of sheer disgust and horror on Tuck's face when I asked him to squeeze my throat as I climaxed. He had been so accommodating to what I wanted—thrusting deeper, harder. Touching me in a way that he had never done before. I thought maybe . . . maybe last weekend had changed him. I mean, to let another man sleep with your wife while you watch and pleasure yourself is pretty damn progressive. And it's not like he just *let* it happen. He *wanted* it. Just as much as I did. Maybe even more.

And the things he was saying to Ransom . . . the way he was instructing him . . .

"Taste her . . . Taste how fucking good her pussy is."

"That's right. Fuck her hard. Harder."

"Pull her hair."

"Slap her ass. Again . . . slap it again. This time make it hurt."

All things I've wanted him to do with me. Things he's refused me at every single turn.

So over the years, I just stopped asking. I stopped fantasizing. Which led to me resenting every fucking gentle caress and tender kiss. That's what he needed. That's the only way he could love me—as if I were a fragile, little paper doll. He was afraid he would rip me in two. And I wanted him to do just that.

Break me. Destroy me. Wreck me.

Love me.

Tucker could've loved me through all the madness. And I would have known that he cared for me beyond the boundaries of his own inhibitions. Isn't that what love and sacrifice are all about? Isn't that *marriage*? Putting your own selfish needs aside for the happiness of the person you vowed to devote your life to?

Don't get me wrong—Tucker is an amazing husband. He's patient, kind, and supportive. He's a great provider and I know he'd be an incredible father, if we ever cross that bridge. I trust him with my life, and I can go to sleep every night knowing that he is dreaming of me and only me. I don't have to doubt him or question his love for me. I feel it in his touch, see it reflected in those eyes as blue as the ocean. See it curl around his full lips to shape a smile so warm it could have been carved from the sun.

I know my husband loves me. But when I am forced to stifle who I truly am and what I want—what I *need*—is love enough? Can I live another ten years like this? Can I spend a lifetime with a man who only chooses to know the part of me that is deemed pretty and decent?

Even after I've prepped, primped, and plummeted into the late morning crowd at Starbucks, the same questions still replay in an endless loop of confused frustration. I grab a nonfat frappe and find a vacant stool at the bar that faces the street. It's busy today, and if anything can get me out of my head long enough to find some perspective, it's people watching. That's what I love about New York. Even when you're by yourself, you're never really alone.

However, after a good half hour, I still can't wrap my head around the state of my marriage. I can't understand Tucker's motivations for last weekend if we were still going to have a sex life that was about as dry and stale as day-old toast. I mean, he's a wonderful lover . . . to someone else. There's nothing wrong with his equipment and his mouth and hands have made my legs shake for days. But it's not enough to fill the emptiness. Not enough to feel completely satisfied behind the sacred doors of our bedroom.

I fish out my cell phone and stare at it a good thirty seconds before sliding a thumb over the Unlock icon. My finger hovers over a name in my contacts for twice as long before I bite the bullet and press Call.

I told myself I wouldn't do this—my marital problems are for me to deal with and nobody else. Tucker and I had struggles long before we made the mistake of involving another party. Going down this road could only further complicate things. And how do I know it's safe? Hell, how do I know I won't look like a total freak?

Only one way to find out.

"Drake," that gruff baritone sounds over the receiver.

"Take the bass out of your voice, JD. I'm not calling to bitch you out . . . for now."

"Surprise, surprise. So . . . what can I do for you, Heidi?"

"I have . . . a few questions. And I need to know that it will stay between you, me, and the phone, or I will fly to Arizona, cut off your balls, and serve them with Riku's Béarnaise and a side salad. Got it?"

He laughs without so much as a hint of discomfort. To tell you the truth, Justice Drake is probably the only person who can tolerate my silver tongue, so I keep it extra sharp just for him. I think he actually likes it. When people pay you to be a merciless asshole five days a week, maybe it's nice to be in the hot seat for a change.

"Questions, huh?" I can almost hear the smile in his voice. Can almost imagine those denim blue eyes dancing with intrigue and his lips slinking into a wicked grin. "You have my undivided attention. And my word."

"Good. Because this . . . this is off the record. So I better not find any notes in your fucking client list. And I damn sure better not find out that it's the topic of pillow talk with Ally. I swear to you, Drake. I will end you if this gets out."

Silence stretches for just a beat before he asks, "Are you done?"

"Yes."

"Good. Now talk. It's my day off and I'm not getting paid for this shit."

"Fine." I take a deep breath and mentally count down from ten before looking around to ensure that no one seems overly interested in my conversation. As I suspected, the rest of the café is oblivious. Another perk of the city—we've seen and heard it all. No one cares enough to eavesdrop because they're too busy trying to conceal their own dirty, little secrets. "What do you know about open marriages?"

"A lot. Be more specific." Not even an inkling of surprise or over-interest.

"I mean, do you think they can work? If both parties can agree to it?"

"They have worked, yes. But I believe that a relationship, namely a marriage that is built on the foundation of monogamy and devotion, can only survive if the circumstances are right. And the reasons for the arrangement are of a decent nature."

"What do you mean?"

"To be frank, is this arrangement based off the fact that either you or your husband merely want to fuck other people?"

"No! Of course not. And I'm not even saying that this is about me and my husband."

"Whatever. I'm not judging. But the fact that I only found out about this husband mere months ago speaks volumes, Heidi. Why the secrecy? Is it because you're ashamed of him? Or you want to live a life separate from him? Is that your motivation for an open marriage? Because in that case, I say get a divorce."

"Save the self-righteous psychobabble, Dr. Feel Good. I never hid my marriage from you. It was none of your business. And you're the one with Magnum P.I. on the payroll. All the dirt you dig up on your clients and you can't get your thumb outta Allison's ass long enough to do a quick Google search about my marital status?"

"Huh. Well, what can I say? I'm more interested in the people who pay me. Not the ones who charge me enough to mortgage a small castle."

"Obviously, I need a raise."

"You're getting it now." He clears his throat and when his voice floats through the phone again, it's devoid of all humor and cynicism. It's almost sincere . . . sympathetic. "Heidi, I don't usually suggest open marriages unless each spouse is completely comfortable of the terms and the reasons behind it. A good reason to go down that road is if one of them are handicapped or medically incapable of providing their wife or husband sexual pleasure. Or if they are merely sexually incompatible, yet very deeply in love. Being a slut isn't a good reason. Getting tired of the same dick or pussy is not a good reason. If one wants to seek pleasure in others, solely for the purpose of sexual gratification, then they don't need to be married. Now, I won't ask you if any of this pertains to you, but I will say . . . be very careful what doors you open in your marriage. Once open, some can never be closed. And you're allowing just about any and everything to taint the sacredness of your vows."

Stunned, I silently chew the straw of my drink for a good fifteen seconds before responding. "Wow. I have to say, that girl is getting to you."

He laughs, the cocky tremor of his deep voice booming from the other side of the country. "And that's a bad thing?"

"No. Yes. I'm worried you're losing your edge. Just when I started liking your arrogant ass."

"Trust me. My ass is still very much arrogant. You just saw it a month ago."

"I know, it's just . . . I've never heard you actually speak like that . . . with so much passion and conviction. I have to say, Justice, I'm impressed. You might not be as full of shit as I initially thought."

He laughs again, and this time I join him. "Look, Heidi.

We both know that monogamy isn't always successful for people like us."

"People like us?"

"Sharks. Predators. We take what we want without apology, no matter who gets hurt. We're selfish motherfuckers, but that doesn't mean we don't feel. And when we do happen to find that one person in this world who can tame us, who isn't afraid of getting ripped to shreds and eaten alive, we have to do whatever it takes to keep them. Because being wild again just isn't an option. Not anymore. So if this is what he needs, or what you need, just be sure you're doing this to help your marriage, not harm it. And above all, realize what you'd be losing. What you could never, ever have again."

"And what's that?"

"Your innocence."

I snort, and roll my eyes. "Innocence? You do realize that when a man and a woman love each other, they sometimes like to show it by taking off their clothes and getting into bed together. Sheesh, I thought you of all people would understand the birds and the bees."

"Not your sexual innocence, wise ass. The innocence and sanctity of your union. When you get married, you create a bond between you and your husband, and if you're religious, God. You become untouchable to everything else. That person becomes as essential to your being as the air you breathe. But the moment you invite someone else to stand within that union, you find that you don't need your spouse as much as you once thought you did. You can breathe without him. You can find gratification without him. You can live without him. And that's a slippery slope for someone you have vowed to love for eternity."

"So you don't think you can maintain the emotional bond of a marriage if the sexual aspect is unconventional? Kinda narrow-minded coming from someone who makes his living off staging fantasies."

"I didn't say it doesn't happen. I didn't even say I disapprove. I'm just giving you my honest opinion. Experimentation is one thing, and it can be uniquely beneficial to a marriage, especially one that's withstood the test of time. However, when does an experiment or a fantasy turn into a habit? And when does that habit turn into a full-blown affair?"

I can almost imagine the smug grin on his face as he leaves me too stumped to answer eloquently. Tucker and I experimented, and it was great. Better than great. So much so, that I haven't been able to stop thinking about it. Haven't stopped wanting it.

My mistake wasn't sleeping with Ransom. It was letting that fantasy blur into reality. What happened between the three of us should have stayed and died in that hotel suite. It should have been nothing more than a few risqué memories for Tucker and me to laugh about in bed between wet kisses and eager touches. Something to get us hot and bothered before expelling all that lustful energy into each other.

"You've given me a lot to think about. Thanks, Justice," I say, my words as sober as my heart and mind. "Hey, I have to make a call. Talk soon?"

"Hopefully not too soon." He hangs up before I get the chance to. I swear, I think we've made hanging up on each other a game.

I scroll through my contacts and land on R. His number is the first name in that section. Even if it weren't, it'd still be the only one I see.

After five rings, I'm just about to hang up when he answers, obviously out of breath. Heat flames my face—guilt, suspicion, desire—and I stammer out a cold greeting. Initially I think he's still busy with his last night's booty call, but then I hear the sounds of drums and a guitar tuning up.

"Heidi? You need something?"

"Oh." I clear my throat, trying to put the business back in my tone. "I wanted to see if we could discuss something. It's important, and I'd like to get this over with at your earliest convenience."

"Well, I'm at sound check for *SNL*. I'll see you later, right? And we can just talk then."

"Well, actually, I—" I hear the piercing sound of a microphone on the fritz, shrill enough to make my eardrums bleed.

"Hey, we'll talk later. I gotta go. Ok?"

Fuck. Not ok. "Yeah. Ok."

I hang up and set my head in my hands, feeling like a complete pansy. Shark, my ass. I can't even quit a fucking job.

Damn him. Damn us both.

I can't quit him.

Chapter Sixteen

Tucker gets home just minutes after I do, which is later than usual. I have to be honest; I was stalling for time, wandering the city in search of clarity. Or maybe just a small reprieve from my marital woes. And nothing soothes the soul better than a little retail therapy.

"You went shopping," he remarks, eyeing the bags strewn about the bed. There're a lot of them—Saks, Bloomingdale's, Barneys. Plus I had to replace the pajama set from La Perla that I ruined the night before.

"Yeah." I make busy work of arranging my new garments in our closet, which is almost as large as the little love nest we had years back. I smile at the memory. Ikea furniture, a bathroom the size of a coat closet, and a kitchen that was barely large enough for us both to fit in at the same time. But we were happy. Happy and in love.

"I made us a reservation at Nobu for tonight. Thought you might like a change of pace," he says from behind me, his voice tentative. He's feeling me out, studying my movements, searching the tiny lines in my face that tense together when I'm agitated and smooth when I'm amenable. I turn my back fully to refuse him those little clues. I shut him out, shut him down, just as he did me last night. If he wants to make this right, he's going to have to do it the old-fashioned way.

"Bunny . . ." I turn to shoot him a terse look that says, *Don't you dare. Don't you fucking dare try to butter me up with that name. It will not work*. He clears his throat and starts again. "Heidi, what I said last night . . . I didn't mean to hurt you or make you feel defective or deviant. You know how much I adore you."

I turn back to my rack of clothing, refusing to let him see the flash of pain that goes along with the knot in my throat. "But you don't take it back. You don't regret saying it, you're just remorseful that it hurt me."

"Of course, I regret saying that, baby." He steps in closer to me, so close that I can smell his cologne and feel the heat of his body caress my back. "I don't want to hurt you. That's the last thing I want."

I shake my head, not to refute his claims, but to try to shake away the frustrated tears collecting in my eyes. I'm not upset at his words. I'm upset that no matter how much he may claim to love me, I'll always feel like a charity case in his eyes. The little monster he tamed and domesticated. He walks on eggshells to avoid disturbing the wildness in me that simmers right at the surface.

"Tuck . . . I don't want to fight anymore. But I don't want to have to lie about who I am and what I want."

He places a hand on my shoulder and I lean in to his touch, starved for affection . . . acceptance. "Then let's not. Let me take you to dinner. Let's just be Heidi and Tucker tonight. Let's laugh and joke about my feeble attempt at using chopsticks and drink too much sake. And maybe . . . maybe we can try again. Just you and me."

I turn around, my breast brushing his chest. "Really?"

"Yes. If that's what you need me to be, then I can try. For you."

I hug him tight to my body, so tight that every cell within me fuses to his. His embrace is warm and comforting, and he kisses me on the top of my head.

"Let me grab a shower," he says after a few moments, pulling away, taking that warmth with him. "Long day today."

"Everything ok?" I ask, flipping through the racks. I stop on something sexy and appealing. Perfect to start tonight's mood off right.

"Yeah. Patient in the hospital. Rough few days but I think we're out of the woods now." Translation: One of his patients has gone off the deep end and OD'd, either intentionally or accidentally, prescribed or street pharmaceuticals.

"Will they be ok?" I'm genuinely concerned. Tucker takes on a lot of entertainers and society types, most of them young. Last year, one of his patients—a teenage, rising starlet—overdosed on Klonopin and washed it down with her dad's collection of aged scotch. All of it. The doctors did what they could, but her mind had given up, soon after her body did. It killed Tucker, and he carried a bit of the blame with him for months afterward. He knew the girl was suffering inside, and he put his all into helping her fight her demons. In the end, they were just too strong to combat.

Tucker sighs, and I turn around just as he sinks onto the edge of the bed. Now that I am just really seeing him for the first time in days, I find that he looks exhausted. His eyes are sunken in, his usually meticulous hair too long and a little disheveled, and he probably hasn't eaten real food in days. God, have I really been that much of a selfish brat to see that my husband is suffering? That he just needed me to put my own bullshit aside for once and just be a wife?

I hang my sexy outfit back on the rack, putting it on ice and step out of the closet, going straight to the bed. Without a word, I climb up behind him and begin to massage his shoulders, which feel as hard and unyielding as boulders.

"Hey, you. Let's skip Nobu tonight and just stay in and hang out," I suggest.

He lifts his head a fraction, but not enough to deter my kneading. "Are you sure? You love that place."

"I know, I know, but we can always go some other time. Besides, I've really been craving pizza. Angelo's?"

Even with his head turned, I know he's smiling. "I'll call it in." He turns to face me, his eyes just a shade brighter. His smiling lips press against mine for just a split second before he's on his feet, instantly reenergized by the word *pizza.* "Thanks, baby. I owe you one."

After calling in to place an order for a large pepperoni, sausage, and mushroom, Tucker takes a quick shower and dresses in a pair of comfy, flannel pants and nothing else. His body is magnificent, the muscles tight and toned without even a hint of aging. Even the ridges leading to the waistband of his pants form a perfect V before disappearing under the nuisance of fabric. I'm a lucky woman—the luckiest. A gorgeous man adores me, worships the very ground I walk on, and has for a decade. Never once has he made me feel less than beautiful or confident in my skin. And he's never, ever made me feel guilty or ashamed for wanting a less than noble career, even though I know he hates it.

We've had a good marriage—a solid marriage. Up until now, neither one of us has had to question our fidelity. And other than his desire for children—that mostly stems from his overbearing, southern belle mother—Tucker has always appeared to be happy with our life.

Maybe that's what all this is about. He gave me something, now it's time for me to give him something. I mean, I'm not opposed to motherhood. I just don't see the need for it. He's aware of my circumstances; he knows I could never conceive on my own. And while IVF is definitely an option, it's not 100 percent guaranteed. Hell, it's not even 50 percent guaranteed. And I can't say I'm comfortable with those odds.

In any case, Tucker hasn't brought it up within the last few weeks, so maybe his sudden interest in my sexual deviance hasn't been sparked by his need for fatherhood. He's getting older, and forty will be knocking at his door in a couple years. And we're both incredibly busy with work. So maybe he feels that ship has sailed for us?

"What?" he asks, breaking me from the reverie of my thoughts.

I smile and shake my head. "Just looking at you. I honestly think you get more handsome every day, if that's even possible."

"Oh, it is, baby," he jibes, slinking over to the bed, where I'm perched. "Just wait a few more years. You won't be able to keep your hands off me."

"I can barely keep my hands off you now."

He leans over onto the bed and I help him by pulling the waistband off his pants. Even fresh from a shower, I can smell the hypnotic scent of his most sensitive skin. His smell is so erotic, so incredibly masculine, that sucking him off is a feast for the senses. I feel myself get wet at just the remembrance of him pulsing down my throat.

His mouth crushes against mine, and I part my lips immediately to welcome him inside. We're all lips and tongue and teeth, absolutely starved for each other. I moan in the back of my throat, and Tucker uses the opportunity to kiss me even deeper. I need to feel him. Right now. I need to erase the ugliness of the night before. All the ugliness that has caused a rift between us.

I'm pulling up my skirt with one hand and trying to yank down Tuck's pants with the other when the intercom buzzes.

"Shit," he curses against my lips. He stands up and straightens himself, and makes his way to the buzzer. "Yeah?"

"Dr. DuCane, it's Norm from downstairs. I've got a pizza delivery guy here for you."

"Right, thanks, Norm. Send him up."

I huff out an aggravated breath and stalk to the closet to get out of my day clothes. Great. Now I'm even more sexually frustrated than I was before. That delivery guy better have a free order of garlic knots for me or I might lose my shit. Can you actually explode from being overly aroused?

After snatching up Tuck's worn dress shirt and sliding it on, sans bra, I might add, I make my way out to the kitchen where my husband is already divvying out slices and servings of salad. And dammit, there are no garlic-fucking-knots.

"So what do you want to do tonight?" he asks, settling in beside me on the bistro table.

"I don't know. Just chill? Have a couple glasses of wine, maybe? I think Lucia picked up some Stella for you."

"That sounds amazing," he says, jumping up to inspect the fridge. Sure enough, his beer of choice is fully stocked.

"Hey, bring me one of those, will ya?" I say, ripping off a bit of crust and popping it in my mouth. Tucker looks surprised—I'm not a beer drinker—but complies, even pouring it in a glass for me.

"This is great," he remarks around a mouthful of cheese and pepperoni. "Pizza, beer, and my favorite girl. I so needed this."

I smile and nod. "Yeah, me too. Busy week." I take a sip of beer, which turns out to be crisp and refreshing on my tongue. It's not bubbly, but it definitely hits the spot.

We polish off the pizza and settle onto the couch with our second round of beers, which is pretty risky considering that our living room set is ivory. But I'm trying this new thing called being a supportive wife that just lives in the moment. And in this moment, Tuck needs to be comfortable in his own home. This is his refuge away from all the horror he must experience at work. I can provide that for him. *I* can be his refuge.

He grabs the remote and starts to flip through the channels, bypassing E! News, VH1, MTV, and Bravo. Nothing that would pique my professional interest and take me away from him and our little slice of normalcy. We're not even twenty minutes into some slapstick funny sitcom when his cell phone rings.

"What? When did this happen?" He's pacing the floor, his brow wrinkled in concern. "Dammit. I'm leaving now."

Tucker looks to me with a mixture of regret and fear. "Bunny, I have to get to the hospital. There's been a turn for the worse."

"Is everything all right?"

He shakes his head, heaves out a resigned sigh. I can already see the rigid tension creeping back into his shoulders and his expression is bleak and ragged. "I don't know. I hope so. I'm sorry, babe. I've got to get over there."

"Go, go," I wave. "I'll be fine, honey. Do whatever you need to do. I'll be here when you get home."

I really wish that statement could be true.

Sixty minutes after Tucker rushed to Mount Sinai, my own cell phone is chirping. I pick it up and look at the number, then immediately set it back down.

Ransom.

I know why he's calling. *Saturday Night Live* begins in less than an hour. But I've already made a conscious decision not to attend. Granted, that decision was much easier to stick to when Tucker was here, but I'm committed to my word. I'm committed to my husband . . . to my marriage. Talking to Justice really put things into perspective for me. Letting Ransom into our proverbial marriage bed wasn't the issue here—we both enjoyed that walk on the wild side. The problem was, and is, that he's still in it, lingering in our unsaid words and unmet desires.

The only way I can exonerate him from our lives is to cut him off cold turkey. I'll draft a letter of resignation, and we'll split amicably. I mean, I was his publicist for less than a week. I've had relationships with badly cut bangs longer than that.

Still, I'm a glutton for punishment. And instead of changing the channel and picking up a book or magazine, I keep it on NBC. And soon I'm watching the show, anxiously awaiting Ransom's musical performance.

As soon as Rebel Wilson introduces them, I'm on the edge of my seat, struggling to breathe through my undefined angst. The lights go up, revealing the band, and their singer positioned front and center, his head down. The music begins, and he lifts his chin slowly, dramatically pulling the audience in to his world. God, he looks good. Black jeans that fit him like a glove, charcoal gray tee, and a black leather jacket with the sleeves pushed up to his elbows. The silver hoop in his nose matches the rings on his fingers and the crucifix hanging from his neck. He briefly spoke of the faith he was raised in, and how it affected his family ties. Maybe religion is his last link to his parents. Or maybe it's merely a fashion statement.

The music curls around the first lyrics of the song, and I audibly gasp when I realize what song they're performing. It's the song—*the* song—he sang to me that night. The song that fell from his trembling lips as he surged inside me, filling my body and soul with his lustful submission.

I never thought I'd be able to hear that song again.

Yet, here I am, glued to the screen, watching him sing it with so much zeal and conviction that I swear I hear the rasp of his voice quiver with emotion. Not sadness or distress. Maybe longing . . . desire. As if he's remembering the last time he sang it too. I've never heard it like this before. I've never listened with ears that have felt the brush of his soft lips and the tingle of whispered words. And now that I do, I'm right back to where I started. Drowning in denial, falling in the farce that I could somehow be over him.

The crowd erupts into wild cheers at the end of the song, and the show cuts to commercial. I force myself to turn off the TV. If I watch any more, I may find myself hailing a cab to Rockefeller Center.

I take a hot shower, and slip on my new pajamas, and resign to call it a night. It's late, yet Tucker still isn't home. I don't expect him to be. The way he ran out of here, wearing that solemn look that spoke of death and despair, I doubt I'll see much of him for the rest of the weekend.

Sleep comes easier than I expect, and I'm caught within the deepest, warmest parts of my mind when something startles me awake. I blink rapidly, wondering if it was a dream, when I hear the piercing ring of my phone.

"Hello?" I answer, my voice choked with sleep.

"You need to get down here."

I clear my throat and push myself up on tired limbs. "What? Who is this?"

"Caleb. Now get your ass out of bed and get to the Monkey Bar, pronto."

I look over at the red-lit numbers on my bedside clock. "Caleb, it's 3 A.M. What the hell is this about?"

"Our client, that's what this is about. And right now, he is pissy fucking drunk, high out of his fucking mind, and asking for you. I was able to get the bar cleared out, but the rest is on you. You wanted the job . . . now it's time to work."

"Caleb . . . I can't . . . I don't."

He heaves out a frustrated breath, and when he speaks again, his voice is low and gravely. "If I could deal with this shit on my own, do you think I would call you? Obviously, you're needed. So wipe the drool off your lip, and get down here before this kid completely ruins his career."

With that, he hangs up, not even giving me a chance to ask for directions, or even an address. Luckily, the cab driver knows the place, and once I throw on some clothes, I'm whisked away into the wee hours of the morning to play babysitter to a shit-faced Ransom Reed.

"There she is!" I hear as soon as I walk in. I look around the dark, dingy place and cringe. Thank God, I'm up to date on all my shots. The bar top looks like it's been spit-shined in Hepatitis. There's music playing—piano—but it's not from a stereo system. And while the place looks relatively empty, there seems to be some commotion toward the stage.

Caleb approaches me first, and the alarmed look on his face tells me that he is in no mood for jokes. "Took you long enough," he grumbles. "Look, try not to stay here too long with him. The papzz are bound to show up any second."

"Stay here with who? What the hell is going on, Caleb?"

"Ransom. He's . . . having one of his moments. We've done everything we can to get him to come down, but nothing is working."

Before I can inquire anymore, the ear-splitting racket of glass shattering sounds from the front of the room. There're shouts, then laughter, just as Cash Colby comes stalking up to us.

"Is this her?" he barks, clearly pissed off. He runs an agitated hand through his sandy blond locks and sucks his teeth.

"Yeah," Caleb answers. "Cash, this is Heidi DuCane. Heidi, Cash Colby."

I extend a hand, but he completely ignores it, looking back to Caleb with eyes the color of polished steel. "I'm fucking sick of this, man. Every week, there's something new with him. We can't keep covering for his ass."

"I know, I know," Caleb assures, his expression anything but confident. "He just needs time. Maybe if he takes some time off—"

"Fuck that. We have an international tour in a matter of months. If he doesn't get his shit together, I'm done."

Cash stalks toward the entrance and disappears into the night without so much as a goodbye to the rest of his bandmates. Rude ass. Maybe he does have Bieber's cuntiness, as well as his looks.

Soon after Cash leaves, Gunner Davies comes to stand beside Caleb, placing a hand on his shoulder. Caleb drops his head and nods. "I know, Gunner. I know. I'm just not sure what else we can do."

With that, Gunner presses his hauntingly light blue eyes into me so intensely that I nearly gasp. They're so pale that the stark contrast of his black hair and clothing make him seem almost otherworldly. He gives me a single, stiff nod and walks away without even uttering a word.

"What was that about?" I whisper to Caleb, unnerved by their one-sided conversation and the force of Gunner's stare.

"He doesn't want you to get involved in this. He doesn't think it's fair to make this someone else's problem."

"Not fair to who?"

Caleb shrugs. "To you. To the band. They're a tightly knit group. Involving someone else is risking exposure."

"Exposure? What would I possibly expose?"

Before Caleb can answer, Striker Voss approaches us, his silver adorned face looking more distraught than I've ever seen it. He always seems so playful in public, so energetic on stage. Now he looks exhausted, drained both mentally and physically. Kinda like a father who has just had to bail his teenage kid out of jail in the middle of the night.

"I got him to take a few swigs of water, but he still refuses to eat anything. Caleb, I hate to leave you with him, but I've gotta get home. The wife will already have my balls for this."

"Yes, of course. Get home to your family, Striker. We can take it from here." He extends a hand toward me and gives a weak smile. "This is Heidi. Hopefully she can talk him into getting into a cab and heading home."

"Heidi," Striker says, holding out a large hand for me to shake. He looks so different up close, even taller than I imagined. And although he's inked and skewered to death, there's a certain gentleness in his eyes. "Good to finally meet you. Sorry it's under these circumstances."

"Likewise," I reply, taking his hand for a short second. "What exactly are the circumstances?"

Striker looks toward the darkened stage and exhales heavily before looking back to me. "Ransom," is all he says, as if that's all the explanation I'll need. And truth be told, it kinda is.

He bids us both good night, waves to the barkeep, and follows his brothers into the night.

"Well, Blondie. You're up," Caleb says once we're alone.

"Up against what?"

"Go see for yourself. I've gotta fix this shit before it gets any worse."

Right on cue, Caleb fishes out his cell and barks a greeting into the receiver, stepping away for privacy. I roll my eyes. I didn't even hear it ring. He probably just wants to escape like the rest of them.

On tentative legs, I make my way to the front of the bar. It's dark and smoky, yet there's a single spotlight focused on the stage. The room is tiny, but I couldn't get a clear view from the entrance since it was blocked by a partition meant to ward off prying outside eyes. As I round the corner, I'm grateful for the visual obstruction. And sad that I can never unsee what sits before me.

Ransom Reed is slouched over a piano, the top of it littered with beer bottles and empty glasses. There's an overflowing ashtray that looks to be filled with at least a full pack of butts, some of them still emitting wisps of toxic vapors. And that's not even counting the stuff he can legally smoke.

My heart lurches at the sight of his disheveled clothing and mussed hair, so far from his usual fresh-sexed look. Now, he just looks sloppy, and a bit dingy. Still, he's beautiful. Inebriated or not, I can't fathom a world where he isn't the most alluring man alive.

I'm only a few feet away from him when he finally looks up from the piano keys he's been staring at. At first, his glossy-eyed gaze doesn't register, but after a few blinks, he focuses on me. Twin flashes of pain and anger contort his features, before he quickly smoothes them into a lazy smile.

"Well, well, well . . . if it isn't my hardworking publicist. Always there to answer my calls and show up to my appearances. Just like the good girl that she is." His tone is casual, but I don't miss the venom in his words.

I force myself to close the distance between us until I'm standing before him at the piano. The rest of the place appears to be empty now, but I don't want to risk any eavesdroppers.

"I'm sorry, Ransom. Something came up, and—"

"Something came up? Something more important than me and what I need?" He barks out a harsh laugh, throwing his head back dramatically. "Of course, it did. Let me guess, your husband came up. Didn't he, Heidi? Oh, he was up for you, all right."

"Stop it, Ransom," I grit out, looking around to see if anyone heard him. "That's enough."

"Is it enough, Heidi? Have you had enough of me? Because, baby, I assure you, I have so much more to give you. And that is what you want, right? For me to give you . . ." He reaches down between his jean-clad thighs and grips himself, gently squeezing more than a handful. ". . . this. All this. Every last long, thick inch fucking you crazy until your eyes roll to the back of your head. That is what you want, right?"

"No!" I retort, my face hot with frenzied anger. "How dare you. How dare you fucking speak to me that way."

"Speak to you that way?" He leans forward, clumsily placing his hands on the keys so that it creates a composition of chaos. I look down to see that they're all scuffed up, the top layer of skin on his knuckles caked with dried blood. What the hell? "You like it. You begged for it. Don't try to act like I sought you out. And now that you've gotten what you want, you just throw me away, is that it? Just use me like a fucking dildo and throw me back in your lingerie drawer with all your other dirty, little toys."

This time, he doesn't even try to mask the truth on his face. There's pain there. Rejection. Remorse. Even through the haze of alcohol and God knows what else, Ransom is hurt. *I* hurt *him*. And I don't even realize how.

I take a deep breath and steel what's left of my nerves before sitting down next to him on the piano bench. He reeks of booze and stale cigarettes, and I resist the urge to turn my head away. An action like that would only further alienate him, and the objective right now is to get through to him. To make him feel like he is wanted and respected, even in his debilitated state.

"Ransom, I'm sorry. Whatever you think I did, I'm sorry. You're right; I should have answered your call. I should have been there for you when you needed me. How about you let me take you home and we can talk more?"

"Why?" he sneers. "Will your husband be there? Does he want to watch that too?"

"No, Ransom. I promise, just you and me. Let's get you out of here, get you cleaned up, and have a cup of coffee. Doesn't that sound much better than sitting in a grimy bar in the middle of the night?"

He almost smiles, but shakes his head instead. "Not yet. I want to play a song for you first."

"A song?" I take a beat to erase the annoyance in my voice when he gives me a pointed look. "Don't you want to play it for me later? After you've gotten some sleep and let your hands heal?"

He looks down at his battered knuckles and frowns, as if he's just realizing that they're raw and reddened. "No," he replies, shaking his head. "I want to play it for you now."

"Fine," I sigh. "But then home after that, ok?"

"Ok." He flexes his bruised fingers before lithely placing them on the keys. Even intoxicated, his hands are incredibly graceful. With the first few notes, his eyes close and his head dips back to face the ceiling, surrendering himself to the music. Giving over to pure, raw emotion that can only be translated through song. He begins to sing, and soon I am just as wrapped up in the ballad, completely swaddled in the sound of his voice.

Your lips taste like lies
So sweet that they sting my eyes
I lift my face to the sky
Drown in the sorrow of angel cries

It's amazing, every note, every inflection of his voice accompanied by the piano . . . pure, unadulterated magic. But it's sad. Much too melancholy to accompany such a beautiful melody.

I let him finish his song as I sit in silence, contemplating the inspiration of those lyrics. Where does such sadness stem from? How can a man who appears to have it all—youth, beauty, fame, fortune—exude so much pain?

When he slides his fingers from the ivory keys, his whole body slumps over and half of his weight topples on top of me while the other lands on the piano. I yelp underneath the heft of his frame and struggle to get him upright. Luckily, Caleb emerges from some hidden room and helps to get Ransom off me.

"I need to get him in a cab and get him home," I grunt, trying to transfer the much larger man's weight.

"I've got a car waiting out back. Take it. The driver's discreet. I'll grab a cab."

He helps me to the back entrance where a black Lincoln MKT awaits. After maneuvering Ransom into the backseat, who appears to have passed out, I slide in next to him, allowing his heavy head to fall across my lap.

"Heidi . . ." Caleb begins from the doorway. He looks away into the black night and then back to us. "I told you to be careful with him."

"What makes you think that I wasn't?" I frown.

He purses his lips knowingly, flattening them into a thin line. "Just get him in bed. And call me later."

He slams the car door on my blank expression and taps the roof of the car, signaling the driver to go. When we turn onto the main road, he asks, "Where to, ma'am?"

Shit.

I don't even know where Ransom lives. And I damn sure can't take him back to my place. And rolling up to a hotel at this time of night will definitely have the blogs talking by dawn.

I look down at Ransom's sleeping form. He looks so sweet and small right now. So peaceful in his chemically induced dreams. I lightly slap his face, and of course, he doesn't respond. I do it again, adding enough force to create a smacking sound. When that doesn't work, I slap and shake his heavy body until he begins to groan.

"Ransom!" I shout directly in his ear. "I need you to tell me where you live."

He groans again, as if every cell in his body aches. Considering the stench coming from his pores, I bet he'll be feeling even worse in a few hours.

"You know," is all he grunts out, before drifting off to sleep.

"Huh? Ransom wake up! What do you mean, I know?"

He mumbles something unintelligible before I pick up on a clue that immediately lets me know where to take him. Hell, I should've known.

". . . I fucked you on my bed."

I look to the driver with my face flamed with embarrassment, silently praying that he didn't catch that last part. "Take us to the Royal, please."

Chapter Seventeen

The Royal is not the usual haunt for celebrities, or even celeb wannabes. To be frank, the only thing royal about it is its name. It's considered boutique in its size and amenities, and while the décor is posh and modern, it doesn't scream opulence. And right at this moment, I could not be more grateful for that.

The lobby is completely empty, with not even a doorman in sight. Our driver helps Ransom from the backseat, who finally has decided to wake long enough to walk inside. Thank God for that. There was no way I could carry him.

By some miracle, Ransom successfully staggers to the elevators and stays upright long enough to press in his code to the penthouse suites. Funny. I don't remember there being one last week when we were here. But then again, I was with Caleb, and far too high on champagne and nervous energy to really pay attention.

When the elevator begins to lurch upward, he slumps back against the far end wall, opposite where I stand. Although we're not even close to touching, his glassy-eyed gaze sweeps over me with what can only be described as pure fire and malice. He looks at me like he hates me, like I disgust him, yet I can't find the nerve to abandon him. Not when I know that he needs me more than he hates me. More than I hate what we're doing to Tucker.

The doors slide open once we reach the top, and I go to help Ransom out to the hall. At first, he flinches at my touch, but his body can't support its own weight, so he lets me lead him to the door of the suite. The odor of alcohol and smoke singes my nose, but it's almost completely overshadowed by the heat of his body against mine.

"I need your key, Ransom," I tell him.

He looks perplexed at my words for a split second before stuffing a hand down his back pocket and fishing out a keycard. He hands it to me instead of sliding it in the card slot attached to the door. When I take it from him, our fingers brush against each other, and while I've had him literally asleep in my lap for the last twenty minutes, this . . . this seems more intimate. Like maybe it's a subconscious thing for us to want to feel the other's skin. Be *in* the other's skin.

I usher him into the suite, which is as meticulous as I remember it with no signs of permanent residency. I can't believe he actually lives here, considering that he's in the city for at least a third of the year. The other two-thirds? I have no idea. And I'm not sure if I want to know.

"Can I get you anything else?" I ask, going straight to the wet bar to grab a bottle of water. I crack the seal and hand it to him. He takes it without provocation and flops onto the sofa. "Food?"

"Nah," he answers before taking a swig. "Order yourself something if you want."

"That's ok. I'm not staying," I reply, looking at the door. I really should get home. Tucker will be home any minute and although I left a note, he'll still be worried sick.

He snorts out a sardonic laugh before draining the rest of the bottle. I grab another and hand it to him. "What?"

Ransom shakes his head. "Nothing. Of course you're not staying. I'm too fucked up to give you anything."

"What?"

He struggles to his feet and staggers to the bedroom. "Nothing, H. Go on home to your husband. Don't worry, whiskey dick usually wears off in a few hours."

I'm right on his heels, filled with renewed pisstivity. "What the . . . what are you talking about, Ransom?"

He spins around, not as coordinated as he usually is, but successfully startling the shit out of me. I follow the swift movement of his hand, completely enraptured and unable to look away as he cups his manhood for the second time tonight. "I said, don't worry, baby. I will still get hard for you. That is what you want from me, right? That is why you've left your warm, marital bed to come save me from myself, abandoning poor Tucker, right? But don't worry. He looks like he has no problem taking care of himself."

I don't know what possesses me in the next pivotal moments. It's like having an out of body experience as I watch my right hand pull back and lurch forward to connect with Ransom's stubbled jaw with enough force that his chin meets his shoulder. Slowly, he turns back to look down at me, his nostrils flaring and his dark eyes brewing with ire. A single trickle of blood escapes the corner of this luscious mouth, and he sluggishly drags his tongue to his lip to lap it up, those sultry, onyx eyes never straying from my face.

"I see how you want it," he rasps, his voice husky with anger and alcohol. "You like to give it just as much as you like to take it."

"Fuck you," I spit out. "Fuck. You."

"You did, baby. Don't you remember? We talked. We laughed. We drank. We fucked. We came. Hard. Or was I that forgettable for you?"

His words are ice but the look on his face is all fire. And even through all that . . . even through the bitter bite of his insults, I see his pain. I don't want to—I want to hate him—but I see in him the same thing that I see every time I look in the mirror. The same thing I see reflected in Tucker's eyes when he gazes at me in pity and confusion.

"I didn't forget you." I say it because he needs to hear it. I say it because it's true.

"Then why do you want to leave me?"

I don't expect that from him—that raw, unguarded truth—but it's right there. And he's not taking it back.

His strangled words are barely a whisper, but I hear them loud and clear. "I can make you feel young again, Heidi. I can make you feel things that he can't. Let me be your second chance."

I shake my head—at him, at myself, at our whole fucked up situation. Now I understand . . . I see why Tucker often looks at me the same way. Shaking his head in resignation, sighing in reluctance.

You can't win with a broken person. Because you don't want to. It's just not a fair fight.

And Ransom—somehow, some way—is more broken than me. And something within me wants to put him back together again.

"I'll stay," I find myself saying. "I'll stay if you lie down and rest. Ok?"

He seems to sober with that promise and allows a small smile to slip from his lips. "Ok," he agrees.

I help him to the bed, assisting him with the buckles on his boots and belt. And while there's absolutely nothing sexual about me undressing him right now, I can't help the way my skin prickles when my fingertips graze his taut waist. Or the way my breath catches when he removes his shirt to reveal the most spectacular torso that I've seen in more than three decades.

He climbs into bed in nothing but his fitted boxer briefs,

and while I know he should probably shower, I can't see how I can coax him into getting up now that his head has hit the pillow.

"I'm sorry," he mumbles, his eyes closed. I bring the duvet up to his chest, more for my comfort than his.

"For what?"

"For wanting you. For hating that I want you. For wishing you'd hate me too."

"It's ok," I whisper.

He releases a sound from the back of his throat, something more out of pain than eroticism, and within seconds, he's asleep, snoring soundly.

I click off the lights and gather up his dirty clothes to send out to be laundered before tiptoeing out of the room. Before I stuff the smoke-saturated garments in a plastic bag, I remove all the personal effects from his pockets to ensure he doesn't lose anything.

At least, that's the reason I tell myself.

Oxy. Ativan. And what's left of an eight ball of coke.

Fuck.

Ransom isn't just broken. He's still breaking.

Chapter Eighteen

Pure morning sunlight filters through the curtains when I finally allow myself to go home. I'm convinced that Ransom won't notice anyway. He probably wouldn't even remember last night or my presence whenever he came to. However, I would never forget the things he said to me. Or the look of sheer desolation on his face. Or the drugs I found in the pocket of his jeans.

I'm still not sure what to do when I arrive at my building. If anything, I'm even more confused.

"Hey, baby," Tucker rasps, his voice hoarse with too-little sleep. "Everything ok?"

"Shhhh, go back to sleep. It's fine. We'll talk later," I smile, leaning over to kiss his lips. He returns my grin before rolling over and drifting back off to dreamland.

I slip out of my clothes that still stink with the aroma of beer and bar, and head into the bathroom for a quick shower. Just before I step under the hot spray, a pang of guilt attacks my chest. I'm washing away what little bit of Ransom I'd taken with me. He was afraid I'd forget him . . . that I'd leave him. And that's exactly what I'm trying to do.

I'm still trying to convince myself that it's the right thing to do when I slide into bed next to my husband.

"YOU SHOULD HAVE told me." I stir my latte for the tenth time, trying to expel the nervous energy. If I look up, I may slap him across his pretty face.

Caleb heaves out a sigh. "I know. But if I had, would you have taken him on?"

"Of course not! Jesus, Caleb. He's a junkie. You tricked me into representing a fucking junkie and had me in there blind. Can you imagine what could have happened once you sent me off in the middle of the night with him?"

He lifts his hands in surrender. "He's harmless, I swear. He's more of an emotional addict. And come on . . . what entertainer *isn't* coked out of their minds every night?"

I shake my head, refusing to agree with him although I know it's true. "This is different. Ransom is . . ."

I can't find the words. *Special?* No. *Better than that?* Hell no. *Using only to stifle a much deeper compulsion?* Ding, ding, ding.

"I know, Heidi." He nods, his eyes fixed on the woodgrain of the table. It's the most sincere and humbled I've ever seen the man in all the years I've known him. "That's why

I asked you to meet me today. I wanted you to understand why I couldn't tell you. And why I can't let you give up on him, even though I know you tried to."

"What?"

Caleb lifts his eyes to meet my gaze. They stir with a kindred somberness. "I know you. You wanted to drop him. I couldn't let you do it. Not now."

"And why is that?"

"Because everyone else has. And if you did, he may not survive it. And the band would be dead."

I purse my lips and smirk knowingly. "And that's your only interest in his well-being? The future of the band?"

Caleb shrugs before picking up his cup of overpriced mocha. "I'm a businessman first. But I'm also human. Ransom is a good kid. He just needs someone to believe that so maybe he can start to believe it too."

I roll my eyes and cross my arms in front of my chest, leaning back in my seat. "Oh, spare me the bleeding heart bullshit. He's a grown man, Caleb."

Caleb matches my cynical glare, and a slow smile creeps onto his thin lips. "You would know, now wouldn't you?"

Poker face intact, my face and body language don't flinch a muscle. "And what the fuck is that supposed to mean?"

He shrugs, backing down from what would have been a fight to the death, and pretends to check his phone. "Nothing at all. It's just interesting that he's grown so attached to you, is all. So attached that he refused to leave that bar until you showed up. He kept saying that he had a song for you, and that you wanted to hear him sing. Quite fond of you in such a short time, wouldn't you say?"

I don't say a word. Fuck Caleb and all his suspicions. I would cut off my arm before I surrender my secrets to that gossip queen.

"Anyway," he presses on. "I need a favor from you, seeing as he seems to listen to you."

"And that is?" My voice is flat, my face unreadable.

"I need Ransom to lay low for a while. Get out of town. After last night's antics, I'm sure the publicist in you would agree that taking some time away would be beneficial."

"And why the hell do you think I'd do something like that? Better yet, how do you think I could convince him to even agree to it?"

Caleb shrugs for the eighth time since we've sat down. It's not like him to be so indecisive. "You're a resourceful woman. Use your God-given resources."

I absorb the jab of his words and retaliate, leaning forward across the table so he can clearly see the seriousness on my face. "Careful, Caleb. I like you and all, but be very fucking careful about what you insinuate."

He brushes it off with a phony laugh. "I'd never, love. Just a thought. Hey, if he lands in jail, he's your problem—not mine. Last night, he only got into a fight with a brick wall and a few barstools. But who knows what tonight has in store for us. Hey, we've got Fallon tomorrow night. That should be a riot."

With that, he climbs onto his Prada loafers, throws a bill

on the table, and straightens the lapel of his crisp oxford. "Now if you'll excuse me, I actually have work to do."

I watch him strut away with more sass than necessary, sipping what's left of my cold latte and wondering what the hell to do next. So I can't quit on Ransom, for fear that he'll spiral even further. But I can't control him either. I thought getting into bed with him was the pinnacle of my problems, but it seems that getting into business with him is just as messy, if not messier. I'm just not sure what I'm willing to sacrifice—my marriage or my sanity.

I don't hear from Ransom for the rest of the day and I assume he's drying out after last night's antics. So I focus on the person who's really important—my husband. Tucker needs me more than anyone else right now. When I left, he was still asleep, which was surprising considering that I've never known him to sleep past 7 A.M. even on the weekends. I was only able to squeeze in a couple hours of shuteye when Caleb hit me up for coffee.

"Hey babe, you hungry?" he calls out from the kitchen over the sounds of Coltrane. The aromas of griddle-melted butter, fried pork, and syrup caress my senses.

"Starving," I answer, kicking off my shoes and stowing my purse before padding toward him on bare feet. "Whatcha making?"

He waves his spatula like a magician's wand toward the various pans on the glass range. "I've got scrambled eggs, bacon—the real stuff, no turkey crap—and I'm almost done with the pancakes. Champagne is chilling in the fridge along with the OJ for mimosas."

I take that as my cue and, after giving him a quick peck on the cheek, go to prepare our drinks. Even though I was hoping to catch a few extra hours of sleep, there's no way I can deny us this rare, uninterrupted quality time. Sundays used to be sacred to us—we'd go to the farmer's market, cook together, listen to Tuck's records, and just relax and recharge for the week ahead. Yet for the past couple years, we've used the day to catch up on unfinished projects and separate activities. Seeing Tucker move around the kitchen, grooving to "A Love Supreme" makes me miss the old us. It makes me crave the togetherness we once shared. Seeing him now is like looking through new eyes. It's still a wonderful sight, but it's not familiar to me. And that makes me sad.

"Feel free to change the music if you want," he offers as he flips the last batch of pancakes. "Or turn it off if you want."

"No, this is fine," I smile between sips of my cocktail.

And actually, it is.

MONDAY REARS ITS ugly head before I'm ready, but at least I feel better than I have in ages. A lazy Sunday was just what the doctor ordered, and I get to the office ten minutes early, bearing donuts no less.

"Oh, shit," Tamara remarks, taking a peek at the glazed confections. "And these aren't even gluten free. Girl, Dr. D must've put it on you real good this weekend!"

She holds up a hand for me to slap but I ignore her and retreat to my office, shaking my head the entire way.

"We will not talk about my sex life, understand? So go eat your deep fried breakfast before I replace them with bran muffins."

Tamara laughs me off and comes to sit on the edge of my desk. Why the hell do I let her get away with this shit? Anyone else would be limping out of here if they'd done that. Metaphorically, of course.

"So you want to tell me what's going on with you and that sexy ass rock god?"

I power on my iMac and busy my eyes and hands with reading messages from last week. Anything that will help school my features into something other than *What-the-fuck-am-I-really-that-transparent* shock. "Who? Ransom?"

"Uh, duh. What other fine-as-fuck musicians were you damn near tonguing down this weekend?"

"Tam . . ."

"I'm just saying . . . that boy wants you like fat chicks want fat-free cupcakes."

"Well . . . I don't want him." Lies.

"You don't? Not even a little bit?"

"Nope. Not interested." All lies.

A devilish grin broadens her plump, red-stained lips. "Well . . . can I have him?"

"Um . . . I don't think you're his type, Tam," I snicker.

"What? You don't think he likes brown girls?"

"No. I don't think he likes dick."

Tamara rolls her eyes and waves off the remark like I just told her he prefers red wine to white. "Girl, please. A man doesn't know what he likes until he tries it. And trust me . . . once you get a taste of this chocolate bar, you won't ever wanna satisfy your sweet tooth with nothing else. I'll turn that pretty boy into a full blown chocoholic!"

Great. Yet, another addiction for Mr. Reed.

"Look, this has been fun," I say, lifting a slender, arched brow. "But I don't pay you to talk about your raunchy fantasies. Don't you have some work to do?"

"Yeah, yeah," she answers, sliding her round backside from my desk. "Just one more thing. Can I go with you to *The Tonight Show* taping today? My new ex-boyfriend is going to be there!"

"No," I shake my head. "Hell no."

"Aw, come on, boss lady. I'll be good."

"No, Tam. I've got enough to deal with. I don't need your out-of-control libido to be one of them. Now go do your job before I find someone to do it for you. Those interns are just itching to knock you off your stilettos, and I'm starting to feel like letting them."

"Fine! I'm going. But you can't keep him all to yourself if you're not going to do anything with him, you know," she retorts before quickly shutting my office door before I can fire back.

The day crawls at a snail's pace, and I find myself staring at the clock more often than not, waiting for five o'clock to hit. Ransom will get to Studio 6B earlier for necessary sound checks, and while I am tempted to show up for that, I don't want to seem too anxious. Caleb is there; he's got it. And while it's perfectly reasonable for one's publicist to be present for all publicized events, it just seems a little thirsty to pop up for rehearsals. Lord knows we don't need any speculation from anyone else.

I make it a point to arrive on time to show that I'm all about business. And while I may be decked out in new Stella McCartney, my look is chic and professional. I'm here to work, and nothing else.

"You're here," Caleb remarked, looking genuinely surprised when he spots me in the green room.

"Of course, I am. Why wouldn't I be?"

"It's just . . ." He shakes his head, not even bothering to finish. And, honestly, he doesn't have to.

"So where are the guys?" The guys . . . yeah right.

"You know the drill. Quiet meditation before performances. Ransom has been insisting on it since as long as I can remember."

I peg him with a look that screams, *Oh, come on!* "So you mean to tell me, even knowing about his"—my eyes dart around to ensure no listening ears are near—"issues, you never questioned what he was doing before every show?"

The answer seems painstakingly obvious. He's getting high, for Christ's sakes! Ransom wants to be left alone so he can get lifted in peace. Meditate, my ass.

"I know what you're thinking," Caleb claims before I have to say it out loud. "And you're wrong. Music is the only thing that kid is serious about. He never performs less than completely sober, not even a drop of beer. It's the one pure part of him that he keeps for himself. The one thing that he can offer with one hundred percent honesty."

I stare at Caleb for a long beat, waiting for the rest of the joke, but he only gazes back with total confidence. He's telling the truth. He really believes that the only time Ransom isn't high is when he is on stage. *Humph.* Interesting. Maybe what they say about artists is true. Maybe their art truly is the source of their sanity and the villain of their demise.

We watch the show from backstage, jamming out to The Roots and laughing at Jimmy's witty banter. He slow jams the news and plays Password with Reese Witherspoon and Josh Duhamel. It's great, all lighthearted fun and games. But when Jimmy introduces tonight's musical guest, Ransom, to the stage, I instantly know that shit just got real.

"Fuck," Caleb spits out under his breath as the lights go up to reveal the foursome, all decked out in black. The music starts, and the roaring crowd simultaneously calms into hushed silence.

"What?" I know something isn't right, but I'm just not sure what it is.

Caleb pulls out his phone and starts texting furiously. He doesn't look up when he answers. "The motherfucker changed the song they rehearsed. This isn't what they prepared at sound check."

"Fuck," I say, mimicking Caleb's earlier sentiment. "He can't do that. He can't do that, right?"

"He just did."

I look around, my mind working double time to find a way to fix this debacle, but it's too late. The sounds of electric guitar are already echoing throughout the studio, along with the hypnotic rhythm of drums. Even though the band could play just about anything on their own, The Roots accompany them to add an extra dimension of sound. Luckily, they know this, which is surprising, since it's not a Ransom original. I can't even place what it is exactly.

Until he sings.

I should have known. I should have fucking known. Of course, he's still pissed at me and wants to let the world know just how much of a mind-fucking slut I am. And maybe he should. If this is what it takes for him to let this go, then better to do it in song than let it play out on TMZ.

But as he belts out the first verse of Prince's "Darling Nikki," a cover they featured on their last album, I know that this is so much more than musically venting. Ransom isn't . . . right. He looks good, and he's engaging the crowd in that wildly sensual way that gets them screaming for more, but there's just something off about his movements. Even his voice isn't as crisp as it usually sounds. There's something lying underneath it, be it pain or desire or shame. I just know this isn't the Ransom Reed I saw kill it in front of the massive audience at Madison Square Garden just two Fridays ago.

Still, the band finishes to a cheering crowd and a standing ovation, which is a good sign, despite the glaring truth staring us in the eye. Ransom wouldn't know it though. As soon as the music stops and Jimmy appears on stage, holding a vinyl copy of their last LP, Ransom drops the mic on the stage and walks off, brusquely pushing past the host and his bandmates. And me.

"Never performs less than sober, huh?" I say to Caleb, both of us too stunned to do more than just stand there.

"Holy fuck. Holy fucking fuck," he groans.

"Yeah. My sentiments exactly." I look over at the shell-shocked agent and sigh, releasing my last bit of resolve. "So about getting him out of town . . . I think I might be able to help with that."

Chapter Nineteen

Convincing Ransom of getting out of the city is much easier than Caleb and I anticipate, and we're left wondering if the young rocker was already getting burned out of "the life." We knew that confronting him after his grand performance would only lead to tragedy, so we waited until Tuesday—today—to give him the ultimatum—take some time out or we walk. Both of us. I can't understand why that would be a big enough incentive, but apparently, it works.

Now, convincing Tucker? That's a different story. One that I'm not quite prepared to hear.

I get home from work at my usual time, knowing that coming in late would only agitate him and make it harder to plead my case. He's sitting at the bistro table, sipping a cup of tea and reading a document from a stack of papers in a file folder. The scents of fresh herbs, tomatoes, and lemon waft from the kitchen, and my stomach growls. Even though Lucia has already left to go home for the evening, she always leaves dinner in the oven. Tonight smells like her famous citrus herb chicken.

Tucker looks up as soon as I approach and smiles, although I can tell it's forced. He looks tired . . . even older. I can't imagine what must be troubling him, and I make it a point not to ask. That's our thing—work stays at work. Still, I can see the past few days have worn on him, and I am yearning for him to let me comfort him.

"Hey babe," I say, wearing a genuine grin. "Something smells good." I kiss him on his full lips and go into the kitchen to pour a glass of wine. I'll need it for the conversation we're about to have.

"Lucia made chicken and a Caprese salad."

"I was talking about you." I turn to give him a wink and see him soften just a fraction. Ugh. I hate to spring this on him, especially with how up and down things have been for us this past week. "Want a glass?" I ask holding up a bottle of Sauvignon Blanc.

"No thanks," he sighs, looking back down at the papers. I watch him for a beat, sipping my wine, when he looks back up at me, the defeat in his eyes so strong it takes everything inside me not to run to him and fall at his feet. "I lost someone. I lost a patient."

"What?" This time I don't hesitate. I put down my glass and go to him.

"Yeah. Young kid, seventeen. There was nothing I could do, but still . . . I feel responsible. I knew him. I knew he was struggling, and I tried everything I could to reach him outside of moving him in and making him sleep on our couch. He was alone . . . he was lonely. His parents were in Monaco when he was brought in after he OD'd. Took them two days to get back here to see about their son. Two days. Apparently, they had been planning that trip for months."

Without a word, I slide onto his lap and wrap my arms around him, just trying to absorb his pain. He cared for that kid, just like he does all his patients. He knows he's not supposed to, but Tucker can't help it. He's one of those genuinely good, kind souls. He went in to psychiatry because he wanted to help the people whose wounds weren't visible to the outside world. He understood that suffering inside the prison of your mind was far worse than any iron shackles inside a jail cell. And he had helped people . . . tons of them. But sometimes, he lost them too. They were just too far gone . . .

"I was thinking . . . maybe it's time we took a vacation. I need a break, Bunny. This one . . . this one was difficult. Think you could take a week or two? I could just really use some time away from here . . . from this. I just need to escape reality with you."

I sit up in slow motion, and look at him with all the understanding I can muster. Oh no. This isn't what I needed. I just don't have two weeks to give him right now, not after the deal I made with Ransom.

I shake the thought from my head. Tucker is my husband. Husband. And he needs me. My loyalty lies with him. He comes first. And my career . . . Shit.

"What were you thinking?" I ask him, trying not to picture the image of my reputation going down like a sinking ship.

"I don't know. Somewhere far from the city. No traffic, no social media, no paparazzi. Just peace and quiet. And us."

I smile and nod. That sounds nice. In a perfect world, that would be all I'd ever need.

"So can you make it?" The optimism in his voice is undeniable. I can't crush him—not now. Not when he's already in ruins.

"See . . . the thing is . . . I have to go out of town for a little while, but maybe I can just cut it down to a few days and be back by this weekend to leave with you."

"Out of town?" he frowns. "Since when?"

"Since today. I just found out and planned to tell you tonight. I have a client that needs to lay low for a while and stay out of the press. I told . . . them . . . I'd ensure they were set up and comfortable. But honestly, I don't see why—"

"A client like who?" I hear it—the accusation. The skepticism. Still, I play dumb.

"Huh?"

"Your client. Who is it?"

This was not how this was supposed to go. He was not supposed to already be on the edge when I told him. I was going to wait until after dinner and a couple glasses of wine.

Then I was hoping we'd break our recent dry spell and make love. I wasn't even going to ask him for anything remotely kinky. Hell, if he wanted to do me in a floor-length gown, I'd let him.

He sits there waiting for me, growing more and more suspicious with every second of my silent unease. I just have to tell him. If I want a snowball's chance in hell at gaining his trust and support, I just have to tell him.

"Ransom Reed."

He opens his mouth, yet snaps it closed immediately, as if he doesn't trust his words. I wait for the jealousy, the rage, the disappointment. But they never come. And part of me—a rather large part—craves them. At least I'd know he cares. At least I could feel like he loves me just as furiously as he cares for his patients.

"So, Ransom needs to get out of town?" he finally asks.

"Yeah, um, he's been in some trouble; Caleb and I think it'd be a good idea for him to gain some perspective, away from the craziness of the city."

He nods, maybe out of empathy. "And where were you planning on taking him?"

"Um, well, I'm not . . ." I'm stammering. Stammering is not a sign that I'm confident in my decision. "I was, uh, thinking of Oasis. Since Justice has beefed up security and gone public, the appeal for the papzz simply isn't there anymore. No one wants to do an exposé on a couple's spa."

He nods again. "Good idea. I'll come too."

"You'll . . . what?" I surely did not hear him right. Did

he just say he'd come with me to take Ransom to a former sex school for bored, undersexed housewives, aka just about every married woman in Manhattan? (Ahem.)

"Yeah. I've always wanted to see that place and meet the guy. Plus it's a five star resort and spa in the middle of nowhere. Sounds like fun."

Sounds like *fun*? Does he know what he's signing up for?

"Well, I haven't actually talked to Justice about this yet. He's sure to shut me down, seeing as it's a couple's resort. And plus . . ."

I can't finish my thought. I can't admit that I confided in Justice in something more than business, and divulged details of our personal lives, even if they were vague. The guy isn't stupid. He knows exactly why I quizzed him about open marriages. And once I show up with Tucker *and* Ransom, I won't be able to dodge that narrowed look of condescension. Because, let's face it, no one does condescending like Justice Drake.

Tucker shifts and grips me by the hips, lifting me from his lap. "Why don't you call and talk to him. I need to make a few calls myself and arrange for the rest of my patients to be taken care of."

"Really?"

He kisses me on the forehead and smiles softly. "Yeah. This'll be good. For all of us." Then he shuffles away to his study, leaving me behind in an obscure cloud of *what the fuck?*

Ransom agreed easier than I expected. Tucker was borderline alien in his acquiesce. But Justice? Shit. I might as well pack my cutoffs and flip-flops and tell the guys we're going to Disney World.

"You want to *what*?" he snaps after I present the idea to him. Most would wither under that clipped, cold tone, but not me. Justice is all bark, very little bite. Especially now that Ally has got him as tame as a teacup Yorkie.

"I want to bring Ransom there to Oasis to lay low for a week. Two weeks tops. The press won't think to look for him there, and around all those old, boring ass married folks, he's sure to stay out of trouble."

"I'm still not seeing how this has dick to do with me and mine. This isn't a fucking hotel, Heidi. I have clients—clients that pay me well to maintain a sense of safety and serenity. And how am I supposed to explain some young, single kid walking around when we have a strict Couples Only policy?"

"Well . . . tell them he's with me."

Silence, save for the sound of his unspoken accusations. He opens with a snort before continuing. "You? You're coming too? And what does your *husband* think about that?"

"He thinks it's a good idea. He actually suggested he come along too."

Another snort, this time one of aggravation. "I said couple, Heidi. As in two. Not three, not four. Two."

I purse my lips as I walk into the bedroom for more privacy. "And since when have you been the patron saint of monogamy?"

"I've always promoted the idea of it, Heidi. It was just in

a slightly misguided, convoluted way. However, you can't deny my success rate. You don't become Justice Drake without knowing your shit."

I roll my eyes, even though he can't see it. "Oh, Justice. What a big ego you have. So are we doing that now? Talking about yourself in the third person?"

"You know what I mean."

"Actually, I don't. Is it cool for us to come or not? Or would you like to continue to judge me as if your closet isn't bursting with more skeletons than a Tim Burton film. Please . . . tell me again how you met and seduced your current love interest aka your sister-in-law. And tell me again how she found you hiding out in Abu Dhabi, when someone went out on a fucking limb—sacrificing her own time and resources—to track you down for her. I particularly *love* that part of the story."

I can almost feel the heat of his temper flaring from over two thousand miles away. And while his voice is arctic, he's saying exactly what I want him to say, as I knew he would. I always get my way.

"Fine. Bring him. But space is limited. He stays out of the way, and he doesn't pry into my business. Understand? And if I catch one single fucking inkling that he's using, he's out. Got it?"

I nearly gasp, but bite it down. "Using? What makes you think he's using?" I hadn't told anyone. Not even Tucker.

"I have basic cable, Heidi. God forbid the rest of the world outside of Manhattan has the use of modern technology."

I manage to smile. He's agreed. And while he may be pissed, I know Justice can't stay mad at me for long. Above all, he owes me. He'll always owe me. I'm the one who helped bring him back from the dead.

"You're such a hater. Admit it—you miss it here."

"Like a hole in the head." I almost hear him chuckle, but being the hard ass that he is, he refuses to show any other emotion outside of pissed and horny.

"So, we'll be there within the week. I'm shooting for Thursday if Tucker can get things squared away with work."

"Fine. Shoot me your info and I'll have your ride waiting."

"Seriously?" I scoff. "I know how to get there. All that security bullshit isn't necessary."

Justice pushes right back, ignoring my attitude. "You're bringing two strangers to my home and business. So yes, the security bullshit is necessary. Take it or leave it."

"Fine."

"Fine."

We both hang up. And I smile. I kinda love that guy.

I don't waste any time contacting the travel agent and Caleb and pass along the travel info. He's stunned that Justice would agree to let us come, but downright flabbergasted that Tucker would suggest he come along too. I don't let on that I'm just as shocked. I like Caleb, but not enough to share with him. There are industry friends and regular friends. Caleb is an industry friend. My regular friends can be counted on one hand with a couple fingers to spare.

Initially, I think I won't be able to rest until our flight on

Thursday morning, but both Tucker and I are so busy with tying up loose ends that the day comes sooner than expected. We don't even get a chance to talk about what to expect. I know that Tucker thinks this will be good for us, but why? Because he thinks it will provide us some much needed alone time? Or because he can keep an eye on Ransom? Or is it that the prospect of having Ransom there for . . . a repeat performance is what he's craving? And if that is the case, what the hell does that mean for us? That he only gets off on watching another man fuck me?

I can't even think like that right now.

Caleb insists on bringing Ransom to the airport to ensure he actually shows up and I'm grateful. I need as much time alone with Tucker before we get on this plane. After today, who knows what will remain sacred between us?

"I can't understand why you'd choose to fly commercial," Caleb sneers, approaching us at the First Class ticketing line. He air kisses me, and continues bitching about everything from tiny bathrooms to Ebola. "I swear to God, Heidi DuCane, if either you or Ransom get some type of deadly virus, I will kill you myself before you contaminate me. Those quarantine moon suits do nothing for my figure."

At the mention of his name, I straighten, mentally and physically preparing myself to see him again. It always takes me a moment to acclimate when in his presence. It's like he sucks the air right out of the room. He doesn't just take my breath away; he deprives my brain of precious oxygen, leaving me a blubbering, stuttering mess.

As expected, Ransom is dressed in jeans and a tee, this one heather gray. He also has on dark aviators and that gray slouchy beanie over messy hair. I don't know if it's the same one from that night or if he has a dozen of them, which probably boasts some ridiculously expensive label that costs a fortune for merely a bundle of wool. Still, he looks amazing, even in that disheveled, just-rolled-out-of-bed way. It's like he doesn't even have to try. Sex appeal is about as natural to him as blinking those dark, sinuous eyes.

"Hey, man," Ransom mutters, extending a hand to Tucker. The two shake and Tuck returns the greeting. When Ransom turns in my direction, he's less than cordial.

"Heidi."

One word. That's all I get. Not a nod, not a smile. Just my name on his tongue. And it doesn't sound like music anymore. It sounds like a curse.

"Well . . ." I say, looking down at our itinerary. "Flight leaves in an hour. We better get moving."

We go through ticketing and security without speaking, which isn't a problem considering Ransom is stopped for autographs every five feet or so. If he had chosen to showcase his signature locks, I'm sure we would have needed security. By the time we get to our gate, the attendants are already calling for first class passengers. We board quickly to avoid further delays from fans and find our seats. To my disenchantment, Ransom is seated directly behind us, not across from us as I initially thought. He'll be able to see everything—hear everything. And while I really shouldn't care, or suspect that he does, I can't help the pang of unease that seizes my gut as I take my window seat, giving Tucker the aisle.

"What's wrong, babe?" he asks, settling beside me. He takes my hand where it rests on the armrest between us. "You look a little pale."

I give him a weak smile. "Just tired, I guess."

"Well, just try to relax," he responds, leaning over to press his lips against mine before tilting back into his headrest. "It's going to be a long flight."

Long flight, indeed. Probably the longest one yet.

The flight attendant comes over to take drink orders and I hurriedly request a glass of champagne. Tucker lifts a questioning brow, eluding to the early hour. I simply shrug.

"Vacation." And if I'm going to make it through alive, with my dignity and marriage intact, I'm going to need alcohol. Lots of it.

The flight is uneventful for the first hour or so, and I manage to doze off after a couple more glasses of bubbly. That's when I feel the back of my seat bow as if someone is gripping it. My eyes pop open and dart up just in time to see Ransom looming over me, his tired eyes gazing down at me with the intensity of a sniper.

"Excuse me," he mutters. Then he shifts over into the aisle and creeps into the lavatory. I look over at Tucker, who appears to be oblivious, completely engulfed in an audiobook he's listening to through his headphones while tapping on his MacBook Air. It's as if he didn't even notice.

A few minutes pass before a suspicion hits me like a baseball bat. Ransom should have been back by now. What if he's sick? Or what if he's in there getting high? Shit. I can't have him on a public plane, blitzed out of his mind. And if Justice finds out? Yeah, I take my liberties with him, but he won't budge on the No Drugs policy. His staff is randomly tested and even his clients have to submit to pre-enrollment screenings. Say what you want about him, but Justice is a standup guy. Total asshole, but a good man deep inside.

I can't sit still. I can't be satisfied with just wondering what he's doing in there, if he's ok, if he's finally gone too far this time. My reputation may be on the line, but, hell, so is his life. And cold bitch or not, I can't not care about him.

"Excuse me," I murmur, unsnapping my lap belt. When Tucker doesn't respond, I tap him on the shoulder to get his attention.

"Yeah?" he says, pulling off his headphones.

I point toward the lavatory. "Bathroom."

After Tucker's moved into the aisle to let me out, he quickly sits back down to get back to whatever he's doing. I know there's some investigating that goes along with the passing of his patient, so I assume he's still dealing with that.

When I get to the ugly, beige folding door, I tap lightly, as not to draw attention to myself or the person inside.

"Yeah?" replies a strained rasp.

"It's me."

A long moment passes before I hear the lock slide open, yet he doesn't open the door. I look up to see that Tucker is still deeply engrossed in his work, and then I do the unthinkable. I step inside the tiny airplane bathroom with another man.

Ransom is leaning over the sink, palms pressed to the edge of the makeshift cabinet. His head is down, but I can see that his skin appears to be slicked with a thin sheen of sweat that looks clammy to the touch. I peer around his massive body, which takes up the entire space, save for the spot I'm standing in, and search for any signs of drug usage. But there's nothing. Not a trace of paraphernalia.

"I don't have anything on me," he mutters, without lifting his head.

"I didn't think you did," I lie.

"I know why you're here, Heidi. I know what you're looking for."

"Well, if you know, why didn't you tell me? Why didn't you tell me you were a drug addict, Ransom?"

He chuckles under his breath, causing his hunched back to vibrate with mirth. "I'm not addicted to drugs, H."

"Then what is it? Alcohol?"

"I wish." The sound of his voice is so weak and defeated in this enclosed space, it seems to amplify every unsaid word and every rejected sentiment. I just want to lift my hand and touch him—for his comfort and for mine. Whatever is eating him up inside—whether it be pills or coke or booze—is hurting him. And he's hurting himself to dull the pain.

"Ransom, you can talk to me," I whisper. "Whatever is going on . . . I'm here for you."

"Are you? Like you were there for me Saturday night?"

"That's different. I needed to be home, and you were fine—"

"I know what you wanted to talk about, H. I know you wanted to leave me. Just like everybody else."

My first reaction is to deny, but his words stun me into silence. *I know you wanted to leave me.* It sounds like so much more than annoyance at having to find a new publicist. So much more than just business. There's pain behind those words—pain deeper than I could ever reach. And while I may not have initially caused it, I've become a physical reminder of it. An itchy, stinging scab over the secret laceration over his heart. And I don't know why. I don't understand why he's given me the power to hurt him, when I never asked for that role.

"I'm not good for you," I hear myself say on the edge of a whisper.

"I know. Nothing fun ever is. But I want you anyway."

I look past his back to find that he's looking at me through the tiny mirror, those dark, glassy eyes rimmed with even darker circles. I believe him about not using. I believe him but I don't want to. The truth seems even worse.

The plane hits a rough patch of air, and we remember where we are. The haze of raw emotion retreats and we both sober with self-consciousness. Ransom turns on the miniature sink to splash water on his face. I fiddle with my hair as if I were actually doing something in here to mess it up. When I place my hand on the handle of the door, Ransom turns to look at me expectantly.

"Try to get some rest, ok? We'll be in Arizona in a couple hours." Then I escape that tiny closet filled with our secrets and skeletons, and hope that none have followed me out.

When I return to my seat, I find that Tucker's eyes are still glued to the screen of his computer. He nods when I approach and gets up to let me in without letting his fingers leave the keyboard. I sit down and lean my head against the window, suddenly exhausted.

"Is he ok?"

I turn to my husband, his expression impassive, his attention still tuned to his work. When I don't answer right away, he simply lifts a brow and gives me a mere fraction of a glance. That's it.

"Yeah." It's a lie. Ransom isn't all right. I'm not all right. And we . . . we haven't been all right for a long time.

He nods. "Good." Then he acts as if we hadn't spoken at all.

Ransom returns to his seat minutes later, his color less pale and his face more relaxed. That alone is almost enough to soothe me into sleep. And just as the first caress of slumber starts to pull me under, I feel warm, callused fingers brush against the back of my right hand. The hand by the window. The hand that Tucker can't see.

I fall asleep that way—my husband at my side, completely oblivious, and my one-time lover running his fingertips over my knuckles. And it feels like we're fucking. Only this time, Tucker isn't watching.

Chapter Twenty

Arizona is fucking hot.

Not New York hot, which is pretty damn miserable in the summertime. But West-coast-so-goddamn-dry-I-can't-breathe-blink-or-swallow hot. I hate it. But the heat doesn't compare to the way my hand still kindles with Ransom's touch. Or the way Tucker's shrewd stare burns right through me, picking me apart, sifting out the secrets and leaving behind the shame to fester and rot. I hate that too.

The limo ride to Justice's compound is uncomfortable to say the least. But we try to make the best of the long journey by completely tuning one another out. Tucker goes back to whatever the hell he's typing up on his MacBook. Across from us on the bench seat, Ransom slips on his headphones and pulls a notebook out of his bag. I watch with rapt fascination as he taps his fingers against the blank, paper canvas, head nodding, eyes closed. To watch him create—to breathe life into oblivion and somehow compose greatness—is probably the most intimate experience I've had with him to date. And even though I must look like a moron staring at him like he's some rare, exotic piece of art, I can't force myself to look away. He's beautiful in his element—unguarded, pure. It's like I'm truly seeing him for the first time.

His eyes suddenly open, and lock on to mine. He frowns for half a second before the corner of his mouth twitches. He mouths the word, *What?*, and the unspoken question, coupled with the flash of his tongue, unleashes a swarm of silk-winged butterflies inside my ribcage. Reflexively, I look over to my husband, who, as I expect, is none the wiser. When I turn back to Ransom, I simply shake my head. He lifts a challenging brow, tempting me to tell him what's on my mind. But then again, I don't have to. He can see the way my skin is flushed like it's just been burned by the stubble of his chin. And the way my chest rises and falls with every single ragged breath as if he's squeezing my lungs with his bare hands. And he surely notices the way my gaze runs over him, trying to capture every detail and download them to the forbidden file folder inside my mind.

He can see all these things, because in some convoluted way, Ransom has gotten inside of more than just my body. He's watermarked my heart, and now he can read me like I'm splashed across the front pages of *The Post*.

This stranger has made me feel for him. And I hate that most of all.

I break the spell by pretending to be engrossed in unread text messages and emails on my cellphone, avoiding eye contact with him for the rest of the trip. When we arrive at Oasis over an hour later, my whole body aches with tension and stiffness. Of course, I don't even have a chance to get out and stretch before I spy Justice on the front steps, his maddeningly handsome face screwed in discontent.

Most women would be overjoyed to be in the presence of such male beauty. Tucker, Ransom, and Justice are all ridiculously gorgeous in very distinct, yet very obvious ways. Tucker is what one would consider classically handsome, with his strong jaw, bee stung lips, and ocean blue eyes. Ransom is the complete opposite, his olive complexion and dark, angular features more intriguing and exotic than my All-American husband's. But Justice . . . Justice is what a woman would deem panty-dropping fine. The man is sex on a stick, covered in rich chocolate and rainbow sprinkles. His eyes are the color of a blue sky that's been threatened by a storm and his lips are bowed, pouty even. They'd make him appear almost feminine if it weren't for the fact that the man's body is an in-depth course in sexual education, and every muscle and plane is a quiz you want to ace with flying colors.

At first glance, you'd think you were staring at a mirage. Then he opens his mouth, and the illusion shatters. It's like he knows he is *that* gorgeous, *that* sexy, and he wants to repel you. Like his intent is to turn off as many people as he can in an attempt to keep them at arm's length.

I scoped out his tactics within the first few moments of meeting him years ago. Cut from the same cloth, that guy and me. And after the top blew off his personal life last year, exposing his piece of shit "family" and the way they threw him out like garbage, I can understand why he chooses to live his life in exile.

"Took you long enough," he grumbles, coming down the terra cotta stairs of his massive estate. Exile or not, Justice is loaded. After his spineless father's bitch of a wife sent Justice and his mom packing, he was left with a little chunk of change. He took the cash, put it toward an idea that would either get him stoned or celebrated and, alas, Justice Drake, sexpert extraordinaire, was born.

"Save the niceties and concern for someone who actually gives a damn," I fire back, walking past him into the air-conditioned foyer. It's not that the heat is unbearable, because it is. But mostly the fact that if I stand there between my husband and my—shit, I don't even know what he is—Justice will see right through me. He'll see the truth displayed on my body like a scarlet letter, inked with bloodred lies and lust. And I'm just not ready to face him yet. I could give two shits what people think about me as a person, especially my clients. But Justice is different. I actually like him, but even more than that, I respect the hell out of him. It's kind of hard not to.

I hear the men behind me, exchanging introductions as

they make their way into the house. And while my exterior is stoically cool and blasé, my gut rages like the mosh pit at a heavy metal concert. What was I thinking? Bringing Tucker and Ransom to Justice's den of sin? Exposing them to what really goes on behind the closed door of most marriages? Am I just encouraging this thing between us? Did I subconsciously choose this place because I knew we'd be safe from ridicule, and encouraged to explore our fantasies further?

"Your rooms are this way. The staff will grab your bags," Justice says, leading us to the grand staircase that leads to the second floor rooms. They were initially used as living quarters for the women enrolled in his program, but they now house couples that have joined Justice's new relationship-enrichment course. I was instrumental in the changeover after he abandoned his business last fall. Being that exposed and vulnerable nearly crushed him. But losing Ally—watching her walk away from him and back into her husband's arms—it almost killed him.

After months of trying to pick up the pieces of his war-torn life, and worrying about him until I was physically sick, I enlisted a little help. Like I told him, every businessperson worth their salt has a hacker on their payroll. So I emailed and emailed, to no avail, hoping to get just a breadcrumb of an IP address, anything that would lead us to him. He never answered, of course. It was like he knew what my intent was, and he didn't want to be found. He was going to disappear, reinvent himself, and eventually die alone. I couldn't let that happen.

Then, we got a bite.

He wrote Ally.

It wasn't much of a letter, most of it scratched out and unreadable. But there was a postage stamp. The smug bastard had given us a clue. He was ready to be found. He wanted to come home.

So I contacted a couple friends—one in customs, the other in private investigating—and we tracked him down. And I told Ally, who had damn near stalked me for months, showing up at my office daily and annoying the ever-living shit outta me, to go get her boy. And never, ever let him go. A love like that—one birthed out of pain and courage and friendship—was so rare to find. And those two had it. They just needed a little help in keeping it.

I look back at Tucker as we round the top of the banister and give him a smile. What we have is real. Tucker's love for me is solid and true, and always has been. No one can take that away from us. Not Ransom, not Justice, not even me. And as much as I don't deserve him, I can't bear the thought of losing him. I can't fathom my life without him in it, keeping me rooted in love whenever I try to float away.

My gaze darts to Ransom, who trails a few steps behind us, his eyes unfocused, his mouth pressed into a straight line. It was easy to be attracted to him, easier than it should have been. He's the promise of excitement and youth. He's that rush of exhilaration from standing right on the edge of a cliff, arms outstretched and eyes closed. He's that punch of adrenaline that rushes my heart so rapidly that I feel high.

Weightless, yet covered in sensation that prickles every inch of my skin.

Ransom makes me believe I can fly, but it's Tucker who keeps me tethered to the earth. Sometimes I can't tell which is worse.

We stop at a rich mahogany door with the word *Reflection* engraved in beautiful script on a stainless-steel placard. "What's this?" I ask.

"Ally wanted to do something with the rooms . . . create specific themes for them. This is the Reflection room. We're pretty booked right now, so you lucked out."

He fishes a key tied with a ribbon bow out of his pocket and unlocks the door. And as we step inside, I know exactly how this particular room earned its name.

The space is bathed in muted colors—gray, taupe, nude. Colors that would calm the minds and invoke peace, and allow the couple a chance to contemplate on their relationship. However, it's completely decked out in mirrors from top to bottom, the main ones seemingly focused around the bed. So while a couple may reflect on their love for each other by day, their naked, twisted bodies will be reflected by night.

It's as if Justice is trying to tell me something. And for someone who has never relied on subtlety to get his point across, I'm kinda pissed that he took this opportunity to try it out.

I turn around to tell him so, when I realize that I'm not the only one musing over the bedroom's double entendre.

Actually, the message seems to be very clear, and the way Ransom is eyeing the mirror situation directly over the bed, he's just as uncomfortable with what this represents. And what this means for him.

"Your room is down the hall," Justice says to the younger man. He waves Ransom toward the hall and I'm tempted to follow when Justice stops at the doorframe, training that cold, icy stare at me. I can almost feel the temperature in the room plummet. "My place in ten."

Then I'm left with my husband, wondering what the hell Justice could want that would demand my attention so suddenly. And what the hell he and Ransom could be talking about right now.

Under normal circumstances, I would have shown up at the guesthouse where Justice lives at least five minutes late. Ten if I was feeling feisty and wanted to piss him off. But knowing that he's alone with Ransom, and considering our conversation over the phone about open marriages, I can only imagine what conclusions are being made. I know that Justice won't divulge any details, but would Ransom? If he felt it would benefit him in some way?

"Ten minutes, eh?" Tucker muses from behind me. He's closer than I expect, close enough that his warm breath stirs the hair at my nape. "I can think of a few things we can accomplish in ten minutes."

He brushes the hair from my shoulders and presses his lips against the back of my neck, a move that has successfully made me dissolve into warm honey on many occasions. I've always craved physical affection from Tucker—yearned for it like a starving child. Now it just feels like a distraction . . . an annoyance. My husband's touch is annoying me. And that's a serious problem.

"Later," I say, shaking him off. "We've been traveling all day. I feel gross."

I escape to the bathroom to freshen up and to put even more distance between us. When I reemerge, I find Tucker on the balcony that overlooks the courtyard. The sparkling turquoise, negative edge pool is surrounded by couples in plush loungers, talking, laughing, sipping fruity libations from the newly installed in-pool bar. Such a vast difference from a year ago, when only fragile, disparaged women frequented the estate. These people are here solely by choice. Not out of desperation.

"Wanna take a dip after your meeting?" Tucker asks without looking at me. His voice is level, as if he can't feel the tension crackling between us, but I know he does. He's a smart man.

"Sure," I tell him, knowing damn well that won't happen. I tell myself it's because I'm working and can't afford the luxury of lazing around the pool, but even my own denial reeks of guilt.

I kiss his cheek and tell him I'll be back, suggesting he order up some drinks and food. I even recommend some of Riku's specialties before anxiously dashing out the door and away from the whispered judgment of those mirrors in the Reflection room.

Just as my hand retreats from the cool hardness of the doorknob, I hear a husky chuckle from behind me.

"Your friend . . . has a way with innuendo," Ransom drawls. I take a deep breath before turning around to face him, only to find that he's half dressed and looking more luscious than I remembered. I open and close my mouth a half dozen times before speaking.

"Uh, yeah. He's a riot. Forget something?" I ask, lifting a questioning brow, my eyes roaming his taut frame from the soles of his sneakers to the earbuds that dangle onto his bare, tanned shoulders.

He looks down at his low-slung (seriously, how can he be wearing underwear?) black basketball shorts and shrugs. "Thought I'd get in a workout. Too hot to wear anything else."

He's right, but I can't help the pang of possessiveness that urges me to demand he turn his sexy ass around and go put on a shirt. So what if all the women here are married or in serious committed relationships? They're not dead. Take me, for instance. I was so very alive when I spread my thighs for Ransom and took him inside me, mummified him in my warmth and wetness, and made him a permanent memory on my soul. Actually, I can't remember feeling more vital than that night I spent with him, crying for God yet worshipping him. And that feeling has only been amplified with every stolen moment since.

So, no, Ransom isn't mine to feel ownership of, or mine to boss around and tell what to do. But he's mine, goddammit. And sharing isn't an option.

"Heidi?"

I blink, abandoning my fervent reverie, and look back up at him. He licks his lips, goading me, tempting me, and smiles. "I said, going somewhere?"

"Justice," I rasp, my voice splintered. I clear it and press on. "I need to speak with him."

"About me?"

I answer with a frown. "No. Why would I? Did you . . . say anything to him that would invite any questions?"

He snorts and looks away before shaking his head. "No. I haven't. Don't worry, your secret's safe with me."

Even though I'm sure he's being honest, I feel the need to reiterate just how dire his confidence is. "Good. Because, if that got out—if someone found out about . . . us—it'd hurt us all."

"Hurt us?" His eyes flare on the word "hurt" as if the prospect excites him.

"Our careers, yes. The press would be relentless."

He nods, the small smile on his face turning smug. "Sure. The press."

He gazes down the hallway, searching for an escape hatch, and I release him by saying goodbye. I contemplate inviting him for dinner later, but think better of it. We're not here together. I'm simply here to ensure that he doesn't completely fuck up or get fucked up. And I'm here for Tucker, of course.

When I knock on Justice's door, a sense of anxiety, almost fear, has me tempted to turn back around. But before I can make a run for it, he swings open the door, nearly ripping my arm out of the socket as he pulls me inside.

"What the fuck did you do?" he asks as soon as the door slams behind me. He's pacing the floor, breathing heavily, pulling at his short, spiky hair. He's positively pissed. And it has nothing to do with being tardy.

I stand perfectly still, the soles of my sandals planted in marbled quicksand. "What do you mean?"

Suddenly, he's in my face, not threateningly, but he's challenging me. Challenging me to lie to his face and try to deny what he so obviously can see. "You think I'm fucking stupid? You think I don't know what you did with that boy? Dammit, Heidi! I thought we talked about this? I thought you understood the gravity of your decision, and how it would cost you everything. Everything! You think some romp with a rock star will replace a damn decade with your husband? Fucking hell, Heidi. I thought you were smarter than this."

"Justice . . ."

He keeps pressing, keeps digging into me. And I just stand there and let him. "I should have fucking known when you said you needed to bring him. This isn't about drugs or alcohol, is it? You want him here so you can fuck him, yet play the good wife for your husband. Well, not in my house. I don't do affairs, DuCane. You wanna fuck around, take your ass back to the city. Tucker deserves better than that, and I won't have him believe that I was an accomplice."

"Justice . . ." I try again. "He knows."

"What?" That makes him retreat a few steps. "What the fuck do you mean, *He knows*?"

"Tuck . . . he knows. About Ransom."

Justice heaves out an aggravated breath and resumes his pacing. "I'm not a marriage counselor, you know. I can't fix your marriage now that you've screwed it to hell."

"I know." I step toward him, humbled, defeated. "And it's not like that. I didn't screw it up. *We* screwed it up. Together."

"We?"

"He was there. Tucker was there when I was with Ransom. He watched. He . . . instructed. And he loved it. At least he did at the time."

"Did?"

I shake my head, not wanting to believe what's happened—what's *been* happening for some time now. "What I need . . . he can't give it to me. And he knew I found Ransom attractive. We were all drunk, high . . . it just happened. And I . . . I can't stop thinking about it. I can't stop thinking about *him*. I thought letting Tucker see what my body needed from him would help him accept it, and he would eventually be able to provide. But he can't. *He won't.* And ever since our little tryst . . . ever since I felt what it was like to be so completely sated, so undeniably fulfilled . . . I can't go back to how it was. Shit, I refuse to go back to that."

That sobers him and I watch the ire drain from his features. "Does he know this? Your husband?"

I nod. "We tried afterwards. I thought he was catching

on, opening up to the idea. And then he stopped. Jumped away from me like I was a leper. Like I was disgusting and deviant. It hurts to be rejected by the man you love. Especially when another man is willing to not only accept you, but also give you what you need. And not because you need it, but because he wants it too."

I move in closer. Closer than we've ever been. Not seductively, but in an act of vulnerability. I'm giving him his chance to reject me. Letting him push me away and make me feel dirty too. "Justice, I'm scared. I'm terrified because I want him so badly it physically aches. And I can't think of anything else but him, and how it felt to be understood. I know that's wrong, and vile. But fuck, I can't help it. I can't stop feeling this way. And it's only a matter of time before the desires of my body override the intentions of my heart."

He looks at me for a long time, either silently judging or thoughtfully comprehending, when the front door opens, causing us to jump apart. Luckily, Ally is joyfully oblivious, flitting in from outside as if she were just dancing on the sun. Fire-streaked red hair is toppled on her head in a messy knot, and she's dressed in purple running shorts, a yellow tank, and candy-colored running shoes.

"Heidi! You're here!" she trills, her smile so infectious that I nearly forget the seriousness of the moment before. I can see why Justice keeps her around. The girl is like his own personal sunbeam. He lives in dark and stormy—thrives there. But one can only go so long in the absence of light before they fall ill in their own coldness and despair. Ally is his warmth. She is his sun and moon and stars. She's what brought him back to life.

"That I am," I reply, with a nod of my head. She comes to hug me then remembers herself. I'm not a hugger. Ever.

"You came at the right time too. You'll never guess who's here! I didn't even know he was a client!" She looks to Justice and punches his massive bicep with her teeny, tiny, cutesy fist. "Did you do this to surprise me? Because you know what a crazy fan I am?"

Justice and I look at each other, our brows raised in confusion. "What are you talking about, angel?" he asks, pulling her into his arms. That took some time to get used to—their PDA. I envied the way Justice had allowed himself to change for her. Well, not even change, actually. Evolve. Ally had evoked the evolution of his heart.

She kisses his lips before turning around to face me, her eyes so bright, they blind me. "Ransom Reed! You know, from the band, Ransom? Oh em squeee! I was on the treadmill, workin' on my fitness, zoned out, blasting their last album on my iPod, and in he walks. Just strolls in like it's no big deal that he's a freaking rock god in our gym. And he was shirtless!"

Justice clears his throat, which causes her to turn around and beam at him lovingly. "Oh, baby, he has nothing on you, of course. But, Heidi," she says, turning back to me, "Holy abs, Batman. You've got to see it to believe it."

"Oh, I'm sure Heidi believes it," Justice murmurs, rolling his eyes.

"Huh?" Of course, Ally doesn't miss his comment. The girl is bubbly and quirky, yes. But she's no dummy. She's seen what goes down within this compound. Hell, she's been an active participant.

"He's my client," I explain, hoping to avoid any further speculation. "I brought him here to get away for a little while. And my husband . . . I brought my husband too."

"Oh." That one word is all I need to know that she doesn't buy it. But she's polite enough not to pry. "Well, you guys have got to come by and hang while you're here. It's not every day that we get to see Mr. Heidi in the flesh. Maybe a couple's game night? I'll make margaritas!"

"No," Justice and I say in unison. When her expression falls, we both try to explain, rambling on top of each other.

"She's here on business, and probably wants to spend her free time with Tucker."

"I don't want to intrude. Plus, I've got a ton of work to do."

"Fine, fine," Ally sighs, waving us off. She shimmies out of Justice's arms and begins to make her way toward the back rooms. "You guys can save your excuses. Business before bullshit, I get it. I'll be in the shower so you can go back to plotting your quest for world domination."

After she disappears from sight and we hear the telltale signs of running water, Justice looks at me with an expression so stern that I feel chastised. "You won't get her involved in this mess. If something happens, and this gets out, you will not mention her. Understand?"

"I understand." I nod.

"She likes you, Heidi. She cares for you. And knowing what you're doing—after all she's been through—would hurt her. You won't hurt her. Got it?"

"I do."

"Ok." He scrubs a hand over his face and takes a deep breath. "If you're going to do this, you're going to do it the right way. No sneaking behind Tucker's back. I can . . . help you two devise a way to make this a safe and healthy situation for the both of you. But I need total and complete honesty. Understand? And he needs to be on board to trying whatever it takes. If he still can't give you what you need, we can look at other options . . . including Ransom. But you have to try to make it work with your husband first, Heidi. Ok? Another dick will not solve your marital problems."

"I know." I nod. "I get it. And, yes, I will do whatever it takes. Whatever you want us to do. But I need to know . . . what's the catch? I mean, I'd like to think we're friends in some sick, twisted way when we're not at each other's throats, but why would you be willing to help me? What's in it for you?"

He looks toward the bathroom, where water can still be heard pelting the glass door. The mangled sounds of Ally's shower singing echoes against the tile.

"Because, like I said, she likes you. And you did something for me that could not have been easy. So consider this payback."

Ah, yes. That I did.

A few months ago, shortly after Justice returned to Oasis, he needed a little favor. Evan, Ally's ex and Justice's half-brother, was on a smear campaign to ruin her reputation and expose personal information about Justice's mother. We knew his hands were dirty, but no one knew just how dirty they were. So I made a few calls, and some people took a few pictures of Evan in a few compromising situations. I mean, no one *made* him pop the molly or snort the coke. We just ensured that when he did it, there was photographic evidence. And we may have brought a couple friends that posed in those photos once he passed out. And those friends may have been transvestite prostitutes.

Ally never found out and, of course, those photos never saw the light of day. Once his eyes fell on the contents of the manila file folder that happened to show up on his desk at work, Evan shut the fuck up. He also accelerated his descent down the rabbit hole, and he hasn't been able to climb out since.

Part of me should feel bad for contributing to his self-destruction, but I don't. Evan Carr was, and is, a piece of shit. And it's only appropriate that shit be properly disposed of.

I don't know why I say it, but I thank Justice. What he's offering is so unconventional that if someone were to overhear our conversation, they'd think we were both certifiable. But right now, I feel like he's thrown me a lifeline. He's willing to save my life.

We say goodbye before Ally comes back out to the living room. If she saw I was still there, she'd lay on the guilt and beg us to come over for dinner or something as equally uncomfortable. Before I can get fully out the door, Justice stops me, his eyes darting around the vicinity to check for eavesdroppers.

"Promise me you won't do anything with him until we try, OK? Promise me that."

By *him* he means Ransom. He's asking me not to cheat on my husband. How ludicrous does that sound? Still, I nod once, giving him my word. And I'm sincere. I don't want to hurt my husband, but I know I'm more than capable of doing it.

He closes the door and returns to his happy life with his happy girlfriend. And I imagine that behind those doors, he's happy too. I'm smiling to myself, imagining Justice Drake as the sweet, doting lover that relishes in lazy Sundays spent in bed and movie nights featuring the latest Nicholas Sparks flick. I bet he even cries when he's with her.

I'm so wrapped up in my amused reverie that I don't even notice that I'm being watched. Not just watched. Studied. Analyzed. Picked apart by blue, shrewd eyes that squint against the bright, hot sun, reading the story that I've just told.

Chapter Twenty-one

I do what I've been asked.

I try my hardest to stay away from Ransom. I do all I can to keep him at arm's length. But that doesn't mean he's promised the same thing.

We finish our first day at Oasis without incident, all of us too exhausted from traveling to do much more than unpack and rest. The next, Tucker and I order dinner to our room—chef's special five-course meal. And now that Riku is running the kitchen, it's no surprise that everything is divine.

You know that saying, "Birds of a feather flock together"? Well, if Justice was a particular species of bird, he'd obviously be a beautiful one, such as a peacock—proud and exotic. And Riku would be strutting right beside him, just as gorgeous and unattainable.

I met him when he was the sous chef for Oasis, but after things went south and Justice disappeared, Riku was one of the few who stuck around, holding out hope that he would return. He never gave up on him, even when JD gave up on himself. So it was only fitting that he make Riku, his only real friend and confidant outside of Ally, head chef and part owner of the new and improved Oasis.

"You know, I could get used to this," Tucker says as I feed him a bite of the most incredible key lime pie I've ever tasted.

We're in bed listening to soothing jazz from the bedside stereo, the confection positioned on a tray between us. Tuck picks up the small dessert fork and divvies off a portion to serve me. I take it gratefully, moaning around the cool metal between my lips.

"You shouldn't do things like that," my husband warns, his voice gravely.

"Do what?" I look up at him with hooded eyes and smile.

It only takes mere seconds before I am flat on my back and my panties are dangling from my foot. Tucker kisses me from the inside of my ankles to the tops of my thighs. And when I'm panting, begging him to touch me more, kiss me more, he spreads me wide and licks me slowly from front to back, savoring every slick part of me. I shake and squirm as he devours the first drops of fresh, warm wetness. And when that wave ends, another begins as he slides his swollen cock inside me with all the patience and control of a deranged serial killer. God, it's maddening. How can he take it? How can he not be so ravenous for release that he just greedily takes me without regard for my comfort or safety?

I grip his ass, scoring the taut flesh with my fingernails, pulling him in closer, deeper. He groans into the crook of my neck, so I do it again and again, begging him with my body to join me in this realm of reckless abandon. *Just let go,* it whispers, its slick tongue trailing the shell of his ear. *It'll be ok. I promise you'll like it.*

He comes hard, quicker than I expect. He grunts in my ear as if the sheer violence of the act pains him. My body cools underneath him, rigid and still, as he empties his demise inside my womb.

"Oh," he groans, kissing my neck. "That snuck up on me. Sorry, baby."

"It's ok," I lie. I shouldn't be upset, considering that he licked me to orgasm beforehand, but I'm a selfish bitch. I wanted him to take me. I wanted him to claim me. And he failed.

"Seriously, give me half an hour, and I'll make it up to you. Promise." He pulls out of me and rolls onto his back, his chest heaving with exhaustion.

"Don't worry about it. It's been a while, and you've had such a hard week. You needed that." I say the words, knowing they're true, but I don't mean them. I wish like hell that I did though.

He kisses my face once more and closes his eyes. Within minutes, he's snoring softly, his softening cock still glistening with my wetness.

Great.

I climb out of bed and clamber into the bathroom. Along with a glass-encased shower, each room is outfitted with a claw-foot tub large enough for two, and luxurious bath soaps and oils. I decide that a hot, bubble bath is just what I need to expel all the nervous energy still simmering inside me, and I fill it up as high as it will go without overflowing, hoping to drown my discontent. An hour later, my water is cool, my skin is pruned, and my joints are still not uncoiled.

I towel off and slip on a plain cotton dress and sandals. Even with the late hour, it's still hot out, and if I happen to step outside, I don't want to sweat my face off. I don't know where I'm going or what I'm seeking. I just know that I can't stay within these four walls. There are a dozen different voices drifting from the pool area when I make my way downstairs. I think about checking it out, but decide not to. Nearly naked couples submerged in water? No thank you.

Right off the main dining room is a bar area, housing a few pub tables and stools. Masculine laughter echoes from that direction along with what sounds like a lively commentator on a sports show. I pause, letting the shadows envelop me, listening to chatter about the latest game and some domestic scandal between a popular baseball player and his wife. I hear them bond over their mutual appreciation for various musicians and colorful stories of their favorite travels. I stand there, an intruder, a voyeur, and I ache with jealousy, longing to be on the receiving end of those chuckles and casual banter. Not feeling like I have to calculate every word to avoid a slip of the tongue.

"Must be incredible to go on tour," Riku says, pausing to take a sip from his beer. "I saw you guys back in 2012 and it was insane. I can't even imagine how your fan base has grown since then. And how much your sound has evolved since the first album."

"Yeah. Been a crazy ride. But I think this next album will shock people, which is fucking hard to do in this market. But I think it's the subtlety that'll get them. The simplicity." I can hear the smile in Ransom's voice.

"Shock them with simplicity? I like it."

They tap beer bottles and go back to gazing at the big screen that displays the sports highlights of the week. Growing weary, I take a deep breath and step around the seclusion of the wall.

"Heidi! What's up, girl?" Riku smiles, damn near startling me by the sheer perfection of it. The tall, golden-skinned half Japanese, half Brazilian stunner is beyond gorgeous. He's actually prettier than most women I've seen. His heavy-lashed eyes naturally look as if they're lined with onyx, and his lips and nose are thin yet perfectly aligned. Jet-black hair is cut and styled in a short, classic style for the kitchen, and it suits him. Anything flashier would detract from the beauty of his face.

"How's it going, Riku," I say, returning his grin as I approach. "Haven't burned the place down yet, I see."

"Aw, girl. You know that's not happening. How was dinner?"

I force myself to keep my eyes trained on Riku, but I can feel Ransom's stare sliding over every inch of my frame. Looking at him would be bad for the both of us. I wouldn't be able to hide the flush of my cheeks and the sharp intake of breath. And he wouldn't be able to resist devouring every one of my reactions like sex-flavored candy while wearing that smug smile on his face.

"Delicious." The word is no more than a whisper on my lips. I mean to elaborate, but standing before not one, but two, incredibly sexy men, my body wound tighter than a rubber band threatening to snap, I can't seem to find the words.

"Good. Glad to hear it," Riku replies thoughtfully. "Can I get you a drink?"

"Please."

He disappears around the bar, leaving me to confront the one person I was told to stay away from.

"I was wondering when you'd quit eavesdropping and come join us."

I snap my gaze to him and frown. "What? How did you . . . ?"

He laughs, tipping his head back to give me full view of his throat. Oh, how I would kill to rake my teeth against the fragile skin, the promise of puncture so thrilling that we both moan when the sharpness of my canines make contact.

"You know that feeling you get when danger is near? The

hair stands up on the back of your arms. That niggling sensation that crawls up your spine. The silent alarm that goes off in your ears. That's what I get when you're close by. I smell danger."

His words are like the sweetest poetry, his voice like syrup dripping from his lips. I don't know what to make of it . . . don't know what to say other than, "I know."

"You know?" One corner of his mouth lifts. "You know you're dangerous?"

"I know we're dangerous together."

"Yes. We are." He nods before sipping the remnants of his brew. I eye it, questioning. Should an addict be drinking? He did say it wasn't alcohol that was his main vice, and other than that one time after *SNL*, I had never seen him drink more than beer.

"Which is why this is a bad idea. We were a mistake."

He looks at me then. Really stops to see me through those eyes made of black lava rock. Maybe he's surprised. Maybe he's hurt. Maybe he hates me enough that he'll be able to walk away. I can't say which reaction I was going for, but any would be better than this.

"A mistake, eh?" He's suddenly too close to me, yet I don't think he's moved. I just know I feel overwhelmed by his presence, almost violated.

"You know what I mean, Ransom," I whisper furiously, my eyes intently watching the doorway. "This isn't right. What we did . . . It's not fair. Not to Tuck, not to you, not to me. So can we try to forget about it? Please?"

"You want to forget about it? Just like that?" He looks amused. "Can you forget me?"

"I can try."

He nods and places the empty beer bottle on the bar, just as Riku arrives from the back with a glass of something bubbly and pink. "Here we are," he announces. "Been saving a bottle of this stuff especially for you."

I plaster on a smile and accept it, and while I know it's delicious, I can't taste anything but regret and longing on my tongue.

"Well, I'm out," Ransom states, dapping up his new friend. "Catch you later." He looks at me momentarily and tips his head. "Heidi."

"Ransom." Then he turns around and disappears from view.

"Well . . . damn."

"What?" I frown, looking at Riku over the rim of my glass.

"It's just . . . if you were somebody else, I'd swear you two are in a lover's quarrel. Must be your sparkling personality," he jibes.

"Ha ha. Sparkling personality, my ass. Someone has to be the hard nose around here, when all you strong, strapping men are writing sonnets and getting mani-pedis."

"Mani-pedis?" he feigns outrage. "Excuse me, I'll have you know that I receive paraffin dips. Don't get it twisted."

We share a few laughs until a few guests begin to filter in from outside. I recognize a few CEOs, TV personalities, and even a big shot record label exec. Of course, my presence doesn't evoke any warm fuzzies so I down the rest of my drink and bid Riku good night. When I return to my room, I find that Tucker is still knocked out, flat on his stomach, snoring softly. Half an hour—yeah right. Tuck hasn't been able to go two rounds since his twenties. And it's not that he isn't in shape or the equipment is malfunctioning. We're just usually too tired or too busy. Honestly, sex between us had become a weekly chore that we just wanted to "get over with" to release the pressure. And while it's still good, it has become much like the rest of our life—predictable.

I figure I could sleep if I tried, so I slide between the sheets next to him. Out of habit, I check my phone, which I had left on the nightstand, set to Silent. To my surprise, there's a message. I don't even have to read the name to know who it is.

I could try too.

I tap out a quick reply, confused by his cryptic statement.

Try what?
To forget you.
Ok.

My heart sinks, but he can't know that. It would only complicate things further, and make it that much harder to let go.

Is that what you want?

He's asking me if I want him to forget me, as if he knows it's ripping me up inside, turning muscle and organs into shreds of bloody despair. In a desperate plea, my traitorous heart is screaming *No. No, Ransom, don't forget me.* But my head slices through like a hot knife to butter, silencing the weaker vessel.

That's what I need.

Ok. I'll try. But I can't promise you anything.

Thank you.

I don't know why I say that, but it seems appropriate.

So will you still be my publicist?

Of course.

So you'll still be there for me when I need you to be?

That's my job.

Your job, huh?

I roll my eyes but find myself smiling down at the screen.

Yes, Ransom.

I hope he can feel the playful exasperation in my words.

Good. Because I need you. Now.

I almost drop my phone, imagining his mouth saying those words to me, his lips whispering in my ear as he expresses this uncontrollable need for me.

I need to ask you something.

The text comes in before I can conjure up any more ridiculous scenarios.

Why?

Just come out to the hall. I'll step out so you know where my room is.

I'm texting that it's not a good idea, it's inappropriate, it's wrong, it's late, yada yada yada, when another text comes in.

Come on, H. I heard you loud & clear. I won't touch you, I swear. Just give me 5 min.

I look over at my husband, the sated man I love sleeping next to me with remnants of our love making a dried, flaky, white souvenir on his soft cock. I don't feel him between my thighs anymore. It still aches, but not for him.

My fingers tremble over the touchpad of my phone. Five minutes with my client. Even Justice can't deny that interaction is necessary.

Ok. Give me 2.

I shuffle to the bathroom and quickly run a brush through my hair and swish some mouthwash around to expel the stale taste of champagne. I'm in a flimsy, coral applique nightgown and nothing else. If I change, it'll look like I'm expecting more than just a five-minute conversation, and I didn't pack any sweats. I decide the matching robe will have to do, and even though I'm supposed to be keeping up the ruse that this is totally casual and even a bit inconvenient, I dab on a little sheer lip gloss and pinch my cheeks. I'm going to hell, but at least I won't be alone.

I step into the hall barefoot and look down the hall. Lounging in the doorway of his room, wearing nothing but basketball shorts much like the ones he wore yesterday, stands Ransom Reed. His hair is sexily tousled as if he had been in bed while he was texting me, and it looks like his already tan skin has taken in some sun. He dips his head forward, training those dark, deceptive eyes on me, before tilting it to one side, signaling for me to come to him. I hesitate for a breath, and collect my senses. I promised Justice. I promised myself. I won't throw away a solid marriage and a good man for some kid. He's twenty-four . . . of course he's hot and ready to go on command. At that age, he's nothing more than a walking, talking hard-on.

"Let's get this over with," I say as I approach, my voice much more icy than I intend. Ransom doesn't even flinch. It's as if he's becoming immune to my bullshit.

"Come in." He moves inside to let me in. When I pass, I catch the word inscribed in silver on his door.

Temptation.

Justice Drake, you patronizing fucker.

I ignore it and step inside, my arms crossed over my chest protectively. I've never felt unsafe with Ransom, not even when he was tripping off oxy and blow. But now that I'm here alone with him, in a dimly lit bedroom outfitted in lush reds, blacks, and grays, I don't think I've ever felt so afraid. Not of him. Of myself, and what my body wants. And what I'm capable of doing to satisfy it.

"Have a seat," he says, offering an oversize, cranberry armchair. He didn't offer the bed. That's a good sign. He goes over to the small kitchenette and opens the mini fridge. "Water? Tea? Wine?"

"Wine, please." I know it's a mistake the very second I ask for it, but I need something to take the edge off. Something to keep me from ripping off this satin robe and mounting Ransom against the mahogany chest of drawers.

He cracks the seal of a small bottle and pours me a glass. I take it with a grateful smile and watch as he plants himself on the bed across from me.

"So?" My throat is coated with broken glass, so I take a swig to wash it down.

"So."

"You said you had a question, Ransom."

"Right. I do."

I make an aggravated noise that sounds too much like a moan. I could have been riding my husband right now after waking him up with my hot mouth. Or shit . . . I could be masturbating. Being here is like walking a tightrope with no net underneath. I know I'll fall, and on some level I want to, just to get it over with. But I know the plunge will kill me. And right now, with the suspense piercing my resolve like a thousand little ice picks, leaping to my death seems less and less daunting.

Seeing the irritation play across my features, Ransom finally puts me out of my misery after taking a deep breath. "Caleb . . . what did he say about me? What was his explanation?"

I take a sip of wine and look around the room. Against the blood-stained walls are black and white photos of men, women, and couples. All naked. All rooted in their own passion, completely oblivious to the camera's lens. They're erotic, yes, but not pornographic. They're beautiful. They've created art with nothing but their skin.

"That you're an addict," I finally answer, tearing my eyes from the series of grayscale flesh. "And while he seems to believe you have it under control, sometimes you break and need to get away for a while. Hence our little cross-country excursion."

He lifts a brow. "And that's all? That's all he told you?"

"Is there more?" I want to ask him, *how much worse can it get?* But think better of it. I honestly don't know what's ailing him, and until I do, it's better not to aggravate him.

He answers, "No," yet the frown deep between his brows seems uncertain. "Yes, I am. And yes, it's under control. I'm sorry for how I acted that night you found me at the bar, and I'm sorry for what I said to you. Well, most of it at least."

"Most of it?"

"I shouldn't have said anything about Tucker or your marriage. That was out of line. And I shouldn't have insinuated that you were there for anything more than to put my ass to sleep and make sure I didn't swallow my own tongue."

My voice is a whisper on ice, skating across the diamond planes. "You remember that?"

"Yeah. Remember that slap you gave me too. Damn, H. You've got one helluva arm." He laughs and rubs his jaw that's lightly dusted with dark stubble. "But I deserved it. And again, I'm sorry."

I nod, accepting his apology, although there's really nothing to forgive. Can I really blame him for feeling used by me?

"You said you were sorry for most of what you said. What aren't you sorry for?" I ask, emboldened by the wine.

Ransom shrugs and looks down at his callused hands. "Fill in the blanks, H. Don't you remember? You were sober that night."

I was. And I do.

I haven't been able to stop thinking about his helpless plea and the heart-wrenching vulnerability on his face since that night. He asked me to stay with him. He said he could make me feel young again, and do all the things Tucker refuses to do. He felt abandoned, but I could tell it wasn't just by me. It was by everyone. Ransom felt utterly alone and fraught for a connection. So much so that he was willing to make an older woman's fantasy come true while her husband stroked himself to orgasm in the corner. What generates that level of desperation? What drives a person to offer their body to a stranger just to feel loved for a little while? Or makes them fill their veins with poison to numb the pain?

Now more than ever, I want to go to him. But not for sex. I just want to hold him, make him believe that he's not alone. But wouldn't that be another lie?

"You're not sorry for that."

He lifts his gaze to mine and I see just a glimpse of that vulnerability now. It's the same look he had in his hotel room. The same one he wore inside the tiny airplane lavatory. But just as quickly as I catch it, it's gone. "No. I'm not. Do you want me to be?"

I tell him what he needs to hear because I don't want to hurt him. I tell him the truth.

"No."

Strained silence crawls all over our midnight-drenched skin like sleepy, little spiders. We stare at each other, waiting for the other to break the trance with a blink, but it never comes. Finally, Ransom releases me by looking away. But he hasn't retreated. No. In the shallowest of breaths, he's in front of me, leaning over me, pinning my body between his bare chest and the high back of the chair.

"Ransom . . ." It's not even a whisper or a moan. It's a sigh. Something done out of reflex.

"I'm not touching you," he drawls, fanning warm mint-flavored breath over my face. "I promised I wouldn't touch you, and I won't."

"Then what are you doing?"

"Smelling you. Seeing you. Trying to let my other senses do what my hands can't."

He lifts a hand from the chair and slowly brings the back of it just mere centimeters from the bust of my nightgown. I open my mouth to protest, and he shushes me.

"I won't touch you. Trust me."

With that, he runs his hand up to my collarbone, so close that I can feel the sun on his skin. With maddening patience and restraint, he lets it travel down down down, until it stops at my breasts. I can almost feel him there, grazing my nipples with his knuckles, running his thumbs over them, pinching them between his fingers so that heat collects in my belly and slithers like wet paint between my thighs.

"Look at you. Look how you respond to me . . . not touching you."

I peer down to see that my nipples are hard and straining through two layers of satin, staring at him with pleading eyes. He chuckles lightly and his hand is on the move again, this time roaming over the expanse of my belly. Then he sits on his knees and leans back on his feet, letting both his palms hover over the tops of my thighs.

"I promise you, I won't touch you. Even if you beg me to. I want to prove to you that I can do this, that I can kick this habit. I want to prove it to myself."

His hands move down to my knees, and he makes a slow

sweeping motion, willing them to part. And dammit, they do. *I* do. I open this door. I unlatch Pandora's Box. He gave me the power to reject him, offered it to me from the tips of those massive, callused fingers, and I didn't do it. I gave it back to him. I relinquished my willpower, my body, my soul to him, even without his asking.

I'm a bad wife. And an even worse publicist. But with my sex opening to him like delicate cherry blossom petals at full bloom, I am neither.

I am his.

At first, his hands just hover over my thighs, trailing a slow, languid path from my kneecaps to the fabric that covers my swollen clit. Over, between, even under, he teases me with his phantom touch, haunting me with his heat. I need him to touch me, but I can't bring myself to beg. And even if I did, I know he won't anyway. He's enjoying this too much, dark mirth flickering in his heavy-lidded gaze. He's showing me that he could drive me crazy without even touching me. That even if I never give myself to him again—and I won't—he can still affect me. He can still fuck me whenever he wants.

"Lift your nightgown," he commands, his voice gruff.

I tell myself that I won't but my hands are already sliding down my hips and bunching the soft fabric. I fist the satin until the hem disappears inside my palms and cool air meets the heat of my sex.

Ransom looks down at it—at me—and sucks in a strangled breath. I watch him as he bites his lip so hard that it turns white under the pressure of his teeth. His fingers skim the air over my mound, trembling, pleading. Maybe he's not as strong as he thinks he is.

"I won't touch you," he rasps, persuading me and himself. Yet, his hands come dangerously close to making contact. So close that I can feel him brush my short, soft hair at the very center, causing me to gasp.

"I won't touch you." He says it like he's a dying man and this is his final plea. He repeats it again and again, making it his personal mantra. And while he denounces his carnal needs, he begins to shift. Down. His body is moving down between my thighs until his face is aligned with my pussy.

I'm afraid to move, afraid to speak. Just the barest flinch, and my clit will be against his mouth, my lips on his, falling into an unintended kiss. So I watch him watch me, not breathing, waiting for him to decide if he's going to be a liar tonight.

He inhales. Deeply. He sparks me up, takes a hard drag, sucks me inside his body. The perfume of my slickness coats his nose and throat before he consumes the tiny molecules of my arousal. We moan together, pulling on a double-ended joint of lust and loneliness, letting it take us higher than high. We see the ceiling, know we should stop, but we're going too fast. And there's no guarantee we'll be able to break through and survive the impact.

He scents my sex a half dozen more times, his reaction to my fragrance growing more vehement with every lungful. I'm so wet, so potent, that I can smell myself too, which only makes me ache more. That coupled with his hot breaths on my even hotter clit and the illicit sounds he makes in the back of his throat, and I know it won't be much longer. I just need a little more . . . just a little more.

His moans morph into whispered words, and I still my own whimpers and the beating of my heart to try to make sense of it. Even through the pounding of blood in my ears, I hear him loud and clear.

She's an angel without wings
Sent down to earth to destroy me
Fucking me so religiously
Take me to hell, you lovely, damaged thing

I thought I may have imagined it before.

That night we spent together in his suite, me flat on my stomach, him inside me, his belly pressed to my ass and his lips on my ear.

Ransom sang to me . . . *is singing* to me. Fucking me crazy with the magic of his tongue without physically touching me at all. I won't make it . . . I won't last like this. And if I give in to the stinging current this time, if I let him own yet another of my orgasms, will I ever be able to find my way back to the surface? To my marriage? To Tucker?

I know I look as ridiculous as I feel as I push his face back with trembling hands and scramble from the chair, careful not to touch him any more than I have to.

"Heidi . . . I'm sorry," he stammers from the floor, but I

just shake my head, unable to hear it. Because I'm not sorry. Not in the least. But I know I should be.

"It's ok. I . . . I just need to go." I pull my robe around me tighter, the move only adding more friction against my already tingling body. "I have to go," I repeat. But it takes nearly twenty seconds before I regain the function to even move.

I run away from the scene of the crime and nearly barrel through the door of the Reflection room. I catch Tucker stirring on the bed out of the corner of my eye, but I can't stop to acknowledge him. That would only make this worse.

I slam the bathroom door behind me and lock it before falling into it in exasperation. The very second my fingertips meet my slick, swollen clit, the silken flesh quivers. I dip inside to wet my fingers, I stroke the hardened knot that pulses with its own heartbeat, and I fuck myself so violently and desperately that I don't even hear someone approaching the door until a knock nearly makes me yelp.

"Babe? Are you ok?" His voice is groggy, concerned, but not skeptical.

"Yeah," I manage to whine. I bury two fingers deep inside me as far as they will go. I thrust so hard and fast that it almost hurts. I bite my own lip until I taste blood, ensuring that it does.

"Something wrong?"

"Not feeling well. Be there in a sec."

I feel it coiling inside me like a deadly snake, its venom trickling down my hand and sliding down my thighs. So wet I add another finger. So wet I feel like I could drown myself.

"Ok. Well, hurry back to bed so I can take care of you."

There it is, pulsing wildly as it swells so much that it pushes my fingers from my body. I fight for control, needing that pressure, needing to burst that bubble with the blunt tips of my nails. It's so full and slick that I can't keep a steady rhythm. Yet, I can't . . . I can't . . . stop.

"Ok . . . ok. I'm coming."

And I do.

Chapter Twenty-two

My husband holds my hand, our fingers coupled together, and brings my knuckles to brush over his lips. We walk down a long hallway housing a half dozen different rooms that service different purposes. I knew Justice's place was big; I just didn't realize how big it was. This much real estate in New York would literally cost an arm and a leg. And probably a kidney too.

"Here we have the studio where we instruct couples yoga every morning, as well as a course on tantric sex three times a week," Justice states very matter-of-factly, waving toward the space that looks like . . . well . . . a fitness studio, with its hardwood floors and 360 mirrored walls. A class is in session right now, and both men and women are propped into a bridge pose, their pelvises jutting toward the ceiling.

We follow him down the hall for a few yards until we come across another door. "Here's the theater room. I'm sure I don't have to tell you what's projected on the screen. The seats are cleaned and sanitized after every viewing."

Tucker and I take in the plush, oversize loungers that are made for two. The room is draped in darkness, setting the tone for naughty fun in a forbidden place. Makes sense. How many people have messed around in a movie theater with a boyfriend or girlfriend? How many guys have let their hands snake up a girl's skirt to stroke her clit while she held a giant popcorn bucket in her lap as cover?

When we come to stop at another room, boasting twin, raised platforms, each skewered with stripper poles, Tucker lets out a low whistle. "Strippers, eh?"

"My friends Candi and Jewel host two interactive shows every week," Justice explains. "How many couples have fantasies that revolve around a strip club? It's a multibillion dollar a year industry, so obviously, the demand is there. The problem is that too many spouses reject them, seeing it as something vile and degrading to their marriage. But, in reality, they are just as intrigued by what goes on behind those doors, and their hatred comes from a place of fear. So not only are we bringing it to them, we're teaching them how to re-create this experience in their own bedrooms. And we encourage them to enjoy it for what it is—entertainment."

I watch Tucker's expression as he nods in appreciation. Of course, this is no shock to me. I already knew the two strippers were on the payroll. I'm just pleasantly surprised by all that Justice has accomplished with his new training program within a few months. I try not to get into the details with him, considering that I can't spin what I don't know. So information is usually offered on a need to know basis. And before now, I didn't think I needed to know any of this stuff.

Justice waves in the direction of a pair of doors as couples pass us wearing nothing more than navy blue bathrobes etched with the Oasis logo on the breast pocket. "Through there you'll find the spa area, both male/female, and coed. Indoor pool, hot tubs, steam rooms, tables for intimate massage, plus a separate entrance to the outdoor pool. And down through here is the . . . communal play area, if you will. We call it the playground. Either you play fair and safely, or you don't play at all."

"Play area?" I frown. This is news to me. "What do you mean by that?"

"Let me show you."

Justice leads us to the door in question and pulls out a key, also tied with a satin ribbon. This one is black, alluding to the dark desires that harbor just on the other side. He unlocks the door and steps aside to let us in first. While the lighting is dim, I can clearly make out a descending staircase.

"Go down. You'll come to another door. Also locked," he instructs from behind us, his tone all business.

We do as he says, maneuvering our way down the cramped staircase. It's narrow so Tucker and I must part grasps, him taking the lead as my husband and protector. When we reach the end of the staircase, Justice comes to stand before us, his back to the door protectively.

"Now before I open this door, I want you to understand something: No marriage is created equal. There's no handbook, no set of rules and regulations. And in this day and age, people are just trying to hold on to the love that initially sent them down the aisle. They've learned to improvise . . . explore. Experiment. And I allow them to do so in a safe, non-judgmental environment where discretion is the golden rule. Any and everything you see behind this door will probably shock you. It may even scare you. But you will refrain from condemning the people that choose to be proactive in their marriages versus succumbing to society's opinion of what their relationships should be. You won't find routine within those walls. You won't see rigidness or censure. What you'll find is freedom and happiness and, yes, love. Because it takes an immense amount of love to selflessly give your partner what he or she needs sexually. That is one of the greatest sacrifices one can give to another."

With those words, Tucker and I lock eyes and lock hands, just as we were before. However, I hold on to him a little tighter, hoping he can still my trepidation, and I feel just how incredibly grateful I am that he is my husband. It's no secret that this may be uncomfortable for him, yet he's here anyway. He's always here, always patient. He's the perfect husband, yet I have been a less-than-perfect wife.

We both look back at Justice and nod our agreement. He turns around and places the onyx-laced key in the lock.

The first thing that hits us is the noise. The bass is so heavy that I can feel the vibrations through my chest and the tempo is sinuously provocative. It's like the quintessential sex mix tape, and not just any sex either. Nasty, messy, kinky sex. And that's exactly what surrounds us at this very moment.

Large beds are scattered around the room, some canopy (to hold up a variety of chains and cuffs), some round (because apparently, they fit more people), and others rotating (providing a 360 view for . . . everyone). Aside from the three of us, everyone is naked, or wearing the same blue terry cloth robes I saw earlier. The same ones hanging in our en suite bathroom. Come to think of it, I recognize a few of the participants from just minutes before when they disappeared into the spa.

I try to withhold my gasp, or what Justice would call it—pearl clutching, but there's just so much . . . sex. Like on every surface, every platform. Even against walls and from ceilings.

There are men and women on huge wooden crosses, naked and shackled, some with gags in their mouths. They moan and writhe as their lovers perform humiliating acts on them—whipping them, caning them, even pouring hot wax on them. And while many of them cry out, I find that they are not cries of distress, but cries of pleasure. They *love* it. Some even beg for more.

I spy at least three sex swings suspended from the ceiling as well as a half dozen oddly shaped lounge chairs that are being used for anything but lounging. There's a scene merely feet away from where we stand, where a woman is being impaled from behind, her upper torso draped over the chair in a way that gives her lover maximum depth. I hate to admit it, but it looks incredibly hot. So hot that I'm mentally strategizing all the positions that chair would allow.

There's not just hetero sex going on in here either, even with people I am positive lead hetero lifestyles. On one of the round beds, there seems to be some kind of conga line of sorts. A man is fucking a woman from behind while her face is pressed between a woman's thighs. Another man fucks her mouth while he eats a man's ass. And that guy is balls-deep in a young man who looks no older than eighteen. And that's really not the most shocking scene around the room.

Reluctantly, I look over at Tucker and find his eyes fixated on the group sex scene. I can't read his expression, and I so desperately need to know what he's thinking. He's never had an aversion to homosexuality—hello, we live in NYC—but he also has never made me think that he could be into other guys. That night with Ransom, as he watched with his dick in his hands, was as close to kink as he's ever gotten. And maybe that's what did it for him . . . not watching me get fucked, but watching another man. Maybe that's why he came harder than I've ever seen him come. Maybe that's why he seemed so buoyant and sexy. Justice said that one of the greatest sacrifices one can give their spouse is giving their partner what they need sexually. What if Tucker doesn't need *me*? Maybe *I* can't physically satisfy him? Would I be willing to let him experiment with another man?

Tucker must feel my hand tense as that realization gnaws at me, and looks down, a mixture of haughty desire and fear on his face. "What's wrong?"

I shake my head and return my gaze to the crowd. Now I realize why the music seemed so ridiculously sexual. It's being remixed by real life moans and mewls.

"Any questions for me?" Justice asks. "And before you say *No*, I'm not buying it. Everyone should have questions. And I'm glad to answer them."

I look up at the gorgeous man to see that he appears nonplussed. All this must not even phase him. I guess being around it day in and day out makes you pretty immune.

"These people are all married. So are these couples sleeping with other couples? Seems like it could get kinda messy."

Justice nods and glances out into the crowd. "We bring in people who are willing to participate, people that are well versed with this lifestyle. Some are professionals. Some just want to guest star for fun. However, this is not sex for hire. All of my employees choose who they play with. Just because they are here, that doesn't mean they are obligated to fuck you. We hold weekly mixers so the couples can get acquainted with our featured players. Sometimes they connect with someone and decide to take it further. Other times, they just like to come here to have sex with each other."

"Wait. So there are singles here too? Staying here on the compound?" I try and fail to keep the alarm out of my voice. That was my only saving grace—knowing that Ransom was surrounded by married couples. It would be much less likely for him to sleep with anyone while we're here. And yeah, while I know he fucks other women and it is none of my business, I definitely don't want to be sleeping a few doors down from it.

"They all go through a strict screening process," Justice explains. "All STD free and bound under airtight contracts. If they even whisper about this place in their sleep, they forfeit every dime they've ever made and will ever make for life."

I nod like he's eased my reservations, though I feel even less confident. Ransom could fuck whomever he wanted, and there'd be no risk of it ending up in the tabloids. This would be like an all-you-can-eat buffet for him. And, of course, the women that I suspect are "guest stars" are all insanely gorgeous and youthful with their round, full breasts and high, perky asses. Perfect.

"Let's take a look around. If we stumble upon something that intrigues you or confuses you, we can stop to dig deeper, no pun intended. Shall we?"

I look at Justice's expectant guise and offered hand, then turn to my husband. Oddly enough, he looks as if he's waiting for me to decide too. As if he's already made up his mind.

I give each man a shaky palm and stiffen my spine, steeling every nerve within me. "Ok. Let's do this."

Chapter Twenty-three

I haven't been able to sleep for two nights since the day we got a glimpse of Justice's playground. I thought I was ready for it. Thought that it was just what we needed to open up the conversation for our marriage and our sex life. But all it's done is leave me even more confused and obsessive about our issues.

I can't get the look on Tucker's face out of my mind. He looked so fascinated, so engrossed in every single devious act. Several times he would just stop and watch, chewing that full bottom lip with wolfish delight. It didn't matter who was involved—men, women—it seemed oddly interesting to him.

We stopped to witness a couple masturbating on the bed. Their eyes stayed locked on each other as they pleasured themselves, and when they came, they did it together. It was as if they didn't even notice us standing there watching. Like they didn't give a damn. They were the only two people that existed in their world. Tucker gave them each his attention equally. I assumed most straight men would keep their eyes pinned on the woman and the way her fingers slipped through her slick, pink folds, but he was just as enthralled in the way the man pumped his thick cock and massaged his balls simultaneously. It was . . . unnerving. And I found myself watching my husband, instead of watching the couple's intimate show.

There were several group sex scenes—threesomes, foursomes, and all-out orgies. Those seemed to be his favorite. And while I found them so hot that it left a wet spot in my panties, I couldn't stop speculating why *he* seemed to find them so enticing.

After our tour of Oasis's underground bedlam, Justice gave us homework—a series of questionnaires that would keep us busy for hours, which I was grateful for, considering I was trying to avoid Ransom at all costs. The motive was to have us be honest about our wants and fantasies, and even discuss them candidly. I shouldn't have been surprised when Tucker checked Yes for sex involving others, but I was. Which was so fucking hypocritical of me considering that we'd already come to that bridge, crossed it, and were considering just burning the fucker down altogether.

As awkward as it was, we did speak about our expectations . . . sorta. He talked, I listened. He asked questions, and

I deflected. The process—which should have been informative and fun, even—was frustrating, and none of it was his fault. I brought him here. I asked him to have an open mind. Now I was being stubborn that he's willing to try things my way. Be careful what you wish for, and all that jazz.

Still, I would have rather been caught up with my feelings about me and my husband's potential alternative lifestyle rather than what was really eating me up inside. I didn't want to see Ransom, which was pretty easy to achieve considering the size of the compound, yet I missed him. I missed him like he was a million miles away rather than mere yards down the hall. I missed him like he had been my best friend for years and we talked every day. I missed him like he was mine. And none of those reasons made a lick of sense, but that didn't keep me from wanting them to be true.

I can't deny that I'm worried for him. Well, worried for me. Ever since Justice revealed that there were singles here that were down for pretty much anything, I've been a nervous wreck about what he could be getting into—quite literally—now that I'm not in the picture. I mean, let's be honest, I was never in the picture. He was still sleeping with women before and after me, and rightfully so. But I don't need to know about it. I don't need it flaunted in my face, wearing a goofy, satisfied grin and messy, just-fucked hair.

Because of all the random ridiculousness swirling in my head, I've been bitchier than usual. Tucker's been trying everything—suggesting yoga, classes, movies, even a playful couple's game night—but I've shot him down at every turn, feigning work situations that needed my immediate attention, or—you guessed it—cramps. And every time, he's shrugged his shoulders and taken it like the gentleman that he is, even bringing me pain meds on occasion.

I stand out on our balcony, overlooking the pool area where nearly a dozen couples splash around and mingle jovially. They all look so normal, so happy. You'd never guess that one is a state senator who likes to get fucked in the ass while eating his wife's pussy. Or one is a Food Network TV personality who likes to be shackled and blindfolded while her husband whips her until her skin is raw then force-feeds her decadent cakes.

I watch these people and I both envy and loathe them for being able to accept who and what they are, and have the strength to act on it. I thought sleeping with Ransom was my way of owning my sexuality. A way for me to feel empowered by letting another man screw me into the mattress in a haze of violent passion. It was my way of taking back control—giving the finger to the sick fuck who stole from me. Yet, here we are, more than a decade later, and he's still taking from me. And I'm letting him.

I decide that I can't keep doing this. I can't keep letting my bullshit hang-ups affect my marriage. It isn't Tucker's baggage to carry, yet I keep placing it on his shoulders. And being the man that he is, he takes it without complaint.

I love him. God, I love him. And there will never be another man better than him. There will never be another man who will put up with my mood swings and my bickering and my sexual complications. There will never be a man who was born to be a father, yet has sacrificed that need within him for the woman he loves. I'll never find a man who loves me harder and fiercer than he does. And if there is something that I can do to show him just an inkling of the gratitude I feel for him, then it's my duty as a wife to do it.

I go back inside my room and gather the folder containing the questionnaires and contracts, looking over the details one last time. Then I slip on my sandals and make my way to the room that Justice uses as his office. It used to house the files of his many clients and gave his concierge a place to work, but now he actually uses the thing. Something about separating his work life from his home life, aka life with Ally.

I find that he isn't in when I pop my head in so I place the documents inside a sealed envelope and leave it on his desk with his name on it. I'm not worried about anyone nabbing the file. After what I saw in that dark den of sin, I have enough dirt to start a dust storm on Mars. We're all in the same boat here, and I feel oddly confident that these walls are pretty silent after last year's debacle.

I'm turning back to my room, deep in thought about the decision I've just made, and contemplating where we go from here, when I nearly take someone out while rounding the corner.

"Oh! Excuse me," I stammer, but I'm only met with a deep, throaty chuckle.

Of course. *Of course,* this would happen now.

"Heidi," Ransom smiles, one corner of his mouth reaching higher than the other.

"Ransom. Hi." I clear my throat and touch my hair nervously. "I hope all is well. Enjoying your stay here?"

He nods. "I am. Thank you."

I take in what he's wearing right now—board shorts, flip-flops, and a sleeveless tank. There's a towel draped over one arm, and a very familiar navy blue robe on the other.

"Going for a swim?" I ask, trying to school my voice into something that resembles nonchalance.

"That's the plan. I heard there was a spa around here with an indoor pool and a couple different specialty rooms. Thought I'd check them out. Should be fun."

My mouth drops and my eyes grow in size. I mean to respond but no sound comes out. Not even a peep.

Ransom is going to the spa. And he's got that terry cloth robe with the Oasis insignia on it. It could be innocent fun or it could be something else. And if it is—if he is going back there for more than just a massage and a mud mask—it won't be just to watch. Ransom is going to play. And I can only imagine that he'd be the shiniest, most enticing new toy on the playground.

Chapter Twenty-four

Things are in motion.

The contracts have been approved. The questionnaires have been evaluated. And Tucker seems to grow more and more excited by the prospect of going through with this. The mixer is tomorrow night and that's where we will meet other couples and singles that are like us. So I'm not surprised when I receive a text from Justice, asking me to meet him in his office. Maybe he's had a change of heart. Or maybe he can see through my bullshit, and is ready to call me out on it. Part of me hopes for the former, but is more confident in the latter.

When I arrive, he doesn't look angry or annoyed, which totally puts me on guard. Justice Drake without a sneer screwed onto his face? This must be serious.

"I wanted to ask you something, and I need you to be totally honest with me," he says as soon as I sit down, not even bothering with pleasantries. "Do you have feelings for Ransom?"

I almost choke on my own saliva, so completely caught off guard by his candid inquiry. "What? Why do you ask that?"

"Because I need to know before we go any further. I need to know that your heart will be in this one hundred percent." He leans forward, digging his elbows into the tops of his knees and steeples his fingers in front of a proud, prominent chin smattered with a thin dusting of stubble. "So tell me, Heidi . . . Is there something there with him? Other than physical attraction?"

I think about what he's asking me, taking a beat to let the question permeate my initial, guarded reaction. Do I care for Ransom? Well, of course I *care* about him. He's my client. And I'm not so cold that I can't feel for someone I've shared such intimacy with. But beyond that—if sex were never that magnet between us, drawing us to each other on the most basal physical level—would I want him? Would I feel the same yearning inside me that keeps me up at night, imagining my hands are his hands as I touch myself while lying beside my sleeping husband?

I don't know.

I don't know what I'd feel for him.

"No," I answer, knowing that is as close to the truth as I'm going to get. It's necessary. It's a lie, yet a necessary one.

"Are you sure?"

"Of course, I'm sure. It's not like that between us. Sure, that night we shared was hot, but I love my husband. And I want to make sure this works with him. I wouldn't be here otherwise."

Justice nods and sits upright. "Good. I'm glad to hear that. Because he's coming to the mixer."

"What?" This time, my disbelief is much more evident. "Why would he do that?"

"Because he's a young man with a crazy libido. Because he's single. Why not? He'll be here for the next week at least. You think he hasn't got an itch that needs scratching? Especially when he's surrounded by sex every damn day? Besides, I'd rather him get his rocks off in a safe, consensual environment than fucking around with one of the wives on the low." His eyes narrow just a fraction, making those dark aqua eyes look downright villainous.

"But I thought the program was for couples only. How could you possibly allow him to engage in . . . whatever . . . with other married people? He's not a professional. He's a musician. Surely, this can't be healthy."

Justice shrugs as if my words have just hit an iceberg without so much as a shiver. "My house, my rules. Besides, I think this will be a better solution, considering . . ."

"Considering what?"

I can see him weighing his words in his mind before simply shrugging again. "He's agreed to it. He's even looking forward to it."

I bite down the urge to label him a liar along with some

very colorful adjectives, and I shut my trap. Ransom *agreed* to this? He *wants* to go to this mixer? To meet other couples to potentially *play* with?

I feel sick to my stomach. This can't be right. Ransom wouldn't do this . . . to me. He knows I'll be there with Tucker. How does he expect me to just stand there and watch him charm and flirt his way into some other couple's bed?

I know it's ridiculous of me to feel any type of possessiveness, but fuck that. He came here with us. He knows us. And if he's going to screw anyone, it will be us.

Us.

Shit.

Why didn't I see this coming? If Tucker is interested in exploring his sexuality, and if I'm going to try to support him in that, could I really consider Ransom as a possible candidate? I mean, shit, I don't even know if he swings that way, but I know plenty of musicians that do. Artistic souls are different. They're all about feeling with their whole body, without labels or restraints. I could name a dozen rock stars that live totally normal, hetero lives but have swam in the male pond a time or two. It's no big deal. But when it comes to Ransom and my husband? It totally fucking is.

"Heidi? Hey, you all right?"

I startle at the sound of my name and focus my dazed eyes on Justice's face. "Huh?"

"I asked if you were okay with that. With Ransom being there, and potentially coming down to the playground."

What could I say? No? After just telling him that I have no

feelings for Ransom? Yeah, I could chalk it up to a conflict of professional interest but he'd know that's bullshit, considering he's my client too. And hell, what if Ransom has already been down there? He said he was going to the spa. Was that code for something else entirely?

"Sure. Of course I am." Liar. I am such a fucking liar. "Whatever he wants to do, it's none of my business as long as it doesn't make any waves in the press. Other than that, we're good."

"I'm glad to hear that." Justice nods, and I take that as my cue to get the hell out of his suddenly cramped office. He doesn't stop me, but I feel that intense blue gaze on me even after I've disappeared from view.

I head straight to my room and have unscheduled sex with my husband. I even come. I just can't tell who it was who owned my orgasm.

THE MIXER IS held in the ballroom after dinner. Most of the couples choose to dine together, laughing and bonding over succulent meats, buttery shellfish, and rich wine. We've taken our meals in our room since we've been here, but Tucker insists we go down and join the group. "How will we connect with these people if we don't interact with them?" he says. "We don't want to come across as unapproachable."

He's right, of course. He's always right.

So I slip into a sexy, black Herve Leger number that hugs every inch of my slight curves, slide my pedicured feet into

Valentino, and let my fine, white-blonde hair fall down my back in soft waves. When I step from the bathroom, my makeup on and expertly accessorized, Tucker nearly drops the glass of scotch at his lips.

"Wow. Baby, you look . . . wow."

"Do I seem approachable?" I ask, doing a spin move so he can see the dress's deep dip in the back. "Does this say, 'Hi, we're the DuCanes. And we'd like to get kinky with you'?"

He laughs at my jibe before coming to stand before me, close enough that I can feel him growing in his slacks. "You're saying that and so much more, Bunny. But, seriously, don't even think about it like that. We don't have to invite anyone to jump into bed with us. There's no rule that you can't be completely monogamous while on the playground. I saw plenty of couples that only had sex with each other, and that's completely fine for me."

"But I thought . . . ?" Wait. So he doesn't want to experiment? He doesn't want to have sex with a . . . ?

"Let's just see where tonight takes us. No rules, no plans. Let's just see. Hell, we might just call it a night and end up here alone with some more of Riku's key lime pie."

I nod in agreement. Maybe that's for the best. I can't see myself wanting to explore with some random stranger. And I damn sure don't want to watch Ransom doing the same. I don't think I could take it.

Dinner is fabulous, as expected, and we end up sharing a table with a couple from Cleveland. They don't tell us much about their lives back at home other than being part owners of the Cavaliers, which, of course, steers the conversation to basketball and whether or not LeBron will lead his team to victory. The guys chat stats while the wives chat about new movie releases and handbags. Just easy, casual conversation.

When a bell chimes, signaling that we should all reconvene in the ballroom, the husband, Frank, looks at Tucker and I and asks, "So . . . do you two swing?"

We look at each other. Look at them. Then back to each other.

Do we? Is that something that we're in to?

I can see Tucker struggling for words—something diplomatic and PC. Me, being the public relations beast that I am, beat him to the punch.

"While that sounds lovely, Frank, I think we had something different in mind tonight. But you two have fun."

"Well, that's too bad. We were looking to get a little naughty with you both. See you in there."

With an accepting nod and a smile, they turn toward the ballroom, leaving me with my still speechless husband.

"Wow." He blinks out of his trance and reaches for the last of his scotch. "I didn't . . . I thought they were just nice people. I mean, we were talking sports. Never once did I think he was interested in sleeping with you."

"Or you." I smile before leaning over to brush my lips over his jaw. "Come on, you handsome devil. Let's go play in the lion's den."

The space has the feel of country club cocktail party meets underground sex club. The clientele is varied, ranging from their late twenties to their fifties, and now that I see them with their clothes on, they all seem so normal. No different from Tucker and me. No one seems outwardly inappropriate or overly sexual. And if Justice hadn't entered, with a dozen beautiful, young singles at his flank, I wouldn't believe that every one of these married couples is battling their own sexual deviances even if you paid me. But then again, within these walls, there is no such thing as a sexual deviance. Only freedom to express and love and feel. Freedom to be who they are, not society's picture of the perfect pair.

No one here is perfect. And for some reason, that brings me a little comfort.

I notice that Ransom isn't included in the roundup of guest stars, as Justice called them, and that also reassures me. Maybe Justice had a change of heart? Or maybe Ransom just wasn't interested in hooking up with someone else? Either way, after a glass of bubbly, I find myself loosening and chatting with the other partygoers.

"Heidi! This must be Tucker," Ally says as she approaches us, a beaming smile on her face. "About time we meet. I was starting to think our girl made you up."

To his surprise, she knocks away his offered hand and hugs him like an old friend. I'm actually shocked to see her here, considering Justice makes it a point to keep her away from all of this. Not to keep her in the dark—complacent and oblivious to his dealings. But to protect her. With Ally's background and growing up the crème de la crème of the Upper East Side, she may very well know some of Justice's clients. And in order to avoid any awkwardness for all parties involved, she stays a good distance away. It's not like she doesn't know what his job entails. She was one of his star students, after all.

"So, Heidi, did you hear who was going to be here tonight?" she asks, turning her attention back to me.

I open my mouth to feign ignorance when I am instantly stunned into silence. Actually, the entire room falls from a jovial roar to a hushed quiet when Ransom enters it, wearing all black from head to toe, a crown full of sexily mussed hair and confidence like a damn war medal.

I think I hear her squeal something to the effect of, "OhmyGodheissofuckinghot" but I can't be sure. I'm so completely disarmed by him that I can't hear anything outside of the rapid pounding inside my chest. I don't know if I should be seriously worried for my health or exhilarated by his mere presence.

He doesn't see me at first. Or maybe he does and just won't look at me. I can't deny that things were left in an awkward space the other night when I ran from his room, embarrassed and aroused. We took things too far, and I'm afraid we'll never be able to retreat from that.

I know I'm being watched, analyzed, so I take a sip of champagne and turn back to my husband. Ally gives me a quick peck on the cheek and focuses her energy on greeting all the couples, between stealing kisses from Justice when she thinks nobody is watching. And I try my damnedest to act like I'm ok with this. More than ok. I'm downright stoked about the prospect of having to watch my young lover/client fuck someone else while my husband and I get busy doing the same. It just seems like too much. Too much at one time. And I don't think I'm ready for that.

Reading the panic in my expression, Tucker leans over and whispers in my ear, asking if I'm ok. I tell him yes. Then I tell him the truth.

"Tuck, I don't know about this. Doesn't it seem like we're moving too fast too soon? It's just . . . maybe we should talk about this before something happens that one of us isn't prepared for. Something that could seriously affect our marriage and our feelings for each other."

Translation: I need you to tell me if you want to sleep with a man, so when it happens, I'm not totally caught off guard. And I need to decide if I can be ok with that, and not see you differently.

I mean, could we stay married if Tucker hooked up with a dude? And what if he liked it? Doesn't that make him gay or bi or whatever? That's cool with me. I'm just not so sure it should be cool for my marriage.

"Relax, baby. We don't have to do anything you don't want to. Ok? Here, try this." He flags down a server holding a tray of miniature glasses, all smelling of strong liquor.

"What the hell is that?" I cringe, accepting the shot glass. It's a shimmery, iridescent liquid, unlike any alcohol I've ever seen. It smells sweet, but is still potent enough for me to know that it packs a punch.

"Easy. It's just a little something to help you loosen up. I figured you might need something a bit stronger than champagne. Go ahead—drink up. I promise, you'll be one hundred percent fine. I am a doctor after all."

I look down at the mystery pearlescent elixir in my glass then up at his charming smile, and shrug. It's one shot. What's the worst it could do? And like he said, he is a doctor. He'd never give me something that would potentially harm me.

I put the glass to my lips and tip it back, letting the cool tang of the liquor slide down my tongue and ease down my throat. It feels warm in my tummy, yet icy on my tongue. And I instantly know that it was a tad bit more than just alcohol I consumed.

Tucker leans in to kiss my temple and whispers, "That's my girl."

The more we talk and smile and laugh, the more I drink and the less apprehensive I feel. I'm so relaxed that I've almost forgotten that Ransom is here. Well. Almost.

"Tucker. Heidi. Good to see you tonight." He grins when he approaches, totally catching me off guard.

He shakes Tuck's hand then turns to me, mischief gleaming in those dark eyes. Then, in slow motion, he leans in and kisses my cheek. But his lips land closer to my ear, giving him the perfect opportunity to rattle me with his words.

"You look fucking delectable tonight. Good enough to eat," he half groans for only me to hear. Then as he pulls away, his lips run over my cheek, leaving behind a trail of flames that seem to flare and scatter throughout the rest of my body. I think I thank him. I can't be sure though.

After that, something in the evening air shifts. Not just for us, but for everyone. Voices dip into hushed whispers. Eyelids lower into sultry, hooded gazes. Wine and spirits are still present, but it seems as if the servers and their silver trays have been dismissed. Which is smart; Justice is a stickler when it comes to overindulgence and consensual sex. Oh so easily are those lines blurred, opening the gates for speculation and damaging claims, not to mention valid accusations. It's just not good for business.

I watch as couples pair up with other couples or singles. They huddle together as if they share some salacious secret that just begs to be told. This is what they came for—to meet others like them. Not only to share their varied interests, but also to explore them . . . enjoy them.

I feel eyes on me . . . hear whispers inquiring whether or not we're available for play. When the crowd begins to thin out as people make their way downstairs, I cling to Tucker like my life depends on it. Oddly enough, he seems oblivious to the obvious interest we're garnering.

"Hey," he coos softly, kissing the crown of my head. "How about we just go down and watch? No pressure. We don't even have to take our clothes off. We don't have to do anything at all."

I look around the room and instantly lock eyes with Ransom, who is surrounded by two couples and even a few singles, all vying for his affections. With his statuesque frame, he easily peers over the horde, gazing at me with perplexity. Maybe he feels it too—this uneasiness. This doubt.

Maybe we're not cut out for kink. Or maybe we're just not cut out for it with anyone else.

That can't be true. It won't be. Not anymore.

I look up at my husband and give him a slight smile, stowing my apprehension for the sake of this beautiful, loving man. I don't get to worry about Ransom's feelings. I don't have the right.

"Sure. Let's go."

Chapter Twenty-five

There's a sort of out of body sensation that one experiences when they step out of their comfort zone and do the unthinkable. It's as if you take on another life, switching from existing as the executor to the bystander, watching, anticipating, but not really feeling. Your body feels pleasure, but mentally, you check out. If you don't, reality will creep in, shattering the illusion and allowing insecurity to slither its way into you like a black oil serpent. And once it settles inside you, purging its disease, you realize that you weren't just witnessing this depravity. You were living it.

At least that's how it is for me.

We do as Tucker suggests. We watch, we talk; we bite our lips in fascination and desire. And when our own feelings of arousal become too intense to put off any longer, we touch. In front of a room full of people, all of whom are too caught up in their own sexual exploits to give a damn, I let my husband touch me.

It's almost chaste at first—a brush of my hair off my shoulders, a soft kiss on my neck, a gentle caress across my collarbone. And while I am somewhat tentative of each touch, my body betrays just how much this experience has truly affected me. Watching people kiss, fondle, lick, suck, and, oh yeah, fuck, is hot as hell. And the carnal, ruthless part of me craves that too. To be kissed, fondled, licked, sucked, and fucked. Desperately. In any and every way I can get it.

We settle on one of the unoccupied odd-shaped lounge chairs, which is barely wide enough for the both of us. It's a good central location, giving us a view of the entire room. At every angle we hear people moan and gasp in pleasure. We see them testing the limits of their sexual restraint before thrusting into it headfirst. We even smell the arousal in the air, mixed with the scents of strategically placed jasmine and lavender candles.

All of it creates a heady cocktail of seduction that tempts my senses yet soothes my trepidation. So when Tucker leans over to kiss my lips, I don't hesitate. I open for him, allowing his tongue to sweep into my mouth to taste the remnants of champagne and strawberries. I let his body settle over mine, even open my legs as far as they will go in my skintight dress. And I'm not even going through the motions now. I'm enjoying it. I'm present for it. That is, until something nudges me in the back of my head. Call it a hunch or intuition.

Maybe it's my body's animal instinct. But I know Ransom is here. And I know he's close, yet not close enough.

I open my eyes, but I can't see much more than Tucker's face. His legs are on either side of the chair, the part of it that's enhanced with a smaller wave than the one my head rests on, and my ankles are hooked around his ass. He gives me his sexy smile—the one that means he wants me. The one he once used only on designated sex nights. But here we are, deviating from the routine. Doing something so out of the box for us that I can't understand how it ever existed. How were we ever placated with mediocrity? When both of us are so extraordinary in our professional lives? Shouldn't we be mad, ravenous beasts in every sense of the word?

His lips fall to my throat, and he kisses and sucks a path down to my chest. I don't object when he tongues the tops of my breasts so he takes that as an invitation to slide the straps of my dress down. When I arch into the movement, he goes a step further, sealing our fate and completely taking us from playground spectators to contributors. He pulls my dress down until it gathers around my ribcage, exposing the hardened peaks of my breasts.

His gaze flickers up to mine as he slowly lowers his face to a pebbled nipple, taking it into his mouth, stroking the stiff bud with the flat of his tongue. I squirm under him, part of me self-conscious of prying eyes and part of me turned on beyond belief. This is different from our time with Ransom. Having Tucker watch me with another man was off-the-charts amazing. But now there are potentially more than two-dozen people watching us, watching the man I love suck and lick my nipples the way he knows I like it, and that . . . that's beyond incredible.

I fist his soft hair, drawing him nearer, begging him with my body to lick faster, suck harder, and Tucker reads me like a book, giving me exactly what I need. When I feel his teeth squeeze my inflamed flesh, I don't even hesitate my moan. I just let it live in this space, in this time without apology, just like us.

The fabric of my dress eases down farther, stopping at the lacy waistband of my thong. It feels too heavy, too hot on my blistering skin, and I want it off me. Tucker doesn't waste a single second yanking it over my stomach and hips when I lift my ass from the lounger. I fumble with the buttons of his shirt, needing him to feel what I feel—this heat that can only be extinguished with the brush of another's flushed skin, and he aids me in my efforts by yanking it over his head. I move down to the belt of his slacks, then the clasp, until he is just like me—nearly naked in his underwear and exposed. Vulnerable.

Our lips lock as if we have just discovered our weakness. As if we are Adam and Eve in the Garden of Eden, post apple. Only the discovery of our sin does not hinder us. It only rouses us, making us crave this evil more. Creating a hunger inside that can only be sated with more wickedness.

He pulls his lips away only to lave my breasts once more before moving down to my navel. He swirls his tongue inside the tiny dip, kisses a trail from hipbone to hipbone, and then nibbles the edge of my panties. I know what he requires: permission. A sign that I want this to go further. That I want to do this as badly as he does. Tonight is in my hands. I can say no, and we can keep this right where it is—safe. Or I can raise my hips a fraction, allowing him access to my nakedness, and open the door to everything my marriage was missing before. Excitement. Danger. Passion.

His underwear meets mine on the floor almost simultaneously, and we are skin to skin. Nothing between us—no secrets, no fear, no frustration. Just me and my husband, as it should be.

There's nothing safe about the way he touches me after that. Nothing gentle about how he pushes my back into the rounded chair. Nothing sweet about how he grips my thighs with enough force to score my skin, and spreads my legs as far as they will go, causing a cool blast of air to touch my wetness. I groan as he sits up and slides his palms to my ass. And when he aligns his dick with my slick entrance, I moan his name, begging him to take me now, fuck me now. And I don't have to beg for long.

He fills me in one swift, hard stroke. With the position this chair allows—my pelvis tilted and my body curved, I feel him deeper than ever before. We stay locked like that for a long time, him barely thrusting, our joined sex grinding together, as we kiss passionately with uncontrollable hunger. When his hips finally flex and he pulls out just a bit, I shiver with the need to feel him again. That depth, that warmth. His body completely submerged in mine.

He fucks me then. Not his version of fucking. Not the soft-core shit I sometimes find on his computer. My husband fucks me how I need to be fucked. Hard, fast, and violent. Like he hates me. Like he needs to fuck the disgust and loathing out of me for all these years of discontent. All the years of shame and frustration. And for all the ways he couldn't love me how I needed to be loved because of what had been done to me.

I think I always knew where the root of our problems stemmed. It was in fear. Fear of hurting me both physically and mentally. Fear of him feeling like the monster that had stripped me of my dignity and robbed me of the privilege of being a mother. We were both so scared for so long that there was no more room to feel anything else. We had built our home on an eggshell foundation, and we tiptoed around the truth, hoping that all we had constructed would not crumble under the weight of our own selfishness. And here we are, taking a wrecking ball to that home. Crushing it, dismantling it, together.

When I rake my nails over his chest, he answers me by plowing in harder, hard enough to make me yelp with pain. It doesn't stop him. He leans over to take a nipple in his mouth, his strokes still deliciously brutal, and bites the puckered bud before sucking nearly my entire breast into his mouth like a starving infant. I pull his hair, telling him to take more, telling him he's a greedy bastard, and he moves to the other breast, assaulting that one as well. It's only when he comes up for air that I realize that we've slid to the peak of the rounded chair and Tucker is standing, his fingernails digging into my ass, his cock so far inside me, I can taste the first drops of his release just begging to be freed.

I gasp for air, the oxygen in the room suddenly becoming too thin, yet thick with lavender-tinged smoke. My chest heaves wildly and sweat rolls between my breasts, making my nipples harder than diamonds. They ache with the need to be touched and pinched. Bitten until the pink peaks become red and raw. I reach for Tucker, searching for him to anchor me, feeling so high that I may float away if he doesn't hold on. He grabs on to my shoulder with one hand to level his strokes, and wraps the other around my throat.

It's all I need—those nails biting into my skin, tightening, creating pressure to my carotid arteries so that my brain is denied of precious oxygen. Getting me drunk off carbon monoxide and the sheer eroticism of being fucked until I'm light-headed. His other hand abandons my shoulder and dips to my clit where he rubs the tiny bud that kisses his dick with every stroke. He's growing for me, swelling, and I tighten around him in response, daring him to do the same. Challenging him to rip me apart and dirty me just a little bit more.

My frantic eyes wide with bliss and lack of air, I'm soundless as the first surge of orgasm overtakes me. I ride it out in rough waves, falling deeper and deeper into black water. I shake violently, unable to control the spasms that roll through my body like thunder. I can breathe now, Tucker's grip completely loosened, yet climax still squeezes my lungs, wringing out every drop of arousal from my body like a wet cloth. I've never come like this before. Never experienced anything like this before. And I did it with the one person I thought would never bring me to this place—my husband.

He collapses on top of me and I wrap my arms around his sweat slickened back, the need to comfort and nurture him almost overwhelming. It's as if he's awakened this . . . vulnerability in me. Yet, it's not borne of weakness. It's freedom and strength. It's the irrevocable feeling of unconditional love and acceptance.

Ragged with exhaustion and ecstasy, my head lolls to one side with no bones or joints to support it. I smile lazily, basking in the feeling of being completely blissed out, and allow my eyes to focus, realizing in the haze of afterglow that we've done it. We've done the unthinkable. And it was everything that I could have asked for and more.

That's when the oily, black serpent sinks his fangs into my flushed skin, penetrating tendon and arteries. Infecting me with its ugly doubt and shame.

I only see him for a moment before he turns and stalks away. But that's all I need; a glimpse of the dark pain that paints Ransom's handsome face, leaving a smeared trail of dejection behind him.

Chapter Twenty-six

I wake up sated and splendidly sore when my cell rings early the next morning. It's Tamara (who still can't calculate the time difference) with my daily update, giving me the scoop on all my clients and events in the city. Being this far from home has been difficult, but not impossible. Thanks to the internet and a strong cell signal, I can do my job anywhere. And as long as my clients stay out of the proverbial kitchen, no one has to get burned. Also, my two most controversial, i.e. difficult, clients are merely yards away. Which has proven to be just as much of a curse as a gift.

I look at my sleeping husband, flat on his stomach, his teddy bear brown hair falling over his forehead. I smooth back the waves that tickle his brow and muster a smile. He was amazing last night. So amazing that we came back to our room and went at it again, licking and sucking each other to another earth shattering orgasm. Of course, I struggled to live in the moment and just focus on Tucker and what his tongue and fingers were doing to my body. I'd give myself over to pleasure, only to be jolted back to reality when the look on Ransom's face would pop into my mind. I hurt him—I know I did. But I don't see how there was any way to avoid it. Tucker is my husband . . . will always *be* my husband. And there's no way Ransom can expect me not to make love to my husband.

I pull myself out of bed much sooner than I should and stretch my stiff, sore limbs before jumping in the shower. When I step out, it takes me a full five minutes to decide what I should put on. I look at my tiny, white bikini, still completely untouched with the tags still dangling from it. I've been here for a week and still haven't gone for a swim in the beautiful infinity pool, or even taken a dip in the more private turquoise lagoon, partitioned by blue palo verde and palm trees. I rip off my towel and grab the bathing suit. It's still early enough that it should be pretty empty, plus after last night most people are probably sleeping in or going for another round. But with the bright morning sun streaming through the curtains, and the smell of fresh, desert air, I can't find a good reason to spend another second inside.

I lift my face to the heavens as I greet the cloudless blue sky and the warmest, most brilliant sunlight I've ever felt. The only signs of human life are Oasis staff, preparing the day for lots of sunbathing, noshing, and sipping. Ordinarily,

I would roll my eyes at those couples lazing around the pool in their designer swimwear and shades, but for some reason, I want to join them. I want to stretch out in an oversize lounger made for two and eat fresh cut papaya and drink ridiculous libations from a hallowed out pineapple.

Overnight, I had become one of those people. The sexually liberated. And even though it was just a one-on-one experience for Tucker and me, which would probably be deemed tame compared to theirs, when we looked up from the fog of orgasm, we realized that we were being watched. Yet, there wasn't an inkling of judgment or disdain etched in their faces. There was admiration, awe, and definitely arousal. At least that was the case for mostly everyone. For Ransom? Not so much.

I assumed he had stormed off to his room after watching Tucker and me, so overwhelmed with hurt and disgust. I couldn't go after him—seriously, how ridiculous would it look if I ran after him ass naked?—and I couldn't fully express my regret to Tucker. We had turned a page, the one that had been holding us back from completing our story. I needed to stay in this moment with him, no matter how badly I wanted to make things right with Ransom. This was our chance to make things better. I had to take it. Any good wife would agree.

So here I am, the morning after. I had not only survived Justice's playground, I had thrived. And maybe this was exactly what I needed to solidify my love for Tucker. Maybe I was only weak for Ransom because my marriage was weak.

And now that we had found the key to our bedroom ills, maybe we could cure everything else that was wrong with us. Whatever that is.

After sitting out for ten minutes, the Arizona summer sun, aka hell's tanning bed, had become unbearable. I decide to roam over to the shaded lagoon situated behind the pool bar and a row of cabanas. I'd seen it before, obviously, but I had never actually been there. So checking out one of the most romantic spots on the property alone seemed a little sad, yet cathartic.

I step through a barrier of trees and my eyes find incredible beauty in that small space. Shimmering teal waters, limestone boulders strategically placed to create a magnificent series of natural fountains, and a sculpted, sun-kissed back slick with water.

I suck in a surprised breath when I see him, drawing his attention, and Ransom turns around, revealing a bare, chiseled chest that I had seen just days ago. He looks at me with the same shock I stare at him with, yet his expression quickly morphs into contempt. He snorts and cuts his eyes at me, just before turning back around to rest his elbows on the edge of the pool. I stand there, shocked at his demeanor. Just days ago, he was begging me not to leave, not to turn my back on him completely and shut him out. Now it seems the tables have turned.

"Can I help you?" he snaps without looking at me. The tone of his voice is so cold even the desert palms shiver.

"Ransom . . ."

I'm not sure what I should say. *I'm sorry?* Nope. What would I be sorry about? Sleeping with my husband? Trying to fix our intimacy issues in hopes that it would be enough to fix us? Yet, to shrug and tell him to get over it would seem callous. I'm a bitch when I need to be, not because I enjoy hurting people. And I'm not a liar. At least when I can help it.

"You knew we'd be there. You knew I wanted to repair my marriage. That was my intention all along."

"Right. Your intention," he sneers, looking over his shoulder. "Was it your intention when I was inside you? When you were damn near begging me to take you every time we were alone? Or how about the other night? What were your intentions when you had your pussy in my face, so fucking wet that there's still a damp spot on the fucking chair? Were you thinking of Tucker then? Was *that* to save your marriage?"

Each accusation is like a blow to my gut, but I recover without so much as a flinch. I won't let him rattle me. I won't give this asshole the satisfaction of affecting me. That's exactly what he wants. Instead, I drop the towel and the paperback I was holding, and march over to him, head held high and back straight. Although I feel about two feet tall right now.

Ransom peers up at me from his place in the pool, his expression a mixture of fury and boredom. Before he can spew one more insult, I let his ass have it.

"What'd you think, Ransom? That this was about you?

It was never about you. You were fun to play with, yes, but that's it. We had fun. But what else could you expect me to want from you? A relationship? A life? You're a good lay, Ransom, and a great musician. But that's it. Stick to what you know and leave the marriage shit to the grownups."

The lie lingers on my lips, swollen with the stinging remnants of my words. I know they're harsh, but they don't even seem to crack his stoic exterior. Instead, he just continues to look up at me, hands on my hips, my mouth a tight slash. All of that, yet no response. It's unnerving.

I start to turn away, when I feel his arms under my knees, squeezing. Then I'm airborne for a fleeting second before being plunged into cool waters headfirst. I thrash and fight, gulping down a gallon of water before I realize what's happened. When I finally break through to the surface after what seems like the battle of my life, I hear him chuckling, yet I can't see him through the wet hair and water in my eyes.

"You son of a bitch!" I sputter through violent coughs. "How dare you! How fucking dare you!"

I still hear him chuckling just inches from me, and I claw at the air in front of me, hoping to connect with his skin. My nails rake across what feels like the hard mound of his bicep, yet he keeps laughing, the dark timbre of his voice both infuriating and disturbing me. When I'm finally on two feet and my sopping wet hair is out of my eyes, I glare at him with pure concentrated malice in my steel gray eyes.

"Who the fuck do you think you are? You don't get to touch me. You don't ever get to fucking touch me!"

"Relax, H. It's water. It won't hurt you." He rolls his eyes and crosses his arms in front of his chest. That's when I see angry bright red scratches lanced in his arm. I drew blood. I made him hurt for me just as he's made me bleed for him. And now . . . I want to do it more. I want him to ache. I want him to suffer. Just make him feel an ounce of the torment I feel inside. I launch myself at him, pounding his chest, scratching at him like a wild animal. Fighting this demon inside me that makes me want him, even though I have everything.

"I don't care! You can't do this! You can't just throw me around. You can't just put your hands on me whenever you want to. You can't have me! I am not yours! Understand? I am not yours to touch!"

I know I'm not making any sense, but it feels good to scream. The freedom of letting go, of purging myself of this affliction for him, is therapeutic.

He grips my wrists, yet I still thrash with elbows and knees and teeth. I fight him for making me feel for him. For making me feel less for my husband. For making me realize that there is something sick and twisted inside me that is wrong, and will always be wrong. And making me accept my disease because there are people like him in this world that are wrong too. Because even though Tucker has tried his damnedest to appease me, to feed my wrongness, I'll always know that he is only pretending for me because he loves me. And Ransom . . . Ransom is wrong without even trying. And that is so right for me.

I don't realize I have collapsed into his chest until he wraps his arms around my trembling frame. I try to pull away but I'm too exhausted to fight him anymore—to fight this. Sweat, tears, and water streak down my face, creating a salty, slippery salve between us.

"I hate myself," I sob. "I hate myself for wanting you. And I hate him for letting me."

Big, callused hands on my neck, my shoulders, my back. Lips in my hair, my temple. I feel him shake his head as he holds me tighter.

"Don't hate yourself. And don't hate him. Hate me, H. Hate me for wanting you just as badly."

I push away from him, my palms over his nipples, but he keeps his fingers locked around my waist. Looking up at him with contempt and desire battling for my next breath, I tell him the truth. I tell him what I don't really mean. "I already do."

"Then show me," he whispers, stepping in closer. "Show me how much you hate me. Loathe me. Despise me. Detest me. But don't reject me. Don't push me away because you think I can't take it. Because I want it, H. I want that beautiful violence. I want you to scratch and kick and scream. Because you know what's on the other side of that madness?"

"Don't say it." I shake my head frantically, refusing to hear it. "Don't fucking say it."

"Passion. Obsession." He pulls me in closer so that my hands are sandwiched between our chests. "Love."

It happens so quickly—his arms around me lifting me up,

my legs wrapping around his waist, and our mouths fused together, drinking in every drop of each other's daring desire. I'm in peril with his arms wound around me so tightly that I can only breathe through him, his lungs sustaining mine. With his rock hard length pressing into me through the thin fabric of our bathing suits, I might as well sacrifice myself to him now, lay my head down on the chopping block, and let him end me. I'm helpless to him—utterly defenseless against this chest that was cut from smooth marble and these lips that have whispered the most erotically beautiful lyrics ever conceived.

He rips my bikini top away just as he presses me up against the pool wall. We've somehow moved to the shallow area adorned with huge boulders that sift water through cracks and manmade spigots. Under the cool spray, deep into this cradle of limestone and granite, we've found *our* oasis. It's not the striptease classes or the erotic yoga. It's not even the den of iniquity. It's just us, unabashedly honest in our skin.

My back rakes against the rough stones as Ransom grinds his pelvis into mine. My elbows are on his shoulders and my fingers are knotted in his hair. I bite his bottom lip, tasting salt and iron, and he digs his fingertips deep into my ass, breaking the skin. We groan together, sharing this pain, relishing this pleasure. He spreads my cheeks wider and slides his hands under my bathing suit bottom until his fingers meet my seam. I shudder at the feel of him there, in that place that Tucker has never touched. In the place I touch myself when I get off alone. He places the very tip of his finger against the pucker and presses gently, waiting for me to squirm and tighten in refusal. I gasp inside his mouth, telling him I won't say no. That word doesn't even exist in my vocabulary right now.

Ransom thrusts against the thin nylon covering my pussy, aligning his steel length with my swell. "You want me to fuck you here?" he whispers against my lips. His finger presses me from behind, and he slowly inserts the tip. "And here?"

Emboldened by his candor, and the image of him filling me from both ends, I nod my head feverishly. "Yes. Please."

Without removing his finger, he pulls at the ties on each side of my bikini bottoms while I fumble with the drawstring of his shorts. I reach under the waistband and wrap my hand around his thick, hard cock, pulling it between us. It throbs against my belly, the silken skin stretched tight around its impressive size. I stroke it against me, loving his little jerks and twitches. I imagine how it would feel in my mouth. How he would taste when the first drops of prerelease would bead at the head. How hot his seed would be sliding down my throat.

"I want to taste you," I tell him, as we both watch the way his dick pulses with its own heartbeat.

"I want you to. But you'd drown in here."

We share a chuckle that's quickly cut off when Ransom sinks his tongue into my mouth. He kisses me hungrily, fucks my mouth just as he told Tucker to do. But his fucking feels different. It's hard, desperate, deep. Unapologetic, just like the rest of him. His finger still lodged inside me starts to move just a fraction. It's slight, almost nonexistent, but with my tightness and the friction of the water, even that tiny movement has me groaning. I stay completely still, fighting the urge to slide back and devour that finger, but I know it'd be too much too soon. Ransom knows what he's doing, and while I may not fully trust him with my heart, I know I can trust him with my body.

He slips his finger in deeper, just past the nail, and slowly thrusts in and out. My whole body shakes with the feeling and I grip him tighter in my palm in response. We stay like that for what seems like forever—him fingering my puckered tightness deeper, stretching me to take him, and me fisting his cock against my belly.

When he gets his finger in past the knuckle, he shifts, bending at the knees while still holding me up, and thrusts inside me. I cry out in uncontained madness, overwhelmed with the feeling of him fucking me from every angle. Even his tongue keeps in time with the rhythm of his strokes.

The first time with Ransom, I wasn't allowed to feel. My body felt him—adored him—but I had to keep it superficial. At least that's what I was supposed to do. But now . . . now I have no other choice but to feel him everywhere—inside me, outside me, throughout me. He sexes my whole being—mind, body, and soul. There is no part of me that is left untouched or unfilled.

My insides quiver when the pressure from behind increases. It burns for a second as my body accepts a second finger, but it isn't unpleasant. Actually, it feels good. Spectacular. Like Ransom's cock is everywhere at once. Filling every empty hallow, even the ones he can't see.

Scalding heat consumes my belly as my womb erupts with the first devastating orgasm. I cry against his lips, biting his tongue hard enough to taste his blood once again. He answers my violence by fucking me impossibly hard before pulling out of my body. I whimper at the loss of fullness, but before I can protest, he's filling me again, this time in the place where his fingers were just buried to the knuckle.

Tears stream down my face as my body swallows his. His breathing is rapid but he doesn't rush. He stays completely still, letting my pliant flesh stretch around him. The water is shallow enough in this spot that it doesn't wash away the remnants of my climax, letting it act as a natural lubricant. Plus with me tilted so only my shoulders touch the rock wall, beads of slick arousal roll down my seam, adding even more wetness.

He pushes in a little deeper, and my voice breaks in a sob. It hurts—my God, it hurts—but he knows well enough not to stop. He knows I can take the pain. He knows I crave the pain. And this is by far dancing the thin line of my threshold. Still, I won't beg him to stop. Even if it rips me open, I will never let him go.

He pushes in farther still, and this time, it doesn't burn as bad. Actually, it's starting to feel ok. He holds me up with one arm wrapped around my waist and brings his other hand to stroke my clit. That, coupled with the intense pressure from behind, makes my whimpers turn to pants. He pinches my sensitive flesh between his fingers, pulling the hot, little button as he pushes in a little more, and I throw my head back. Oh God . . . OhGodOhGodOhGod.

He's inside me to the root, fully immersed in the one place Tucker refused to explore. He always thought it would hurt me—that the scar tissue in that area would make things painful for me. So after he shot me down again and again, I stopped asking him to touch me there. Instead, I learned how to touch myself, and make it feel good.

This is so beyond what I had been doing. My thin, dainty fingertip was nothing compared to Ransom's thick hardness inside me so deep, I can feel his sac against my ass cheeks. And nothing ever will compare for as long as I may live. There's no way I could ever go back to what I had before. I've bitten the apple, I've sucked the seed, and now I want that sin to grow deep inside me.

He strokes me slow, knowing my body well enough that that's all I can take. I hang on to his shoulders as he angles us in a way that keeps him thoroughly buried but also lets me taste his tongue. He makes those erotic, little noises again, those throaty rasps that he does on stage to make the girls wet their panties. I swallow every one, wanting every bit of him to live inside me. He smiles against my lips as if he knows exactly what I'm doing.

His tempo increases and he begins to throb within my tight walls, causing my own orgasm to build. This one is different though. This one won't be like the others. It feels too strong, too uncontained. Like even if he stopped right now and pulled out of me, I'd still come so hard I'd faint.

I grasp his back and bury my head in the crook of his neck, trying desperately not to stop it, but slow it down. I'm not ready to let go. I'm not ready to surrender this feeling for anything.

Despite the madness of our bodies, Ransom's lips are oddly soft and controlled as they caress the side of my face. He kisses my temple, the shell of my ear, my neck. And then he opens for me and bears his soul. He shows me the beauty in chaos, the grace in all this filth and sin.

He sings for me. He sings *because* of me. And it's a song I've never heard.

Falling through the rabbit hole
Down down down I go
Let's go mad together, babe
Nobody has to know

I'll take you into my veins
Drink the elixir of your soul
You're mine now little bunny
I'll never let you go

We come together in a way that bonds us for life. No secrets lie between us—no denial, no regrets. Only sweat, water, and our release. I refuse to let him go for a long time, and it's not until he slips out of me that I lift my head to look at him. His eyes are low, but unguarded. He's still here with me, still all mine for the taking. I kiss him with all I have to give, hoping to convey everything I don't have the courage to say. When he sets me on my feet, I have to steady myself against the wall until the blood returns to my extremities.

Something happened here. Something deeper than we intended. Something deeper than I've ever felt. And it wasn't the sex. That would be too easy. We became kindred in a way that's beyond the physical. And that scares me to the marrow of my bones.

I'm silent as I gather my bikini and he slips into his shorts. We don't even speak as we leave the safety of our little cave dwelling. On some level, I don't think we have to. Words are irrelevant to what's transpired here. They would never be able to describe the sheer horror and savage beauty of the monster we've created.

I leave the lagoon area first to find that people are already lounging around the pool area. I smile and wave, going through the motions on autopilot. No one seems suspicious. No one notices the bright-red scratches on my back or the fingernail marks peeking out from the sides of my swim bottoms. And even if they did, they wouldn't care.

The room is empty when I arrive, and I breathe a deep sigh of relief. I strip off my abused swimsuit like it's on fire and turn the water in the shower to scalding hot. I've done something dirty, and while I don't want to wash it away, I have to. I have to be clean for my husband again.

A door opens just as I step under the hot spray. The steam

is so thick that I can't even see the door to the bathroom and Tucker approach the glass shower partition. It's not until he's right in front of me that I see his naked frame, staring over my body with those shrewd, knowing eyes.

I look at him through tears, desperately trying to swallow my sobs. He says nothing as he steps closer. Nothing as he runs his thumb up and down the column of my throat. I've never felt threatened by my husband, never felt like he could hurt me. But right now, with him looking at me with the calmness of a serial killer, stroking the skin that Ransom had licked and sucked and bit just minutes before, I've never been so terrified in his presence.

He knows.

He knows.

He's always known.

"Tuck . . ." I try to choke out, but it falls on deaf ears. He just keeps touching my kiss-burned skin, his fingers moving down to my shoulders. He moves in even closer and tastes my jaw with the barest brush of his tongue.

"Tuck . . ." I whisper again, begging for him to hear the plea in my voice.

He doesn't.

I'm spinning around in a blur of movement, my face and chest pressed into the cold, slick tile. I cry out with shock, but am unable to move with Tucker holding my wrists against the wall. I stop struggling and he lets them go, only to sink to his knees on the shower floor. He grasps my ass, which is still sore and raw, if not swollen. I want to stop him—I should stop him—but if I do, he'll know for sure. He may already have a hunch, but he can't know for certain exactly what went down.

He spreads me, revealing that puckered hole that was once unsullied. Tears stream down my face as my husband sees the proof of my indiscretion. As he bears witness to my filth and indignity.

I release a full sob when his tongue meets that ravaged skin. Not because he's hurting me—it actually feels amazing despite my debilitating guilt—but because I know I'm hurting him. He's kissing, licking, sucking the very place where Ransom was buried inside me. He's not only tasting me; he's tasting him too. And that makes me so utterly disgusted with myself that I can do nothing but press my face against the tile to hide the shame rolling down my face.

I cry against the shower wall, my howls a mix of torment and pure ecstasy. And when I come for the third time in the past hour, I nearly collapse on the floor.

Tucker lifts me into his arms and carries me out. He wraps a towel around my dripping wet body, all the while leaving his own naked frame cold and dripping. When I am securely tucked into the bed, he goes into the bathroom to towel off.

I turn on my side and curl into myself, trying to sift through the endless stream of doubt running laps inside my head. Maybe he doesn't know. Maybe I still have a chance to make this right. Maybe now that I've gotten Ransom out of my system, we can move on for good. I can't lose him. I can't give up on what we have, regardless of what I feel for someone else.

I'm so preoccupied with my own selfishness and deceit that I don't even notice the pile dumped beside the door. And once I do, I know that worrying is futile. Agonizing over the inevitable is wasted. It's over. It's all over.

My husband is perfect in every way. Kind, generous, and considerate. So considerate, that he brought in my towel and the paperback book that I had forgotten at the lagoon. The towel and the paperback that I don't remember seeing when I left.

Chapter Twenty-seven

I make up an excuse to leave the room, telling Tucker that I need to discuss a new press release for Oasis with Justice, and I throw on a cotton dress and slip into flat sandals. I don't even bother drying my hair or doing my makeup. I just comb out the snags and smack on some mascara and lip gloss and race out of our shared space, far away from the truth that we now both know.

When I make it to Justice's guesthouse, he's already in the doorway, his arms crossed in front of his chest and his face screwed in a scowl.

"You just can't leave well enough alone," he says, closing the door behind us. We're alone, thank God. And while I'm sure there are no secrets between him and Ally, I couldn't stand for her to see me like this.

"Justice . . . Justice, I think I made a big mistake."

"You *think!* You didn't make a mistake, Heidi. You fucked up. I told you to stay away from him; I told you it was a mistake to bring him into your marriage, but you took it a step further, didn't you?"

I frown. Wait a minute . . . why is he so pissed? And what could he know about my fuck ups? He wasn't even present for last night's debauchery. Has Ransom been confiding in Justice?

Seeing the confusion flash across my face, Justice rolls his eyes and says, "I have surveillance cameras everywhere. It's in the contracts. You think I would have a business this provocative and not have camera evidence to cover my ass? Come on, Heidi. You should know that. You're slipping."

I take the insult like a slap in the face. He's right. I've been less than stellar when it comes to my role as a professional.

"You were spying on us? You . . . you saw us?"

"Hell no. At least not the shit you were doing in my pool. But I saw enough. Dammit. You've really fucked it up this time, haven't you? I tried to give you the benefit of the doubt when I saw you go to his room. But this . . . this is just too obvious."

I shake my head, refusing to believe what I can plainly see. Tucker knows it. Justice knows it. And soon, everyone else will know it too. I'm a cheater. I've cheated on my husband. And even though he helped open the door to it, it was still me who chose to keep this up with Ransom. I knew I wouldn't be able to resist him forever. I knew sooner or later, our eggshell house would crack and shatter under our feet. And now . . . now it has.

"He knows," I manage to whisper to Justice, who just stares at me in disappointment. Tucker isn't the only person I've let down. Justice went out on a limb for me. He welcomed us into his home, counseled us, gave us an outlet to explore ourselves, and I still managed to do the one thing he requested I not do.

"I know he does. I saw him. He came to me . . . wanting to try again. Willing to do whatever it takes to make you happy because he loves you."

I don't even bother to dash away the tears in my eyes. The secret's out. I'm a screwup. No need to pretend now. "What do I do, Justice? What am I going to do now? I can't lose Tucker. He's my whole life and I love him. But Ransom . . . oh my God. What if he thinks we're together? What if he tells someone? Shit! What if he confronts Tuck?"

Justice takes a deep breath through his nose and lets it out slowly, a move he uses to calm himself. Ally's been insisting on him joining the morning yoga classes. "Look. Go back to your room. Spend the rest of the day with your husband. Order up food, watch TV. Let this situation simmer for now. Then tomorrow night, we're going back down to the playground—at Tucker's request. I'd advise against it, but then it'd raise too many questions—questions you don't want me to answer honestly. But after that, you're going to break things off with Ransom—personally and professionally. Then you're going to send him back to New York. Alone. We'll figure out the rest once he's gone."

I nod, fully accepting his advice. I need to drop Ransom for good. I need to cut him loose. I'll never give my marriage a fair try with him here.

In a move that surprises us both, I go to wrap my arms around Justice in a warm embrace. He stiffens for at least five seconds before he exhales and begrudgingly hugs me back.

"I'm sorry," I whisper, meaning it. To him, to Tucker, hell, even to Ransom.

"I know. And you're going to be sorry for a very long time. But not forever. Remember, I've fixed worse."

I leave his home and do exactly what he says. I don't pass Go. I don't collect $200. I go straight to my husband. When I reach the door that says Reflection, I find that he isn't there. Normally it wouldn't surprise me—it's still early and the compound is huge—but every fear I've ever harbored comes bubbling to the surface. What if he's talking to Ransom right now? What if they're fighting? Or what if Tucker decided to do exactly what I have been doing to him? What if he's screwing another woman right now?

I make a mad dash for the spa, sweeping the area for any signs of my husband. The lower private level doesn't open until after noon, so I don't have to worry about him going for a romp in there, thank God. I check the instruction room, the theater, even the library that I never even knew existed. As I leave, I hear the sounds of piano close by, originating from an area I've never seen before. It's open like a ballroom but much smaller. And it's unfurnished, save for a single baby grand piano in the middle of the room, being played by none other than Ransom Reed.

He's freshly showered, dressed in his signature frayed jeans and white V neck tee. He almost looks like the Ransom I'd seen on TV. The Ransom I was secretly infatuated with. And now that I know him, in every way that a woman can know a man, I feel more intimidated by him than I ever have before.

He looks at me through hazy eyes and smiles. There's something in that smile that alarms me, something familiar that I just can't put my finger on. It's enough to draw me closer to try to figure it out.

I don't say anything at first. Just sit beside him and listen to him play. I know the music, but I can't remember the name. It's not until he starts to sing that I understand—that I get it. The song. Him. Us. Why we were destined to be, yet doomed to coexist.

People like me and Ransom Reed, and even Justice, were always meant to be a little wrong. Without us, those perpetually good, righteous souls would have no one to save. They would have no purpose. Ally would have never met Justice and showed him what it was like to be loved and accepted, despite his background. Tucker would have never found me, and taught me how to live again, and accept love. And Ransom . . . see, that's the problem. He thinks I'm his person. He thinks I'm the one who's supposed to fix him. When we both know that two wrongs don't make a right.

He flows into the chorus of "A Song For You" by Donny Hathaway, his voice wrapping around the melody like a warm, electric blanket. He's always had a rich timbre to his voice, as if he could have been a soul singer in a past life. Considering his family was heavily religious and he grew up in the church, I'd imagine he spent many a Sunday singing hymns and gospel songs. And even though he's excommunicated himself from the church and his family, he can't deny that his upbringing helped shape the musician that he is today.

When the song ends, we sit there for a while, savoring the silence. We both have so much to say—how can we not?—but no one's ready to take that step.

After several minutes, I suck in a breath, I tell him what I should have told him a long time ago. What I should have said the very first night we met. "I can't do this, Ransom."

He smiles but his eyes stay fixed on the keys. "We're not doing anything right now."

"You know what I mean. I can't . . . be with you anymore. And I can't represent you. I'm sorry. It's highly unethical of me, and it could damage both our reputations. Not to mention, I'm married and I love my husband. I need to do this for all of us. And you and I having any type of interaction just isn't healthy."

"Healthy," he snorts. "How do you know what's healthy for me, huh? Maybe it's you that I need to make me better."

I turn to him and frown. "No, Ransom. I'm not. This isn't

right. We're hurting him when we both know he doesn't deserve it."

"What do you know about what he deserves?" he sneers, his voice suddenly icy cold. "He had it all, yet he wanted more. What makes you think he's hurting? What about me? What about my pain?"

I start to reach out to comfort him, his vulnerability catching me off guard, but I stop myself before I make contact, hoping to soothe him with my words instead. "I'm sorry we dragged you into all this. I didn't mean for it to go this far. I didn't mean to . . . to . . ."

"To fall in love with me?" He looks at me then, his eyes red-rimmed and glassy.

"I never said that, Ransom."

"But you are in love with me, aren't you?"

I shake my head. "I love my husband. I want to make things work with him."

"That doesn't answer my question."

"Ransom . . ." I stand up then, realizing what a mistake it was to try to talk to him. "Tucker is a good man, and a good husband. I need to be with him."

In a flash of red rage, Ransom pounds against the keys, creating a disjointed song of fury and pain. "Fuck him! What kind of husband has another man fuck his wife? Huh? What kind of man would manipulate someone's weakness for his own agenda?" he yells, spewing contempt from his lips.

Startled, I take a step back, putting myself at a safe distance just in case he decides to lunge at me. Hours ago, I relished his violence. Now, it terrifies me in all the wrong ways.

"You don't know what you're talking about," I try to say in a level voice.

"He's not what you think he is, Heidi. He's not as good as you think he is."

"Shut up, Ransom. Don't you dare act like you know the first thing about my husband and my marriage," I retort. "You're a kid. You have no clue what marriage entails. It's not easy; it's hard work. But when two people love each other, they do whatever it takes."

"Right. Sure," he snorts. "So I guess that's what you were doing with me this morning. Putting in some of that hard work. Tell me, was it easy to take my dick deep inside your tight, little ass? Or was that just you, doing whatever it takes? Because, baby, you sure can take a lot."

I'm trembling with rage, completely shocked and appalled that he would say that to me. What was I thinking? Was I really even considering being with Ransom—this punk kid? How could I be so stupid?

"Fuck you," I spew. "And pack your shit. You're on the next flight back to Manhattan."

"No can do, sweetheart. Didn't you hear? We've got a date—you, me, and the good doctor. Unless you'd like me to explain your sudden change of heart. Or maybe he'll be able to see the evidence for himself. I don't know if my scratches will heal by tomorrow night. Maybe I should go explain to him how his wife likes to draw blood."

"Don't you dare. Don't you go near him, Ransom, or I swear—"

He's in my face, just inches from my kiss-swollen lips that he'd ravaged just hours ago. "Or what? What are you afraid of Heidi? That he might see it—the truth between you and me? You think he's fucking blind? Newsflash, baby. I'm all over you—permanently embedded in every inch of your skin. I'm *inside* you, H . . . even when it's him you're fucking. I'm fucking you too . . . always. And you know that. You know that every time you come, it's me that's making your legs quiver. It's me you're screaming for. It's my back you're scratching when you want it deeper. *Mine.* Shit, you can feel me right now, can't you, baby?"

"Shut. Up. Ransom!"

"Stop lying to yourself. Stop lying to me. This is us, baby. We're both fucked up in ways that he'll never be able to understand. We're the same, baby. And only I know what you want . . . what you need. You know that, don't you? You felt it, just like I did. And you're still feeling it right fucking now."

Flustered and furiously aroused, I turn around and stalk out with a huff, the echo of his laughter chasing me from the room. Ransom Reed is the biggest mistake of my life. And it's time to right my wrongs once and for all.

Chapter Twenty-eight

I thought I could do it—I thought I could finally put my own selfish, narcissistic needs aside for the sake of my husband . . . my marriage. But I'm a coward. A coward that was too afraid of not only losing him, but, dammit, losing Ransom too. Because I do feel for him, I do want him, but I want my marriage more. I may want Ransom, but I need Tucker. He's my husband, my life. So despite what he says, Ransom is nothing more than a passing phase. That's all he can be to me.

So here I am—in Justice's playground. Ready to give it all one last kiss goodbye. I could have told Tucker that I'd had a change of heart and wanted no one else but him. But my insatiable hunger for more—for Ransom—is stronger than the desires of my heart. Or maybe they're not. Maybe they're more aligned than I've allowed myself to admit.

"Don't be afraid," Tucker whispers in my ear, before leaving a trail of soft kisses along my collarbone. I am afraid, but not for the reasons he believes.

We're on one of the round beds—the ones designed for a crowd. There are fewer people here tonight, however, Justice is present. He watches us intently, those molten blue eyes unblinking. Yet, I don't find his presence unnerving. If I'm being honest with myself, having him here—watching, studying . . . potentially wanting—only makes me want this more. He's a powerful man, with a body fit for every woman's erotic fantasy, and a presence that makes him seem ten feet tall. And in our world, there is no greater aphrodisiac than power.

The lights are dim enough in the room that I can't really see the other couples around us. I can hear their moans and mewls, but they're barely visible unless I concentrate. I imagine it's just us here in this room—just my husband and me. We're in our bed back at home. We've just polished off a bottle of Cab and are feeling free and frisky after a long week. I close my eyes and focus on the feel of his lips moving down my chest and the soft scratch of his 5 o'clock shadow on my delicate skin. He loosens the tie of the terry cloth robe and lets it fall open, allowing cool air to entice my already pebbled nipples.

"Do you want this, Bunny?" he asks before sucking one into his mouth, not even bothering to wait for an answer. I try to speak through a moan but it comes out as an unintelligible mewl. A chuckle rumbles from the back of his throat, causing his teeth to nip my puckered skin. "What was that? You'll have to tell me, baby. I need to hear you say you want me."

"Yes," I whine, opening my eyes to gaze down at him as he worships my body with his mouth. "Yes, I want you." And, dammit, I do. I want this man. I've never stopped wanting him, as difficult as that may seem. I may have developed a taste for more, but I never stopped desiring him. He's my husband, and I love him. Nothing or no one can change that.

My head falls back as he makes his way down my torso, with hands caressing what his lips cannot. I missed this—this attentive, gentle lovemaking. I feel beautiful in his arms. He cherishes me with every kiss, every touch, and every heated whisper across my humid skin. With Tucker, I don't have to guess or worry. I know I am loved. And considering that he knows what I've done—he knows the depth of my perversion—and can find it in his heart to love me anyway, truly makes my heart swell with gratitude. Tucker is the best man I've ever known, and he is mine. And by some act of divine intervention, I am his. He still wants me. After all I've done to soil my marriage, he still loves me.

"Tonight is all about you, baby. You're in control," he rasps as he slowly parts my legs, unveiling my sex. "I want to please you in every way. I just want to make you happy."

His words catch my attention and I meet his lustful stare. "I am happy, Tuck. You make me happy. Every day."

He responds with a nod before sinking between my thighs and pressing his hot tongue against my mound. The room seems to get dimmer . . . less solid. Lines blur and colors swirl and the air hums around me. I gasp his name as the wet, gentle scrape of his tongue fondles my sex with expert precision, mapping his way to my entrance. I reach between my legs and fist his hair, holding on to this feeling. Trying to keep us here in this moment for as long as we can. I'm on the brink of orgasm when Tucker pushes up to rest on his knees. Sex still gleams on his lip, along with a sinuous smile. I fix a finger to beckon him closer when a chill whispers across my dampened skin.

I part my lips to protest but my breath is barren of all coherency when I allow my eyes to focus on the dark figure slowly stalking toward us, drenched in shadow. My body responds immediately, vibrating with exhilaration and fear. This was what I was afraid of. Not having sex in front of strangers. Not being completely naked and vulnerable in front of Justice. I was afraid of this . . . this feeling. Of wanting another man so badly that his mere presence makes my sex tingle with expectation and my heart break into a drum solo. I'm afraid that he's right, that I do want him for more than just some premature quarter-life crisis. And I'm afraid that within these dark-stained walls and under the thin veil of candlelight, I won't be able to hide it anymore.

Ransom approaches with the cocksureness of a bullfighter, taking his time to circle the bed so he can see us from all angles and plan his attack accordingly. His eyes are like a moonless midnight, his too-sensual mouth a tight line of concentration. He isn't dressed in the navy blue Oasis robe, but in a pair of ripped jeans and nothing else. I want him completely naked, like me. I want him to be just as exposed and aroused as I am.

I watch Tucker watch Ransom with expressionless eyes. When the younger man finally pauses to place a knee on the bed, I feel the air escape my lungs. I feel Tucker shift upright between my legs, yet I'm too captivated by Ransom's presence to see what's happening. There's pressure at my entrance, and before I can brace myself for impact, Tucker is filling me.

"This is what you want, baby," he grunts out, pushing in to the hilt. "This is what you want, isn't it?"

I nod, too overwhelmed with eroticism to speak. This time, the roles are reversed. Ransom is watching Tucker fuck me. But I want him as more than just a voyeur. There's no way I can not touch him with him being so close I can smell clean sweat and smoke on his skin. But then again, if I touch him—if I feel his skin on mine, our combined heat creating an inferno of lust that's hot enough to melt the paint off the walls—I'll never be able to stop. I won't be able to kick this nasty habit that causes me to keep running from the safety and love of my husband into emotional anarchy. So I shouldn't touch him, as badly as I want to. As badly as I need to.

As if he's crawled into my mind and played Scrabble with my disjointed thoughts, Ransom crooks a wicked grin and utters in that voice on the cusp of a moan, "This is what you want too. Isn't it, H?"

I look up at my husband who still appears unshaken, only his brow furrowed in concentration. He's inside me yet he's not moving, his restraint causing a sheen of sweat to bloom across his forehead. He stares back at me, but answers to Ransom. "Yeah. Yeah, she does want that too. Why don't you give it to her?"

Without hesitation, Ransom makes quick work of his fly and zipper, but hesitates just before letting his jeans slide off his hips. I've been so captivated by the sight of his chiseled body, that I didn't realize that our threesome had become a foursome.

"Whatever you want to do tonight, Heidi, it's your choice" Justice says from the other side of me, his smooth, deep voice adding a new dimension of excitement. "If you want both Tucker and Ransom, you can have them. They are here for your pleasure. But if you choose to do this—if you push the dynamics of your relationships—be absolutely sure you're prepared to handle all that comes with it."

Through the haze of hedonism, a contradicting mix of insecurity and arousal clouding my judgment, I take a beat to consider his words. I've had sex with Ransom, and I've obviously had sex with Tucker. But both of them? Together? Could my marriage survive it? Shit, could I? And do I even want to?

"I'm sure," I hear myself reply, the certainty behind the words as shaky as my current moral ground.

Everything seems to move all at once. Justice steps away yet stays nearby. Ransom lets his jeans hit the floor, unsheathing a hard, proud cock. And Tucker . . . Tucker moves inside me with deep, languid strokes. The kind of strokes that remind me of forgotten lazy Sundays spent in bed making love. I relish the feel of him and the sight of Ransom as he moves closer to me on the bed. He's nearly hovering over me, the tip of his erection so close to my lips I can taste him. He reaches over to graze my nipples with the pads of his callused fingers while Tucker continues his unhurried thrusts.

I want more. I want so much more of him . . . of this. So I do what any sane, hot-blooded woman would do with nine inches of hard-as-steel male in front of her.

I take it.

I'd wanted to taste Ransom since that very first night in his suite, but it was Tucker calling the shots. So since it's my turn to take control—to demand my own pleasure—I'm going to have these two beautiful men every way I can get them.

He's pulsing in my palm, little ripples of vein and flesh quivering as I caress it gently. A low growl rumbles in his throat and I look up to see that Ransom's eyes are closed and his head is tipped back. I turn my gaze to Tucker, who is watching me—watching us—intently. How would he react to the sight of another man's cock in my mouth? Only one way to find out.

Ransom trembles on my tongue as I take as much of him as I can. My eyes still trained on my husband, I start with gentle licks up and down his shaft before falling into a rhythm that matches Tuck's strokes. He thrusts, I suck. It's fiercely erotic and soon I feel myself tightening below, overwhelmed by this new level of pleasure. Ransom takes it even further by pinching and twisting my nipples with one hand and reaching down between my legs, down to where me and Tuck are connected, and rubbing small circles in my clit. It's the devastating blow that does me in, and with me moaning wildly around Ransom's thick length, I come apart.

Tuck's never been able to hold on for long after I've orgasmed. The feel of my body greedily sucking him deeper always sends him over the edge, so he quickly pulls out. We're in motion again, and while I'm still trembling with aftershocks, I still want more.

"Lie down," I instruct Ransom after I release him from my mouth. He does as directed, stretching his long frame beside mine.

I look to Tucker, who is still between my legs, his sex still wet with my release. "You too."

I'm sandwiched between two of the sexiest men alive, wondering what the hell I plan to do with them. I turn to Tucker first, who is at my right and kiss his lips. Still ravenous and on the edge of orgasm, he eagerly snakes his tongue in my mouth, devouring every one of my soft whimpers. His hand trails up to knead my breasts, just the way he knows I like it. Breathless, I pull away and turn to Ransom. He gazes back with dark, hooded eyes, his sensual lips parted in expectation. I give him my mouth, my tongue. I give him my heart in that kiss, and let him taste my soul. I drink his anguish and lick love letters on his lips.

I kiss Ransom like it's the last thing I'll ever do, hoping that somewhere in the midst of our lust he can taste the goodbye that I can't bring myself to say. Because that's what tonight will have to be: goodbye. When I pull away, the desolation in his stare tells me that he knows it too.

Tucker is still hard and ready behind me, his hands roaming my body in search of release. If we're here to push the limits of our marriage, I'm going to take this opportunity to put it all on the table. I may not ever get another chance.

"I want to feel you," I whisper to him, turning my head to look at him from over my shoulder. I reach behind me to stroke the hardened flesh that's sliding between my cheeks and take it one step further, placing the tip of him at my puckered entrance to show him exactly where I want to feel him. Tucker has never been willing to try it. He'd always been too afraid of hurting me. But now that we're here, throwing every speck of inhibition to the wind, there's no better time like the present.

As I expect, shock and alarm flash across his features, but he quickly tamps it down. "Is that what you really want?"

I stare back with unshakeable certainty, despite the coiled doubt in my belly. "I do."

I lift my gaze to find Justice staring back at me. Without a word, he strides over to us and extends his palm to Tucker, revealing a small tube of lube. With the tentative tips of his fingers, my husband receives it then looks over my shoulder to Ransom. Something passes between the men, something that encourages Ransom to grasp my thigh and drape my leg over his hip.

This is happening. Against all my better judgment, against the niggling voice in my head that tells me to shut this shit down right now and escape with my marred dignity and what's left of my marriage, I'm seriously going to do this.

I look up to find that Justice is still looming over us, his expression terse. When our eyes meet, the line of his bowed lips tightens until they're completely white. I know how he feels about me and what I'm destroying in this moment. But he's made his living off building fantasies, even for those who don't deserve them, like the sexist, spineless husbands who would send their wives to him for instruction. Even for people like me, the twisted, the weak, the unfulfilled. His nostrils flare just subtly before he takes a step back. However, that's all the distance he puts between us. He wants to see. He may deal with every sordid type of sex there is, but he is still a man.

With my leg angled like this, my sex open and so close to his, I hold my breath, awaiting contact. I turn back to Ransom and gaze up into those dark, sultry eyes, seeking comfort and solitude. I can hear the shuffling of Tucker fiddling with the lube. When the cold gel touches my inflamed skin, I nearly yelp in surprise. It's only Ransom's face and his tight hold on my thigh that stills me.

Without warning, he crushes his lips to mine, wrapping

me up in an intense kiss that steals the oxygen from my lungs. He tastes like the sweetest sin, his mouth as captivating as the lyrics that fall from his tongue. I'm losing myself in him when I feel a prick of pressure behind me. Instinctively, I try to fight against it, but Ransom just holds me tighter and pulls my leg wider, giving Tucker more room to push inside me. I squirm and groan, but Ransom just absorbs it all, continuing to kiss me deeper and hold me tighter.

When Tucker pushes in to the hilt, we all sigh audibly. He kisses my hair and shoulders, kneading my ass as he allows me to adjust to his size. I know he's still afraid to hurt me, but the way that he's pulsing deep inside me and groaning with the need to move, tells me that he likes it too. He feels so good here that I want to cry. Not only from the physical sensation, but from the fact that he's overcome so many of his hang-ups, all out of love for me. I turn to him and smile lazily, basking in his body connected with mine. He kisses me slowly, tasting Ransom on my tongue, when he begins to move his hips. I gasp into his mouth, but he doesn't stop. His strokes are gentle and unhurried, but each one fills me to the brim, making it difficult to do much more than let my head fall back onto his shoulder and moan his name. Tuck isn't as long as Ransom, but he's a good bit thicker, and right now, I can feel every strong inch of him caressing places that he's never dared to touch before.

Ransom's hands slide up to my breasts where he rolls my nipples between his callused fingers. I cry out at the sensation, but I need . . . more. I need to be stimulated everywhere. I need him to fill me too.

I pull his lips to mine as I reach between us to stroke his length. Ransom moans into my mouth, only encouraging me further. I guide him to my slickness and rub the tip of him against my swollen mound. It feels indescribable, and soon I'm panting with the mounting need to come.

"I need you," I nearly beg. "I need you right now."

Ransom wastes no time hoisting my leg up to his waist and angling his body to meet mine. Tucker keeps a steady rhythm, restraining himself, and Ransom is able to slip in easily.

We all pause to take a breath and contemplate the severity of this crucial moment. Both men are inside me, making love to each other through me. While their hands and mouths and cocks may only be reserved for me, they can't deny the intimacy of this act. We'll forever be connected—the three of us. Even after tonight, after I send Ransom away, Tucker and I will be forever stained by the pleasure we all shared.

The guys move slowly at first, testing to see how much my body can take. Tucker pushes in, Ransom pulls out. They alternate like this with shallow, languid strokes. I'm so unbelievably full that I feel like I'm to the point of bursting. Still, when Tucker increases his tempo and presses in deeper, prompting Ransom to do the same, I can't imagine euphoria feeling much better than this. I'm floating, so high that I may kiss the sky. I never knew that it could be like this, and now that I've felt bliss and tasted heaven, I don't know how I could ever go back to how things were before.

I want both men. I need them. And if that makes me immoral or selfish or whorish, then so be it. But I won't deny what I am. I won't pretend any longer.

It doesn't take long before we're all shaking with the need for climax. Ransom is panting in front of me, eyes shut tight, lower lip sucked between his teeth. I nuzzle into the space under his chin and kiss his neck. With trembling fingers, he cups my cheek, turning my face up to meet his. The very second I see those heavy-lidded eyes, rimmed in anguish, I gasp aloud. I want to say something—do something—but it's too late. My body wins out over my emotions, and sends me into a climax that shakes heaven and earth. I pulse wildly around them both, and I start to feel Tucker quivering behind me, his own orgasm coursing through him. But Ransom . . . Ransom continues to watch me as he thrusts into me, the fear and pain in his stare so jarring that I'm afraid to look away.

I'd have shot down the moon for you
So you could lay with the stars
But we're out of time, little bunny
I've fallen too far . . . too far

When he comes, he grips my thigh so hard and thrusts so deep that I feel like he may break my body in two. It'd be fitting. Those desolate words, the pained look on his face as he rides out his orgasm, the small, single tear that rolls down his cheek . . . he's already demolished my heart.

I came here tonight to say goodbye. To get Ransom Reed out of my system for good. And now that it's done, and I feel more connected to him than ever, I know that I made a grave mistake. One that will cost me everything.

Chapter Twenty-nine

I wake up the next morning alone with an unfathomable sense of urgency that I can't shake. Something isn't right. I can feel it inside me, churning like hot lava in my gut. I text Tamara to see if everything's ok. I shoot Caleb a message to inform him of my plans to send Ransom back to the city. Then I hit up a travel agent to arrange the next step.

As much as it pains me, I have to get Ransom out of my life. Permanently. I fell for him . . . fell for him hard and quick and so completely. And if I'm going to stick to my word and try to make things right with Tucker, I have to let him go. It's not right of me to hold on to him just so I can play with him like a toy. I saw it on his face last night, even in the haze of orgasm. I'm hurting him. I'm hurting my husband. And when it's all said and done, I'm hurting myself. And while the immediate sting of letting go has me texting through tears, I know that this is the only chance of recovery.

Tucker still isn't back by the time I've dried my tears and finished my calls, so I decide to click on the TV to busy my mind. I flip through the channels until I land on another late 90s favorite of mine—*Cruel Intentions.* Sarah Michelle Gellar's character Kathryn was the epitome of devious debutante and Sebastian, played by Ryan Phillippe, was the wayward boy who never felt whole, no matter how many girls he slept with. Until he met her, of course. Wholesome, kind, virginal. Annette was the good one, sent to mend Sebastian's brokenness and show him how to love. And even though he was a complete asshole in the beginning, you wanted him to be with the good girl, even though he may not have deserved her. You hoped that maybe she could make him good too.

But as the movie came to its climax, we saw that trying to conform—trying to steal that slice of happiness when it wasn't meant for you—only got you hurt. So why was it even worth trying at all? When all people would ever see was the defect in you?

I look at my cell phone and instantly think of Ransom, wondering if he's watching the same movie. If he can identify with Sebastian the playboy, or maybe he even feels like Selma Blair's character, Cecile. He didn't know what he was getting into. He didn't realize what he had signed up for when he invited us back to his suite. It was just to be one night of fun. One naughty tryst between consenting adults. And now look at us.

I don't know how we got here. But I know we can't continue any further.

I snatch up my phone and text him, asking him if he received the flight info the travel agent should have forwarded to him more than hour ago. No response. I text him again, asking him if he's ok. Again, nothing.

That same feeling of dread sets in and grows until I'm almost choking on it. I knew it when I saw him in the music room. I felt it last night in Justice's playground. I had seen that same hopelessness reflected in those dark eyes before. Yet, once again, I didn't ease his discord. I didn't give him what he needed.

I get to the door of the Temptation room to find that it's ajar. I can hear The Verve's "Bitter Sweet Symphony" blaring from the TV, the same song that I was just listening to as Kathryn was publically exposed and ostracized at her stepbrother's funeral by none other than sweet, non-suspecting Annette, played by a cutesy Reese Witherspoon.

"Ransom?" I call out, pushing open the door. "Hey, it's Heidi. Did you get my text?"

I don't see him anywhere and the bathroom door is wide open and empty. The room is a mess, pillows and blankets strewn across the floor, cushions turned over, as if someone was frantically looking for something. At first glance, nothing looks out of place, aside from the disheveled linens. But when I walk over to the other side of the bed, my heart stops. Completely flatlines with shock and horror.

Several opened prescription pill bottles, most of them empty. A half-drunk bottle of Jack. Ransom had been popping pills—a lot of them. And considering how much he took, I'm positive it's more than any person should be able to survive. I pick up a bottle to get a better look, recognizing some of them as antidepressants, antianxiety meds, even a mood stabilizer.

I'm Googling the uses for Androcur, when an even more shocking realization causes me to drop the bottle, scattering pills across the floor. Right there, next to the field reserved for the prescribing doctor, it states DuCane, Tucker J.

No. That can't be right. But every bottle reiterates the same.

DuCane, Tucker J.

DuCane, Tucker J.

DuCane, Tucker J.

Tucker prescribed these pills to Ransom.

Tucker is Ransom's doctor.

Ransom is Tucker's patient.

I cover my mouth with a trembling hand, unable to grasp what I'm seeing—what I should have seen all along. It wasn't a coincidence. None of this was. They knew each other. My husband and my lover, they knew what they were doing.

I walk backward out of the room and scurry to the safety of mine as quickly as I can, and plow right into a hard chest covered in white linen. I'd know the feel of him anywhere.

Could identify his masculine, fresh scent blindfolded in a room full of men. Yet, I couldn't see Tucker for what he truly is. The puppet master. He wasn't sweet, loving Annette as I initially thought. He was Kathryn. My husband is the scheming, conniving control freak.

He closes the door without saying a word, even though he can clearly see the disbelief etched in my wide, unblinking eyes. He's perfectly calm like always. Perfect, impassive guise without even a hint of discontent. And that pisses me off.

"You." It's the only word that I trust myself with right now. "You. It was you all along. You did this. You wanted this. And in the back of my mind, I knew. I just didn't want to see it. I didn't want to believe you were this . . . monster. The first night when we met him . . . I remember thinking that you never introduced yourself. You never told him your name. And the way you damn near pushed me into his bed. You wanted me to be with him. Why?"

Tucker sits on the edge of the bed and shakes his head. "No, baby. That was what you wanted. I just facilitated it. You needed something that I couldn't give you. And I knew he could—he would. So while I may have given you the gun, I never made you pull the trigger. No, my love. You did that all on your own."

"But he's your patient, Tucker! He needs help! Not to be manipulated!"

"What makes you think I'm not helping him? You think I couldn't be helping both of you right now?"

I shake my head in disbelief, refusing to accept what's happening. Tucker was the mastermind. Tucker used Ransom, told him things about me, told him how to seduce me. And I fell for it. Maybe Tucker wasn't manipulating Ransom. Maybe he's Sebastian and they were in on this plan the whole time? To seek out the girl and break her down. Make her fall in love. Then crush her like brittle, paper-thin petals of a preserved rose.

"I knew it . . . I knew it when I heard it," I stammer, thinking out loud as I try to put the pieces together. "When he sang . . . he called me little bunny. You told him all about me, didn't you? The rape? My sexual deviances? You told him!"

Tucker looks at me with remorseful eyes, his first crack of emotion since I exposed his lying ass. "It wasn't like that, Heidi. You both needed something from each other. You just couldn't see it yet."

I look down at the empty, orange bottle straining under my tight grip and throw it at him. "What's this used to treat? What does it do?"

Tucker looks over the plastic bottle that once housed a prescription for Androcur and shrugs. "A number of uses, one being prostate cancer."

"Stop bullshitting me, Tucker. Does Ransom have prostate cancer?"

He releases a breath, letting his shoulders sag in defeat. "No."

"So why did you prescribe it? What is he taking it for?"

I watch him swallow down the last of his lies, before he closes his regret-tinged eyes. "Hypersexuality. Sex addiction."

Sex addiction? Ransom's a sex addict?

The first time I saw him drunk and high—it was as if it was a reaction to something. Like he was compensating for something much deeper with booze and pills. He told me he wasn't a junkie, and I believed him. I wanted to. Now I see he was being honest, which is much more than I can say for my loving husband. I just don't understand how he could put me in the hands of someone who needs sex like a drug. He was serving Ransom a hefty dose of X on a cocaine-dusted platter.

I look at the man I love, the man I'd built a life with. The man I had once considered having children with because that was what he wanted. We struggled together, fought together, cried together, laughed together. He was a piece of me, and up until this moment, I had believed he was the very best piece. But he was a liar. He was a fraud. And now, I can't tell if I'm just looking at a stranger. I know absolutely nothing about him at all.

"I have to go," I say, turning toward the door. "I have to go find Ransom. He could be lying at the bottom of the pool, no thanks to you. Were you trying to kill him? By prescribing all those pills?"

His face contorts in horror, and he inhales sharply as if he's just taken a blow to the kidney. "No! Of course not. Ransom is a sex addict, but he also suffers from bouts of depression, anxiety, ADHD. Those pills were necessary to his treatment program."

"And me? Was I necessary to his treatment program?"

Tucker diverts his eyes to the floor, unable to face the evidence of his transgression. He gave another man his wife—the woman he had vowed to love and protect—in some convoluted attempt to help her help his patient.

"Where is he? I'll go talk to him," he finally says.

I shake my head in frustration. "Don't you get it? I don't know! There're empty pill bottles and alcohol. And he's not answering my text messages."

That certainly gets his attention, and Tucker jumps to his feet, pulling his cell out of his pocket. "We have to find him," he says, headed for the door.

I put my anger aside and accept his assistance. Two people are better than one, and right now, Ransom needs me more than I need to crucify my husband. But there will be hell to pay later. You can bet on that.

"You check outside," I instruct, going into boss bitch mode. "Check the pool areas, the bungalows . . . the lagoon. See if anyone has seen him. I'll search inside and check with the staff. I know there are surveillance cameras. Justice can check for me."

Tucker nods his head and looks at me solemnly before turning toward the doors. "I never meant to hurt either one of you—you know that. I thought that if you got what you needed, we could have a fresh start, and maybe . . . maybe I could learn to love you the way you needed to be loved. And I thought if Ransom got what he needed in a safe, controlled environment, he could see that he could tame the urges of his body and focus on the needs of his heart. That maybe he could open himself enough to see that he too could find love and happiness and acceptance. I just didn't bet on him finding all those things with you."

I stare at the stranger in front of me and feel . . . nothing. I know I love him deep inside, and I know he cares for me. But now I've gone to that place where none of that exists. That emotionally barren wasteland where love can no longer grow and thrive under the harsh conditions of his lies and deceit. Maybe one day I'll be able to forgive him. Maybe we'll even look back on this and be able to take a deep, cleansing breath, exhaling it all into the wind like ash. But for now, he doesn't get to matter. He doesn't get to make me feel sympathetic to him. Not when there's a man out there who needs me to save him. A man who looked at me like I was his person, like I would be the answer to all the difficult questions of his heart. The same way I had once looked at Tucker.

My husband didn't expect for Ransom and me to fall in love, but he let it happen. And for that, he's just as guilty for our transgressions.

"Be careful what you wish for," I say with an air of finality.

I don't say goodbye as I turn and walk away. But I should.

Chapter Thirty

It doesn't take long before I realize that Ransom has left the property. When I find Justice in his office and tell him what's happened, he instantly springs into action, reviewing the surveillance tapes of the last hour or so.

"What's going on?" Riku asks as he passes the open office door, his arms stacked with what looks to be giant leeks.

"Ransom. Have you seen him?" I try to keep the alarm out of my voice, but I know I'm failing. It hasn't been long since I left his abandoned room and those empty pill bottles, but every minute that ticks by is another minute that his life could be in serious peril.

"No, not since early this morning. We got up before sunrise to hit up the fish market and grab produce. Actually, I was looking for him too. He offered to park the company truck in the garage for me after we unloaded. Still need to grab the keys from him."

Justice and I lock eyes, both of us wearing identical looks of dread. It only lasts a second before he turns back to the surveillance footage, narrowing his search down to the compound's gates.

"There," he says pointing to the screen. "The Oasis truck, leaving at . . ." he squints at the time stamp and then at his watch, "shit, just ten minutes ago."

Ten minutes?

I could have stopped him. I could have found him before he had a chance to leave. Instead, I was confronting Tucker, something we could've done together.

Justice opens a drawer and produces a set of keys. "Here. Try to get to him. I'll find Tucker and we'll be right behind you."

I take the key fob dangling from his fingers and hold them to my chest, nearly emotional with gratitude. There's still a chance I can catch him. And considering the logo on the keychain says Porsche, my chances are pretty good.

I race to the garages and hit the Unlock button to see which beauty lights up. While Justice may have a huge estate, he isn't really big on flash and pretention. However, his love for fast cars must be the exception. Ally once told me that Justice didn't have a guilty pleasure. She had tried to corrupt him with ice cream and bad TV, and while he was a good sport about it, he was pretty clean in the vice department. But now that I see the full extent of his car collection—Ferrari and Bentley and Jag, oh my—it's plain to see where he gets his naughty kicks.

I slide into the 911 GTS and rev the engine, relishing the sound of pure power and fury. While I'd love to savor this experience, I don't even get time to enjoy the butter-soft leather and the luxury accouterments. Not if I want to catch Ransom.

Luckily, the journey between the compound and the next signs of civilization is merely a long, flat, dusty stretch of two-lane highway. If Ransom is on the road, I should find him, and catching up to him shouldn't be an issue in the Porsche.

A few miles and several passed grandma drivers later, I catch a glimpse of a white Ford truck with a familiar emblem on the tailgate. I release a sigh of relief and begin to slow. He's pulled over onto the shoulder. Not the safest place for him to be on these narrow roads, but it's better than him driving under the influence.

I pull over, getting as far off the street as I can to avoid any unfortunate dealings involving Justice's baby. I'm pretty sure if I got even so much as a scratch on her, he'll have my head. Ransom has left the vehicle, but has good sense enough to lean up against the passenger side door. I wait until the coast is clear and hop out into the sweltering desert sun. There are no trees or shade for miles. And with Ransom's bellyful of pills and whiskey, he could easily suffer from dehydration.

"Ransom!" I call out, jogging over to him. "What are you doing out here? What happened to you?"

He slowly looks up at me from his spot in the dirt and shrugs his hunched shoulders. "You want me gone. I'm gone," he slurs. His eyes are glassy, his face is ghostly pale, and it looks as if he's struggling to stay upright. I crouch down beside him and put an arm around his shoulders to steady him. His skin is slicked with sweat and clammy, yet cool to the touch.

"No, Ransom. I don't. Not like this. I know everything now. I confronted Tucker. I don't know what all of this means, but we'll be ok. All right? I'm sorry if I hurt you. You have to know I never meant it."

"No, you were right," he drawls, trying to shrug me off. "Your place is with him. You should go be with him, H. I'm no good."

"Don't say that, Ransom. You are good. You're so good for me. And you and me . . . we're good for each other. Or at least we can be." I cup his face in my hands and turn it to face me. His gaze is unfocused, his pupils dilated, and his mouth is slack. I don't even think he can see me right in front of him. If we waste any more time out here, he'll lose consciousness. I can't wait for Justice and Tucker to get here. I have to get him in the car and blast the AC. Tucker is a lying sack of shit right now, but he is a doctor. He'll know what to do.

"Come on. We can talk about this back at Oasis. I need you to push yourself up so I can get you to the car. Ok? Can you do that for me?"

He does something that looks like a nod of his head, but

ends up slumping forward, pressing his full weight on me. I struggle to get him upright again, but my meager 128 pound frame is no match for his six feet, four inches of hard, lean muscle. Still, I have to try. I can't leave him out here in this condition. He looked to me to save him, and I'll be damned if I let him down.

With nothing but adrenaline and desperation, I somehow get Ransom on his feet. He stumbles the entire way to the car, but thankfully doesn't give in to gravity until I open the door to the Porsche and maneuver his long legs inside. It would have been easier and closer to get him into the truck, but the sports car is much faster. Plus, there's no way I could justify leaving a car like that on the side of the road.

I'm buckling a nearly unconscious Ransom in when he lifts a hand to gently brush against my cheek. His eyes are mere slits and his lips are dry and cracked. Still, he manages to lucidly utter those three little words that will aid in the undoing of my marriage. Those three words that I've felt but hadn't found the courage to say out of respect for the man I once thought was the perfect husband.

I quickly retreat from his lap like it's on fire, and shut the door. I can't go there right now. Not when there is still so much left unsaid. So much we all need to discuss.

Is my marriage over? I don't know, but considering the mistakes we've both made, it probably should be.

Do I still love my husband? Of course, even though I hate him right now, I'll always love him.

Do I love Ransom? Yes, I do. In the way a little girl loves a stray, mangled cat. Fiercely and fearfully.

I'm so preoccupied by my discovery that I don't realize how far into the road I'm stepping, nor do I take notice of the speeding car that is driving dangerously close to the shoulder. But as the side of the car clips me with enough force to send me flying twelve feet into the air, launching me several yards away into oncoming traffic, I think about that movie, and the bloody irony of this very moment.

There's a reason why the broken ones stay broken. When they pretend to be mended, their glue never truly gets the chance to dry.

Chapter Thirty-one

Breaking News: Ransom lead singer, Ransom Reed, has been involved in a gruesome accident in Arizona. Although foul play is not suspected at this time, authorities are investigating.

~

Ransom Reed, playboy rocker, refuses comment when asked about a tragic accident involving his publicist, Heidi DuCane. Rumors indicate that the two were romantically involved, however, sources deny the claims, calling them "outlandish" and "despicable."

~

Justice Drake, client of Heidi DuCane, released a rare statement about his colleague and friend, saying the accident was a "truly horrific event" involving "a loving, devoted wife and confidante who would do anything for her husband and friends. And it is truly heartbreaking what has happened." Justice's girlfriend, and speculated soon-to-be fiancé, has organized a prayer vigil in honor of the DuCane family. Heidi's husband, Tucker, is asking for prayers and privacy during this time.

~

Rock star Ransom Reed has reportedly checked into a rehab facility upon the wake of the brutal accident involving his publicist. While he is not known to have been involved, sources close to the band have reported that he is "not handling it well." His camp has requested support from fans and press during this sensitive time.

~

The much-anticipated Hostage World Tour featuring bands Ransom, Fall Out Boy, and Panic! at the Disco has been postponed due to the recent events leading to Ransom Reed's rehabilitation stay. While there is still no known history of substance abuse, rumors swirl around the lead singer's involvement in a serious car accident just months ago.

~

Fans rally together in support of Ransom Reed's continued recovery. After his release last week, he was in good health and good spirits. "Mental illness is not weakness," the twenty-five-year-old stated at his recent birthday party, where he shared smiles with bandmates and close friends. "Being able to confront your demons, and seek help for them . . . that is the true example of strength."

~

Tour dates for the Hostage World Tour have officially been announced, slating the concert series' kickoff for November in Copenhagen. All three headlining bands are looking forward to playing for fans in Europe, Australia, and select cities in Asia, and hope supporters are forgiving of the delay, stemming from Ransom Reed's rehabilitation. However, with the release of Ransom's new album, We're All Mad Here, going platinum in a week, we're guessing that cities across the globe will be sold out within days.

~

HBO will be documenting the upcoming Hostage World Tour, giving fans a behind-the-scenes look at the band Ransom. The tour will end with a show in London that will also be aired as part of a special on the premium cable network.

~

In an exclusive, two-hour interview with Katie Couric, Ransom Reed spoke candidly about his experience with mental illness and substance abuse. When asked about the accident involving his then publicist, Heidi DuCane, which sparked his decision to seek help, he said that he "regret(s) what happened that day. It's something that will stay with me for the rest of my life. And if I could go back and do it all again, I would have done anything . . . anything to save her."

Chapter Thirty-two

You ever think about what people will say about you once you're gone? Of course, at your funeral, it's pretty much a given that they'll say nice things. They'd have to. Standing in front of your closest friends, family, and colleagues to reiterate just what a cheating, lying whore you were would be entirely too awkward.

I had wondered what Tucker would say in my eulogy. Would he miss me? Were his last memories of us together fond? Did he still love me right up to the end? Or would he have realized that me getting hit by a car was the best thing that had ever happened to him?

He'd have a fresh start, a second shot at life. Maybe a chance to pursue his passion. After what we'd gone through and what he'd done—committing a dozen different shades of malpractice—he'd get to retire early and focus his talents on something new. Maybe take the life insurance money and invest in a little record store uptown or something. He'd also get another shot at love with someone who didn't work tirelessly long hours and shared his love of chicken enchiladas. Someone he could seek out quaint, little vintage shops with and spend Sundays in pajamas, listening to jazz and eating pancakes. Someone who loved and desired him just as he was.

I wouldn't be surprised if he moved on quickly after my passing. Tucker is a catch. He's gorgeous, obviously, with a body that hasn't yet been cursed by time. He's affectionate, compassionate, a great listener, and a passionate kisser. He cares for people deeply, maybe more than he should. And he always puts the needs of others over his own.

My husband is a good man—the best man. And any woman would be lucky to call him hers.

And I am.

Lying on your back 24/7 for six weeks straight will provide you with plenty of time to think. Actually, that's all I had for several days. Just my thoughts. I didn't have use of my limbs until the swelling on my spine had subsided enough so they could operate, and even then, both arms and both legs were broken. And my jaw had to be wired shut after doctors fused the bones back together with the help of a metal plate and screws. My eyes were so badly bruised from twin shattered eye sockets, so even seeing was problematic. Actually the only thing that I hadn't broken on my face was my nose. Go figure. So at least I could breathe, even though it hurt like a bitch with broken ribs.

I was a hot mess. Truly. When they showed me pictures of what I looked like when paramedics scraped me off the road, I cried. No one was supposed to survive that type of carnage, yet somehow, I had. I thought my fate would parallel Sebastian's of *Cruel Intentions*. I thought I would leave my loved ones with only my memory, and the urge to rip one another apart once the truth had come to light. But no dice. I lived. And I'm not sure who was more disturbed by that revelation—them or me.

I certainly wasn't surprised that Tucker was right there beside me when I had awoken three days later. I wasn't even shocked by how glad I was that he had been there for me—unmovable, unshakable. He slept at the hospital in an uncomfortable little chair that barely reclined. He ate gross hospital food when he ate at all. And he washed up in the sink of my hospital bathroom. Justice brought him clean clothes, and Ally made sure he got some nourishment. She was a wreck. That surprised me too. I never knew she cared about me that much. I never knew any of them did.

However, the thing that stunned me, almost to tears, was the fact that Ransom never came. Not even once. And it wasn't that Tucker had refused him entrance and then lied to me. He just never came. I held out hope for a few days, thinking he just wanted to be sure I was out of the woods. But after days turned to weeks, and weeks turned into a month and a half, I realized that he just wasn't coming.

Things had gotten ugly and he bailed. He left me, even after begging me not to leave him.

Oh, the irony.

I later learned that he had entered rehab a couple weeks after my accident. Something about "mental distress" and "exhaustion." Fucking famous people. Who the hell goes to rehab for exhaustion? It's called a nap. If you're tired, go the fuck to sleep.

We all knew the truth, as eye-roll-inducing as the spin was. Ransom had hit rock bottom, and it was either go to rehab or face scrutiny for being involved in my accident. It was a smart move, something I would have suggested had I still been his publicist. But I wasn't, and I'm not. I'm not his anything.

I'd like to think that Ransom's absence from my bedside was his way of giving me a gift. I lied to him right before the car hit me. We weren't good together. We were bad—toxic even. We would hurt everyone we care about if we kept on like that. So maybe he was doing what I had failed to do a long time ago. He was cutting himself out of my life. He was letting me heal with my husband and friends. And he was going to get himself healthy and move on.

In my mind, that's what he did, and that's what I'll remember. That's what I felt in my heart when I said goodbye to him. And that's what I would have stated in his eulogy. Ransom is dead to me, but not in a bad way. But in a very final way. We came, we saw, we loved, and we left. He isn't meant to be a part of my life, and I'm not supposed to be a part of his, in any capacity. It was real. It was fun. But it wasn't always real fun.

Learning how to walk, write, feed myself, tie a bow, cross my legs, and throw a ball again thankfully occupied most of my time. It was a grueling twenty-two weeks of physical therapy every day to regain usage of my limbs. I'm pretty much back to normal, although I walk with a slight limp. And wearing heels is out for at least a few more years. They might as well toss me in the casket now.

Tucker was incredible throughout it all. Of course he was. And I don't say that with resentment. He was amazing to me—encouraging, positive, and patient. I had a lot of bad days. There were times when I had given up altogether and would just crumple on the floor and cry. And Tucker . . . he'd get right on that dingy linoleum with me and hold me close as I cried and cursed and hated everyone who could walk without issue. He didn't try to tell me how to feel. He didn't make me feel guilty for my irrational envy. And he didn't take it personally every time I tried to push him away permanently, telling him that we should get a divorce. He let me feel my anger. He let me be afraid. Probably because he was afraid too.

That time spent on the floors and beds of hospitals reminded me of why I fell in love with Tuck in the first place. Back in undergrad, when I had shed that fear and rage from my attack, he let me own it. He never tried to make me feel differently. And it just felt so damn good to be heard and understood.

He really was a great doctor. Despite what he facilitated in an attempt to help both Ransom and me, his heart was in the right place. Crazy but true. And maybe Ransom saw it too . . . maybe he realized that the only way for us to all heal from the wreckage was to say goodbye for good.

Chapter Thirty-three

It's been a long time coming, but I am finally able to get back to work. And oddly enough, we've been busier than ever. I promoted Tamara to Social Media Manager as soon as I returned, considering how well she kept the ship running in my absence. I hate to lose her, but once upon a time, someone gave me a shot after proving myself. And she has gone above and beyond proving herself. Plus, it's downright hilarious watching her boss around her own assistant.

Although business is booming, personally I'm only taking on a couple clients, Justice being one of them. If I didn't believe it before, Justice and I have officially crossed into close friend—almost family zone. After we got settled back in New York, he and Ally came for a visit to help out. Of course, Justice kicked and screamed the second they touched down at LaGuardia. But after being pulled in by the sheer magic of the city—the bright lights, the colorful characters, the constant symphony of car horns—he began to settle in and make himself at home. As he should.

I look around my office, which apparently moonlights as a flower shop considering the sheer fuck-cophony of fragrant, floral arrangements that fill it. We received flowers after the accident. We received them when we came back to the city. And now I'm getting "Welcome Back" bouquets at the job. Awesome. But I'm not complaining. Not on the outside at least. I'm just grateful to be alive, to be able to work and bitch and gripe and deride another day.

After an uneventful first week back, my body is certainly feeling what several months out of work will do to you. I love it though. But the only thing I love more is opening the front door to our condo to find my handsome husband stretched out on the couch, those Tom Ford readers on his nose, and a book nestled between those large, yet delicate, hands.

"How was your day, baby?" He smiles, placing the book down flat so he doesn't lose his page.

"Long. Busy. Great," I answer, kicking off my Tory Burch flats, which honestly, aren't nearly as comfortable as my favorite heels. "How about you?"

He smiles again and shrugs. "Nothing too exciting here. Oh, the life of a well-kept house husband."

"Well, who needs excitement?" I sigh as I sink into the couch beside him, curling into his side. "I think we've had enough excitement for five lifetimes."

He wraps me in his arms and holds me close, running his lips over the crown of my head. "Well, it's date night. I don't suppose you'd want to go out, would you?"

I shake my head and smile, burying my face into his shirt to steal his scent. "No. Let's just stay here tonight. Just the two of us."

"Good. I was hoping you'd say that. Angelo's?"

I chuckle at the hopeful inflection of his voice. Leave it to Tuck to find an excuse for pizza. "Sure," I acquiesce. "But don't forget the garlic knots."

Like two old married people, we spend our Friday night on the couch, eating pizza and drinking wine. He fills me in on whose team is going to the playoffs and who will be out for the season after an ACL injury, and I give him an earful on all the latest gossip around town, and who's hot and who definitely is not.

Neither one of us truly cares about what the other is saying, but we listen anyway, and comment when appropriate and laugh when something is funny. We do it because we love each other. And we do it because that's marriage. Celebrating and arguing and kissing and crying and loving and sexing. And everything in between. And I wouldn't trade it for the world.

We switch the TV over from the nightly news to see what else is on. Tucker flips through the movie channels while I grab the popcorn with extra butter, before squeezing into his side as close as I could possibly get. He laughs, and somehow manages to pull me closer while nabbing a handful of popcorn. I pinch his side. He licks my nose. We laugh and toss salty, butter-coated popcorn on my expensive all-white sofas.

When we finally calm down long enough to settle in for a movie, we hear something on the television that catches both our attention.

There's a heavy drumbeat, the zing of electric guitar and heart-pounding melodies. And then just as the singing begins, the title of the program appears on the screen.

AN HBO EXCLUSIVE SPECIAL

THE HOSTAGE WORLD TOUR

STARRING RANSOM

We look at each other, smile, and turn off the TV.

Epilogue

It's been 9 months, 3 weeks, and 5 days since I saw her last.

9 months, 3 weeks, and 5 days since I hit rock bottom.

The police and press labeled it an accident—an unintended devastating tragedy—but I know the truth. Shit, pretty hard to ignore when it's all I can fucking think about when I'm not on stage or in rehearsals.

I've worn the guilt every day since, cloaked in shame and anger and pain. I fucked up . . . fucked up so bad that I ended up almost killing her. And while I'm still learning how to forgive myself for that day, I'm not ever sure I can forgive myself for falling in love with her. Sordid shit aside, I love Heidi—*loved* Heidi. And that was my biggest mistake of all.

So here I am, nursing a beer in a damn near deserted hotel bar in the most romantic city in the world. The band just killed it at one of our most incredible venues to date, and while they're all out wreaking havoc on the streets of Paris, I'm pathetically alone, licking old, scabbed-over wounds. For one, it's better for my recovery, and healthier for me both physically and mentally.

See, the booze and the drugs weren't my issue. I don't even know if sex was either. It's just . . . me. I have what people would say is an addictive personality. I chase highs of all varieties. I drank because it masked my pain and got me outta my head. I drugged because it made me forget the bad shit and elevated my state of mind to another plane. And I fucked because, plain and simple, it felt fucking good. Sex was my biggest issue, by far. So much so, that it was threatening the future of the band. Let's be honest, pussy is easy to come by when you're an international rock star. But the more I indulged, the more I wanted. And the more I had, the emptier I felt. So I tried to bury it with more, desperately searching to fill that fucking canyon inside me. When it started affecting the music, I tried to self-medicate. And when that didn't help, I was instructed to seek "professional" help. For a minute, I thought that shit was even helping.

Until Heidi.

Heidi was an addiction all on her own. Funny that I called her H, although I never had an itch for heroine. However, she wasn't drugs or booze or even sex to me. She was every fucking vice rolled into a never-ending joint and sprinkled with candy-flavored crack. I knew it when I saw her, long before I had her . . . before her husband had coerced me into fucking her. He said it was like using Methadone. Having her would staunch the need for random hookups until I could successfully kick the habit altogether. She wouldn't be the real thing. Except . . . she was so much more.

Loving her wasn't part of the plan. Shit, neither was losing her. But I knew that if I didn't let her go cold turkey, neither one of us would recover.

So here I am. Exactly where I was before. Hollow. Hurting. But this time, I'm surviving. I owe it to the guys too. I owe it to myself. And I owe it to Heidi. If she could overcome the horror of that day, I could learn to control my dick.

The television over the bar is broadcasting some news channel that's obviously all in French. A photo of some random Kardashian pops up that requires no translation. The groan from the Parisian woman a few stools down, the only other patron in the bar, says it all.

"No wonder they all hate us," she mutters without so much as a hint of a European accent before sipping her wine. The shock must be written all over my face because she casts a quick glance in my direction and apologizes.

"No, it's cool, it's just . . . you're American," I reply with a little too much awe in my voice. Hell, she even has the nerve to have a little southern twang.

"I am. As are you." She smiles, shaking her head. "Of course they see just a tiny glimpse into our culture and think we're all like that. I just wish that glimpse had nothing to do with sex tapes or selfies or publicity stunts."

I simply smile back and nod, merely grateful for a little taste of home.

"After the year I just had, I'm pretty much done with all things attention-seeking," she continues. "Again, sorry. I'm just rambling now. Please, let me buy you another beer for disrupting your evening. It's just nice to be able to speak English without feeling like an ignorant moron."

"Not necessary," I assure her. "I know how you feel. It's been months since I was on U.S. soil."

"Months? Extended vacation?"

I shrug, not really knowing what to say. Of course, I have an alias with a whole backstory when I want anonymity, but I don't get the vibe that this girl is a crazy. For one, she's alone in an empty bar like me, watching news she can't understand. Plus she's dressed modestly in something a Sunday school teacher would wear.

"I'm a musician," I offer. "We're on tour."

"Oh, that's interesting. What do you play?" she asks, seeming genuinely interested without coming off as overly eager. She doesn't know who I am, which honestly is pretty fucking great. In her eyes, that I now see are a glimmering emerald green, I'm not some self-destructive rocker.

"Just about everything. And I sing lead."

She nods appreciatively, and smiles, those green eyes sparkling with admiration. "Wow. That's exciting. Anything I may have heard? You'll have to forgive me . . . I'm not really up-to-date on current musicians. Honestly, my last rock and roll purchase was Soundgarden in high school, and the reverend, aka my father, was furious about it."

I stifle a laugh, because she's sorta fucking adorable. I find her cluelessness endearing . . . refreshing even. I'm surrounded with people that only really put up with my bullshit because they think my name means something or they want to carry out some stupid rock star fantasy. And to be in the presence of someone that could give a fuck less about any of that, yet wants to talk to me anyway, almost makes me feel . . . I don't know . . . normal? Like an actual fucking person for a change, instead of an icon or a conquest to brag to her girlfriends about.

She blushes scarlet and shakes her head before shielding her face with her hands. "Oh God, I must sound pathetic, huh? And I've offended you. Forgive me. Please . . . just ignore me. I promise to shut up now."

I don't know what prompts me to abandon my bar stool in exchange for one closer to hers, but I do. And soon I'm smiling at her . . . like seriously fucking smiling with teeth and shit.

"You're not pathetic, and you didn't offend me. Not at all."

When she lifts her face from her palms, those bright green eyes widen with shock at my proximity. Shit. I didn't mean to scare her, but it felt stupid to keep hollering across the bar.

"I didn't?" she asks, her voice timid.

"No. Not at all. I know what it's like to grow up in a deeply religious family. Preacher's kid here too. Baptist." I nod.

"Yikes." She grins, loosening up a bit. "So you know all about the evils of secular music. Apparently, the devil was a guitar player."

"Really? I thought he was a drummer."

We share an easy laugh. The kinda laugh that you have when you're genuinely having a good time. When Green-eyes lifts her champagne flute to her rose-painted lips and polishes off the bubbly, I offer to buy her another.

"I shouldn't. That's probably enough celebrating for me."

"Celebrating?" I look around the empty bar, wondering if I missed something.

She nods, mindlessly tracing the lip of the glass with a blush-painted fingertip. "As of this afternoon, my divorce is final. I never thought I'd have the guts to do it. My ex-husband . . . his family . . . they've got money and clout and power. And I endured a lot just to live in that shadow. But not anymore. Not ever again. So in the spirit of independence, I decided to hop on a plane to Paris by myself. Which honestly . . . ?"

"Yeah?" I urge, captivated by every word that falls from her lips. They're fuller than I expected. Shit, her mouth is almost X-rated.

"It really sucks." She tips her head back and laughs with delight. I study the sound, draw it inside me. It rings of new-found happiness. It sounds like freedom.

"Don't get me wrong," she adds, once she's calmed down,

"Paris is a gorgeous city. And while I don't miss my ex or my old life *at all*, experiencing all this beauty alone is depressing. I've been here half a dozen times, but I never just got to be here . . . no plan, no schedule. Just me. And I'm just not that interesting, if you couldn't tell from my rambling."

"No, I feel the same way. About being lonely in the city, not about you."

My words give her pause, and I mentally kick myself for going too far. Shit, I'm out of practice. I'm rusty as fuck. But am I really even trying to go there with this chick? I don't want to feed her any bullshit lines or anything like that. I just like talking to her. It's been so long since anyone's actually talked to me with the intention of just interacting. Not trying to gauge my mind-set to ensure I'm not spiraling or using. This stranger is the closest I've been to anyone since . . .

"Doesn't feel so lonely right now." She smiles at me before shaking her head as if she can't believe she just said that. "I'm sorry. It's just . . . weird. This is the most fun I've had since I got here. Isn't that ridiculous?"

I shrug. "Well, I guess I'll be ridiculous too. This is the most fun I've had . . . in a long time."

She gives me another sweet smile and extends her hand. "Well, it's nice to meet you kindred, ridiculous stranger in a bar."

I take her soft hand in mine and fight the urge to bring it to my lips. "You too. I'm Ransom Reed."

"Ransom." She grins like the very sound of the syllables

on her tongue pleases her. "I like that. I'm Lorinda. Lorinda Cosgrove. Well, formerly Cosgrove. Old habits die hard, eh?"

"Yeah, some of them," I reply, flashing her a wink. "Usually the ones that are bad for you."

"Do you have many bad habits, Mr. Reed?" she flirts back, her smile radiating warmth and solitude. I just want to sit here and bask in the feel of it on my skin.

"I used to," I answer truthfully, still cradling her hand in my grasp. I gently brush the top of her knuckles with my thumb. "Not anymore."

Acknowledgments

First and foremost, I have to thank my family for allowing me the space and time to create my eighth novel. Writing and publishing is a team effort, and if it weren't for their patience and motivation, I never would have made it through this. There is nothing I could ever write that could fully express how much I love and appreciate you all.

To my readers—Never could I have imagined that there would be people from different parts of the globe, reading something I created. In these words, although fictional, I have shared a piece of myself with you. Thank you for allowing me to do so. Thank you for your undying support and love. The posts, the comments, the emails . . . you all are incredible.

To my blogger friends—I truly appreciate all the hard work and dedication you put toward your love for books. I know sometimes it is a thankless task, but I am saying to all of you right now, THANK YOU. From the bottom of my heart, thank you. Without you, this book community would be nothing. Extra special shout out to Milasy, Lisa, Celesha, Michelle, Kiki, Tiffany, Debbie, Ali, Yaya, Grace, Michelle (ADBL), Jennifer M., Jesey, Trish, Jessie, Christine, Jennifer W., Ana, Tammy, Lisa, Jodi, Denise, Angie L., Vilma, Angie M., Jessica, Miri . . . seriously, I could do this all day. I am so grateful to know and respect each and every one of you.

To my author friends—Your support and encouragement have carried me through this journey and have motivated me to keep writing, even when I was overcome with doubt. I want to thank Gail McHugh, Claire Contreras, Emmy Montes, Mia Asher, Rebecca Shea, Corinne Michaels, Tillie Cole, A. L. Jackson, Jessica Prince, Leylah Attar, Mary Elizabeth, S. L. Scott, Trudy Stiles, C. D. Reiss, K. Bromberg, Elle Chardou, and so many more for being the amazing talents that you are. Sometimes all it took was just a quick text or message from you to inspire me to keep going.

To Mo, my rock, my ace—I honestly don't know what I would do without you. You have been an angel to me, and the best book bestie a girl could ask for. Thank you for rocking with me this far!

To the JFJ Girls, who are some of the sweetest, more supportive women I've ever known—I'm so amazed everyday that I am lucky enough to have you all in my corner.

Shanta, Jennifer D., Sofia, Louisa, Andrea, Alicia, Julie, L. J., Sandy, Jennifer N., Sharon, Kara, Shannon, Nasha, Toni, Samantha, Lesley, Cheri, Reyna, Martha, all of you . . . Thank you so much for your amazing dedication and love.

To The BBFTalkers—You girls are balls to the wall amazing! Big, sloppy kisses to you all!

To my amazing editor, Tessa, who manages to be both badass and sweet at the same time, thank you for taking a chance on me. Thank you for believing in my words and in my stories.

Also, huge thanks to Elle, who allowed me to pester her with endless questions and pics of hot guys. Research, right?

Much gratitude for my entire team at HarperCollins, who endured my indecisiveness with cover design, release dates, marketing, etc. It's been a pleasure to work with you all.

To Rebecca Friedman, my incredible agent—Thank you for recognizing my dreams and helping me to make them a reality.

To anyone I may have missed—Thank you. Please understand that while you may have slipped my mind, you are surely in my heart.

Xoxo,

S

Keep reading for a peek at
the *New York Times* bestseller,

TAINT,

the first sexual education novel from S.L. Jennings

Right now, you're probably asking yourself two things: *Who am I?* And, *what the hell are you doing here?*

Let's start with the most obvious question, shall we?

You're here, ladies, because you can't f★ck.

Oh, stop it. Don't cringe. No one under the age of eighty clutches their pearls. You might as well get used to it, because for the next six weeks, you're going to hear that word a lot. And you're going to say it a lot. Go ahead, try it out on your tongue. F★ck. *F★★★ck.*

Ok, good. Now where were we?

If you enrolled yourself in this program then you are wholly aware that you're a lousy lay. Good for you. Admitting it is half the battle. For those of you who have been sent here by your husband or significant other, dry your tears and get over it. You've been given a gift, ladies. The gift of mind-blowing, wall-climbing, multiple-orgasm-inducing sex. You have the opportunity

to f*ck like a porn star. And I guarantee that you will
when I'm done with you.

And who am I?

Well, for the next six weeks, I will be your lover, your
teacher, your best friend, and your worst enemy. Your
every-f*cking-thing. I'm the one who is going to save your
relationship and your sex life.

I am Justice Drake.

And I turn housewives into whores.
Now . . . who's first?

Day One is always fucking exasperating.

The tears. The glassy-eyed looks of confusion as they try to piece together where their vapid relationships went wrong. The stupid, incessant questions about how I could possibly live up to my word and earn every cent of the small fortunes their husbands have paid to send them here.

Sit there and shut up, honey. One of us is a professional. Now, if I need help making a fucking sandwich or getting a wine stain out of a linen tablecloth, I'll ask for your opinion. Otherwise, shut those powder-pink lips and look pretty.

That's all they're good for—looking pretty. Shopping. Primping. Taking care of disgusting, snotty-nosed spawn.

Stepford wives. Trophies. High-class, well-bred prostitutes.

They seem perfect in every way. Beautiful, intelligent, graceful. The perfect accessory for the man who has it all.

Except for one thing.

They're as dull as lukewarm dishwater once you get them on their perfectly postured backs.

As they say, looks can be deceiving. Sexy does not equate to good sex. More often than not, this theory holds true. If it didn't, I wouldn't be in business. And let me tell you, business is good. Very good.

I take a sip of water as I scan the varied expressions of shock and horror that typically follow my usual first-day speech. This class is larger than the last, but I'm not surprised. It's the end of the summer—a season when wearing less clothing is socially acceptable. Husbands' eyes have strayed, and so have their dicks. And in an effort to save their picture-fucking-perfect marriages, some have commissioned me, in hopes that by some miracle, I can make their husbands look at them like they see more than a well-groomed melee of coiffed hair, veneers, and filler. Others weren't as lucky to be in the know, having been sent here by their loving benefactors like summer camp castaways. They actually thought they were coming to a spa. Silly, clueless girls.

A slender hand goes up, and I nod toward the young, waif-thin brunette who's shaking like a leaf in her floral Prada frock. It's ugly as shit, and makes her look like a middle-aged bag lady. She reminds me of one of those half-twit wives from *Mad Men*. Not the hot secretary—the one that just sat her ass at home, eating bonbons in front of her black-and-white television set while her husband screwed everything that moved.

"So . . . what exactly do you do? Are you, like, a teacher or something?" she asks, just above a whisper.

"More like a consultant. You all share a very serious issue and I hope to . . . guide you toward some techniques that may improve your situation."

"What situation?"

Holy fuck. Testing, testing. Is this thing on, or has Botox already begun to corrode her brain cells?

I smile tightly through the aggravation. Patience is key in my profession. Most days, I feel more like an overworked, underpaid day-care provider than a . . . *lifestyle* . . . coach. Same, same.

"I thought I explained the situation, Mrs."—I squint at the file in front of me, matching her face to the name—"Cosgrove."

Lorinda Cosgrove. As in Cos-Mart, the place where you can go shopping for honey buns, cheap lingerie, and a nine-millimeter at 3 A.M. while wearing cutoff booty shorts and Crocs. No lie, there are websites dedicated to these train wrecks. Google that shit.

"Yes, I am aware of your assessment, as crude as it is. However, what do you expect to achieve?"

I shake my head marginally. There's one in every class. One that doesn't want to accept the ugly truth staring her in the face. Even though she's read the manual, signed the contracts, and undergone all the necessary briefings before arriving, she still can't grasp her reality—flashing bright, neon arrows toward her dried-up vagina. Good thing I have no qualms about reminding her.

"You suck at sex," I deadpan, my expression blank. Audible gasps escape from almost every collagen-plumped lip, yet I continue to drive my point home. "You don't satisfy your husband sexually, which is why he wants to cheat on you, if he hasn't already. You may be a fantastic wife, mother, homemaker, *whatever,* but you are a lousy lover. And that trumps all."

Lorinda clutches her chest with a shaky, manicured hand. The woman sitting next to her, a heavier-set, forty-something housewife—whose husband's midlife crisis, and his love of barely legal debutantes, have turned their marriage into a media circus—steadies her with a motherly squeeze on the shoulder. Aw, how sweet.

"And that goes for all of you," I say, casting my glance around the room. "You're here because you know you're about to lose the one thing you've worked your pretty little asses off for—your man. You love the lifestyle you live, and instead of licking your wounds and moving on, you'd rather fix your broken marriage. And I'm here to help you."

"But how?"

A slow, sardonic smile unfurls across my face. "I'm going to teach you how to fuck your husband."

More gasps. More pearl clutching. Even a few shrieks of *My word!*

"But that's not . . ." Lorinda screeches above the flurry of discontent. "Not proper. Not dignified."

And there it is.

It's the reason why her husband, Lane Cosgrove, likes to bend his pretty blond secretary over his desk and fuck her senseless while she calls him "Daddy." He has a thing for anal—giving and taking it. His secretary keeps a strap-on in the locked file cabinet beside her desk for Thursday nights. Lane always works late on Thursdays, leaving Lorinda to her usual book-club meeting, women's Bible study, wine tasting, etc., etc. Nothing Lane does on Thursdays is "proper." Letting his secretary probe him with a ten-inch dildo while his mouth is stuffed with her panties to muffle his cries is anything but dignified. And he knows it. That's why Lorinda can't satisfy his needs. And letting your very rich and powerful husband leave home sexually unsatisfied is like giving him a loaded gun. Sooner or later, he's going to pop off a few rounds.

On cue, my head of concierge services, Diane, enters, followed by several members of my staff. Time to move this little welcoming party right along before any more tears are shed.

"Ladies, if you think that you do not need this program and have ended up here by some mistake, please feel free to leave. Our drivers are prepared to take you straight to the airport, and you will be given a full refund. We just ask that you honor the nondisclosure agreements you and your spouses have signed."

No one makes a move to stand, so I continue. "If you would like to stay and learn how to improve your sex lives and, ultimately, your relationships, our staff will show you to your rooms. You will find that they are fully equipped with en suite facilities and amenities, plus we have a twenty-four-hour chef and staff at your disposal. The property also houses a state-of-the-art fitness center, spa, and salon for all your personal needs. Comfort is key here. Welcome to Oasis, ladies. We want you to consider this your home for the next six weeks of instruction."

Eleven sets of eyes stare back at me, waiting for the first command. No one wants to be the first to jump out of her seat, arms flailing as she screams, *Pick me! Pick me! Teach me, I want to learn!* They all want this; they all want to know the secrets of marital bliss. And they know everything I've said is true.

Each and every one of these women knows that someone else is fucking their husband because she herself doesn't know how to do it herself.

And deep down, I feel for them. Hell, I even sympathize with them. They made it their life's goal to meet and marry someone who would catapult them from their mediocre backgrounds and send them flying to the comforts of wealth and luxury.

It's a regular *Pretty Woman* syndrome. They go from lying on their backs for lavish gifts or some inconsequential promise of commitment in the form of a cheap, dime-store diamond ring, to more jewels than they even have limbs to wear them on. But what these ladies fail to realize is that whatever they had to do to nab their Richard Gere, they have to do that—and more—to keep him.

The staff ushers the women up to their private rooms, leaving me alone in the great room just as the Arizona sun begins to set, slowly sliding down the azure sky. It morphs into a life-size canvas of ombré oranges, pinks, blues, and purples, the breathtaking view not sullied by towering buildings or jigsaw highways. Oasis is tucked far away from civilization, away from paparazzi, designer bullshit, and reality television.

This is my favorite part of the day—when gravity pulls that scorching, desert sun above, coaxing it into the outstretched, jagged arms of mountains and cacti. Even the most tortured souls seek comfort and solitude.

I make my way across the courtyard toward the guesthouse. I own all the property, but I don't sleep in the main house. There's a level of privacy and professionalism that I must uphold, and being locked in a secluded mansion with eleven women can be . . . difficult. My business is sex. I instruct sex. I live and breathe sex. And I need it, just like their duplicitous husbands.

So thanks to my don't-shit-where-you-eat policy, I endure six, sexless weeks during instruction, only sating my sexual appetite between the four courses I host per year. Even then, I'm discreet. Being any other way just isn't profitable in my line of work.

After letting the shower rinse away the day's aggravation, I dress and head to the dining room for dinner. The ladies trickle in one by one, quietly taking seats around the grand table. They're all still here. Eleven women desperate to reconnect with the men they hope to be tied to until death. The men that promised to move heaven and earth in exchange for their promise of commitment. The men who have broken their vows in order to sate sexual deviancies and feed their egos.

The women are silent as we're served the first course. Hardly anyone touches the starter of foie gras, elaborately dressed with poached apple in a fig reduction. Not even the scrape of silver against china echoes through the vast space.

I chew slowly, surveying the eleven, perfectly poised women from the head of the table. All are determined to avoid eye contact as they pretend to nibble their appetizers and numb their nerves with wine.

"So . . ." I start, drawing their reluctant eyes. "When was the last time any of you masturbated?"

A symphony of coughs and gasps coaxes my mouth into a satisfied grin. This group should be fun.

"Excuse me?" one sneers, after downing her red wine. A server moves to grace her with a refill of velvety courage, knowing she'll need it.

"Did I stutter? Or do you not know what it means to masturbate?"

"What? I know what"—she cringes, flustered, and shakes her head in embarrassment—". . . *masturbating* is. Why do you feel the need to ask such crude, inappropriate questions?"

I examine the striking redhead still glaring at me, her cherry lips tight with irritation. Her too large, almost animated eyes narrow in abhorrence, burning right through me with unspoken judgment. Even with her face twisted into a scowl, she's stunning. Not overly done up or glamorous. She's old Hollywood beautiful, yet there's something fresh and simple about her.

I frown, because that type of beauty is too much for this place. Yet it's not enough for the world that she lives in.

Allison Elliot-Carr. Daughter of Richard Elliot, owner and CEO of one of the largest investment banks in the world. Her husband, Evan Carr, is a trust-fund baby from an influential, political family, and Allison's father's golden boy. He's also a pretty boy, a philandering bastard with no qualms about fucking anything in Manolos from Miami to Manhattan. Of course, that tidbit of information is not publicized. It's my job to know these things. To get inside their heads. To expose their darkest secrets and make them confront them with unrelenting honesty.

Allison purses her lips and shakes her head, her mouth curling into a sardonic smile. "You like this, don't you? Humiliating us? Making us feel flawed and defective? As if *we* are the cause of our less-than-perfect marriages? We're responsible for the way the tabloids rip us to shreds? You don't know me. You don't know any of us. Yet you think you can help us? Please. I call that bullshit."

I set down my silverware and dab my mouth with a linen napkin before giving her a knowing smirk. "Bullshit?"

"Yeah, complete bullshit. I mean, who the hell do you think you are?"

A smile slowly spreads my lips. I imagine licking my chops as a lion would before devouring a graceful, delicate gazelle. "I am Justice Drake," I state smugly without apology. It's a promise and an omen, gift-wrapped in two little words.

"Well, *Justice Drake* . . . you, my friend, are a bullshit artist. You know nothing about our situations. There's no magic, cure-all remedy for our marriages. But you wouldn't know that because you don't know a damn thing about us. You're not a part of our world. Hell, you probably do your research on Page Six or TMZ." With a wave of Thoroughbred arrogance, she settles back into her chair and sips her red wine, her blue, doe eyes trained on my impassive features.

Mimicking her actions, I ease back into my own seat and steeple my fingers under my chin, elbows propped on the arms of the high-backed chair. A beat passes as my gaze delves into hers, unearthing traces of pain, embarrassment, and anger—feelings she's been taught to hide in the face of the public. Still, no amount of MAC or Maybelline can mask the undeniable hell etched into her ivory skin.

"Allison Elliot-Carr, wife of Evan Winston Carr and daughter to Richard and Melinda Elliot. Graduated from Columbia with a degree in business and finance in 2009, though your true passion is philanthropy, and you spend your free time working with various charities and nonprofits. You pledged Kappa Delta Nu sophomore year, where you met Evan, a senior, legacy member, and president of your brother fraternity. You were exclusive to Evan throughout college, and during Christmas of 2008, he proposed in front of both your families at your parents' winter estate in Aspen. You were wed the following summer in New York City and honeymooned in the Caribbean. You hate spiders and scary movies, and think sweater vests should be outlawed. You can't function without Starbucks, have a borderline unhealthy addiction to *Friends* reruns, and you eat ice cream daily. Mint chocolate chip is your current drug of choice, I believe. And according to the tabloids, your husband is sleeping with your best friend, and charming the panties off half of the Upper East Side. Plus you two haven't fucked in months. But that's just a little something I didn't pick up from Page Six." I lift an amused brow and lean forward, taking in her horrified expression. "Shall I go on?"

The deafening silence swells and becomes uncomfortably dense, painfully pressing into my temples and crushing my skull, serving as punishment for my questionable conscience's failure to intervene. Allison's eyes mist with tears, transforming into an endless blue ocean of hurt. I don't care. I shouldn't care.

"Well," she croaks, her mouth dry and her wineglass empty. "Congratulations, asshole. You know how to navigate Wikipedia." And as graceful as the elegant gazelle she was bred to be, she slides her chair back and stands, head held high, and glides out of the room.

I go back to enjoying my meal while the rest of the table stares vacantly at the space that once briefly housed Allison's retreating back. One down, only ten more to go. She isn't the first, and she won't be the last.

"Make her stay," a meek voice barely whispers. Lorinda. The prim and proper housewife who's more concerned with being dignified than where her husband puts his dick.

"Why should I?"

"Because she needs you. We all need you." Several heads nod in agreement around the table. "Maybe her more than anyone else."

More nods. Even a few cosigning murmurs.

I exhale a resigning breath, knowing exactly what I'm about to do, though it goes against every principle I've learned to live by for the past six years.

Never get emotionally vested in a client.

Never pressure or persuade them; it has to be their choice.

And never, ever *apologize for my unconventional technique, as cruel or brash as it may seem.*

The door to Allison's suite is slightly ajar, but I knock anyway, letting it creak open to reveal her petite frame. "What do you want?" she snaps, refusing to look up from the suitcase she's furiously stuffing with clothes.

I step inside, not bothering to wait for an invitation, and close the door. "Going somewhere?"

"Home. This was a mistake."

"That's funny. I never pegged you for a quitter."

"Really?" she asks sardonically, casting an angry glare through thick, wet lashes. "Because you know everything about me, right? You know my entire life story. Height, weight, Social Security number . . . hell, do you have my gynecologist on speed dial?"

"Don't be absurd." I smirk with a wave of my hand. "You know there's no way in hell I could ever learn a woman's true weight."

Allison raises her gaze from her Louis Vuitton luggage and shakes her head, dismissing me and my dry attempt at humor. But before she can turn away, the tiniest hint of a smile reveals itself at the corner of her mouth.

I move closer, close enough to smell the Chanel dabbed behind her ears. "Mrs. Carr, it is my job to make your business my business. In order to best serve my clients, full disclosure is key. There is no room for dirty little secrets here. We've all got them, and trust me, yours pale in comparison to most. And believe it or not, no one in that dining room is here to judge your situation. They're all too worried about their own reasons for being here.

"With that said, I apologize if you felt my brand of honesty was too potent for you. It was callous of me. Still, that's no reason to throw in the towel. Not when we've hardly scratched the surface."

She barks out a forced laugh and looks away toward the window. A sea of glittering stars dot the blackened sky, lighting a path toward a full moon. The paleness of night floods the room, bathing her fair complexion in the glow of diamonds and sorrow.

"You said I was exclusive," she says just above a whisper, her voice distant yet melodic enough to echo in my head.

"Excuse me?"

She turns to me, eyes painted in angst. "You said *I* was exclusive to him in college. Not *we*. As if I was faithful while he was not."

She isn't angry, or surprised, or even embarrassed. She's stuck somewhere between jaded and indifferent. In perpetual limbo, writhing in the space between being hurt beyond words and too fed up to give a fuck anymore.

She needs to give a fuck. I need her to give a fuck if I'm going to help her save her marriage.

"I'm aware, Mrs. Carr. And so are you."

Allison smiles the kind of smile that's meant to be a grimace. The kind contorted by deep-seated hurt and shame. "You think I'm stupid, don't you? That since I knew what kind of man he was from the start, yet married him anyway, I deserve this?"

"It's not my job to think that, Mrs. Carr."

"Right." She smirks. "Just your job to point out what we're doing wrong in the bedroom." I open my mouth to object but she raises a palm to stop me. "I get it, you know. We all signed up for this. We all knew what we were getting into. That doesn't make it any less humiliating."

I look at her—*really* look at her—and my head swirls with inner turmoil. Of course, she's beautiful—they all are—but Allison is absolutely flawless. She wears very little makeup, and her face is unmarred by the telltale signs of plastic surgery or injections. Tiny, tan freckles dot her slender nose, giving her an almost innocent, youthful appeal. The fact that she hasn't tried to hide or surgically remove a little piece of herself that society would deem a blemish, intrigues me. Shit, it makes her kind of badass. Such a small act of rebellion, yet such a monumental *fuck you* to a world that celebrates narcissism and bullshit images.

Allison's fiery halo of red hair falls to her shoulders in deep waves. It's full and healthy, but not overly styled with product and extensions. It's . . . her. Simple. Classic. Perfection.

"What are you looking at?" she asks, her voice laced with a mixture of annoyance and amusement.

"You." The word is out of my mouth before a lie can even begin to stifle the truth. Shit.

"Why?" Less annoyance, more amusement.

"You have freckles."

She twists her mouth to one side and raises a cynical brow. "That I do. Would you like to count my moles? I may be able to scrounge up some scars for you too."

"No, I don't mean it like that. It's just . . . you didn't get laser surgery or bleach them. You don't even try to hide them."

"Look, I know that I'm less than perfect, but you don't have to be an ass—"

Just as she turns away from me, her face flushed with anger, I clutch her elbow. Our heated gazes collide before sliding down to her arm, where my hand is grasping her soft, ivory skin. I pull away before the act is misconstrued as inappropriate as my traitorous thoughts.

"I like it."

Can't. Stop. The. Word. Vomit.

I'm a lot of things—crass, stubborn, brutally honest, egotistical—but one thing I am not, is careless. I know my boundaries, and I never cross them. In a business where lines can be easily blurred, those boundaries are outlined in black Sharpie, traced in gasoline, then set the fuck on fire, ensuring that no one even gets close enough to inhale the fumes of temptation.

Yet here I am, touching, tempting, testing the limits. Begging to get burned by an angel with a halo of fire.

"My apologies, Mrs. Carr." I straighten, my defiant hands balled into tight fists at my sides. "I assure you—"

"You like it?"

I meet her eyes, which are as big and bright as the moon, casting an ethereal glow across her face. This close, much closer than most people would deem innocent, I see they're not quite blue, as I'd initially thought. Flecks of green and gold illuminate the irises, and I find myself getting lost in the liquid depths, wondering what secrets lie beneath. What past pain is hidden behind those long, auburn-hued lashes?

Yes, I like it. Much more than a narcissistic asshole like me should.

Liking these women isn't what made me the man I am today. It isn't what built my solid reputation. I'm not known for my bleeding heart of gold or sugarcoated tongue. What I am known for is results. And that's all Allison—or anyone else, for that matter—will get from me, and not a damn thing more.

I'm facing the entrance to her suite by the time I realize I've abandoned her, leaving her mouth agape and her question unanswered. I imagine those blue-green eyes narrowed in confusion at my erratic behavior, but force myself not to look. There's nothing to see there that I haven't seen already. Just another poor, little, rich girl.

"Class is in session at ten A.M. Don't be late." My gaze stays fixed on the dark, cherrywood door. I am dying to break free. The walls are closing in, suffocating me, demanding I turn around and face my cowardice. That I confront my weakness, currently bubbling up like bile as I pass the threshold of her suite—away from those enigmatic eyes and the temptation to play connect the dots with those freckles, in hopes of uncovering more of her beautifully blemished skin.

Day-fucking-One. I'm so screwed.